AMONG THE INNOCENT

AMONG
THE INNOCENT

Elizabeth Borton de Treviño

1981
DOUBLEDAY & COMPANY, INC.
GARDEN CITY, NEW YORK

Library of Congress Cataloging in Publication Data

de Treviño, Elizabeth Borton, 1904-
Among the innocent.

I. Title.
PS3539.R455A82   813'.52
Library of Congress Catalog Card Number 79-6858
ISBN: 0-385-13397-9

I wish to thank the following persons for their valuable suggestions and aid: Lic. José Chanis Nieto; Dr. Israel Cavazos; Rev. Mr. Logan Taylor; Father Bonaventure, O.C.S.O.; Sister Aline Marie, C.J.S.; Sister Hildegard, C.J.S.; Sra. Camille de Hay de Coindreau; Sra. Elizabeth T. de Lopez; Mr. Walter Sanchez; Mr. Ross Parmenter; Mrs. Jeane C. Chapman; Mrs. Philip Kahn; Mrs. Ethel Neuberger; Mrs. Leo Hoffman; my husband, Luis Treviño Gomez; my son, Lic. Enrique Treviño-Borton; and lastly and most especially

Dr. Leslie Grey,

to whom this book is dedicated.

Elizabeth B. de Treviño

FOREWORD

Philip II of Spain was conscious of his place in history. He was to be the servant of God who wrested Europe from the heresy of Luther and made the whole continent subject to Holy Catholic Church.

He never forgot that Elizabeth of England had scorned his hand in marriage and had undertaken or permitted the hunting out and killing of Catholics in her realm. Some thought England was lost, but not Philip. He had plans to send against her a tremendous Armada and bring that country back into the Faith. For the equipping of this punitive fleet he needed gold, much gold. The Indies were to supply it.

He kept his plans to himself, for he was a secretive man, and trusted very few. Dour, fanatical, unbending, and cold, he was hated by many of his contemporaries. Yet his Queens loved him —all four of them, even frail little Anne of Austria, his latest wife. Enigmatic and stubborn, he was cruel, in the name of the Faith, even with himself. None ever saw the *cilicio*—a spiked penitential belt—that he wore.

Besides his Armada, a temporal and civil arm, Philip trusted in another religious and permanent safeguard for his dreams of a Catholic world. This was the Holy Office, the Inquisition, which was dedicated to saving the souls that had slipped away, or had been caught in the claws of a demoniac heresy.

Philip's great-grandmother, Queen Isabella, she who had finally driven the Moors from Spain and had expelled all Jews who would not accept baptism in the Faith, had passed on her fierce and total allegiance to Catholicism to her children and to theirs.

Spain had expended much blood and all her treasure over centuries, driving out the infidel. Spain meant never again to tolerate within the State anyone who was not faithful to both Crown and Catholicism, for State and Church were one, indivisible.

Charles V, Philip's father, who had dominated almost all of Europe and then had lost much of it, had spent his last years living a monastic life, attending mass twice daily and reading devotional books, performing many cleansing sacrifices. This fanatical belief in the Church, this longing for a completely Catholic world, this determination to root out all and any deviation from the holy Faith—all this ran thick in Philip's blood, and he was wholeheartedly devoted to this cause.

Torquemada had organized the Inquisition which had been set into motion in Spain by the Catholic rulers, Isabella and Ferdinand. It was Torquemada who set forth the reasons for Inquiry: heresy, witchcraft, bigamy, sodomy, blasphemy, and a long list of other sins. Heresy, of course, was most important, for it was treason as well, an offense against the Catholic State and punishable as an act of treachery. Especially was this considered to be heinous in persons who had professed themselves Catholics in order to be able to emigrate to the New World under the protection of Spanish arms, the King's military branch of power.

But Torquemada, like most fanatics, was eager to justify his obsession under legal trappings. In his rules about the conduct of an Inquiry, he was careful that Holy Church never punish, but always turn over miscreants to the civil arm. Holy Church must never cause blood to be shed. Burning was allowed, if the heretic was recalcitrant and defiant and refused to return to the Church. If instead he repented and accepted the Faith, even at the last moment before execution, it was allowed that he be garroted, a swift death, instead of being consigned, alive, to the flames.

The person under Inquiry was permitted to have a defense lawyer, and indeed there was a body of such lawyers always available to every Inquisitional Court. If the person being questioned was too poor to hire a lawyer, the Court would appoint one for him. This was general practice, anticipating provisions in courts of law today. Also, since in the New World there were only a few cells for the persons under Inquiry, many who had been tried and seemed willing to mend their ways were "paroled"—that is, ordered to perform some daily task for the Church, while living in relative freedom outside jail and reporting with regularity to a priest for instruction. For the announced purpose of all Inquiries by the Courts of Inquisition was to bring the strayed back into the Church, to save souls.

Certain other aspects, though, of the Inquiries, struck terror into every breast. Victims never knew who had denounced them, nor for what crime. Yet the judges were warned that they must be vigilant to make certain that no person was judged only on hearsay, or had been denounced for ulterior motives—that is, from jealousy or spite, or to secure access to a fortune.

The Inquisition, like many other institutions of its time, reflected the general thinking and attitudes of the public. The crowds who attended the autos-da-fé in Spain and the New World were not larger than those who gathered to enjoy the beheadings and drawings and quarterings which took place in Protestant England; and Luther's followers on the Continent, bent on destruction of the "venomous Papists," used carefully thought-out tortures to secure confessions, as they did in England, and as every Inquisitional Court did in Spain and the New World. It was a cruel age and no single race can give itself purity baths except the Jews, who were constant victims, and did not themselves proselytize, or torture.

It is interesting to note that the active Inquisitors in the New World were expressly forbidden, by Philip, from trying the Indians. They were to be taught and converted, not harassed.

The rest of the populace in New Spain lived under the cloud of terror of the Inquisition, for power over life and death, which resided in the judges, generates cruelty in all but the greatest and wisest.

Especially under the constant fear of spies (the Inquisition had an active body of spies), denunciations, torture (in order to secure the names of accomplices), and death were the converted Jews, the so-called New Christians, who had accepted the Cross under duress. It was supposed, often enough with reason, that they had taken the Faith only in order to save themselves and their loved ones. Therefore, they were suspect, always.

New Spain, intent on making all Jews into practicing Catholics, achieved only stubborn resistance and many martyrs, by the use of force and terror. And yet today a strong strain of Jewish blood runs in the veins of countless Latin Americans, as studies and scrutinies of family names and histories have proved. This was natural. The Jews had been persecuted for centuries; they knew how to survive, and they knew how to prosper under adverse circumstances. In time, they simply absorbed and were absorbed into all the great families of the New World.

What fear and torture had never been able to accomplish, love and acceptance did.

I will wash my hands among the innocent and will encompass Thy altar, O Lord. I have loved, O Lord, the beauty of Thy house and the place where Thy glory dwelleth.

From the words used at
the Lavabo in the old mass

PROLOGUE

The year was 1585.

As soon as the snows had melted, even though the roads were icy and stiff with ruts, or so muddy that a man or a horse floundered miserably, people began streaming south, toward Seville. Men from the Low Countries, forgetting for a moment their ancient enmity with Spain, moved southward hopefully; from the German states came many a soldier, heavy-shouldered and thick-kneed, dreaming of fortune. The ebullient French sought adventure, jewels, romance, gold. And from all over Spain came a rabble of rascals, soldiers, beggars, and penniless hidalgos armed only with their *cartas de limpia,* proof of their nobility, of their blood free from taint of Jew or Moor. In litters, or on asses, the clergy converged toward Seville, for they had specific duties in the New World.

The Guadalquivir floated hundreds of ships, all the way to Sanlúcar and Cádiz, and the masts were like a forest against the blue sky. The Fleet for the Indies was being made ready for the spring journey across the still little-known seas to New Spain, guided and shepherded by the armed ships of His Most Catholic Majesty, King Philip II, of Spain.

While the merchants and soldiers and adventurers and religious waited in Seville for the order to board, the English pirates were busy outfitting their fast maneuverable vessels for the chase. They were bold and clever, the English, and the Spanish Fleet provided rich prizes. The English Queen rewarded captains who were successful with honors and titles and royal favor, as well.

It was a year of great adventure, great hope, great danger.

BOOK ONE

Guiomar

1.

The convent of Our Lady of Pardon, known as the Madres Penitentes, or the Sisters of Penitence, was a strong, fortresslike building with no windows in the outside walls, for the sisters were not encouraged to look out and think about the world. Inside there were many enclosed patios, some given over to the growing of vegetables, some to fruit trees, and one to chicken runs and rabbit hutches. The sisters never ate meat, but they were prepared to serve it when their confessor came to shrive them, or when the bishop visited.

Mother Superior worked among her vegetable beds, and studied the rows where she had planted flowers for the altar in their chapel. Despite the rheumatism which called forth her most fervent prayers all winter, and still stiff, she insisted on hoeing the soft earth and on propping up the tenderest plants. As she did so, she meditated on the problem of Guiomar. The time was close when she must make a decision about the girl, and God had not yet sent her instructions. Working in her garden, and waiting for illumination, she pretended not to hear Sor Angustias's shrill voice. At last, with a sigh, she gave in, stuck her hand trowel into the soft earth heaped between the planted rows, and struggled into an erect position. Willing herself to be kind and patient, she answered softly, "You wish to speak to me, Sor Angustias?"

"Reverend Mother, it's Guiomar again. She is rebellious and defiant. I beg you to speak to her."

"She was in your care this month."

"Yes, but I cannot control her. I beg—"

"Sor Angustias. You are impatient. I relieve you of her care, and I will look after her spiritual needs myself. But you must pray an extra hour at the altar and ask God to teach you patience. And remember, our order is penitential, and it is our duty to accept all pain and trouble and transform it into grace, through our prayers."

"Yes, Reverend Mother."

"But what was this rebellion about? What has Guiomar done?"

What has she done this time? Reverend Mother thought to herself. She loved the girl, and she struggled against this affection, for it was not within the spiritual program of her order to cultivate any human frailties, but only to suffer and pray.

"She refused to kill the rabbits. And, as you know, Father Abbot is coming to dinner and he likes rabbit stew."

"You are excused. Oh, but please hand me my cane before you go."

Sor Angustias held out the cane. Mother Superior took it a bit brusquely. She had had many struggles with Sor Angustias, over the years; Sor Angustias, who was the older, had hoped to be Superior.

Mother Superior made her way slowly down the corridors toward the kitchens. From afar, she heard Guiomar's desperate sobs.

"Now, what is this commotion?" she asked, pausing in the doorway.

Guiomar, who had been full length on the stone floor, got up and threw herself toward Mother Superior, clasping her about the knees.

"Sor Angustias says I must kill my rabbits," she began tempestuously, "and I will not! I will not!"

"Get up at once!" ordered Reverend Mother.

Sobbing and sniffling, wiping her eyes on the coarse cloth of her gown, Guiomar obeyed. She tried to calm herself, but her bosom, full now for a fifteen-year-old damsel, still heaved and her face still streamed with tears.

"Put the rabbits back in their hutch," Mother Superior ordered

Sor Basilia, who was cooking. "They are young and can breed well. Make a vegetable stew for His Reverence, with a large piece of bacon, that will be served to him alone. And take eggs and make a *flan*. Guiomar, come with me; I must decide on your punishment, because you have made a great scandal, and have demeaned yourself and our house." (And you usually do make great scandals, thought Mother Superior sadly.) She had tried very hard, but the girl was passionate and emotional.

They walked slowly, Mother Superior leaning on her cane. Indeed, walking itself, even with a cane, was a constant pain, and therefore to be embraced. Mother Superior had given herself the most northern of the cells, the one which received the least sunlight, because Our Lord suffered for us, and she rejoiced to have suffering of her own, to offer Him.

But this is just what has always been my difficulty with Guiomar, she thought. Guiomar is made wild by suffering, cannot bear it herself, and tries to stanch it in anyone or anything. Well, I have tried.

They entered Mother Superior's cell, and the old nun made her stiff and painful way to her small hard bench, and sat.

"Stand there, where I can look at you," she ordered Guiomar.

She is beautiful, thought Mother Superior. As beautiful as I was, though of course, her beauty is of her race, and I was blond. (Guiomar was tall for her age, already rounded in womanhood.) I won't be allowed to keep her much longer, reflected the old nun.

Under the tight scarf, Guiomar's hair fell in cascades of coppery waves below her waist. It was so dark a red that it shone with purple shadows, and so thick and curly that it might have clothed her. Probably the Magdalen's hair was like that, mused Reverend Mother.

Guiomar's eyes were black, large and velvety, shaded by long lashes, and her skin was creamy fair. Her nose was a bit too broad at the tip, her lips too full and fruity, and a strange dimple danced in and out near her left eye. But these were flaws that would not put off a suitor, thought the old nun. It was time now, to make ready.

I must tell her, thought Mother Superior, regretfully.

"I pardoned you, Guiomar, and I even pardoned your rabbits, because I must lose you very soon."

"But why? Why must you lose me? This is my home. I don't want ever to leave you. I want to stay here, and be a nun, like you."

The girl was making an effort to control herself, but she trembled and tears stood and sparkled in her eyes like diamonds.

"I will tell you. Later. Oh, I know you love Our Lord, that you are diligent in prayer and strong in faith. I know this, my child. If you were not, I would have failed most dismally in my duty. But ours is a penitential order and you could never be one of us. You know that you cannot tolerate pain. You even faint at the sight of blood!"

"I know. It is a weakness. I will strive . . . I will try . . ."

"You have tried. I know."

There was silence for a time, broken only by Guiomar's dry gasps, as she struggled not to break into sobs again.

"Sit down, my child. Make yourself calm. I must tell you something about yourself."

The girl sat, still twisting her hands and biting her lip.

"Certain children are given into certain families, or into certain convents, to be brought up strong in the Faith."

"Orphans," murmured Guiomar. "I know."

"A special kind of orphan," went on Mother Superior. "The children given into our care are those whose parents have been condemned."

"Criminals?" breathed Guiomar, a look of dismay on her face.

"Worse. Heretics."

"Ay!"

"Guiomar, your mother was a Judaizer, condemned to the stake."

Guiomar's eyes widened, and all the color fled from her face. With a cry, she half rose, and then fell to her knees.

"I am too abrupt. I have no wit. God help me," prayed the old nun, trying to raise the fainting girl.

"Water!" she shouted, and before long she and a young new novice were holding damp cool cloths to Guiomar's forehead and to her neck.

"No more. I won't tell you any more just now," promised Mother Superior, as Guiomar opened her eyes. "Go and rest and pray, and when you feel strong enough, come to me. I will tell you everything else that you must know."

Another nun came and led Guiomar away to her own pallet, where she lay motionless for hours. She watched the shadows lengthen on the wall, and heard the chimes that called to compline.

At last she rose, straightened her dress, and bound back her hair. Unsteadily, but with determination, she made her way to the cell of Mother Superior.

"I am ready, Reverend Mother," she said, in a small grave voice. "Tell me. I must know. And I must know what I have to do."

Mother Superior had been waiting, with sorrow, for this moment. Strengthened by her prayers, she said, "Sit here beside me, Guiomar, and I will tell you.

"You are not an orphan. Your father is a Christian gentleman who went out to the New World, to New Spain, to make a fortune for his family. He took with him his son, your brother Gonzalo. Your mother was in delicate health, as she was expecting you, so she stayed behind, here in Seville. While she was alone, staying with relatives, she fell into the clutches of a wicked rabbi, who went about preaching the old beliefs and teaching people to deny Jesus Christ, Our Savior. This rabbi taught people to flog the Crucifix and to spit on it."

Guiomar could not hold back a little moan, but she did not take her eyes from the sad face of the old nun.

"He was denounced by pious Christians, and he escaped. But the people he had seduced were caught and tried by the Inquisition, among them your mother. She confessed . . . after the torture."

"Ay! She was tortured. Ay! My mother!"

"And she was condemned to the stake. They waited only for you to be born, and then they took you, just a tiny baby, and gave you to us, to be brought up in the True Faith, and, if you did not eventually take the vows of a religious, you were to be married to some Christian gentleman."

"My mother. My poor mother," breathed Guiomar.

"Do not grieve. She repented, at the end, and embraced the Cross. But the sentence was not changed."

"So she was . . . burned," Guiomar whispered.

"No," answered Reverend Mother. "She escaped. The heretics had many to help them, secretly, and almost all escaped, your mother with them. But she was ill and frail, and she died on the way to another country. Her body was found, and given burial somewhere in the north of Spain. The escape route was discovered later, and also the many disguises that had been used by the Judaizers, to deceive the people. But some of them managed to get to Italy, where the laws of the Holy Office are not so rigidly enforced."

Guiomar was very pale, not weeping, and she sat still as a stone.

"So she died, my mother. She did not suffer at the stake."

"No. And you must pray for her soul, as I have done every day since they brought you to me. I have loved you as if you were my own child, I love you for her, and for myself, and for Our Lady."

Guiomar flung herself on her knees and buried her head in Mother Superior's lap. The old nun stroked the girl's hair.

"And so, since I cannot receive you into our order—you know why—and since I think you would be happy married, Holy Office has found a husband for you. He is a Christian gentleman, old and strong in the Faith, who will watch over you and protect you so that you may never be infected with the spiritual illness that was the destruction of your mother."

"Oh, you know I love Our Lord, and the Holy Family and the saints," cried Guiomar. "But why must I marry? Let me stay with you and be one of you. I will be strong, I will gladly do the penances, wear the *cilicio*, oh, please—"

"Guiomar, my dear child, one of our laws is obedience. And a husband has been found for you. A Dominican priest is coming for you, to take you to the bridegroom's family, where you will be prepared for your wedding."

"When?"

"In a few days. Be calm, Guiomar. Accept. Be happy. You know how you love all little creatures, rabbits and kittens and puppies and small birds. Just think how you will love having your own babies, so small and dear!"

"Will I have to live far away from you?"

"I don't know. I hope not. I hope the bridegroom is here in Seville, so that you may come and visit us."

"Reverend Mother."

"Yes."

"I will be obedient. I will try to be dutiful, and never shame you. You have been so good to me."

"I know. You are my dear child."

Mother Superior made the sign of the Cross on Guiomar's forehead and then kissed her.

"Go now to the chapel and pray. God bless you."

2.

Guiomar spent the next few days in alternating moods of despair and a frightened curiosity. She prayed continually for her mother, poor lost soul, and wept at night, trying to visualize her in her terror, in her desperate attempt to escape, in her lonely death. Guiomar had nightmares and cried out, awakening the novices, and Sor Angustias scolded her sharply and made her go without breakfast, as a punishment for having spoiled the night's rest of the others.

In spite of trying to make herself ready for departure, Guiomar was stiff and unable to move when Sor Angustias came, a look of curious triumph on her face, to tell her to take her things and go at once to Mother Superior in the reception room.

"Tie back your hair and put on your cloak and hood," she ordered. "They have come for you."

Guiomar put on the long dark garment that covered her from shoulders to feet. She took up a square of cloth into which she had tied her small treasures—her rosary and missal, gifts from Mother Superior, two fine linen handkerchiefs, a stone from the garden that was striated into a design that pleased her, a comb made of tortoiseshell. In another bundle was her change of underwear, made of coarse cotton, a second dress, of dark-brown fustian, considered by Mother Superior to be proper for summer, and two pair of knitted hose.

Cold with apprehension, Guiomar followed Sor Angustias down the corridors and into the small reception room where Mother Superior received church dignitaries when they visited the convent. Guiomar had never been there before. She kept her eyes cast down, but through her lashes she saw two large feet, in velvet shoes, and the edges of a white robe covered by a mantle.

Guiomar lifted her eyes to find Mother Superior, and went to her at once, to kneel beside her chair.

"Now, my dear, rise, and I will bless you. Father Fernando has come to get you, and you have far to go. Besides, we have said our goodbyes. There, do not weep."

In a daze, Guiomar heard Mother Superior's murmured blessing, felt the cold old fingers trace the Cross on her brow; blinded with tears, she could not see where she stepped, and choked with sorrow, she could make no answer.

It was a soft afternoon, and Guiomar had never left the convent. Following Father Fernando, she began, after a bit, timidly to look about. Everything was strange. The narrow streets were thronged with people who were excitedly talking, carrying packages, lumber, boxes. The air was alive with noises of activity, shouts, the ringing of horses' hooves against the stones in the street. Two soldiers went by, dressed in their gaudy red-and-yellow uniforms, carrying arms. Guiomar shrank back, confused and frightened.

"Come along, come along," advised the Dominican crossly. He did not like his duty, especially that of escorting such a young girl through the crowded streets; he had not thought she would be so overwhelmingly beautiful, and therefore he was annoyed with her. "Stay close behind me, and do not look at anyone. Nor speak," he added, muttering to himself, "Girls this age are nothing but trouble and well the devil knows it."

The monk demanded passage in a strident, authoritative voice. Guiomar followed close, bewildered by the crowds and the noise. They were making their way past a street display of mountebanks, who performed feats of dexterity and acrobatics, when suddenly Guiomar saw the Dominican fall forward, struck from behind, and she herself was enveloped, all at once, in a thick black cloak and hoisted onto strong shoulders. She tried to cry out but her fears paralyzed her and she could not make a sound. The heavy cloth too, was dusty, and it made her struggle for breath. She could do nothing but pray silently for help to the Virgin. She fainted, and knew no more.

When she awoke, it was to darkness. She lay, remembering with terror what had happened, and she was afraid to move. But as the minutes slipped by, she could make out a window, high above her, through which shone a dim light. She lay on a heap of rugs, soft and warm, and she was covered with a dark embroidered woolen spread. As her senses returned, she listened for some clue to where she might be. There was a deep silence, and yet she was conscious of life around her, of footsteps muffled, of an occasional sibilant whisper. Suddenly the room where Guiomar lay was lighted; a woman had entered with a candle.

She was a small dark woman, of middle age, dressed very simply. She smiled at Guiomar and said, "Don't be afraid! You must
come with me now. No one will hurt you. You are safe here."

She set down the candle, and helped Guiomar sit up and then
rise to her feet. She was unsteady, but the woman supported her,
and guided her. Guiomar was stiff and terrified.

They emerged into a courtyard, small but sweetly fragrant with
flowers, and refreshed by a murmuring fountain. Crossing this,
they entered another corridor, and walked along it, silently, for it
was thickly carpeted. The candle lighted their way. Opening a
door, the woman pushed Guiomar gently inside, and left her.

Another woman lay in bed, propped up against pillows. Her
face in the candlelight was white and bone-thin; two black
braids lay on the pillows beside her hollow cheeks. She half
raised herself to stare at Guiomar.

"Come closer," she ordered, in a breathless voice. Her chest
heaved and her throat throbbed from the effort she made. Guiomar could see that she was very ill.

"Guiomar," she said, "I am your mother."

3.

Far north of Seville, which lay panting in the heat of an early
summer day, Valladolid was enveloped in a sandstorm. The par-
ticles of blown dust stung the eyes and darkened the day, as if a
heavy rain were about to fall. Father Isidro, the abbot, among
many pious ejaculations, did indeed pray for rain to settle the
acrid clouds that were swirling about the city. One of the Irish
seminarians (and there were ten in all, studying for the priest-
hood) began his usual gasping attack for breath. He did this
every time there was a dust storm, but also, reflected Father
Abbot, in annoyance, he did it whenever he was assigned some

unpleasant duty. Or in fact, anything having to do with inside duty. The lad was happy and able, no matter what the weather, whenever he was allowed to take care of the sumpter mules and horses, or the asses, if a visiting abbot rode in. The young man, Columb, seemed to care for all the dumb beasts more than for men, and Father Abbot had once accused him of it.

Columb, who was bright enough, and had learned to speak a fluent Spanish, and was advanced in all his studies, had been thoughtful and silent, when the abbot had scolded him for preferring the stables to the chapel.

At last he spoke, hesitantly.

"The animals do not deceive, nor lie, nor are they hypocrites," he said at last.

Taking this as an oblique criticism of himself and his monks, Father Abbot had banished Columb to a cell for a week, on bread and water, admonishing him to meditate on the Passion of Our Lord, and to put his soul in order with prayer and discipline.

But the most unexpected and extraordinary thing had happened. When, at the end of the week of discipline, Father Abbot had gone to release Columb, he was met with the words, spoken in a weakened but defiant voice, "And they are not cruel, either!"

Father Abbot had had no alternative but to give orders that Columb remain another week in the punishment cell. This grieved the abbot for the young man's soul, but also for his physical health, for he saw him very pale and thin. Indeed, before the second week of discipline had elapsed, he felt forced to open the door and send Columb to the infirmary, because he was coughing, and burning with fever. There Father Abbot himself nursed him tenderly, saw that he was fed nourishing soups and custards, and brought back to health. Then Father Abbot was rewarded, because Columb knelt before him, asked his pardon for his insolence and rebellion, and begged for his blessing.

These incidents had happened some months before, and Columb had seemed to be docile enough, fervent in his faith. But now this sandstorm had descended on the city, and Columb was again gasping and coughing. The physical troubles might bring back with them, in their train, those same emotional errors, feared the abbot. He earnestly prayed that they would not, because Columb had completed all his studies and was about to be ordained. It remained only for the bishop to assign the day when three of the seminarians, who were ready, should prostrate themselves before him, and receive the sacred chrisms.

He called Columb to him, ordered him to go to the infirmary and lie down, covering his face with a cloth dampened in water.

"In holy water," ordered the abbot, as an afterthought, thinking that he might need divine help in saving this young man, who could be valuable for the Church. Besides, Columb's father had promised a chalice of worked Irish gold (and the Irish were famous goldsmiths) on the day he was ordained. Columb's father was the Carolan, chief of a great tribe in Ireland and his son therefore, was O'Carolan, though the abbot and his scribe always wrote the name Ocarolan, in one word. Columb did as he was bidden. He too was thinking about the fast approaching day when he would be ordained, and his soul was full of doubts and uncertainties.

As he lay, he prayed fervently to the Virgin, and to his name saint, gentle Columb, for guidance.

"A sign," he implored, with all his heart, begging and wishing so desperately for some signal, some indication of what God wanted him to do, that he screwed his eyes together until the tears came, and clenched his teeth. After what seemed a long time of intensive prayer, he removed the cloth from his eyes and sat up on the infirmary cot. There was a small high window in the room, and Columb walked over to it, impelled by some wish to see if the longed-for sign from heaven might indeed descend from the billowy white clouds that shone against the blue.

He waited in vain for three days. Then suddenly there was a flutter of wings, and a small white dove, escaped from the monastery dovecotes, came and perched on the wide sill of the window.

My own name, thought Columb. A dove.

The little bird walked up and down on the sill, and then looked straight at Columb, seeming to bow and bob its head. It opened its wings and then closed them again.

It hesitates, as I do, thought the lad.

Then suddenly the dove spread its wings and flew away. Columb watched until it disappeared into the sky, far away, a speck, and then nothing. It had flown south.

"So shall I," determined Columb, sure now of what God wanted him to do. He lay down on the cot once more, and began to plan his escape.

4.

Guiomar fell to her knees, took the sick woman's thin hot hand in hers, and covered it with tears and kisses.

"They told me you were dead," she whispered, brokenly. "My mother! My mother!"

"They would have had me dead, the devils," breathed the woman, fiercely, seeming to draw strength from her own hatred. "They would have burned me."

"Oh, thank God you escaped. You are here with me," cried Guiomar.

"I came, when I knew I was dying . . ."

"Oh no!"

"Yes, I am dying. So I came, to find you. You must obey me, in everything I say!"

"Of course! Mother," continued the girl, sobbing with joy. "My mother! I never dreamed I might see you in this life!"

"We dressed a dead girl in my clothes, and I managed to get to Italy."

"Thank God," cried Guiomar.

"This house is safe. Our own people waited and planned, and

stole you. They brought you to me. You are safe here, with us."
The dying woman raised herself painfully, and pulled Guiomar
close, looking deeply into her eyes.

"We are Jews, Guiomar. I am a Jew. You are a Jew!"

Guiomar was silent, paralyzed with fear. All her training had
been contrary to this intense declaration.

"You must do as I say. It is planned. All is arranged. You must
obey me! I am your mother and I am dying. I demand it!"

"What?" whispered Guiomar. "What must I do?"

"You must go out to New Spain to your father and brother
and you must bring them back into Judaism. This is a duty I lay
upon you! A dying request! Sacred!"

"But I . . . know nothing of Judaism," whispered Guiomar. "I
am a Christian!"

"Never!" The sick woman almost screamed. Her eyes dilated
and her chest heaved. With fierce intensity she seized the girl's
hand and laid it against her own heart.

"We are Jews, Jews! We never torture and burn! We teach
justice and mercy. You will be instructed here, in this house,
until you are one of us again, true to your blood. And then you
will go . . . out to New Spain . . . you will save your father . . .
and your brother . . . No one will suspect you . . . you will go
pretending this cursed Gentile wickedness . . . Promise . . .
Promise!" Her voice had risen and she strained the girl's hand
hard against her burning flesh. Guiomar was transfixed with
horror, and with a surge of frightened love for the woman whose
dark eyes glittered with emotions the girl had never seen, never
imagined.

"Promise!" urged the dying woman again, but before Guiomar could make any answer, suddenly life departed from the
tense, thin figure. Her eyes still staring, she fell back upon the
pillows and was motionless.

Guiomar gave a scream, and then screamed again.

"Help! Help!" She fell upon the bed, and kissed the face of
her mother, now unresponsive, slack. Almost at once the room
filled with people, men and women. Guiomar had experienced

too much excitement, strangeness, terror, and love, all feelings she had never, in such intensity, suffered before. She could not speak. She trembled, and her legs would not support her.

She was gently carried away, and left to rest, wakened softly and urged to drink a hot broth, which she did obediently, still dumb with shock. She drank, at the urging of the woman who had first guided her into the room of her dying mother. Herbs and medicines had been added to the broth, and Guiomar slept deeply for many hours, while in the house the dead woman was prepared for burial according to the rites of her religion.

The body was bathed, dressed in clean white linen, and the chin bound. While all the household sat weeping and reciting prayers for the dead, she was lowered gently into a secret grave inside the patio of the house and laid deep in earth.

Guiomar was tenderly cared for, and kept quiet with potions for some days, until all the household had once again assumed its usual quiet. It was a simple, rather large house, in a section of Seville known to harbor some New Christian families. They seemed to be pious people, who were daily at mass, and who recited the rosary in the evenings, who gave liberally to charity, who tended the sick and indigent with gentle kindness. They were accepted as exemplary Christians.

Several of the family, whose name was Mendoza, had applied for permission to go out to the Indies, and though this was not easily accorded to *conversos,* or New Christians, the family presented documents enough, from centuries back, under King Riccared, to prove their faithfulness to Mother Church, and indeed two of the men in that family had taken Holy Orders, and were Dominican monks. One of them, indeed, had been ordered to the New World, where he was to undertake a mission for the Holy Office there. What more obvious proof could there be of the complete conversion and strong faith of this family? After all, St. Paul himself was a converted Jew.

The Dominican who was to go out to work with the Holy Office in New Spain was Fray Domingo, who before his vows had been baptized Felipe Mendoza.

With devoted and constant prayers, he prepared himself for his mission.

The Mendoza family, secretly Jews, felt safe for Fray Domingo was a sincere and devoted Catholic, and his piety threw a veil of protection around them. His connection with the Holy Office was another safeguard.

5.

When she was well enough to walk about, to eat, to talk timidly to her captors, Guiomar was taken to a plain quiet room in the central part of the house, where, with doors all closed, no one could hear a word of what was said within. Seated at a small table, she awaited the arrival of the "teacher," who was to instruct her in Judaism. Guiomar's emotions swirled inside her and tormented her. A sudden overwhelming love for her mother had taken possession of the girl's heart, and this love was made more poignant by the fact of her mother's suffering and terror. Also, some deep call, inexplicable to Guiomar, drew her to her mother's people, as if her blood could not be denied. But she had been trained since childhood in the Christian dogma, and lately had felt a paralyzing terror of the autos-da-fé, which took place with regularity. She had heard about these only in snatches, when the novices whispered together, but the mere words "the stake" and "the torture" robbed her of strength, and she felt herself powerless to move or to speak when visions of these terrors assailed her. Now she sat trembling and cold, full of fear but determined not to show it. She was very young, but instinct told her to hide her feelings and beliefs and pretend to agree. She was alone in a situation for which she had never been prepared, and so, secretly, she prayed and begged the Savior and His Holy Mother for strength and endurance.

When the teacher was brought to her, she felt a surge of gratitude. He was an old man, with a white beard and silky-soft white hair beneath his house cap. Looking into his face, Guiomar saw an infinite sadness and an infinite kindness. She went at once to him and knelt to him, and he laid his old wrinkled hand upon her head in blessing.

"Do you wish to learn, child?"

"Yes," whispered Guiomar. "Teach me."

The teacher sat, crossed his feet, clasped his hands in his lap, and leaned back, closing his eyes. Then he began, in a sonorous, singsong voice, to intone a prayer.

"Repeat with me," he said, and Guiomar obeyed.

The rabbi came every afternoon and stayed for four hours, teaching Guiomar the prayers and the history of her race. She was quick, attentive, and intelligent, and she had a good memory. She was sure that the teacher was pleased with her, for he often laid his hand on her head, in farewell, and smiled gently at her.

At the end of a month, he said, "You have learned well, child." He sat then, and wagged his head worriedly for some time. Then he shrugged his shoulders, in their shawl, unhappily.

In departing, he stopped to speak with the owner of the house, Antonio Mendoza, and his wife Carmen.

Guiomar had learned the names of her hosts; Doña Carmen had nursed her tenderly, and Don Antonio, short but enormously strong, must have been the man who kidnapped her in the street. The couple had a family of sons, all married, who came to the house for meals on certain days; on these days, until lately, Guiomar had been given food alone in the room where she slept. There were several slaves in the household, who did the cleaning, washing, and other chores, but on a certain day every week, it was Doña Carmen who cooked.

"I have done my best," said the old rabbi. "She has learned the prayers, the forbidden foods, the holy days, the rules."

"But . . . ?" began Doña Carmen, reading the old man's tone.

"She has a Jewish heart," he said then, "tender and loving.

Yes, capable of much goodness. But I fear you may have brought her to me too late."

"It was not possible," said Don Antonio, biting his thumb in nervousness. "It was so difficult to arrange to get her away from the cursed convent. And her mother, Leonor, had not been able to come to us until after so many years, so many years."

"God will act in His good time," remarked the old man. "If God wills, the girl may carry out her mission. If He wills."

"She must," answered Don Antonio, through clenched teeth. "The Fleet is sailing next week, and she must go with it. I cannot fail Leonor, my own kinswoman. And Guiomar promised. She promised her mother!"

"Are you sure?" asked the old rabbi, "I am not so sure."

"Yes! She promised!"

The teacher removed his house cap and his shawl, and handed them with his prayer book to Doña Carmen. Then, putting on a garnet-colored coat, a few gold chains, and a small-brimmed tall black hat, with a white plume worn on the left side, as the Sevillanos did, he prepared to leave. He had changed his appearance entirely, with the changed clothes, and when he went out into the street, it was not with the slow step of an old thoughtful man, but with the brisk walk of a merchant, on business.

Don Antonio turned to his wife.

"He seemed not to be certain of Guiomar," he said, worriedly.

"He will come back, to make sure she knows everything. If she is hesitant, we must keep her here, until there is another chance, another fleet—"

"It would be in another year! Are you sure you heard her promise?"

"Oh yes! I am sure!" cried Doña Carmen. "And she seems so good, so obedient. And she weeps for her mother."

"Well," said Don Antonio, and then he moved his shoulders in a mighty shrug, expressing doubt, hope, and resignation, all at once.

At night, alone in her bed, with no one near, Guiomar prayed fervently and silently.

"Help me, sweet Savior! Save me! Pity the soul of my mother and give her peace. Teach me strength and guide my steps and my words. I must go out to my father in the Indies. But I did not promise to try to change him! I did not! I did not! I did not promise!"

Unskilled in deceit, she had learned from fear and the instinct for survival. Her constant, secret prayers comforted and strengthened her. Living a deceit with kind Doña Carmen troubled her, and she began to long for her departure with the Fleet.

6.

Columb regained his strength, and took up his duties again, and his studies, and his prayers, in humble obedience. But his longing was to go away, to be as free as the dove that had been sent to him, as a sign.

"And the dove, which is my name, is sacred to Our Lord," he thought to himself, exultantly, time and again. His chance came unexpectedly.

A bishop from Burgos arrived one late afternoon, and Columb, who was good with animals, was sent by Father Abbot to take His Reverence's horse, and curry and feed it, to unload the sumpter mules and care for them, and leave all in order at the stables.

Columb led the tired beasts into shelter and spoke to them softly in his own language, which they seemed to understand. He made the animals comfortable, and left them, rubbed down and warm, happily munching, their leather gear and woolen coverings hung in the proper places. All but one saddle blanket, which he took for a cloak. With this around his shoulders, he left, not through the wide doors which welcomed visitors to the monastery, but by a small postern gate.

It was beginning to grow dark, so Columb hurried into the fields, hoping to find some shepherd's hut where he could shelter. Father Abbot was paid in many sacks of wool yearly for the privilege of grazing sheep on monastery lands, and there were many shepherds.

The evening drew in cold and gusty and a persistent rain began to fall. Columb raised his face to the sky in thanksgiving, for the rain brought him thoughts of home, of the dampness and the sweet fragance of the meadows, of the distant blue hills veiled in mist, the chattering little crystal streams of Ireland.

"Is it an omen?" he asked, wondering, hoping. But as he walked on, putting the monastery far behind him, he began to worry that it might not be an omen of welcome, but one of farewell. Surely his father, the Carolan in Ireland, would not be pleased with Columb, and his mother had never crossed that mighty chieftain. John O'Carolan was determined that his eldest son must be a priest, and had so ordered. And Columb was not aware of what arrangements had been made with Father Abbot. Perhaps John O'Carolan would lose money, as well as honor, if Columb's defection were known. Father Abbot might send after him, pass out word to other monasteries and convents to be on the lookout for him. Columb might be put in the punishment cell again, away from the sky and the sun.

When it grew very dark, Columb gave up all thought of finding a manmade shelter, and crouching in the saddle blanket under the overhang of a small ravine, he said his prayers and slept until morning light wakened him. Taking direction from the sun, he set out again, his soaked woolen covering steaming in the early hot rays. When he came to a highroad, he turned south. To keep himself company on the lonely way, he began to sing and to talk to himself.

He was hungry and thirsty. He drank from the rainwater pools that were left from the night's storm and lay winking like jewels in the fields. And, looking about, he found a few mushrooms, which he picked and ate, rejoicing in their earthy-tasting pulp.

Back on the road, he capered and sang aloud.

In a clump of elm trees a little distance from the road, a band of smugglers took bearings for the day. They had managed to cross from France by a secret pass, and were hoping to get to Seville with most of their silks, perfumes, and a bundle of scented leather, which they could sell at high prices to the aristocrats about to set sail for the Indies. The rich men's wives and mistresses, many of whom did not want to leave their comfortable lives in a Spanish or a French city, were loud in their protests, and openly unhappy at the prospect of life among the wild Indians of the new country. Knowing that they would not be able to buy laces, soft leather for slippers, silk or velvets in the Indies, they bought greedily just before setting sail, trying to take with them enough of the things they loved to mitigate the hardships they feared.

The smugglers were three in number. They had crossed the frontiers alone and apart and had met, by previous plan, in Zaragoza. But there were soldiers on the roads, and they were already footsore, and their backs were weary of their burdens. They had camped for the night, around a small fire, protected somewhat by the trees from the downpour. Now the leader, one Ghingheri (Dandy), so called because he always wore a velvet coat finished with jet braid, called the other two to him. They were adventurers from the island of Sardinia who had met in the brothels of Rome and become fast friends in wine and perfidy. Ghingheri now silently pointed out to them the solitary figure on the road.

Columb danced and sang. He was free, he was on the road to the south, and he trusted in God to lead him to the ships. He would try to get a place on one and work his way home to Ireland.

"What do you make of him?" Ghingheri asked the other two, who were called Nero and Scabro.

"A holy innocent," answered Scabro, who, despite his name, was religious and often went to church to give thanks for the success of some scheme. "Look. He wears a habit. A rope sash!"

Ghingheri was thoughtful only a moment. He owed much of

his success as a smuggler, and as occasional assassin, to quick decisions.

"Get him! If the King's men are after us, they are looking for three, not four. We can make him carry part of the load, too. Get him!"

Nero, who was the swiftest, ran out from behind the trees and stopped Columb in the road.

"Brother!" he called. "Come! I can see that you are a religious. We will give you breakfast!"

Columb hesitated only a moment. The mushrooms had not really satisfied a young appetite used to bread and wine. But, though he was unused to the ways of the world, he was not a fool.

"I ask no alms, friend," he said, "and I would therefore wish to know what you want in exchange from me."

Columb had no money, and also he was defenseless. He stood quietly awaiting an answer. Scabro caught up, and shouted, "By Our Lady, we ask nothing but a hand with our burdens, Brother!"

"That I will give gladly," answered Columb and he followed the two across a meadow to where Ghingheri awaited them. He had built up the fire, and with a broad sharp knife he was cutting sausages. These he impaled on sticks, passing them to Nero and to Scabro, and also to Columb. As the sausages heated, the juices rose, and drops fell on the fire, hissing and giving off a delicious odor. Columb felt the saliva fill his mouth. Ghingheri gave out chunks of hard barley bread, and each man held his hot sausage on his piece of bread, pressing the spicy grease into it to flavor and soften it.

As they ate, in silence, Columb observed that there were nine large packages of gear. Two for each man, but three for me, he surmised.

"What is your name, friend?"

Columb had pondered this for many weeks, thinking that he must choose a name for the road in case the abbot, missing him, send out after him. He considered taking his father's name, John O'Carolan, but that would be too close to his own. What about

Paloma? He liked keeping some part of his own identity, and *paloma* meant dove, as did Columb. No. *Conversos*, or baptized Jews, too often took the names of animals; Jews were named Lobo, Leon, Becerro. Quite as often they took as names colors, or the names of trees, or even of towns. But all the same, Columb decided against Paloma. But Palomar? That would be good, the word meant dovecote. Once there had been a visiting bishop from the south by that name.

"My name is Juan Palomar," he answered.

"And mine is Pablo Aguilar!" laughed Ghingheri. "So the eagles have captured the doves, have they?"

"Captured?" questioned Columb, with a straight look at the leader of the band. He had correctly decided that these men must be smugglers, for genuine merchants always had sumpter beasts, and often soldiers to protect them as well.

"A joke! A manner of speaking," answered Ghingheri, jovially. Columb dropped his eyes but he kept his own counsel, and as they trotted southward on the road through the bright morning, each with bundles tied to his back, he made up his mind to attach himself to some other travelers at the first opportunity. Men like these were capable of anything.

When they stopped for a rest at midday, Ghingheri designated Columb to watch while the others had a short nap. Afterward, when they were ready to take to the road again, he tied his bundle on more securely with the rope girdle he wore, and borrowing Ghingheri's knife, he hacked off the lower part of his gown. Below he wore only his long brown woolen stockings, that came up and covered him to the waist, tied there with the points of the weave. His perspiration made the wool itchy and his coarse robe served him no better, and he had decided to make himself look less like a seminarian or a monk. He was just in time, for they had not been moving along the road, where it ran beside a murmuring river, for more than an hour when a horseman appeared, enveloped in a cloud of dust. He came rapidly nearer, and stopped to look appraisingly at the four men, sweating under their bundles. The horseman was armed, and dressed like

one of the King's men, in a red coat, with a wide crossband of
green brocade across his chest, and with a large plume curled
around the rolled brim of his fine hat.

"Hola! Where are you bound for?" shouted the horseman.

"We go south," answered Ghingheri.

"Have you seen some wagon go by with a youth, a stripling, a
seminarian?"

Ghingheri turned to Columb, who stood transfixed with apprehension.

"Son! Did you see anything like a young fellow? He will nod,"
said Ghingheri to the horseman, "because he cannot speak. He
has been dumb since his birth, poor lad. Did you, son?"

Columb nodded negatively, with vigor.

Touching a spur lightly to his horse's side, the man cantered
on, but Columb wondered if he had been deceived by the lie.
Columb indeed, with his black curls, did not look unlike the
swarthy smugglers, but his skin was fair, and it was reddening
and burning now, from too much sun. I must leave these people
as soon as I can, he thought.

He was silent for some way as they strode down the highway
and then he said, "I am grateful to you, friend Aguilar, for not
letting the doves out of the dovecote!"

"One favor deserves another," answered the smuggler. They
jogged on, more slowly as the sun sank, because the day had
been hot and all were weary. They heard church bells from afar,
and then, as the dusk deepened, they saw the flickering lights of
a town; housewives had begun to light their candles, and inn-
keepers to hang out their lanterns.

"We will stay at an inn tonight," called out Aguilar to the
other three. "We are all weary, and we need meat."

The inn was old and evidently a favorite with muleteers and
travelers who came in coaches, as they saw many beasts in the
stables, and carriages unhitched and standing about in the patio.

To the innkeeper—a burly fellow wearing a large dirty apron
that covered him down to his thick calves in their woolen stockings—Aguilar addressed himself.

"Friend, we are weary of the road. We want a hot supper, and beds."

The innkeeper held up his lantern and peered at the four, who were dusty and sweaty from their day's tramp.

"I can sleep three of you in one bed. The other will have to sleep with the hostlers."

Aguilar bargained, and at last it was arranged. Columb was told to stay in the stables, which he was glad enough to do. Was not a stable good enough for Our Savior? he thought, but mindful of their previous encounter with the King's man, he said nothing and continued the farce of being dumb. He marked out a place where he could lie, and after washing himself at the water trough and gratefully eating a bowl of hot stew made with meat, onions, and garlic, he lay down. The animals moved, stamped, snorted restlessly sometimes, and champed their hay and oats. It was a soothing sound, and Columb was utterly weary. At once he fell asleep and knew nothing until midnight, when Ghingheri wakened him.

"Scabro will take your place now. You are to come and rest in bed with us. You're a good lad."

Scabro, somewhat sullen, stood at Ghingheri's side, and, after some grumbling, lay down in the straw where Columb had been. Columb sleepily followed Ghingheri up a short flight of stairs, and then lay down. There were vermin in the bed covers and he could not sleep; indeed he would have preferred to go back to the straw in the stables, but he was afraid of offending Ghingheri, and so he tossed and scratched, and tried not to disturb. At length, made bold by the deep snores of the other two, he left the bed, arranged the bundles and boxes of their baggage, and lay down atop them, where he was more at peace. Finally he slept, but lightly.

He was wakened by a sudden scuffling and cursing. He sat up, but his eyes could not adjust to the darkness at once. He was conscious of struggling bodies, and of danger. Beginning to distinguish the men, he grabbed one of them by the collar and locked his arm around the man's neck. As a lad, before leaving

Ireland, Columb had learned something of wrestling from his companions.

He heard a muffled curse, and the cracking of bones. To his horror, he perceived that there were two assailants, and that Nero had fled. He and Aguilar (Ghingheri) fought hard against the two who had surprised them, but Ghingheri sank to the floor, bleeding. He had been stabbed. Columb used his feet then, knocking the knife from one assassin's hand, and striking him hard in the crotch. The man went down with a scream. The innkeeper by then arrived with his lantern, and Columb saw that the man who lay on the floor wore the King's uniform. The other one had fled through the window, but in falling had wrenched his knee, and two stout stableboys were holding him, and shouting up to the innkeeper.

"Now what is this?" cried the innkeeper. "I won't have scandals and fighting here. You are to get out at once."

Columb was kneeling by Ghingheri. "Aguilar, you are badly hurt. I will nurse you." Turning to the innkeeper, Columb said, "You are to blame, for not providing any safety for your guests from such ruffians."

"Ruffians? They are the King's men!"

"Whatever they are, they have wounded my comrade and I will stay here to take care of him," cried Columb.

Grumbling about letting them stay only until morning, the innkeeper shuffled away.

Aguilar lay breathing painfully and noisily. Columb tried to stanch the flowing blood from Aguilar's chest, but even a piece of the man's shirt held tightly across the wound could not hold back the blood, which bubbled upward.

"I think I am dying," said Ghingheri. "And I think that traitor of a Scabro betrayed me."

The man wearing the King's uniform lay groaning on the floor, writhing. Two stout stableboys rushed into the room, shouting, "They are not the King's men! They are robbers! They stole the uniforms! The one who fell into the patio has confessed it!"

The innkeeper returned, and said, "I will have a maid bring a basin of water and cloths to bind this man's wounds. You have done me a service, revealing the perfidy of these robbers! As for that one, take him away," he ordered the stableboys. "We will send the two of them to the galleys!"

"But, master! Something else has happened!"

"*Dios mio!* What now?"

"The other two, who were with these two," pointing to Columb and Aguilar, "have stolen horses and have run away."

"With my merchandise?" Aguilar managed to half raise his head and ask.

"They had two bundles each, tied to the saddles. But the horses are not theirs! They belong to another traveler!"

Aguilar groaned.

"Is there some baggage left?"

"A few bundles."

"Bring them. I will pay for the horses with merchandise. I am dying. God help me."

"No, no! You will get well!" promised Columb as the maid, with cloths and basins of water, came into the room. She was a buxom woman, with strong arms, who knew what to do. Pushing Columb aside, she opened Aguilar's shirt, tore it away, and began to sop the oozing wound with wet cloths folded into sponges. These she bound tightly around his chest. She sat patiently changing the cloths and sponges, but at an inquiring look from Columb she raised her eyebrows and shrugged her shoulders.

Columb knelt and began to pray aloud. As he began, Aguilar turned his head. He was very pale.

"Palomar! You, the stranger, were loyal to me. You shall have whatever is left of the baggage, after paying for the horses. And," he added, "and my velvet coat. This maid . . . can be . . . witness to my wish."

Columb continued his prayers, but the wounded man lost consciousness, and before noon he died.

Columb had not been a part of violence before, nor ever observed death as part of a sudden wrenching from life of a man in his prime. His experience had been only of passive cruelties, resisted but not fought openly, of quiet preparations for departure, and of deaths of old and quiet monks. The fabric of his thinking was torn; he did not know how to recognize nor to name the emotions he felt. His reaction was to retreat into himself, to pray, and to remain silent, as if the uttering of any word would be sacrilegious.

In silence he stood by while the innkeeper opened the several boxes and bundles of baggage left by Scabro and Nero because they could not carry them. Two contained laces, lengths of satin, velvet, and stiff silk. The merchant whose horses had been stolen accepted them as fair payment, and the innkeeper kept a third to cover his expenses, and to pay gravediggers to take Aguilar's body away for burial.

There remained a bundle for Columb, which contained scented leather, very supple and fine. At once Columb gave half of this to pay for masses for Aguilar's soul. The man had been generous with him, had defended him. Columb chanted De Profundis for him, and grieved. When the innkeeper's maid, who wrapped the body in a shroud for burial gave him Ghingheri's shoes, trousers, shirt, and coat, he accepted them wordlessly.

She said, "I have washed the shirt for you, young sir, and steamed and brushed the coat. It is a fine coat; the trimming is of jet, and valuable, they tell me."

"Thank you," whispered Columb.

Two days later, with his bundle of fine leather, with the jet removed from Aguilar's coat tied in a little bag inside his belt, and wearing the dead man's shirt, shoes, and velvet coat, Columb took a seat in a *diligencia* (stagecoach) going south. He had been able to buy a place in it with one of the skins. The clothes were uncomfortable, because for years he had worn a loose garment, tied on at the waist, and soft sandals. The coat pinched him in the waist, though it was wide enough across the shoulders, and the shoes were too large, and seemed heavy and stiff, but he was glad to have them, for they had stout soles over an inch in thickness, and he kept them on by pushing soft rags into the toes. The hat, cleaned of its vermin, fit him well enough, though he had removed the plume.

He said farewells, heard the coachman crack his whip and the horses jerk the coach into motion. Columb set his face toward the south. The carriage would reach Seville, they told him, in five days' time.

Bouncing in the carriage, he pondered the ways of God, who had shown him a sign to leave the monastery, and had protected him through violence and adversity, and had even provided him with clothes and some valuables. There must be something God wanted him to do, for preserve him He had. I will wait for a sign, thought Columb, and sure that he would be guided, he was able to doze, and even occasionally to talk to some of the other passengers, when they stopped to change horses, or to sleep at a roadside inn.

7.

In her lonely battle to be true to her Faith, and to resist the teachings and insistence of the rabbi, Doña Carmen, and Don Antonio, Guiomar had to fight a growing affection for all three. Doña Carmen was warm and motherly, a bustling, busy, comfortable little person, always ready to give a pat or a kiss, to pop a sweetmeat into Guiomar's mouth, or bring her a cup of hot herb tea. She often came to sit beside the girl when she was ready for bed, to tell her stories of the past, of persecutions of her race, and even some fairytales that lulled Guiomar into gentle dreams.

Don Antonio, too, soon won her respect. She had had no contact with any men save a priest in the confessional, and she saw that he was upright and good, even if harsh in his daily insistence on her repeating to him the lessons she learned from the rabbi. He, too, often laid a kind hand on her head in departing, and she would have given both of them what they asked with a full heart, if only she could have done so without betraying her Savior. She knew she must keep Jesus the Christ enthroned in her soul, full of power and mercy, protected by her secrecy.

In her daily wrestling with her problem, she was helped by the fact that the household went to daily mass, and she with them.

She had been lectured sternly about this by Don Antonio.

"We are Jews, but, in order to survive, in order that our race and our beliefs may endure, we must make pretended compliance with the customs of this country. That is how we regard the mass, as a custom only, a custom based on a false Messiah. We await the True Messiah, who will lead us out of bondage. You are to attend this mass with us, Guiomar, because we must, for our protection, and because spies and informers must have noticed that we have a young woman living here with us. We have given it out that you are our niece, and that you are to go out to the Indies, with the Fleet, to be reunited with your father and brother. This last is true. But I insist that you listen to this mass, as we do, thinking of other things, holding to your own race and blood, one with us, for we are Jews! Do you give me your word?"

"I hold to my race and my blood," answered Guiomar, "and how could I not, having found my own mother at last, only to lose her within a few hours?" The tears came, as she remembered the pity of that pale face and the burning eyes, and her mentors did not notice that she had not actually given her word.

And so, in the mass, she was able to sink her spirit in adoration and beg forgiveness for all the deceits she must practice.

Meanwhile, she was being made ready for her journey. Doña Carmen was a good seamstress, but she engaged two others to help her, and they busily sewed garments for Guiomar: a velvet gown, of sapphire blue, linen undergarments, velvet shoes, and canvas shoes, a long deep blue mantle trimmed with fur, netted hair coverings, and veils, small brimmed hats. Also, Doña Carmen, practical and a good housewife, made long aprons for her, of coarse stuff, to wear over her dresses, in case her father had no servant, and Guiomar must do the housework.

"And you must know how to cook properly, avoiding all the forbidden foods," she told the girl, taking her into the kitchen and teaching her how to make the unleavened bread for the holidays, to stew and braise without lard, and to keep separate the dishes made with meat and those made with milk, for the Mosaic law said that the kid should not be seethed in the milk of its mother.

One day Guiomar fell ill. Usually hearty and of good appetite, she was astounded to find she could keep nothing on her stomach, and the teas Doña Carmen made for her came up at once. Weak and nauseated, she lay on her heaped rugs, holding a linen rag to her lips and praying silently. In the next room she heard Doña Carmen and Don Antonio discussing some matter that aroused their emotions to a pitch, so that they shouted, and she overheard a few words before they hastily silenced themselves.

"I tell you, she can't go," cried Doña Carmen. "Even the rabbi is not sure—"

"She shall go! She is a danger to us here! And he promised he would place a rabbi on the same ship, to watch over—"

"But she is sick . . . And the sailing is next week!"

At this Guiomar was seized with another violent attack of vomiting. She heard no more, and in her distress she forgot the words she had overheard until they returned to her inner ear many months later.

After three days, the illness departed as mysteriously as it had come, but it left Guiomar weak and pale. Doña Carmen clucked as she hastily took in the dresses.

"But I am tightening these seams temporarily," she worriedly explained to Guiomar. "You must eat well and walk in the sun and get strong swiftly, or they may not honor the passage we have bought for you. They are terrified of the pest. There is an illness raging in Italy, they say, which is as bad as the plague."

"Perhaps I had it," whispered Guiomar. "Perhaps my mother had it. She came to us from Italy. She brought it to me, it was all she could give me . . ." The girl began to sob weakly.

"Nonsense!" cried Doña Carmen, and she shook Guiomar roughly. "Nonsense! She brought you our faith, and her last instructions! She made you ours again! Never forget it!"

Coming in later with a strong chicken broth in which floated small dumplings that melted on the tongue, Doña Carmen was her gentle self again.

"Now, my dear, you must drink this and eat the dumplings. They are good for you. You must be well and hearty for your voyage. It is long and tedious, and you will not get food like this on board."

Guiomar obediently ate and drank.

"How long will it take us to reach the Indies?" she asked, beginning to think ahead with interest. "And how will I know my father and my brother?"

Doña Carmen settled herself on a heap of cushions and began, delightedly, to tell what she had heard of New Spain.

"Your ship does not go alone, of course," she said. "The merchant ships go all together, protected by the King's Fleet, and it is a beautiful sight when they all move down the river, hundreds of them, like a flight of great white birds, with wings outspread! You sail out into the Atlantic, coming in sight of some islands after six or seven days, where all the ships stop to take on fresh water and food. And then the journey is very long—days, and weeks, even months—until you see land again. So they have told me."

"And the food and the water last all that time?" marveled Guiomar.

"They bring animals aboard, and kill them as they need them."

"Ay! I cannot watch the killing, or smell it . . ." Guiomar began to tremble.

"You need not. Nor eat any of the meat, for they do not kill the animals according to the laws of Moses, and we Jews should

not touch such contaminated flesh. I am going to get you a pullet
for eggs. And my husband will give you money to buy a piece of
fish, if any are caught."

"You are very good to me, very kind. And the passage, and
these clothes, must cost much money. I will ask my father to
repay you."

Doña Carmen waved her hand.

"You are our kinswoman," she stated, "and anything we have
is yours. You must be true to us, and remember your promise!
And as for food, I shall give you a box with good things that
keep well: bread and little cakes made with sugar and dried
fruits and nuts. Eat very little, and save your water bottles until
the very last, because sometimes, if the ship is delayed, you may
be allowed only a mouthful or two of water each day. So avoid
any of their salty foods, too. And I have made some special soap
for you which lathers in the salt water; it is an old secret. Ask
some sailor to let down a bucket to bring up sea water for you,
and with this soap you can keep yourself clean and fight away
the vermin. The ships attract vermin as sugar attracts ants, they
say, and, for me, this would be the most cruel of the sufferings on
shipboard. And then the sea itself makes people ill. I have some
remedies for that, too, and I have packed a *botiquin* for you with
remedies and instructions."

"You are most thoughtful and kind."

"I try to think of everything. But I know some of the things to
be preventive because many of our people have gone out to the
Indies."

"Are Jews allowed out there?"

"We pretend to be Christians. Otherwise, we could not get
places on the ships. But yes, many of us, many, have gone out
there." She smiled secretly. "The authorities would be surprised
if they knew how many!"

"So I must pretend to be a Christian, too," remarked Guiomar, thoughtfully.

"Yes. But then, you know very well how," commented Doña
Carmen dryly. "Good, you have finished your soup. Now you

must eat this cake soaked in honey. It will strengthen you. Come."

Guiomar obediently ate the sweet, enjoying it, because sweets had not been often on the refectory table at the convent.

Comforted and reassured by Doña Carmen's words that she must "pretend" to be a Christian, Guiomar dismissed her worries. There had been no promise, and she was certain that her father and Gonzalo were Christian. Then why not look forward to being united with them, to the strangeness and wonders of the New World, to the very voyage itself?

She began to count the days between then and departure, and to turn her thoughts, with longing, to the life ahead.

8.

By the time the stagecoach reached Seville, Columb, who now thought of himself as Juan—Juan Palomar—was bone-weary and longing for the chance to stride out into the streets, to swing his arms, to run, and to sing. Indeed, not being able to sing was painful to him; it had been a part of his daily life at the seminary, and he loved the chant, so deeply expressive, so strong and yet tender. Breaking into song at one of the inns where they slept from darkness until early dawn, he had been quickly silenced by the other travelers in the room, and none too pleasantly. He had kept silent from then on, but the old music ran through his mind, and he longed to be where he could draw a deep breath and launch into it again. He even began to remember some of the lilting songs of his own country, and to sing them softly to himself.

On a ship, going home, I shall sing, he resolved. Perhaps my father, when he gets over his rage at my having left the seminary, will let me study with one of Ireland's great bards. I would like that. I would like to be a bard!

Before leaving the coach, from which baggage, bundles, great-coats, and all sorts of packages were being lowered to the ground, and not without occasional sinister sounds of breakage, Juan Palomar said goodbye to the horses. They stood now, winded, with hanging heads, waiting dumbly for their freedom from harness, for a rubdown, a blanket, a measure of oats, and a drink of water. Poor beautiful darlings, thought Columb, loving them. When I am my own man, when I have a farm and space and meadows, as I shall have someday, I will raise beautiful horses, like you, but I will not work you thus, with no hope for rest until you die!

He had caressed and helped comfort the horses every time the beasts were changed. Father Abbot had often reproached him for this affection. "The creatures of the earth are for man to command and to use," he said on more than one occasion. "They have no souls."

"When I get to heaven, I shall change that!" Juan had told him once, in exasperation, earning himself three days on bread and water for blasphemy.

Now free, and having arranged for part of a bed for the night, Juan went at once to the wharves. Many were still being constructed out into the river, for the ships to tie to; the river was clotted with the gently drifting galleons, all the way to Sanlúcar, as far as eye could see. Antlike activity took place ceaselessly as men toiled up the gangplanks taking passengers and bundles and bedding on board, and as they stowed bolts of cloth, wool in skins and carded and spun and wound, spices and salt, dried cod, iron for weapons and tools.

Juan went about asking where he could find a ship sailing for Ireland. Or for the French coast. For the north.

A rough sailor stopped, on his way down a gangplank after carrying up a cask of wine, to answer Juan's question. The din of activity and shouting in several languages was so great that the two men had almost to roar into each other's ears.

"None, friend! The Fleet is going out to the Indies. There isn't any other ship about, nor won't be, until the Fleet sets sail. But look! That will be soon. They are bringing in the galley slaves now, to man the oars of the King's fighting vessels that protect the galleons. After them, the food animals and the water, and then the passengers. And then . . . with the first tide!"

Juan had been afraid to let go of his bundle, and he was tired. He decided to look for a ship receiving female passengers; he would have the best chance to sell his delicate leather for shoes to the women. Some distance ahead, by one of the larger wharves, he saw a party of several women and men, followed by their servants, carrying small leather chests and boxes on their shoulders. They hesitated and looked about, apparently waiting for the purser to come and take their tickets. As Juan approached, he saw a man hurry down from inside the ship, making obeisances to the men and women still onshore who were waiting to board. Juan hurried toward them and came up to them as the purser began counting out the extra ducats which were always taken just before departure.

"Is the ship to sail so soon?" called Juan. "Then would the ladies like to buy fine shoe leather, easily sewed, to take with them?"

Before anyone could answer, they were all shouldered aside, and a heavy smell of sweat and dust enveloped them all. Two men rode on horseback, wearing the red-and-green liveries of the King, guiding and directing a line of eight men who were chained together with neckbands of iron, and who also wore chains attaching them to each other by the ankle. They shuffled along despondently, clanking, while the horsemen shouted and cursed. The galley slaves were of varying ages, some still in their teens, some older men with few teeth and gray hair.

Juan saw a girl start and cry. She had dropped the small shawl with which she had been covering her face, letting only one eye show (for this was custom in Seville, still obsessed with many Arabic customs), and Juan looked upon the loveliest face he had ever seen. In the girl's large black eyes tears sparkled and her tender mouth trembled with sympathy.

"Oh, Uncle, will the poor men have to row us all the way across the sea?" she cried, her voice full of pity.

"Certainly not," was the gruff answer. "Can't you see the masts for the sails? The galley slaves work the oars only on the King's war galleys. But don't cry about them! They are criminals! The King empties his prisons for his ships. The wretches are better off on the water than in the dungeons."

Juan stared. At a sharp word from the older woman, who was holding her shawl up across her nose and mouth, the girl covered herself again, but not before she had looked into Juan's blue eyes and seen his astonished and delighted love.

He had seen no women except the travelers on the stagecoach and the boxom maids at the inns, although he had vague memories of his sisters, who were fair-skinned, blue-eyed and black-haired like himself. This girl had skin like cream, and under the net, which could scarcely hold her thick waving mane, her hair gave off glinting coppery lights.

I must go on the same ship, thought Juan, giving his whole heart with one look. I must be near her, so beautiful, so tender and kind. A sign. Is she the sign? he asked of his saints. He turned for a moment to look at the ship, and he saw the name, in large letters beneath the figure of the siren at the prow. *PALOMA DEL MAR.* Dove of the Sea.

My sign!

He crowded up to the purser and said, "I will take passage on this ship also."

"No you don't," answered the purser. "There is not an inch of space left. These people bought their tickets and their deck space weeks ago! You are too late!"

"I will work! I will work at the sails!"

"Sorry, we have our full quota of sailors."

The purser stopped counting money to stare at the importunate young man.

"If you go downriver toward Sanlúcar, you may be able to get a place on one of the smaller galleons," he said kindly.

The lovely girl had covered her face again, and would not look

at him. All he saw was the bent head, the little velvet hat, and
the long downcast eyelashes.

Juan turned and started south, taking the road that led along
the river. Ireland was forgotten. He would go out to the Indies.

9.

Fray Domingo had been assigned to a ship called the *True
Cross*, which was moored alongside the jetties at Sanlúcar. He
took nothing with him but his breviary, a number of cheap
crosses that he might wish to award if he had the good fortune
to bring some sinner back into the Faith, and a very small bundle
consisting of another soutane and a change of undergarments
and stockings. Having received many blessings from his superiors, and carefully guarding against his heart his instructions
and his documents giving him authority to act for the Holy
Office, he decided to walk to his ship, as an exercise in humility. Accordingly, he took the road that followed along beside the
river, delighting his eyes, as he went, with the sight of so many
of King Philip's wondrous Fleet moored along the way and busily loading.

He meditated as he walked, giving his mind over to prayer
and thoughts of the greatness of God. Almost as if it were part of
his meditation, he began to hear a very sweet voice singing the
Divine Praises. Lifting his eyes, he saw trudging along ahead
of him a young man, carrying a large bundle on his back.
It was this youth who was singing, with heartfelt joy. Fray Domingo hastened his step.

"Ave María Purísima," he greeted the young man, who turned
a candid face toward him.

"Sin pecado concebida," was the immediate and proper answer.

"As we are on the road, for the glory of God, let us walk along together," said Fray Domingo.

"Gladly."

"I heard you singing just now."

"I always sing when I am happy. When I am sad, also," added the young man, as an afterthought.

"Your name, young sir?"

"I am called Juan Palomar," answered Columb. Juan was careful not to tell a real lie to a religious.

"I am Fray Domingo."

They swung along, in step, for a little way.

"Are you going far?" then asked Juan.

"Across the sea."

"So am I!"

"To which port are you bound?" asked Fray Domingo, who had a lively interest in the doings of young men. He had taken the habit young, and while he never yearned for any of Satan's delights and never knew temptation of the worst sort, he was often wistful to know about activities, games, and thoughts.

"I don't know yet," confided Juan. "I have yet to buy a place on a ship. Where does the Fleet go? They told me only 'The Indies.' Where is that?"

Fray Domingo was shocked.

"Why, the Indies are the King's possessions in the New World," he said. "Months of sailing across the unknown waters! You cannot hope to get a place now! Besides, you seem not to have any food, any water—"

"But neither do you," said Juan.

"But I am sent by my order, and the ship's captain will victual me."

"Alas," cried Juan. "Am I to lose her then?"

"You mean, a ship?"

"A ship. And a lady. A beautiful lady I saw who was boarding the *Paloma del Mar*. I never saw such beauty," said Juan, breathlessly. "She has big dark eyes, and wonderful, shining red hair, like copper!"

Fray Domingo pondered this.

"You fell in love," he commented, at last.

"I loved her at once. A face like the Virgin. So good and kind. And lovely."

"I know nothing of this love, except what they tell me in the confessional," commented Fray Domingo. "It is not always good. Not always happy."

"Well, it should be," said Juan. "I felt good, strong, and virtuous, just by looking at her. I could do great things for her!"

Fray Domingo was past thirty years old, and was considered to be a man well into middle age, past the caprices and ardors of youth. Suddenly he was conscious of his mission, of the letters patent from the Holy Office, which were secretly worn inside his habit.

"Would that all the men I speak to were as candid and pure as you, young man," he sighed.

"I am inexperienced in the world," said Juan. "I have been in a seminary, studying religion. But God showed me a sign that I must leave. He sent a messenger to tell me that I must be free, and to go south."

"Let us sit here on this stone and rest a bit. And tell me more about yourself," ordered Fray Domingo. Either this lad is an innocent or he is a rascal, and properly part of my concern, thought the priest.

But after listening to Juan's story of how he came to be on the road, with a bundle of fine leather (Juan did not mention the little sack of jet beads worn inside his shirt), Fray Domingo decided that this young man indeed seemed to be under the protection of some saint.

Yet one must be cautious. The devil works with subtlety as well as with obviously wicked intent.

"You said Father Abbot was cruel to you?" he prodded gently.

"Ay! You sound as if you might be confessing me," laughed Juan. "Indeed, I should confess, and soon. Will there be priests on the vessels, with the body and blood of Our Lord?"

"Oh yes. And we will sing mass. Every day."

"God be praised. I love the mass," said Juan. "Yes, Father Abbot was cruel. As my own father is, often. It seems to be the way," he said, "for men who are training others, to bend their wills and teach them, with pain. But if I ever have sons, I swear I will not chastise them and make them weep, and see them cower when I pass by. 'Love ye one another,' said Our Lord. Why cannot fathers love their sons? And abbots their seminarians?"

"Whom God loves, He chastises," reminded Fray Domingo.

"Well, it was not so with our Sweet Jesus. He did not love the fig tree which denied Him fruit, and therefore He blasted it. But the woman taken in adultery He would not hurt, as the others would. He sent her away. He only said, 'Go and sin no more.'"

Fray Domingo began to feel uneasy. This young man liked to argue, and to argue with the truth. He might be dangerous, he worried suddenly.

"And what about the Holy Office?" he asked. "As a good Christian, do you lament that it is stern against heresies and witchcraft?"

"Oh no!" cried Juan, in horror, crossing himself. "God save us from heretics and witches!"

"There are heretics and witches and evildoers where you might least suspect."

"God save us from them."

"And what was this sign, that you said God sent you? In what form did it appear to you?"

"In the form of a dove," said Juan. "A little pure white beautiful dove, like the Holy Spirit! I see what you have been thinking, Your Honor. That I might have been deceived! Oh no! Can evil take the form of good?"

"Yes, it can. But," sighed Fray Domingo, "I think not, in your case. I think you are innocent of evil. And I will help you. Come. Let us hurry, for the sun begins to sink."

They came to where one of the largest of the galleons, the one which would carry officers of the King out to New Spain loomed up against the sky, casting a great shadow, for it lay so that the sun was behind it.

"This is my vessel, the *True Cross*," explained Fray Domingo. "But I am going to arrange to get you a place. Come."

Fray Domingo pushed his way courteously but firmly through the crowd of people waiting on the jetty beside their boxes and bundles, to where a purser was checking letters and tickets.

"An order from the Bishop of Seville," he announced, in a firm voice, and the people fell back respectfully, "I wish to be taken to the captain at once."

The purser bowed and stepped back so that he might pass.

"Wait!" called Fray Domingo over his shoulder, to Juan.

Juan was glad enough to put down his burden and sit. He was tired and very hungry.

After what seemed a long time, and after two parties of richly dressed men and women, followed by servants in livery, with boxes and chests, had shown their letters and been admitted to the ship, Fray Domingo came back. By this time he had to pick his way very carefully among the boxes and bedding and cages of animals on the decks.

"Juan!"

Juan straightened up, shifted his bundle, and went to stand closer to the monk, though the purser kept a wary eye on him and partially barred the way with his shoulders.

"Juan! You are to have my place on this ship! There is no other way! I will go farther south, and take a place on the sister ship, *El Salvador*. This is your ticket. And the captain will victual you! There, do not thank me! We will meet when the Fleet makes land in the New World!"

Juan, overcome with gratitude, fell to his knees, took Fray Domingo's hand, and pressed it gratefully to his lips.

"I will pray for your intention every day of my life!" he promised.

Juan went up the gangplank, was led to a small cabin amidships and introduced to a quiet man dressed in black, who was arranging his possessions around and beneath the narrow wooden bunk, which was to be his bed.

"Juan Palomar, to serve you and God," announced Juan, courteously, putting his own bundle on the other bunk.

"Fermín García Mendoza," said the man, who turned and looked at Juan with wise dark eyes. The man was thin, swarthy, grave. "I trust we will be good shipmates."

"No reason why not!" cried Juan, who was jubilant at the way in which God was making his way smooth, guiding him with a loving hand. "I can tell you now that I do not get seasick! When I came to Spain from Ireland, our ship was tossed like a ball that children are playing with, but I was never a moment ill!"

"That is good news," said Señor García Mendoza gravely. "May God keep you well."

"And you also," answered Juan.

Farther south along the road, Fray Domingo found the galleon *El Salvador*, and made his way aboard. He was reflecting that his guardian angel had put him in the way of beginning his work at once, for the candid young man, Juan Palomar, would find out much more about his cabinmate than Fray Domingo, a distant relative, could have done. And the Holy Office was suspicious of Fermín. His wife and her relatives were thought to be Judaizers.

All unknowing, Juan will spy for me, thought Fray Domingo, and meanwhile, he said to himself comfortably, I have done a good deed, for which surely I will be rewarded, in good time.

Settling himself onto his narrow bunk in *El Salvador*, he began to read his breviary.

10.

In the narrow cabin, Guiomar put the caged hen under her bunk and disposed her packages of food, her warm rugs and bedding, and her box of clothes. She fought back tears of fear and uncertainty. Doña Carmen had been fierce in her final ministrations, and Don Antonio also had frightened her with his promise of imprecations if she failed in the mission they wanted her to perform.

"But I cannot, I cannot," whispered Guiomar to herself. "I cannot deny Our Lord and his Sweet Mother. And if I did the Holy Office would pursue me, to burn me, as they meant to burn my mother, aiii!" She threw herself on her knees before her bunk and gave herself over to intense prayer and to tears. Later, somewhat comforted, she rose and made an effort to compose herself.

Doña Carmen and Don Antonio know about the Inquisitors and the Holy Office. They know its terrors, she thought, but they are not afraid. What wonderful courage! But I do not have it! Even if I did not believe in the True Faith, I think I would pretend, to save myself!

Confused, bewildered, and fearful of the future, the girl once again made up her mind to be extremely cautious, to hide her thoughts, and to pray silently and often.

"I put my trust in Thee," she murmured under her breath, as two women who were to share her cabin entered with their boxes, chests, and bundles.

They were a woman in middle age, and thin, dressed in dark clothes, and a young girl, evidently her daughter, for she had the same pale oval face, straight dark hair, and dark eyes.

"Ave María Purísima," greeted Guiomar, rising. She was answered at once by the two.

"If we are to share this cabin, let us tell our names," said Guiomar, shyly. "I am Guiomar Montemayor."

The older woman answered.

"Mariana Medina de Cerezo, at your service. And my daughter, Judit."

"I am afraid we shall be very crowded," murmured Guiomar. "Perhaps we could store some of our baggage on the deck."

It was agreed that Guiomar and Judit were to go aloft, to see if they could arrange for space on the deck. They found a place where they were permitted to stow several boxes, and, with the help of a cabin boy, they were able at last to clear their bunks enough so that they could lie down to rest. The two Cerezos, being very slender, lay on the narrow bunk in relative comfort, though Guiomar, who was taller and well rounded, found the bed so narrow that she could scarcely turn upon it. Judit noticed her efforts, and commented, "Ay, Doña Guiomar, you will be as thin as we are when we get to New Spain! They tell me that often the food and water do not last for more than half the voyage, and even what we carry is not enough!"

"Then we must share it," remarked Guiomar.

"So we should."

The two young girls began to exchange comments on what lay ahead, to share plans.

"We are going out to live with an uncle in Zacatecas, where there are great mines," confided Judit. "We have not heard from him, but when my father died, we did not know where to go. My mother sold some jewelry for our passage, and we are going to seek him, though we never knew him."

"I, too, am going out to be united with relatives I have never seen," said Guiomar. "My father and my brother. Only, they know that I am coming; they will meet me in Veracruz, and take me home to Mexico City."

"How fortunate you are! We have no one, and will have to ask our way. Zacatecas is far to the north, they tell me."

"Meanwhile, here we are, together," cried Guiomar, her heart lifting at the prospect of having a young companion on the voyage. "How soon will we sail, do you think?"

"We were told that the King's Fleet will sail down the river tonight, and they will take the morning tide, out of Cádiz. Come, let us explore. My mother would like to rest, anyhow. She has not been well since we lost my father; she has wept until she has no juices left in her body, and no strength."

The two girls went aloft again managing to use the narrow iron steps swiftly enough, despite their full skirts. The decks were anthills of activity, of coming and going, of shouting and the stowing and the moving of baggage, and of caged food animals, of last-minute passengers demanding to be shown their cabins.

Suddenly Guiomar thought of the young man who had stared at her with such awe and delight, as if she were the Holy Virgin, the young man with eyes blue as the sea. She wondered if he had found a place on another of the galleons.

"Why not? There are so many," she murmured as she looked southward, along a forest of masts, where so many ships lay tugging at their anchors in the river. "And he was willing to work."

"What did you say?" asked Judit.

"Oh, I was thinking of the people who wish to go out to New Spain, but who cannot find a place on the ships. How sad for them!"

"Yes. There is only this one fleet, protected by their own numbers and by the King's warships. Of course, there are other ships, that start out alone. But I have heard it said that this is the best time of the year. In summer there are terrible calms, when there is not a breath of air for the sails, for weeks, sometimes . . . And in the fall, there are storms. In the winter, they say, great islands of ice come floating along on the water, and they are like knives, to cut a ship in two, as one beheads a chicken!"

A tall man with gray hair cut close to his head, like a monk, and yet not tonsured, and gray eyes like two silver pieces in his brown face, strode toward them. He was followed by a black slave, a boy of fifteen or sixteen, who was carrying two large boxes and a small kit.

"Careful, Gomo!"

The tall man was dressed in sober brown wool, and wore a long cape of the same stuff. The black boy was warmly dressed too, and in the same stuff, but he had tied an orange-colored silk handkerchief around his thick black curls.

The tall man stopped and bowed to Guiomar and Judit.

"I am Dr. Morales," he told them. "I hope you will not be ill, young ladies, but should that happen, I have herbs and poultices and medicines of all kinds, and I can make you well. For a very small fee."

"Thank you," the girls murmured, with downcast eyes. The man continued to stand near them, staring at them fixedly, first at Judit and then at Guiomar.

"Are you traveling alone?" he asked then.

Guiomar looked up with sudden suspicion. But the man's strong-featured face was grave and kind, and his deep voice betrayed no special interest.

"With my mother, who is below," answered Judit.

Dr. Morales bowed.

"I send her my greetings," he said, and he made a curious gesture with his right hand, touching his breast, then his forehead. He strode away, followed by Gomo, and they disappeared among the many other passengers disputing deck space for their gear.

Guiomar suppressed a little shiver. She had felt the man's curious strength and magnetism.

"I think he must be a Morisco," confided Judit. "Did you not see his salaam?"

"I saw."

"They are said to be the best doctors. The Moriscos and the Jews."

"But Morales is a Spanish name. Perhaps it is not his true name."

"Oh look, that lady has brought a little monkey with her," cried Judit.

And they admired the lady, who, dressed in finest velvet and wearing gold chains, and with pearls sewed on her hat, tripped by, carrying a little chattering monkey on her bent arm. It too was dressed in velvet and wore a jeweled chain on its hat. The monkey chattered and pointed to the two girls, but the lady swept by, without a second look toward them. When she was gone, Judit said, curling her lip, "I hope she has need of Dr. Morales's medicines, the vain creature!"

"Why do you care?" asked Guiomar. "She is not a friend of ours. I only looked at her little monkey. I hope she is kind to it."

Her thoughts returned to the tall doctor, who had spoken to

them, and she wondered why he had singled them out; he
seemed not to greet any other passenger. And she remembered
again the handsome youth who had admired her.

Having been told in the convent that she was to be married,
Guiomar had timidly begun to wonder somewhat about men and
their ways and what love might be. But she shook those thoughts
off when they came.

I am going out to care for my dear family, she told herself,
and I shan't marry for years and years. Maybe never.

11.

In the ports of England—Plymouth, Hull, Southampton, and
others—many swift sailing vessels were being made ready, too,
for the Spanish Fleet to the Indies was their fair game, and
dozens of wealthy lords put up the cash to outfit ships and sometimes even insisted on captaining them. The ships were manned
by stout sailors, expert seamen, and good fighters, for though the
Spaniards called them pirates, the English Queen praised them,
and gave them honors and titles and sometimes lands. As free
Englishmen, they liked nothing better than to tweak the beard of
King Philip, and besides, life on the sea was better than in the
stews and filth of the cities. Few of them were countrymen, they
were the products of poverty and of survival, the brats of cut-
purses and serving wenches, of stablehands and washwomen,
but many, too, were descendants of the fierce Vikings, who had
overrun England in centuries past and left their seed in many a
red-haired, thick-armed churl who would rather freeze in salt
spray than clean the spittle from stone floors in a tavern. And
there was always the chance of gold. The law of piracy was
fairly democratic; after the captain had taken his share of the
looting, the men with him could fight to divide the rest. There
were men, scarred from sea battles, who had hoarded enough

gold to outfit their own vessels, and Captain George Trout was one of them.

It is true that he had mortgaged his ship to Sir Harry Lynn, for enough money to outfit and victual her, but he had done this before, to the great satisfaction of both, and Sir Harry Lynn, after Trout's second voyage, had been able to court and to marry a widow of one of the Queen's cousins, a lady with lands and a castle. He and Trout had high hopes for the Spanish Fleet in this year of Our Lord 1585. Trout's vessel was swift and light, and it was well armed. The overloaded, top-heavy Spanish galleons would never be a match for the *Mary Ann*. The trick was to follow the Fleet's route, well out of sight, and wait for the straggler, or the last two or three of the Fleet—and then pounce.

Spies from Spain had reported that the Fleet intended to go to sea a week before the English had calculated that they might set sail, so activity was heavy in the small hidden cove where the *Mary Ann* was berthed. George Trout knew his sailors, and he had procured barrels of rum ahead of time, so as to be certain of holding their loyalty, because if winds failed, or some bad luck dogged them, the men, seeing their dreams of gold fade, became restless and ugly. He stored a barrel of rum in his own cabin for emergency.

Somewhat against his better judgment, he was signing on eight country lads this voyage. In case of need, he could always sell them as slaves. The Irish were the best, but it was not always possible to buy them. Every now and then there were raids by Protestant soldiers of the Crown to take prisoners of the recalcitrant Irish Catholics and sell them as galley slaves for Mediterranean warships, but there had not been a good successful raid of the sort for years. Trout perforce had to make do with some stout Devonshire men, who knew they were to work the ropes and the sails and take part in the fighting and boarding of enemy ships. And of course, it was in the boarding and looting of the enemy's vessels that the most in gold, jewels, fine stuffs, and other treasures was taken.

Still, a country Englishman was more to be trusted than one of the town bullies, thought Trout, a heavyset man who had no compunctions about breaking open a head with a stout club, or sending a manacled man overboard into the sea, for discipline. He himself always wore a honed dagger, and a thick short club at his waist, as well as a wheel-lock pistol, an improvement on the matchlock, giving him an advantage over any adversary. When a sea battle was imminent, Captain Trout passed out matchlock pistols to his trusted men, though many of them actually preferred clubs and knives for quick personal encounters. Needless to tell, Trout collected and stored and held all the matchlocks in his own cabin after an encounter. Pirate crews were prone to mutiny, as they lived on greed and cruelty.

This year, the winds being favorable, Captain Trout took his vessel out, sailing carefully south not far from the coast of France, and calculating with care the probable arrival of the Spanish Fleet at the Canaries. From then on, he would dog them until his chance came. He was sure it would come. It always had.

12.

Dr. Morales and Gomo had a cabin to themselves, where they needed space for the doctor's boxes of herbs, bandages, and nostrums. They had sailed for the Indies several times—three, to be exact—and had come provided with everything they would need in order successfully to stow and preserve their luggage.

Gomo, who was an ingenious carpenter, brought with him two sets of shelves, which he was able to screw into the walls of their cabin. One, of light wood, held small boxes, each of which was labeled so that the doctor could immediately lay his hand upon any powder, crumbled leaf, or combination of them that he might require. The second set of shelves was sturdier, and held some liquids in bottles, as well as strips of clean bandages, soap, and alcohol. The doctor, unlike many of his profession, believed in washing wounds, and even patients. And indeed, he was very careful of his own strong well-muscled hands, which he kept scrupulously clean, with fingernails pared close and free of dirt. His boxes of knives, saws, grips, tweezers, forceps, and packages of splints, some of bone and some of wood, he kept to one side, in a locked chest.

Having set up the medicines in their shelves, Gomo cleverly made new locks for the door, a procedure the doctor always insisted upon at once, knowing full well how tempting to thieves were some of his drugs, not to mention his knives.

Dr. Morales was very open and confidential with his slave, whom he had owned and trained since babyhood, and for the safety of whose soul he had taken every precaution.

Once the cabin was in order, Gomo attached to the outside of their door a sign which indicated the doctor's trade: a white tube ringed round with red. This meant that he was also a barber and a bloodletter, should need for these activities arise.

All being in readiness before the ship had even cut its moorings, he and Gomo then locked their door with a strong bar from inside, and under their breaths, silently, but with deep concentration and respect, they made their devotions.

13.

The captain of the *True Cross* was not pleased at the peremptory orders he had received from a simple Dominican friar, though, when the monk had displayed his letters patent, he had had to mask his resentment and pretend agreement and approval.

"The young man is to act for me in a confidential capacity," Fray Domingo had said, "giving me his information for the use

of the Holy Office. It is well known, Captain, sir, that the ships
bound for the Indies carry many disguised and hidden heretics
who hope to escape detection in the New World, but plan to
continue to undermine the authority of Holy Church. Therefore,
please victual him as you would me, and be assured that God
will bless you."

The captain had then bowed and agreed to everything, and indeed had permitted that Juan be conducted to the cabin reserved for Fray Domingo. However, he planned to ease Juan out
of that space and utilize him in some way later, reselling the
cabin space. This plan he put into action shortly after the orders
to move downriver and put out to sea were received. At first he
was required to be on deck, at the helm, where he made a fine
showing in his green-velvet suit, and wearing his plumed hat
tied on with a chin strap and a back strap, against the wind. This
was for show. As soon as they were under way and out at sea,
the captain would change into a uniform of rough warm homespun, and wear his hair tied back with a green scarf. His badge
of office was a band of green silk across his chest and the belaying pin in his hand. No sailors were allowed any arms or weapons at all, unless a battle was imminent, in which case harque-
buses and bows and arrows were apportioned out to all
able-bodied men, seamen and passengers.

With the first tug of the ship away from its moorings and its
gradual movement out onto the waters of the river, Juan was
overjoyed. He rushed up on deck and proposed to stay there, enjoying the departure, watching the orchards and fields slide
away on either side, taking in deep lungfuls of the river's watery
breath. Characteristically, he broke into song, intoning an old
Irish melody that had been going through his head ever since he
had first set eyes on the lovely lady of the coppery hair. But before he could finish his tune, a sailor touched him on the arm,
and said, "The captain wishes to speak to you." Juan followed
the man into the captain's cabin, still humming under his breath.

The captain looked up at Juan, taking good note of the broad
shoulders, the strong arms, the youth and health of the young

man, and, perhaps even more important to him, the candor and friendliness of the face.

Instead of simply giving his orders, which he was perfectly entitled to do, the captain devised a small lie, because Juan stood so respectfully smiling.

"I am in trouble, Señor Palomar, and I believe you can help me."

"Gladly!" cried Juan. "What can I do?"

"A messenger of the King has come aboard at the last moment, and he has no cabin space. Would you . . . ?"

"He can have mine," offered Juan at once. "I can bed down anywhere else, I am not used to luxuries."

"And there's another problem. I am lacking a boy to serve at my table, where the King's messenger, his wife, and other important persons will dine. Could you possibly . . . ? Would you . . . ?"

"I could serve, yes," agreed Juan at once, suddenly beginning to see a pattern emerge, but he did not allow his open friendly expression to vary. "I am never seasick, Captain, so no doubt I could be helpful to you."

The captain glanced at him sharply. He had not been convinced that Fray Domingo was telling the entire truth about this young man, but he decided to find out before they were at sea, where he would be obliged to be on duty, carefully shepherding his galleon into line and watching out for the sandbars of Cádiz.

"Fray Domingo told me of your mission, and, I felt you would have more opportunity to gather information, and to form judgments, if you were able to move over the ship as freely as any of my servants do."

Juan merely smiled in a conspiratorial way, and the captain, somewhat against his will, was forced to decide that Fray Domingo had indeed trained the young fellow as a spy for the Holy Office. That smile . . . that disingenuous manner . . .

"And so, when we are out to sea, you will present yourself in the kitchens," he finished. "You may sleep with the cabin boys.

They too overhear many things, you know, and I understand
that every idle word may have meaning."

"Assuredly," agreed Juan. Being then dismissed by the captain, he went back to his place at the rail and pondered the
meaning of what had just taken place.

There's some conspiracy, he decided at last, and I am thought
to be privy to it. Well, I can hold my tongue and listen and
watch until I find it out.

Worrying about his bundle of leather, he went below to re-
trieve it. Fermín García Mendoza had made no changes in the
arrangements of the cabin.

"You are to have another cabinmate," Juan informed him.
"The captain has told me so. I am to sleep with the cabin boys
and waiters, and work serving the tables and washing dishes."

Señor García Mendoza raised his black brows in inquiry.

"I thought you had been sponsored by the *fraile* [monk]," he
murmured.

"Oh yes, I am," answered Juan. "But he gave me his place out
of sheer kindness, and what he could do, I can do also, at the
captain's request."

"You are charitable," said García Mendoza, with a slight bow.

"One should be accommodating," said Juan. "I shall hope to
see you and speak with you sometimes," he added, "if I am not
kept too busy."

"I fear you may be," answered García Mendoza. "But we will
meet, I am sure."

Juan shouldered his bundle and made his way below to where
the sounds and smells told him the kitchens were located. One of
the assistants, a burly black man wearing a voluminous grease-
stained apron, met him at the door with a surly, "Keep out of
here!"

Juan stood his ground.

"The captain said I was to help wait on table."

"*Cáspita!*"

"I never get seasick," offered Juan, and at those words he saw the dark face split into a smile, showing broken teeth but unmistakable cordiality.

"You have sailed before, young scrub?"

"Yes."

"Good. You can stow your gear with mine. Here, give it to me." As Juan hesitated, he went on, "We all sleep together here, there are no separate bunks. What have you got in here anyway? Most table servants come aboard with nothing, not even an apron!"

"I have my inheritance, which I am to sell when we get to New Spain."

The man looked dubious.

"Scrub, you will be lucky to keep a thread of it . . . I can feel that it is soft—velvet, is it? Or Damascene stuff?"

"It is soft leather for ladies' shoes," explained Juan, thinking he might as well tell the truth, for it seemed the bundle would be examined anyhow.

"But I can help protect you," offered the Negro. "For a price."

"Agreed," said Juan. "I will give you three of the skins when we land."

"Five."

"Three."

"Four."

"Three."

Suddenly the black face split again, and Juan was clapped on the shoulder with a heavy hand.

"Good little bargainer you are, eh? Three, then. My name is Roque. Yours?"

"Juan Palomar."

"Juan. I'll call you Scrub, though. Then everyone will know you are under my protection. That you are my scrub boy. Here, we will stow your bundle with my gear."

Roque opened a cupboard where heavy plate of a dark metal was stacked, as well as piles of squares of fine linen.

"The captain's plate and napkins," explained Roque, "but there's room in back, and that's where I keep my shore clothes."

Somewhat uneasy, Juan saw his bundle shoved behind the plate and the cupboard door closed.

"Don't worry, nobody dares touch this cupboard but me," explained Roque. "Now, we had better contrive an apron for you. Wait here."

Juan waited, as told. His head was whirling with speculation. What had Fray Domingo given the captain to suppose? That he was a spy? The idea was repugnant. Did the terror of the Inquisition reach into this galleon? And the captain! He had failed Fray Domingo at the first opportunity and sold out the passage the friar had passed over to Juan. Faithless, not a man of his word.

They see me as helpless, thought the young man, and he made up his mind that the first thing he would do, when he sold his leather in the New World, was buy himself a dagger. And let his beard grow. His smooth young face looked too simple and open for the men he was dealing with. And he fostered no illusions about Roque. Juan had been protected in the seminary for years, but gossip and worldly ideas had filtered in. He knew about the men who took boys for their lovers, and he feared that the long voyage, without women for men such as Roque, might bring out into the open vices usually kept hidden and paid for in secret.

Pondering, and praying for guidance, he saw a little mouse pop out of a small hole in the wall near the floor. It looked at him in fright, and scuttled away to hide, at once.

A sign, thought Juan. Keep quiet, hide, let no one know anything about me. A mouse can keep away from animals stronger and more dangerous. So will I!

14.

Guiomar was happy to see that when the bells sounded for rosary on the galleon, Judit and her mother knelt with her and said the prayers with a devotion as profound as her own. Murmuring the words of the prayers, Guiomar felt take possession of her spirit the feelings of security and safety that had always been hers inside the convent. She could see, in her imagination, the dear face of the Mother Superior, and could feel the coarse stones of the convent under her knees instead of the ship's timbers. Guiomar possessed a small rosary of thirteen decades, of the kind invented by St. Dominic; Mother Superior had helped her make it, from the small hard black seeds of a tree that grew in the convent gardens, and she herself had given Guiomar the silver cross affixed at the end. Guiomar wore this inside her clothes, close to her heart, and she did not always draw it out to say her prayers. She knew the prayers and the mysteries, and she could count them on the ten fingers of her hands. Judit also said the prayers without a rosary, but she confessed to Guiomar that her mother had a golden rosary, worth many ducats, that she wore inside her clothes. They might have to sell the beads, one by one, she confided, to get to Zacatecas, at last.

When the day of sailing dawned and the galleons moved in majesty out onto the broad bosom of the river and thence down to Sanlúcar and Cádiz, the two girls went up on the top deck to watch and to breathe. Their cabin was below the water level, on the second deck, and it was stuffy and hot.

It was a pearly morning when the galleons put out to sea, moving in a line about five leagues apart. It was an impressive sight. Each vessel, standing high in the water, with its three masts piercing the blue sky, looked like an immense swan and seemed even somewhat the same shape except for the long arching neck. The galleon was heavily loaded, and there was little deck space. The sailors, burly men of all ages, some with beards, some scarred, and many with tattered garments, were running about the deck on their duties, and climbing up and down the rigging to adjust the sails. The girls were peremptorily ordered below by one of the boatswains and were timidly returning when a strong bass voice, said, with authority, "I am ship's surgeon. I will vouch for these ladies and keep them out of danger."

Guiomar saw that the speaker was Dr. Morales, and again she felt a thrill of fear and respect. His large pale-gray eyes seemed to capture the light and reflect it back in a shining ray; she felt herself momentarily dizzy until he turned his gaze upon Judit.

"Follow me," he said. He took them skillfully through the maze of packages and bundles on deck and down a short narrow stair.

"This is my cabin. You will be safe here, and you can watch through this porthole. There is none in your cabin, is there?"

"No, none. It is very hot and breathless below."

As they stepped into the cabin, the black boy, Gomo, moved silently past them, not looking at them, and when Dr. Morales left, Gomo followed him a few paces behind.

The girls took turns at the small round window, but after a time, Guiomar turned away.

"I would rather be up on top," she said. "But maybe we can manage that later when we are out at sea, after the baggage is all lashed away. I saw the sailors working on it. Then there should be a little space in which to move."

"Maybe," murmured Judit. "Though, if there is a storm, it would be dangerous. The masts might topple and fall, the waves might wash over the decks, and we would be drowned."

"What good to be below if the waves pour into the whole ship?" asked Guiomar. "I would rather be thrown into the sea than die below, like a rat in a box."

"Uuuuu!" Judit shivered. "I am always afraid," she told Guiomar. "I always think of things that would be terrible. Do you not, sometimes?"

"Sometimes," answered Guiomar. "But I try not to. It is Satan who fills us with fear. Our Lord said, time and time again, 'Be not afraid.'"

Judit had turned her attention to the doctor's cabinets.

"So many bottles, and packages, and boxes," she murmured. "What do you suppose is in them?"

Before Guiomar could answer, she became aware of a presence beside her, and whirling about she saw that Dr. Morales was standing silent and watchful in the narrow doorway.

"I knew you young ladies would never touch my medicines," he said calmly. "Come now, I have found a place above where you can watch the coastline for a little while. Where is your mother?" he asked Judit.

"Lying down. She does not feel well."

"I will examine her later. If she has some dangerous disease, we must put her ashore."

"Oh no!"

"Oh yes! We cannot have illness on the ship. The sailors might catch it, and then what would happen to us all, sailors and passengers? No, taking care of the health of everyone on the ship is a very important and serious duty which God has laid upon me."

As she heard his words, Guiomar crossed herself. Judit and the doctor himself also piously touched brow, chest, and shoulders with their fingertips.

The doctor made a peremptory gesture to them to follow him, and they did so, silently. He had discovered a small alcove formed by a space between two towering boxes which were lashed to the side of the room built upon decks for the chapel, where mass would be said daily.

"You may stay here to watch the shore," the doctor told them. "I will come for you later."

Guiomar felt the gentle heaving of the seas under the ship, and rejoiced in the sweet breath of the breeze off the water. Overhead the sails had caught the wind and were billowing under it, moving the galleon silkily across the swells. Ahead she saw another galleon, and beyond that another, and behind she could see a trail of others.

"I wonder how many of us are going out to the Indies," she said aloud.

"Oh, I heard we were more than two hundred galleons. And going with us are the King's armed vessels, with cannons and soldiers to protect us."

"Against what?"

"The pirates," Judit told her. "They lie in wait for the galleons, and come aboard and seize everything and throw all the women into the sea!"

Judit shivered and crossed herself again. Guiomar put out her arm and drew her close.

"You are a little scaredy lizard," she said fondly. "Never mind. I will take care of you!"

"I am glad I am to be in the cabin with you, Guiomar," whispered Judit. "Mamacita is always ailing, and I am always so afraid!"

"Well, let us not be afraid of anything now. Look out at the beautiful sea, so blue and pure! And the ships riding on it, so beautiful! Beautiful, all of them! I am glad to be going out to the New World!"

15.

Juan found that serving the dignitaries at table was not so much difficult as delicate. He was obliged to hold the dishes so that the ladies and gentlemen could serve themselves, not a hard trick to learn, but what was much more complicated was learning the protocol. The ship's chaplain must be served first, then the general of the sea, as the captain was called, then, in order of their importance, the governor and other authorities who were traveling, clergy, and ladies, and lastly, whatever assistants and companions were traveling with them.

Roque laughed after Juan explained his troubles in remembering how to rush around the table to one important personage after another.

"And one lady always reaches down to touch my knee as I stand there, while she serves herself with one hand," he recounted with fury, "and one of the assistant pilots pinches me every time I pass."

"Uh! That's nothing!" crowed Roque. "Wait until they are all seasick as well, and demand that you serve them in their cabins!"

Juan looked at him in consternation.

"Hold on, Scrub. I will look after you! I'll go with you, and stand at the door with the dishes while you serve. I know how to outwit these *sinverguenzas*."

"Maybe if I complain to the chaplain—"

"Stay away from *him*," advised Roque. "Mind my words!"

Suddenly Roque stopped himself, and a look of cunning overspread his features. "Of course, when you have to speak with him . . . er . . . I understand."

"What do you understand?" asked Juan quickly.

"I overheard the Dominican talking to the general—I was just coming aboard, you see—and I heard him mention the Inquisition—so—"

"You think that I am a spy," said Juan.

"I will keep your secret, of course!" cried Roque.

Juan was silent, but then he looked Roque full in the face. "It would be wise of you to keep it," he said only, and he saw, with a stab of contrition, the dark face take on a look of obsequiousness and fear.

As soon as he could, Juan made his way out to the rail, where he could stare at the sea and try to organize his thoughts. Instinct had told him to utilize the comparative safety of being thought a spy for the Holy Office. Yet spying, and indeed any kind of deceit, was against his nature. The Holy Office had not been established in Ireland. No Irishman would stand for it! thought Juan hotly.

However, he saw that he would have to accept the covering lie for his own protection, since the incidents at table had warned him clearly enough of what persons in high places thought could be done with a simple serving boy. Juan had confidence that Roque would not give out any information, but if he had heard the Dominican tell the general that Juan was a spy, that fact might be used to demand protection, should it be needed.

The water rushed against the sides of the galleon with a soft swishing sound, and the air was clean and fresh. Ireland! He had hoped to be going home. But no! With all its dangers and mysteries, this was better! And he would see that lovely lady again. He would make his fortune, somehow, and he would find that lady of his heart. He broke into happy song.

16.

Two hundred and forty galleons, in a long line, moved out to sea, their sails opening against the wind like blossoms. Beside them, being sent swiftly through the water by the chained oarsmen, the King's war galleys skimmed along, their cannons ready to be used against any danger, by land or by sea. The galleys kept to the landward side, but when the Fleet reached the narrow passage past the Rock of Gibraltar, the warships went on first, and then stood by until every last galleon had maneuvered itself through the strait, and out into the Atlantic. The war galleys kept vigil for a hundred leagues or more, to make sure no hidden pirates—Moroccan, English, Turkish, or French—presented alien sails against the sky. Then, feeling that the Fleet, in open water, was as safe as could be managed, the war galleys turned back toward the Mediterranean, which was, after all, their home.

There was a risk, of course, that there might be an ambush, or trouble of some kind, at the Canaries, but the risk had to be taken. The galleons stood out beyond Tenerife while extra stores and fresh water were brought aboard, and then, outfitted against all danger, as far as could be ascertained, the Fleet started across the pathless gray waters of the Atlantic. All hands and all passengers prayed daily for good weather, and for fair winds all the way. The pilot, a seasoned veteran, had made the voyage many times, and knew just how far north to go to catch the prevailing winds for the West, which should blow them safely into port at Hispaniola in a month's time.

But the galleons were wide and heavy in the water, and carried more cargo than they could safely manage in a storm. They were unarmed, save for a few cannon, and there were few soldiers on board to protect the vessels in case of being rammed by a pirate and put to a hand-to-hand fight on the decks. Some of the passengers were uneasily aware of these dangers, among them the ship's surgeon of the *Paloma del Mar,* Dr. Morales. But he had made the voyage many times, always safely, and indeed, fortune seemed always to protect him under a strong mantle.

"And thank God for that," he murmured under his breath, "for I have the Lord's work to do, and it must be done."

Dr. Morales was in no fear of betrayal to his enemies, because he had only his slave boy Gomo in his confidence, and Gomo could not read or write. And Dr. Morales had, with a small operation, made certain that he could not talk, either. He had done this with many apologies to the Deity, being a very pious man, but the Lord's work was sacred, and some sacrifices had to be made.

The doctor had gone about on his ship making the acquaintance of all passengers, noting with his experienced eye which ones might become genuinely ill of some humor or other, which ladies seemed likely to swoon for no reason or to become hysterical, which ones might be drafted into service should there be trouble on shipboard, with a resulting need for nurses. He thought actually in terms of "trouble," for the great plagues that swept Europe occasionally, might at any time creep aboard in the person of some apparently healthy person, and break out into an epidemic very difficult to control. At the moment, the doctor was worried about Mariana Cerezo, who had kept to her cabin since the beginning of the voyage, and who, as he learned by questioning Judit, ate very little.

Two days out of Tenerife, he took occasion to call at the

Cerezo cabin to inquire about her. The sea was calm, heaving gently like a person asleep, and he had had no cases of seasickness, save two, those being an elderly woman and her maid, who had frightened themselves into nausea.

Leaving the terrified women sleeping after doses of a mild soporific, he had searched out the cabin where Guiomar and Judit were resting. It was early in the afternoon, and they had eaten their barley bread and some dates. The little hen, upset at the strange noises and movement of the ship, had as yet laid no egg, though Guiomar petted and coaxed her.

The doctor knocked briskly and called out, "Open, please! Dr. Morales here."

Guiomar sprang up and opened the door at once. He noted the rich waist-long cape of waving coppery hair, for her net had become undone as she rested. What a beauty, thought the doctor. If I were not committed to my work . . .

"I understand the Señora Cerezo is unwell," he said at once.

Judit rose from the bunk where she lay beside her mother, hastily arranging her dress and smoothing back her hair.

"Mother is not sick," she explained. "She is grieving. We lost my father but a few months ago."

"My sympathy." The doctor looked about, with his strange light-colored, overlarge eyes. When those eyes passed over Guiomar, even briefly, she felt as if he had touched her with a magician's wand, because at first she went cold, and then burning hot. Her blush, staining her cheeks and neck with rose, did not go unnoticed by the doctor, who thought, with pleasure: she is so innocent, unused to the company of men. As I was told.

Mariana Cerezo sat up. She was an older version of Judit, small, black-haired, pale, and thin.

"I see you have a chicken here," said Dr. Morales. "It would make you a nourishing soup. If you wish, I will have my boy Gomo prepare it for you."

"No!" cried Guiomar. "Oh, I couldn't let my little Pollita be killed!"

The doctor looked sharply at her.

"It is yours, the chicken?"

"Yes. Oh, but I am ashamed. If it is needed, for Señora Cerezo . . . I will give it," added Guiomar impetuously. "I spoke before I thought."

"I think I can find some other bird that will do to make soup," answered the doctor, "if yours is a pet."

"It is to give us eggs," explained Guiomar, "but as yet it hasn't laid."

"Keep it. Eggs are very nourishing, too. I will see what I can do."

He approached Señora Cerezo and laid a large cool hand on her forehead.

"No fever," he said approvingly. "But, señora, if you do not eat, and provide your body with some food, you could become seriously ill, and a burden to your daughters."

"Only one is my daughter," she put in, and Guiomar spoke. "Yes. I am traveling alone."

Truthful, he thought, approvingly. He had known about Guiomar, but he had wanted to test her and her cabinmates, to see how careful they were to make the relationship clear. He saw that they were without guile, all three.

The doctor gathered his skirts about him and sat down. He customarily wore a longish covering smock, which showed stains of blood and medicine from previous washings, although it was clean enough. Beneath the smock, his clothes were sober and unadorned.

"We must help you out of your melancholy," he told Señora Cerezo. "Did you not know that it is an affront to God, to resist His will, to receive His commands with so much sorrow?"

The doctor reached inside his smock and drew out a crucifix.

"I know," murmured Mariana Cerezo. "But the tears come. I can't help it. And when I mean to eat, my throat swells with sobs, and closes."

"Let us pray together," said the doctor, and he led them into a long prayer.

"Now," he said, "I will send my boy to you with a powder and

a half cup of wine. You must dissolve the powder in the wine
and drink it. You will sleep well and waken with a better spirit."

"Thank you," said all three. Judit took his hand and kissed it
gratefully, but Guiomar shrank back and made as if to let him
pass.

When he was gone, Judit said, "I feel happier already. He has
helped you, hasn't he, Mamacita?"

"Yes, I feel his power," murmured Mariana.

"I feel it too," said Guiomar, "and it upsets me. I don't know
why. I hope I never get sick here."

The doctor's boy Gomo arrived with the wine and the powder,
and the next day he also sent down a jug of hot chicken soup.
Mariana wished to share it, and Judit took several sips, but Guiomar shook her head.

"No," she said. "It is for you, Doña Mariana. I am well
enough without it." Secretly, she feared the doctor's nostrums,
and determined to avoid having to swallow them. Ever. There
was a power in him which frightened her.

17.

In his cabin on the *El Salvador,* Fray Domingo was recovering
from his first attack of seasickness. He still felt queasy, and could
not take anything more than broth without a return of the retching and nausea. Try as he would, he could not reconcile his
sufferings with the agony of Our Lord on the Cross; his own
misery was too trivial, he knew, though it was making him
wretched. Even in deep prayer, he was interrupted constantly by
the most humiliating of seizures.

In order to calm his conscience, he set himself to work out a
number of rules for the spy-assistants who would be prepared to

ferret out heresy and witchcraft and purify the Body of Christ in the New World.

First, of course, they must be absolutely discreet and maintain strict secrecy. Whenever it was known that someone was acting as a spy for the Inquisition, his usefulness was nullified.

Secondly, they must learn how to merge with the suspected heretics in the life they led, their activities and their work. Many an apostate had been detected by remarks made to a fellow worker, in whom he might feel total confidence. Thus, Inquisition spies must learn to be leatherworkers, muleteers, dealers in slaves, accountants, and merchants of various kinds.

Thirdly, although they must blend into the work and life of suspected transgressors, they must never remain too long in any one locality. This was to protect the active work of the Inquisition, so threatened by schisms, liberal thinking, and other subversive tendencies.

These rules were to apply most particularly to workers dealing with suspected heretics.

Now that boy, that young Irishman, thought Fray Domingo, puts me in mind of something else very valuable that could be worked out. He is to spy for me without knowing that he does so. If he knew, or suspected, what I want from him, he would be of no use.

So why not teach my trusted assistants, who report to me, to choose other innocents to do their work for them? It can be arranged. It takes subtlety, he thought comfortably, knowing how well he had duped Juan Palomar.

"Now, as to witchcraft," he murmured.

Closing his eyes, clasping his hands on his stomach, Fray Domingo began to plan the best procedures for rooting out this wickedness from the body of the faithful.

There were seldom male witches, he mused. Women were the transgressors. Perhaps women should be recruited to alert the Holy Office to suspected persons. Love, he thought, sighing, was often at the base of witches' spells. How to arouse love in the breast of some unsuspecting male, or how to rid oneself of a rival. Yes. Perhaps young and beautiful women, who presumably might attract the desires of many men—these should be the best informers on witchcraft, having little use for spells themselves. Yet they would be aware of their envious sisters, and would undoubtedly draw forth spiteful words, and perhaps information, from them. The lovely copper-haired girl Juan had seen, who had boarded the *Paloma del Mar*, now. Such a beauty would turn the head of any man, except a religious, of course, and would be the target of much female jealousy.

"I wonder if she is going as far as New Spain," Fray Domingo murmured under his breath. Then he allowed his imagination to call up an image of the lovely girl before his inner eye.

If I could recruit her, he mused.

18.

Fermín García Mendoza had been sorry to see his young cabin-mate leave. The passenger the captain sent down to share the cabin, after Juan's departure, was a rich merchant who filled every available inch of space with the bulky packages and bundles of his calling. He was a seller of cloth. Worse, he was talkative, and Fermín went to sleep every afternoon and late evening, with the nasal murmur of the merchant's voice in his ears. Fermín had learned, in prison, to screen out noises he did not wish to hear, and to sweeten stinks he did not wish to smell, and to eat food he could not bear to chew. His control over his senses was strong. And yet it was exhausting, and he really needed his afternoon rest in order to husband his energies.

This was his first journey to the Indies, although he had traveled extensively in Spain, Portugal, France, and the Low Countries, searching. It was a long hard task he had set himself, and perhaps he would never find her whom he sought, his wife of only three months, who had been wrenched from his arms. His torment was wondering whether she had been pregnant when he was taken away, but though he had been able to find clues to where she had been dragged by her irate brothers, he never could find out whether there had been a child or not. His four years in prison had delayed him in his searches, but he was persistent and insistent, and little by little he had found out enough to keep him in hope that he would catch up one day, that he would avenge himself and get her back.

In Ghent he had found a paralytic who could still talk, although he sat all day in a chair and could not move arms and legs. The man had been treated by a certain Dr. Morais, a hypnotist, who could cure by putting the patient into a trance, and then telling him that he was well. In some mysterious way, when awakened from the trance, the sick man or woman would remember what he had been told by that strange doctor, and would insist that he was well. This doctor had put the paralytic into a trance, and indeed, when he woke he thought himself well, had gotten out of his chair and even walked a few steps. But then he had fallen and broken bones, and he had suffered very much. Dr. Morais by then had gone on to some other town, but the hatred and resentment of the paralytic followed him, and he had told Fermín that the doctor had calmed a sick woman who had been brought to him. The description of the woman, plus other information Fermín had been able to elicit, convinced him that at last he was on the trail of his beloved Sarita. Who else had such long black hair, and her two beautiful eyes of different colors—one gray and one brown? And who else wore always his last gift to her, a bracelet of beaten silver worked into a design of a lion crouched to spring, and with an emerald set into the design, for the beast's eye? It must have been Sarita. Must have been. And the paralytic had heard that the woman's brothers were taking her back to Spain, and were planning to go out to the Indies to seek their fortune.

The woman had been sick and wild, possessed, the paralytic had told Fermín, and the brothers were desperate about what to

do with her, for she tried to escape them at all hours, and when
caught and brought back to her duties of cooking and washing
for them, she wept and cried out and was rebellious, and had to
be beaten.

Fermín had winced at this news; he could not help it. But the
paralytic, eager to tell anything he could to the detriment of Dr.
Morais, did not notice.

"They brought her to that doctor, and he looked at the young
woman and made her sleep, and waved his hands and murmured
over her, and when she awakened, she was docile again.

"But it did not last," crowed the paralytic, in triumph. "It only
lasted a few days, and then the brothers had to tie her up, she
became so unmanageable. They were rich, those brothers, they
had plenty of golden ducats, and they bought horses to make
their trip to Spain, and they tied her onto the back of one of
them."

"And so they went to Spain," Fermín had murmured. "They
were Spaniards, then?"

"Jews," spat the paralytic. "But hidden, of course. Crypto-
Jews, but I knew they were Jews; I knew by the way they spoke.
Portuguese Jews. We see a lot of them here. They come to escape the Inquisition. But sometimes they are caught and
dragged back. I never saw them flog the Crucifix, but they say
the brothers did it, and tried to make the woman do it too, but
she would not."

Fermín had lingered a few days, working some silver he had
with him, and selling the trinkets. It would not do to be seen as
immediately going in pursuit. But, going north a day or two, he
then turned south and made his way into Spain with all haste.
Fermín mused about why the brothers had not cast out Sara, as
pious Jews were said to do with any of their women who married a Christian. They even mourned their erring sisters as dead.
Ah, but, thought Fermín, perhaps they had been bound by a
vow, to make sure she returned to the old faith. And no doubt
they feared that she would betray them, as Judaizers. Would his
Sara's love and her conversion stand strong against their insist-

ence and their cruelties? He did not know. He could only pray that she would be true to him and to the Cross.

The brothers and Sara had taken a ship for the New World the year before, he learned. He settled to his trade then in Cádiz, and made as much silver jewelry as he could afford, buying the metal and the stones, but carefully saving every maravedi toward his payment for the voyage to the Indies the next time the Fleet sailed.

So now he was aboard the *True Cross*. Another step in the long search for his love. It should not be so hard to trace her in New Spain, he reflected. Hope kept him patient, and he was by nature tenacious.

19.

The Fleet moved south, to catch the westerlies, which would drive them over the water. The sea was calm, but the heavy laden ships weaved in the water, and the sounds of retching, moans, and complaints sounded daily from the passengers. The captain of the *Paloma del Mar* insisted on the priest (who was also sick) conducting daily mass, all the same, though the sick cleric, supporting himself with one hand on the altar and controlling his nausea, ran through the ritual as fast as he could. For a few days there were few at mass, and fewer at table.

Juan and Roque played drafts, or, as Roque called the game, *damas*. He had a board and the round men—some of ebony and the others carved from bone. He loved his *damas* and was a good player, and at first Juan lost to him consistently. Roque wanted to play for money, but Juan said simply that he had no money to bet, but would like to learn. Being quite mad for his game, Roque gave in, not having found anyone else to play with him. Juan soon perceived that this game, which looked so simple, was complicated and challenging. He had a fair sense of mathematics, and little by little he began learning how to plan his moves beyond the open and obvious one, and sometimes Roque had to think, furrowing his black brow for many minutes, before he could decide how to deceive and catch his opponent. The game became important to both of them, and Juan saw, with some amusement, that Roque's protection of him now became fiercer because Juan was a player he could count on to give him a good game.

"Where did you buy your set of *damas?*" asked Juan idly one day.

"In Turkey. The Turks are wonderful players, and they make splendid sets. I am saving up to buy an inlaid board. Mother-of-pearl and tortoiseshell. Those are really beautiful. There is a man in New Spain who makes them. I plan to find him, this trip."

"You won't go back to sea right away? For the return trip?"

"That voyage back isn't made for several months, anyhow. But this time I may stay. If I could get a good post somewhere." Roque's black face became wistful. "I could serve as a bodyguard for some swell."

"Well, maybe you ought to go up to the capital, where the Viceroy has his court."

"Would you go with me?"

"Why not?" asked Juan, taking advantage of Roque's momentary distraction to jump two men and set a queen on the back line. "Crown me," he ordered. Scowling in anger, Roque crowned his queen.

20.

George Trout knew the skies very well, and besides, he had dependable bones. An arm had been broken when he was young, and imperfectly set (though it was efficient enough in a fight), and this arm always told him when a storm was brewing. Then of course, the skies changed color, later the wind rose, and before you could take cover, sometimes, the storm would be upon you in these southern waters.

He saw the tempest coming and confidently turned his ship back. He was barely in time to hide in the small protected bay he had discovered toward the west end of an island in the Canaries. There was a narrow entrance that discouraged ships of greater draft, but he was a skillful navigator, and he knew how to maneuver his craft past the shallows, through the small gap, and into the tiny safe bay inside. It would not harbor more than one vessel the size of his, and luckily, nobody else had found it. He put in just in time, and was able to take down his sails and stow everything before the heaviest of the winds hit them. Even so, his mainmast was thrown down and snapped off, and his boat tossed about on that little bay like a leaf on a stream.

Undaunted, he put his men to repairing the mast at once, and he stood out on deck through drenching rain, using his glass and trying to discern the look of some ship in distress out at sea. There would be one, of that he was certain. By the end of the second day, when his men had been able to reinforce and lash the mended mast together, he saw one. It was a galleon Fleet, and it was foundering miserably, without sail, and taking water. For some time he couldn't make out which one it was, but as it plunged nearer, in the heavy seas, he made out the name. The *True Cross*.

George spat. Papists, he murmured. I'll strip them clean. He began to shout his orders.

21.

Guiomar found, to her pleasure, that she did not experience the nausea and vomiting that overcame Judit and her mother and

many of the other passengers on the *Paloma del Mar*. The sick
people became too weak to mop up their vomit, or even to clean
their mouths and soiled clothes, and Guiomar found that she had
much to do trying to look after her cabinmates, and the others
nearby. Dr. Morales came, with his slave Gomo, and brought
teas and broths, and medicines, and little by little, Guiomar became one of his nurses. Often she worked at his side, helping to
hold up sick women's heads, coaxing them to drink some con-
coction of the doctor's which put them to sleep, so that they could
rest from their illness.

The animals on the afterdeck, in their pens, being kept to be
slaughtered by the day for food for the passengers, were miserably sick as well, and Guiomar, when not needed for a moment,
went to try to comfort them, and help them to get up and stay
steady on their feet.

Whenever the ship's cook came to lay hold of one of the trembling unhappy lambs or kids, to slaughter them and cut them up
for cooking, Guiomar fled in tears. On her way to hide in her
cabin one morning, when she saw the cook approaching with his
long sharp knife in hand, she ran into the doctor, on his busy
rounds. He detained her, and putting a finger under her chin,
tipped up her face. She kept her eyes closed, but the tears still
welled up and made their way out, wetting her eyelashes and
streaking her cheeks.

"Such a tender heart," murmured the doctor. "Do you never
eat meat, then?"

"Never," answered Guiomar. "We never ate meat in the convent where I was raised, and when I stayed with relatives, I
could not. I could not swallow it. And I could never, never kill
anything."

"But sometimes there is nothing else to eat. And besides, the
flesh and blood are strengthening."

"I cannot bear it," said Guiomar.

"But you were raised in a convent, you say. Did you not learn
that God gave man dominion over all creatures, for his use?"

"I did not know that word from God. Is it truly in the Gospel?"

"Oh yes. Do you deny the Holy Writ?"

"Oh, never. God save me from doubting His word. But I feel sure God would not make me kill anything."

"Not even a fly? Or a flea?"

Guiomar hung her head and would not answer.

The doctor patted her shoulder. "There, there. I will not tease you. You are too kind, you help me too much. Of course you need not kill. Nor eat meat either, if you don't want to. I trust God will see that you always have bread," he added, ironically. "Now, will you come with me, to hold the basin while I lance a boil? Or would that upset you?"

"If there is not much blood. I like to help. I was the one who always took care of the sick old nuns in the convent, the ones who couldn't get up from their pallets, or help themselves."

"It did not disgust you?"

"No. God made me strong. But I faint when I see blood!"

The doctor looked at her again, but he saw nothing in her young calm face but trust and confidence. The tears were drying, though the long black lashes stuck together in spiky points.

"Then come. Gomo has gone to fetch my knife, and a liquid I put on the skin to make it insensitive to pain. You needn't watch."

"You have such a liquid? You make it yourself?"

The doctor smiled. "I have many secrets," he told her, "that are part of my profession. I collect herbs and bark for my teas and my cures. That is why I am going out to New Spain again. In the country, the fields and forests are full of wonderful natural remedies, and I walk all over the land collecting them."

"You are doing a good work," said Guiomar, shyly.

"Indeed I am. God's work," he answered, but he was thinking of something else.

22

Guiomar worked with Dr. Morales increasingly as the days went by. Judit's mother was frequently in need of someone to help turn her, to look after her physical needs in the crowded cabin, to wash her. Judit was too nervous and scared to be useful; her hands shook, and she wept openly, showing her terror that she might lose her mother. Indeed, it seemed that she soon might, for the sick woman became weaker with each succeeding day. Guiomar learned from the doctor that she must be firm and kindly without spending too much energy on sympathy, and that what had to be done must be done forthrightly and openly.

Her own instinct was to whisper praise and prayers, as she worked, but the doctor would not permit this. He stared at her with his strange light eyes, scolding her, and she felt, as usual, a mixture of obedience and a curious revulsion.

"No prayers. They make what we do seem like witchcraft, and surely you know the Holy Office is extremely sensitive to witchcraft," he warned, more than once. "You must remember this. It is important. Do what I tell you, and say nothing."

"Not even 'Thank God' when the fever goes down, or they vomit up something noxious?"

"It is best to work swiftly and kindly, but in silence. Believe me, it is best. Once the Holy Office suspects you, they never forget you, and your whole life can be overshadowed."

Not looking at him, Guiomar asked, "Have they ever questioned you, Doctor?"

"No. I am very careful," he answered, and then he added, "And respectful, of course."

Then they became very busy, and the doctor and Gomo could scarcely keep up with the calls for their help as the ship ran into heavy weather. The great winds whistled through the sails and sought to bring the masts down, but they had been shaped from living trees moments after being cut down, and they were flexible. They swayed and bent, but they did not break. The vessel heaved and flopped and sometimes it fell from one towering wave crest into a trough, with a sound like a crack of thunder, and all the timbers shivered.

"Pay no attention to the ones who are sick now. Help tie them down, that is all we can do. We have to bind up the broken arms and legs of the sailors," ordered Dr. Morales.

He was quick and clever at this, and luckily he seemed to have an endless supply of splints and bandages.

The rumor went around that the captain would order everyone to throw part of his baggage overboard to lighten the vessel, and Guiomar made ready to sacrifice her chest of clothes. She could not think of getting rid of her little hen, though the poor bird cowered in her cage and would not eat.

On Dr. Morales's orders, Guiomar had kilted up her skirts, to give her legs more freedom in getting about on the tilting decks. He had snapped his fingers with annoyance, when she had made some feeble protest, out of modesty, when he first mentioned it. "Legs are legs," he said. "The nuns cover them up, but they have legs, and everybody knows it. And nobody cares right now. Why should they? We are busy with important matters."

The storm lasted three days and they were blown about bewilderingly, but the pilot was a seaman who knew the winds and the tides, and with the captain general, they maneuvered themselves back on course, and putting on more sail, they once more came into view of the other ships of the Fleet far ahead.

Dr. Morales, who like the captain had a glass, put it to his eye and was much pleased to see another great galleon ahead, faint against the still stormy sky, but apparently in no distress. He let Guiomar look, and she was enchanted with the vision, though the glass bobbed and wavered in her inexpert hands. The doctor stood behind her then, and held the glass for her; she was conscious of his nearness, and his scent, and of the pressure of his

arms. She was disquieted, but she managed to hold herself still
and she felt elation at realizing that they were not alone on the
vast ocean, but near another of the Fleet.

"Praise to Jesus!" she breathed, and this time the doctor did
not reprimand her.

During the storm, busy taking the doctor's orders, she had
ceased to feel fear and anxiety near him, as she had at first. She
had wondered, uneasily, why he had seemed to seek them out, to
appear at their sides so often. Why does he take such an interest
in us? she worried. Could he be a spy of the terrible Inquisition?

By the time they had found their place in the Fleet once more,
she forgot all her questions about the doctor, and began to look
upon him as a friend.

Perceptive and watchful, he realized this, and sighed with relief.

He would keep close to her on the trip up to Mexico City, he
resolved, no matter what the danger.

23.

The *True Cross* had fared badly in the storm. Roque had fallen
to his knees and wept and cried like a baby when the mast came
down and fell into the sea, dragging its sail with it. Juan, bracing
himself against the bulwarks of the wallowing ship, trying to
avoid the heavy boxes of baggage that began flying about on
deck and blowing overboard, tried to help the laboring sailors.
To his horror, one of the men who was attempting to get the
broken mast back onto the decks was simply lifted like a leaf in
the wind and dropped into the churning sea. Juan tried to take
his place and put his young strength to the task, meanwhile praying aloud with all his might. "Sweet heart of Mary, help us!" and
"Jesus, Mary, and Joseph, come to my aid!"

The hours went by, and he continued to toil with the sailors who were left. Two had been swept into the sea, one or two had been struck by falling timbers and had been taken below. "O God, I don't want to go below," prayed Juan. "If we founder, they will drown like kittens in a bag. In the open sea, I might catch a spar, and float a while." And he continued to hang on, to make ropes fast, to follow orders as long as the captain and the mate stood and bellowed them out against the howling winds of the storm. Wet to the skin, shivering with cold and terror, he worked through the night. By dawn, the winds had died away and the rain had ceased, but the seas were still very wild. The sailors began to sing, hoarsely, but with praise to God for deliverance.

Until they saw the swift cutter making for them, and flying the skull and crossbones. A pirate, and by the look of the vessel, English.

The captain ordered the protection nets set up, but without the mainmast there was nothing to fasten them to, and when the English pirate ship came alongside, there was no way to prevent the pirates from boarding the wounded galleon.

The pirates wore cutlasses and wide-bladed knives, and some of them carried wide-mouthed muskets. Juan saw with horror that the pirates clubbed down and killed the captain general, and some of them made for stairways down into the passenger cabins. Screams and shouts greeted them there, and all around were the sounds of fighting.

If I had something, I would fight, thought Juan, but he was weaponless.

There was nothing to do but fall to his knees and clasp his hands in prayer. He felt the blow that blacked out sea and ship and silenced all sound, but then he knew nothing.

He did not hear the pirate captain George Trout shout to his mate, "Take three stout fellows, that one there, and two others, for we have lost a few men. These can work ship for us, and on the return voyage I'll sell them to the galleys."

Hours later, when he regained consciousness, Roque and García Mendoza, both bandaged roughly, were near him.

"We are their captives," whispered García Mendoza. "We are to work their sails and swab their ship. We are on the *Mary Ann*."

"Look alive, there!" came a rough voice, and the toe of a great boot nudged them, none too gently. "Get up and get to work, or you won't eat!"

Caution had taken control of Juan's brain, and he pretended not to understand English. Roque, who had swaggered about in many ports, knew some. But the tone of the man's voice, and the boot, were enough to cause alacrity. Still dizzy and weak, Juan stumbled to his feet and began to do what the booted pirate indicated. In a dream, his head throbbing with pain, scarcely able to focus his eyes, he staggered about, hauling on the ropes, heaving at the winches. Time somehow passed, and he vaguely saw his friends, Roque and García Mendoza, at their labors. At nightfall, he was allowed to stop and to drink a bowl of hot soup in which floated pellets of hard bread. Juan was glad to eat. The food warmed him, and seemed to promise that life aboard the pirate ship might be hard but not unendurable.

He mumbled something to this effect to Roque, but before Roque could answer, Juan felt the boot again, and this time, hard in his ribs.

"No talking here! Quiet!" yelled the mate.

As the days slipped by, Juan found he could only occasionally whisper a word or two, in Spanish, to his friends. Roque had been struck in the head as well, and still bled occasionally. García Mendoza had been beaten across the back and shoulders.

When he had the chance, Juan asked, "What became of the *True Cross?*"

"They scuttled her. She went down, with everyone aboard. I think we alone were saved."

"For what?" groaned Juan.

"Patience," whispered García Mendoza. "God has saved us for some reason. Patience."

Juan was mollified, though not comforted, to see that the mate treated his own men just as cruelly, though he always saw that they had food and water, and he never stinted on these.

"If we are weak, we can't work," muttered Roque, grabbing extra bread or another hunk of salt beef whenever he could.

Juan lived in a mixture of hope and fear that the pilot might sight another galleon, and run to ram and plunder it. What then? He would fight, try to get free. But that meant somehow getting onto the galleon. But also it meant a fight in which the pirate's swift and efficient vessel would be victor. Sadly, Juan concluded that this was most likely, as he knew that the galleons generally sailed lightly armed. There was nothing to do but wait and pray, and try to keep out of the way of boots and the belaying pin.

24.

On the *Paloma del Mar* Guiomar and Judit watched over Mariana Cerezo with anxious eyes, and tended her with loving hands. The storm had thrown her out of her bunk onto the floor, and she had not recovered. Dr. Morales, putting his ear to her chest, heard a fitful fluttering sound, and none of his herbs or teas seemed able to right it. She was pale and would not eat, and at the same time she seemed to swell and grow fat. Dr. Morales bled her, but even this did not help for very long, and on the third day, she sighed, turned her face to the wall, and gently died.

Judit grew hysterical with grief and fear, and would have thrown herself into the sea when her mother's body, wrapped in a sheet, was given to the deep. The day was still dark and heavy with storm clouds, and the sea heaved and thrust itself against the *Paloma del Mar* with angry hissings and thumps. Only Guiomar's strong young arms held Judit back, and when there was not even a ripple on the sea to show where her mother's body had entered it, Guiomar's tender words comforted the sobbing girl. The priest had blessed Mariana Cerezo's mortal body, and had chanted the prayers for the dead, and all the passengers had joined with him in praying that eternal light shine upon her. Feeble sunlight shone upon the deck and then danced upon the water where Judit had thrown a little wreath of silk flowers.

"See, the sunlight is a message from above," Guiomar told her, "telling you that she is safe and happy now."

"Ah, I know, because she was so good, my mother," wept Judit. "But what of me? Where am I to go, all alone?"

"You are not alone, you have me," cried Guiomar, fiercely. "You will come with me wherever I go. I will be your sister."

So Judit was comforted.

Dr. Morales made notes in one of the small books he carried about him. Guiomar asked him if he kept an account of every sick person he attended, and he looked up from his crabbed, difficult writing and stabbed her with his large pale eyes. She felt their hypnotic power, but she was no longer afraid of him, having seen how he had labored to save Doña Mariana, and how kind he had been.

"I tell myself what happened, and I hope to find remedies for the next person with the same illness," he told her.

But he had written other notes in his small book, reminders to himself. These were secrets, kept close to himself, upon his person, and besides, few understood the strange script in which he wrote.

Guiomar spent all her time with Judit when she was not busy helping the doctor and Gomo. She was frequently called, for the galleon had been out upon the water for more than thirty days, and the dwindling food supplies had been hurt by the heavy seas that washed over the decks in the storm. In pity for some of the older passengers, who vomited when they tried to eat hard bread that had been soaked in salt sea water and then dried out again,

Guiomar had surrendered her little hen, but she would not taste a morsel of the stewed flesh, nor a drop of the soup.

Dr. Morales had thanked her gravely. Almost all the animals brought along for slaughter had been washed overboard, and even water was running very low, and tasted brackish. Dr. Morales and the captain general of the galleon ordered it rationed, and every passenger received but one cup of water a day thereafter. Every day, at mass, the priest prayed for landfall soon, and the passengers who were well enough to walk on the decks began looking hopefully at the sea, to try to find some sign that land might be near. In his perch atop the highest mast, a sailor spent the daylight hours scanning the horizon, which for seven days more heaved and shifted, but showed nothing but the eternal sea and the stooping sky.

On a clear soft day, with a smart breeze filling the sails, Guiomar saw floating ribbons of dark-brown weed in the swells, and she ran to call Judit and to tell one of the sailors. He laughed and leaped on the deck, and blessed her. Not long after, a bird came and rested on one of the masts, and the whole ship began a song of thanksgiving. Land was in sight, and before the next day had passed the zenith, they put into port at Hispaniola.

BOOK TWO

Gonzalo

1.

Don Pedro Montemayor had worked hard all his life and had endured many troubles and reverses. These had left their mark upon him, and he was now stooped, gray-haired, and stiff. He suffered from a constant pain in his back, and his legs, somewhat bowed, ached distressingly after a few hours in his workshop. He had learned the trade of leatherwork in his youth, and had been happy with his own small factory. His people had been converted to Christianity centuries before by King Riccared, and the Montemayor family was accepted everywhere, except by the most intense of the Jewish communities, who were always marginal, and tended to move about from town to town, in any case.

Pedro had met and loved Leonor, the beautiful black-haired daughter of a New Christian family. She was only fifteen when they married, and she had borne him a son at once, Gonzalo, who now lived with him in Mexico City and made trips around the countryside to the Spanish military encampments, selling leather vests, saddles, and bridles. Leonor had been a loving wife and mother, but she was subject to intense emotional seizures when she hid from him, would not speak to him, or let him love her, and then he suffered, for he was a warm and demonstrative man. Yet after Gonzalo there was another child, a little girl, Guiomar. But she had been born after he had sailed with his small son for the New World. His Leonor had died not long after giving birth to Guiomar, he had been advised, and their little daughter given to the good nuns to be brought up. But now at last, he had been able to arrange to bring Guiomar out to him, and his son Gonzalo would go to Veracruz to await her arrival and bring her home. Don Pedro longed for his daughter; he wanted to pour

out his love on her, and protect her and cosset her, and he hoped
again to hear a soft female voice singing in his home, and see the
feminine arrangements in his rooms that meant softness, color,
and comfort.

He wondered about Guiomar's looks. His own people were tall
golden blonds, with blue or green eyes, but his lovely Leonor
had been slight and slender, with long rippling black hair and
large black eyes that sparkled like the petals of a flower wet with
dew. He hoped his daughter would look like her mother, and recall to him the ecstatic few years of his marriage.

In truth, he had been eager to go to Veracruz, to receive Guiomar, but was persuaded not to, because the dampness of the
coast crippled him with painful rheumatism.

Gonzalo was a good trader, and had the gift of making friends
easily, and this in spite of the fact that he was by nature rather
sentimental and poetic. Yet his delicacies about food and personal hygiene, and his transports over the beauties of the countryside, did not impair his popularity, despite the rough fellows
with whom he had to associate whenever he undertook a journey
to sell leather goods. The soldiers respected him, and never
urged him to try his strength (it was obvious that his slender
frame would not last a minute in combat with any of the thick-
muscled and hard soldiers of the King), and they frequently
asked him to recite poetry, which they seemed to enjoy. It was
his open simplicity and sincerity which won him defenders and
devoted admirers.

In appearance he was more like a bullfighter or a dancer than
any other thing, being slender and wiry, with more agility than
physical strength, and with a crackling vitality. He kept his thick
black hair cut rather short, and yet one or two locks often came
down over his broad forehead. His skin was white with the dark
beard showing through in a bluish line that outlined a thin, flexible mouth, and flat cheeks. His large dark eyes, with long curling
lashes, did sometimes call forth jokes from the soldiers and
traders, yet despite his delicacy and good looks and obvious lack
of rough masculine strength, he was in no way effeminate, and

had seldom been molested by the men in the army who looked for handsome boys.

Gonzalo had planned his trip to Veracruz as a commercial venture, as well as for the reception and protection of his sister. He had two mules laden with leather goods and with miscellaneous objects from the city which he could sell in villages on the way. He hoped to buy a supply of salable goods to help finance the return. For the journey to the sea he would accompany a caravan of other merchants, who had their own armed slaves for protection along the way, and for the return trip, he knew he could attach himself to another such group. It was not safe to travel far, in the interior, without protection.

Having lashed his produce to the mules, he saw to his own baggage. One good dark suit, in which to receive dignitaries from the ship and his sister, an extra pair of boots, well fitted to his slender, high-arched feet, a cape of silk quilted and padded with cotton, for the cold, and a native raincoat, made of thin reeds sewed to coarse cotton, which would shed even the heaviest downpour.

In the bosom of his traveling coat were a volume of poetry, and a few books of the Old Testament for which he felt a special affinity. Gonzalo had taught himself to read Latin in order to be able to enjoy books, for there were not many about in New Spain, and few indeed in Castilian. Having learned to enjoy poetry, Gonzalo had begun, in secret, to write it.

Now making ready for his journey, he wondered, shyly, if some time he might read some of his verses to his sister Guiomar. She had been convent-taught, and no doubt could read, though not all the religious could. Gonzalo had been startled into a convulsion of laughter once, when a tonsured monk had taken up a book of Latin and read sonorous verse from it, because Gonzalo had seen that the monk held the book upside down.

How much else of what he does and preaches is pretense also, pondered Gonzalo.

But at once he put that thought away. Gonzalo knew of the

Holy Office, and had not forgotten that one of his own muleteers had been caught, interrogated, and tortured by the Inquisition for blasphemy.

Gonzalo and his father were careful, in all their words and actions, to do nothing that might arouse the interest of the Holy Office. Even Jewish families long since converted to the True Faith were often suspect, simply because the Inquisitors and their spies knew that the bond of blood is a strong one, and that Jews tended always to defend each other.

They attended mass as often as they could, they gave tithes and presents of candles and oil to the Church, and they walked circumspectly. Yet, nominal Christians as they were, they knew little of what their faith entailed. Don Pedro simply kept the rules, insofar as he knew them, and said his prayers. Gonzalo had had no instruction beyond the basic prayers and how to behave at mass. Gonzalo's poetic spirit sought verse, and beauty. He dimly felt that prayer, deep prayer, might carry his soul into ecstasies beyond imagining, but no sorrows or troubles had inclined him toward such prayer as yet, and his daily work going about the countryside taught him to take joy in a field of waving corn, or in the flight of a blue-winged bird, or in the changing and mysterious shapes of clouds in the blue sky.

He looked forward to receiving his sister, but also he anticipated the journey with lively pleasure, because he had not before journeyed farther south than Taxco, and this time the trip would be by another route, from the highlands down to the sea.

2.

The caravan of merchants, less by ten of the forty who had left Mexico City, arrived in disarray in Veracruz. Some strange malady had attacked the whole group simultaneously, as they had reached the highest portion of their road. Encamped in the thin cold mountain air, unable to stagger about to start cooking fires, all had been ravaged by chills and high fevers which followed, and only a few of the slaves had been able to carry food to the sick, and feed and water the animals. Four of the slaves had died, two had run away, and four of the merchants, when able to sit on their mules, had turned back toward Mexico City.

Gonzalo was with the others who straggled on toward a settlement, there to rest and eat, and to try to regain strength for the rest of the journey. Gonzalo, counting the days, began to fear that the Fleet might have made port before his arrival. And then what would happen to his little sister? He made himself ill again with worry, and it was a frail, pale, almost ethereal young man who finally walked the short streets of the village of Veracruz, searching for a room that he might rent for Guiomar. The Fleet had not yet shown sail on the horizon, so he was fortunate, because when the galleon put into port, there would be a great scrambling for rooms, for space in the patios, and for warehouses, and the prices would climb to great heights.

He had a week to wait before the village seemed suddenly seized by excitement; shouts and people running toward the fort of San Juan de Ulúa, told the news that the Fleet had been sighted. The whole town ran toward the shore, splashing through some of the swampy fields and crowding onto the part of the fort that had been equipped as a dock. Here the galleons would tie up, six or eight to the broad landing wharf, others tied to them and yet others to them, so that the streamers of galleons, tied nose to tail, swept out toward sea like so many ribbons, wavering and heaving with the swells.

Gonzalo had no way of knowing, for certain, on which ship of the Fleet his sister had embarked, but he thought, Oh, I will know her! She will be standing out on deck, waving, waiting as eagerly as Father and I have been waiting for her.

Little sister! he thought. I will take good care of you!

The first of the galleons to make its way to dock and tie up, amid shouting and singing from the sailors, showed the effects of the long sea journey, and of the storm it had passed through.

Gonzalo's heart contracted in anguish. Those tattered flags and pennants, the bare decks, the paucity of the sailors working the ropes, made it all clear. A weary line of passengers tottered over the narrow walks thrown out to the deck from the dock. They were soldiers, men and women, a few children, many religious in differing habits. No Guiomar there.

Five more galleons slipped in over the blue water and tied up. There was no one Gonzalo could believe might be his sister. He still waited, impatiently, on the dockside.

Then the *Paloma del Mar* moved over the swells and made fast to the last anchorage on the docks. And there he saw them!

Two girls stood on the deck, straining their eyes toward shore, young girls. One was slight and dark, with a handspan waist in her dark dress, heavy black hair hanging to her waist, a small white face, heart-shaped. Guiomar! thought Gonzalo. Pretty and small and dear. Just as I thought she would be.

Ah, but the other one! Tall and full-bosomed, a queenly young woman, with the face of a goddess! A broad brow, a wide red mouth, dark eyes, and a cascade of coppery hair that took the light like metal. As he looked, Gonzalo felt the warmth and generosity of the tall, beautiful girl. She was the woman he sometimes saw in his erotic dreams; he could envision her clothed only in that glorious hair. Gonzalo felt his knees go weak and his heart thump heavily. A hot wave of desire swept over him. He thought, I must have her. I will find out about her. Pray God she is not married!

A middle-aged man, followed by a black boy, came out and stood protectively near the two girls as the galleon was maneuvered into position. When the boarding catwalk was set up, Gonzalo saw that he detained the young women until the other passengers had landed, and then he led them and carefully supervised their descent on the somewhat wobbly walk.

Gonzalo stepped forward.

"Guiomar!" he called. To his delight, and then to his horror, it was the tall girl with the coppery hair who tore herself away from her companions and rushed into his arms. Holding her palpitating body against him, he knew he must not kiss her. He did not dare. He gently put her to arm's length, and he saw that she was even lovelier than he had thought at first, and that she was in tears.

"My brother! Thank God that I am here with you at last! And my father? Where is he?"

Gonzalo found that his throat had closed. He could not speak. Guiomar turned then and brought forward the dark girl, and the man who had accompanied them.

"My brother Gonzalo, who has come for me! Gonzalo, this is Dr. Morales, who has been so kind to us on the journey, and Judit Cerezo, who is to come with me and be my sister and companion. We lost her mother on the journey, and now she has only me."

Judit had turned aside and was covering her eyes with her hands; her slender shoulders heaved. Guiomar at once went and turned her about and made her rest her wet face against her own shoulder. She caressed her, and cried, "Oh, don't cry, Judit! I know that you feel lonely and sad, but we will love you and take care of you!"

Gonzalo, with an effort, had recovered his composure.

He bowed slightly. "Indeed, Señorita Judit, you will be made welcome in my father's house."

"And my father?" demanded Guiomar again.

"He is awaiting us in Mexico City."

Gonzalo turned to Dr. Morales.

"Since you were kind enough to look after and protect these young ladies on the voyage, I hope you will accompany us to Mexico," he said gravely, with his sweet smile.

Dr. Morales turned his large gray eyes on the young man, and said nothing for a few moments. Gonzalo felt uneasily that the older man had read his mind, had devined his trouble and his unsisterly feeling for Guiomar. He flushed slightly.

"I will be honored," said Dr. Morales, in his deep voice. "And perhaps I can be of aid. I see that you have been ill, and recently."

"It was a strange malady that struck down the whole caval-cade," explained Gonzalo. "But come. I have rooms, and I be-lieve I can arrange for you to stay in the same house. It will not be easy to find accommodation now, but I have been here for a week, awaiting the Fleet."

"We had a terrible storm," Guiomar told him, "and afterward we were short of water and food. Oh, I am hungry, Gonzalo. We can eat some fresh green things here, can't we, and some fruit? I am longing for an orange!"

"You shall have fruit, and fresh meat, and plenty of cooled water now," he promised her.

3.

Gonzalo led the two girls and Dr. Morales to a simple wooden house where he had engaged two small rooms. It was arranged that Dr. Morales sleep in Gonzalo's room, and Guiomar and Judit would share a bed. It was already hot, for the sun had come up full and red that morning, and the air buzzed thickly with insects that stung and teased.

"I will prepare a liquid that can be stroked onto faces and hands and will keep these pests off us," said Dr. Morales, and he disappeared with his black slave, into the kitchens behind the simple house, where some slovenly and sullen Indian slaves were preparing food. Here the owner of the dwelling, Mateo Bravo, a former Spanish soldier who had lost a leg as the result of an untended wound after a battle, stood over his slaves and occasionally laid a lash across the shoulders of one or around the ankles of another. The Indians, in stout cotton garments, much dirtied from their labors, never responded with more than a wince or a grunt. Don Mateo knew Dr. Morales and greeted him with a shout.

"*Dichosos los ojos!* Did you come in with the Fleet, Doctor?"

"Yes. Once more."

"I can put you up. All the rooms are full, but I will throw out somebody."

"No need. I will share with Don Gonzalo Montemayor. He has invited me."

"Oh. Well. At half price."

"Understood."

"I want to make a lotion against the insects, Don Mateo. May I use one of your fires?"

"This one. Here." Unceremoniously, one of the women was shouldered away from where broth in a great earthen pot was bubbling around large chunks of meat.

"I won't be long, and the cooking may proceed as before," advised Dr. Morales, and he gave some instructions to Gomo in a language they both understood. In a short while Dr. Morales had a green potion boiling in a little pot. To this he added some of his special herbs, and some drops from one of his flasks. He then set the mixture aside to cool, and gave Gomo several small bottles, with corks, into which the liquid was to be divided. He himself then left Gomo to his work, and he strode out and into the small dusty streets, to see if he could find any people he knew from the other ships of the Fleet.

Gonzalo too, having led the two girls into the room which would be theirs while they awaited the forming of a caravan, to conduct them with their baggage over the mountains to Mexico, left them and hurried out toward the docks. He still had two mule-loads of objects to sell, and felt that he must acquire all the ducats possible before starting out toward home again. Besides, he was bewildered and upset at his own feelings, and he thought that perhaps walking and working would settle his mind.

He was not pleased to find that Dr. Morales had joined him, and seemed ready to accompany him to the docks, where more and more travelers were crowding about as other galleons made

their way in. Many small boats were busily plying back and forth
over the water, helping to unload baggage and cargo.

There were many things being brought in by the Fleet which
Gonzalo had instructions to buy: oil, soap, soda, and tempered
steel knives. To his despair, he learned that much of the cargo on
every ship had been lost, and after the trading at Hispaniola, little was left for the merchants of New Spain at Veracruz. However, he managed to acquire a little of what he had hoped to
buy, and even to sell some of his own supply of warm woolen
capes, padded cotton coats, and woven-leaf fans to keep insects
away. He learned that the female passengers had lost clothing
during the storm when baggage was washed overboard, and in
the sudden heat and dampness of the coast of New Spain, they
were driven almost mad by the clinging, biting mosquitoes.

Dr. Morales trudged beside Gonzalo, and seemed content to
help him load and unload his beasts, according to whether he
sold or bought.

"You are a sensible young man," he said, at last. "I can see
that you have made this journey before."

"No, never all the way to this port, not since I landed here as
a lad of six," answered Gonzalo. "But I go often to Taxco, where
the miners buy from me, and sometimes I go north, as well, to
where the soldiers are keeping the warlike Chichimecas at bay.
Zacatecas is a good town for trade, too."

"Are those Indians still so savage? I left four years ago, and it
was supposed then that the soldiers of the King would soon have
them pacified."

"Oh, nobody can pacify them!" cried Gonzalo. "They, and the
Yaquis, farther north, are unconquerable. And when they capture
prisoners, they torture them unmercifully. Zacatecas is dangerous, yes, because of them, because they may raid a village at any
time. But so far, I have been fortunate."

"The Chichimecas," mused Dr. Morales. "One could respect
them for their fierce indomitability. I myself respect courage.
Submission is not in my nature. I had thought of going into their
territory. I wonder if they would molest me, seeing that I cure,

and do not kill. The other Indians I have dealt with help me, and call me kind names in their own language . . . names like Man of Herbs, and He Who Comforts."

"You have made several journeys through the country?"

"Oh yes. It is a beautiful country. And you. Do you like trading?"

"Yes, I like it. And I help my father."

"But you have not the look of a trader. I would say you have the look of . . . I would say, a scholar."

Gonzalo turned to him with a sudden smile.

"I love study and learning. I know some Latin. Now I would like to learn Greek."

"Or Hebrew," suggested Dr. Morales. "The words of Jesus Christ, Our Lord, were written down in an ancient form of Hebrew, and come down to us in the Hebrew of His day. And, of course, also in Greek."

"I can see that you are a scholar, a learned one," murmured Gonzalo.

"I too love study. It is the one joy God has taught us that never fails to comfort the spirit. In love, we can be defeated; we can lose our dear ones; we can be tortured with sickness or wounds; but the one unending pleasure is learning something new, opening a new window in the mind."

"Ah," said Gonzalo. "Your words seem so . . . so right . . . to me."

"Young men often think love is the only reality," went on Dr. Morales, with a keen look at Gonzalo. "But it is a passing thing. It evaporates. It leaves in the spirit, sometimes a perfume, sometimes an odor we turn from with distaste. But study is always rewarding."

"You could teach me many things," ventured Gonzalo.

"No doubt. I was going to ask if I might accompany you on one of your trading trips. I am a doctor and I make my own medicines. I come here to New Spain to collect herbs and berries and barks in the countryside, for I have learned of their curative powers, and many of them are miraculous, if one dare say such a word. Holy Mother Church prefers to define what is miraculous for us."

They continued to talk, as they bought and sold, and when the sun began to sink, they turned their steps back toward the house where they would be lodged.

It had come to be understood that Dr. Morales would accompany Gonzalo and Guiomar to Mexico, and then go out into the country, toward Zacatecas, with Gonzalo.

4.

Guiomar and Judit had loosened their clothing, and washed, enjoying the strange sensation of being clean again, after so many days on shipboard with rationed water. They had drunk their fill of the boiled and cooled water Don Mateo brought them, warning them never to drink water except from running streams or bubbling fountains.

"Still waters are noxious," he told them. "They can cause fevers. To keep water in my house, I have it boiled, to drive out the poisonous vapors. Or one can purify the water with wine. I learned this as a soldier. Until we were careful of the water, we always had half the battalion down with the flux."

Lying on the bed, lightly dressed after bathing, the two girls dozed until they heard the voices of Gonzalo and Dr. Morales in the next room. Then they rose, combed back their hair, and put on their dresses.

"I am longing to wear fresh clean clothes," confided Guiomar, "instead of these, so filthy and limp from so many days at sea, but I suppose it would be best to keep on wearing them, instead of opening the baggage and having to repack everything."

"I wonder if anything of ours was left," said Judit. "Our boxes may have been washed overboard."

"Oh, Judit!"

"I heard the captain general say almost everything was lost."

"Perhaps Gonzalo can find us some native dress to put on, so that we may get out of these heavy skirts and tight bodices. I wish I had one of my convent habits with me. They cover one all over so modestly, but they are loose and one feels so comfortable."

"If we could find cloth, we could make some. Or something like them."

"I will ask my brother. What did you think of him, Judit?"

"I hardly looked," murmured Judit, flushing.

She had looked, she had seen Gonzalo's sudden sweet smile, his large dark eyes. She had sensed something of his poetic vulnerability. Loath to talk about him, she wanted to think about him, to cogitate over his words, to draw special meaning from them.

"I love him already!" proclaimed Guiomar. "And I will love my father! Oh, I never knew how wonderful it would be to have a family, a brother, and a father! Nor did I really know a mother, though Mother Superior was so good to me, and I venerate her. But a real mother . . . always with you in the house, teaching you all the 'home' things, the cooking, the sewing, the gardening . . . Of course, I learned those things, but the family of nuns was so large, and there were no little intimate things, little songs as you work, little jokes, small games, and even quarrels . . . Oh . . . Forgive me, Judit! All I have done is make you remember and cry! I am so clumsy and thoughtless. Oh, forgive me!"

Judit could not hold back her tears, but Guiomar's arms were open to her, and she drew her close, to comfort her.

Just before sundown, Don Mateo called Guiomar and Judit, as well as Gonzalo and Dr. Morales, to supper. From clay bowls they ate a thick stew of meat with strange vegetables, spiced with some piquant flavor which at first Guiomar and Judit disliked. But Gonzalo and Dr. Morales explained that this curious burning taste was common to most of the food of the country; it was caused by the use of a vegetable growing on low bushes called chili.

"I believe it has some virtuous properties," pronounced Dr. Morales, "though it will mask the taste of good wine, which is a pity. Yet, on the whole, one grows used to it, and it prevents the daily fare from becoming too monotonous."

"Was there news of the other ships in the Fleet?" Guiomar asked.

"Yes, and the news is bad. Several ships were lost."

"God save us!" murmured Guiomar.

"Your compassion becomes you," remarked Dr. Morales, "but I must warn you, as I have once before, to be careful with your words, Doña Guiomar. The Holy Office is much offended by blasphemy!"

"Oh, I could never blaspheme," cried Guiomar, losing all at once the soft peach glow that the heat had brought up into her cheeks.

"Your heart may be pure, but if some overzealous person, or some spy, should hear you, your words might be misinterpreted."

"Spy?" echoed Judit, who had not spoken until then. "Are there spies, then?"

"The Holy Office has spies everywhere, and paid informers, and perhaps even persons who attempt to provoke trouble, in order to assess the faith of strangers," explained Dr. Morales. "This is logical. Stop and think a moment! If you had the enormous task of keeping a religion pure, in a country as yet without many soldiers or police, in a country to which strangers arrived by every ship—how would you go about it?"

"I don't know," replied Judit.

"I think I would judge people by their actions," said Guiomar slowly.

"But what if many people pretended to be Christian, but secretly practiced another faith? How would you find out, unless you had spies?"

Guiomar clasped her hands together.

"But are you saying, are you saying that this is what happens?

That there are spies listening to everything we say, looking in the windows of houses, even pretending to be friends, so as to gain the confidence of people and then betray them?"

"That is what I am saying."

Guiomar's eyes filled with tears.

"But this is frightening!" she protested. "Even good Christians might make mistakes, and . . . and maybe even lying reports could be used against them!"

"That is so."

"And . . . and the people who practice another faith in secret, what happens to them?"

She knew. She was remembering her mother.

"If the Holy Office finds them, and subjects them to Inquiry, and they do not repent, they are burned."

Guiomar sat silent, but the tears that had filled her eyes began to slip over and run down her cheeks.

"You must never weep for those people," instructed Dr. Morales. "The Holy Office does not permit us Christians to pity them, for they are traitors to the Faith, as well as to Spain. They come to New Spain under the protection of Spanish arms, swearing that they are True Christians. And if they have lied, and give allegiance secretly to another faith, what are they? Vile traitors!"

Guiomar could make no answer, but his words, though they could not apply to herself, had thrown an invisible veil of fear and foreboding over all her surroundings, and over all the people in this New World.

"I am sorry to distress you, Doña Guiomar, but you have set foot in New Spain only today, and you must be warned of many things," the doctor said in a gentler tone. "And by the way, I am not a spy! I am a simple herbalist and a man of medicine."

"Enough, Doctor," interrupted Gonzalo. "I am here to watch over and protect my sister."

"Your sisters!" corrected Guiomar. "Judit is my sister now!"

Because Guiomar's tears had wrenched his heart and because whenever he looked at her he loved her, Gonzalo turned away to Judit. This small gentle girl, who looked so much like himself, might assuage his tumultuous desire for Guiomar, a feeling to which he was unused, and for which he had no defense.

"My sister, Judit!" he said, and was encouraged to see that Judit sent him a look of gratitude.

After finishing the meal, and equipped with bottles of the lotion Dr. Morales had prepared, all went to their rooms to rest, as Don Mateo had no candles or lamps, and in Veracruz one lived with the light of day, and slept with the dark.

Guiomar and Judit said their prayers with fervor and lay down, both to troubled dreams. In the morning, before Judit set foot to the wooden floor, she gave a cry of fright, awakening Guiomar, who sat up at once. Judit pointed.

Walking slowly across the floor was a large purplish insect, shaped roughly like a lobster.

Guiomar dragged on her shoes, slipped a bodice on over her underclothes, and pulled on her skirt. She ran out, avoiding the ugly creature on the floor, and called loudly for Gonzalo. He appeared almost at once, for he never undressed when he slept. It was a habit acquired during his travels about the countryside, selling his wares.

"In our room, on the floor—" began Guiomar, but he strode ahead of her. He stamped on the insect with his booted foot, and at once an unpleasant acrid smell permeated the air.

"It is a scorpion, but not one of the bad sting," explained Gonzalo. "But I must give you some lessons about how to take care. There are many poisonous creatures about here in the coastal areas."

"And . . . and snakes?" quavered Judit.

"And snakes. But I will teach you both. And Dr. Morales undoubtedly has medicines against all kinds of bites and stings. Now I must go and buy some white woven stuff for you both, from which you can make aprons, or skirts. You must always carry a small branch, with leaves, in your hand, and watch your white skirts; in that way you can see any creature that falls on you, and of course, brush it off at once."

"Yes, brother," said both girls at once, in small voices.

The New World was full of dangers, from creatures and from men, Guiomar was reflecting, and she directed her mind in prayer to Jesus and His Blessed Mother, imploring protection and grace.

Added always to her prayers were words of deep thanksgiving for her brother. My dear brother Gonzalo, thought Guiomar, who is a Christian, and who will take me to my father, where I will live in a Christian household. I thank all my saints that I never did promise my poor mother to do that wicked thing she asked of me.

And then, with love, and sometimes with tears, Guiomar prayed for her mother and for the repose of her soul.

5.

Fray Domingo's ship, *El Salvador,* had weathered the storm. He had remained on his knees, praying without ceasing, as soon as the heavy waves began crashing against the vessel and tossing it from side to side. He had been miserably seasick as well, and when he at last tottered onto firm land at Veracruz, he fell at once, for it seemed to him that everything heaved and moved, and his knees gave way. It did not take him long to learn that the ship he had originally intended to take, and which he had given up to the young seminarian Juan Palomar, had foundered and gone down with everyone aboard.

Then Fray Domingo devoted himself to extra prayers and supplications, for the miserable young man had lost his life whereas he, Fray Domingo, had been saved.

But also, that suspicious creature, that suspect named Mendoza, on whose trail he had been for some weeks, had gone down, too, with the *True Cross.*

But I cannot relax, Fray Domingo told himself, in great severity. He is only one of the many heretics who are deceiving and undermining our Holy Faith. However, since he was a distant relative, I will sing a mass for his soul.

And so he did, in the small edifice which had been set up for masses while construction of a real church took place. The work on this was interrupted constantly by the heavy rains of the region, which came to halt work and to make sodden the earthen bricks that had been prepared.

After the mass, Fray Domingo sought a place to rest and eat, and to rebuild his strength. He arranged to sleep in the bed of a fellow priest who lived in Veracruz and spent much time making journeys to nearby villages, attempting to convert the Indians and to convince them to come to the port to work. But of course, this priest was always on hand when the galleons came into port, to attend the sick and dying, and also to bless the ships that would leave, fully cargoed, for Spain, a few weeks later.

But Fray Domingo had heard of the excellent meat stews of Don Mateo; he had Indian hunters working for him, who brought him deer and wild pig from the lands thereabout. Don Mateo also raised a small kitchen garden of vegetables and herbs. Thus, Fray Domingo appeared for dinner, together with several soldiers from the ship *El Salvador*.

Guiomar and Judit curtseyed and kissed his hand, which had lost its plumpness. He studied them closely with his shrewd dark eyes.

"Pray and be vigilant, daughters," he instructed them, "for this New World is full of danger."

"I have done my best to warn the young ladies of the dangers," said Dr. Morales, "and to provide them with remedies."

"Remedies? No remedy like prayer and daily mass," pronounced Fray Domingo.

"We are God-fearing people," put in Gonzalo, also taking the priest's hand, to carry it to his lips.

Fray Domingo smelled the fragrance of the stewed meat with pleasure. He savored the chili, and even added more of a hot sauce spice with the vegetable, to his bowl.

"And you are bound for Mexico City?"

"My father awaits us there," Gonzalo told him.

"No doubt you are eager to start your journey," commented the priest.

"We must wait until there are enough of us, and get permission from the battalion commander here for some soldiers to accompany us."

"Have you not enough faith in God to make your way alone?" asked Fray Domingo in a soft voice.

"I have faith," rejoined Gonzalo quietly, "but I am in obedience to my father, and he wished me to take the greatest possible care of my sister. Sisters."

In his persistent, courteous, but inexorable way, Fray Domingo learned about the death of Señora Cerezo, and Guiomar's affection for Judit.

"But perhaps the young lady, Judit, may prefer to enter a convent and devote herself to good works, once in Mexcio City," went on Fray Domingo. "If so, I shall be very happy to advise her and assist."

Judit had sat silent through this exchange, and over her small expressive face, a look of anxiety had spread.

"I . . . I don't know," she stammered.

"You may always find me with the Dominican *frailes*," the priest went on easily, accepting a second bowl of stew.

"Do you work with the Holy Office?" asked Dr. Morales, looking fixedly at the priest.

Fray Domingo flushed. He had not meant to expose his connection with the Holy Office so soon.

"Occasionally," he replied.

"Here you have four faithful sons and daughters of the Church, who are ready to serve you, whenever there may be need," went on Dr. Morales. After this, conversation failed for a time, until Fray Domingo finished, and said the prayer of thanks after the meal.

Approaching Gonzalo, after the girls had gone to their room to rest, Fray Domingo said, "I feel sure, my son, that you would like me to accompany your party when you get ready to begin the return journey. Do not thank me! I will be glad to come with you!" And making the sign of the Cross he hurried away down the dusty road toward where he would sleep.

Gonzalo stood looking after him in some perplexity. There was something too persistent, too insistent, about the attitude of Fray Domingo.

"He is with the Holy Office," explained Dr. Morales. "Did you not realize that? Perhaps he suspects that one of us is not as fervent as he should be."

He smiled, slapped Gonzalo on the back in rough friendship, and went away to find his slave and give him some orders for the night.

6.

Guiomar and Judit were able to cut and sew some rough uncolored cotton cloth, which Gonzalo brought them, and make garments that covered them loosely, the result being more comfortable in the damp persistent heat, and which helped them keep free of mosquitoes.

"You must also watch carefully to make sure no leeches fall upon you," instructed Dr. Morales, "for they may be dislodged from the trees as you pass by. Better make hoods as well, so that nothing can fall on your hair, as some insect might go unperceived until it stings you."

"Ay, I did not think New Spain would be so full of dangers," murmured Guiomar with a sigh.

"These are not dangers; they are nuisances," objected Dr. Morales. "And they are characteristic only of our low coastal lands. Within four days' march, you will be into higher, cooler country, where your only danger is catching a chill."

"Fray Domingo is arranging for soldiers and some other travelers to accompany us to Mexico," Guiomar told him.

"Wonderful. You will be well protected. I will stay behind for some weeks, as many of my most useful herbs can be collected here," explained Dr. Morales, "but when I arrive in Mexico, I will come to see you and Gonzalo. Meanwhile, you worked with me, when we were at sea and you have learned some procedures from me. You must remember them. I will provide you with medicines for your journey, so that you will be able to care for anyone who falls sick, or is wounded."

"Wounded?" echoed Guiomar, with anxiety.

"You may be set upon by hostile natives. Or, even worse, by bandits. There are always some people who, instead of working themselves, dedicate their lives to taking away from others what they have gained from their toil. This is as old as history. The New World has been ours for only a few short years, and already we have these criminals among us."

"But you, will you be safe here alone?" questioned Guiomar.

"As safe as God wants me to be. Generally speaking, a collector of herbs and medicines is looked upon kindly by the natives, who know many secrets of drugs and cures, and as for bandits, they are not interested in my little collection of leaves and berries; what they want is gold."

"I will pray for your safety," promised Guiomar.

"God bless you."

Dr. Morales and Gomo disappeared into the countryside very soon after, and Gonzalo could not find them to say farewell.

The caravan, organized by Fray Domingo, gathered to begin the journey to Mexico, and was equipped and ready to start three days later. When he learned that Dr. Morales and Gomo had disappeared, Fray Domingo was annoyed. He had counted on the presence of the learned doctor, as he had not yet recovered his health, and was subject to unexplained swelling in his feet and legs, which troubled him very much in the evenings and early mornings.

Guiomar and Judit put on their white cotton dresses, with the hoods Dr. Morales had recommended. When he saw them Gonzalo laughed aloud.

"Are we so ridiculous?" asked Judit, with some asperity.

"No indeed! You look beautiful, like angels!" he answered. "We need angels to accompany us on this journey. Do you know how to ride, Judit?"

"A horse?" Both girls started back, in fear.

"So. I thought not," commented Gonzalo. "And Guiomar, from years in the convent, has never mounted, either. So I have bought quiet little donkeys for you. You will have only to sit on their backs, as comfortable as in a litter!"

"I have never ridden in a litter, either," said Guiomar. "Where are our donkeys?"

"Come. I'll show you."

Very conscious of her presence by his side, Gonzalo turned taciturn, for he was continually tormented by the desire to touch and caress his sister, and he knew that he must not.

Two small gray beasts waited with the horses that had been acquired for the trip. They stood with drooping ears, looking very meek and gentle. Yet one of them shied, and tried to bite Gonzalo when he laid a hand on its neck.

"Don't be afraid," Gonzalo said. "Dr. Morales gave me some herb to mix into their feed which will calm them and make them very docile for the first two days. After that they will be used to what they have to do, and will be no trouble."

It was so. Mounted on their donkeys, Judit and Guiomar were placed in the center of the caravan which consisted of Fray Domingo on a good mule, Gonzalo on his, two Spanish merchants, Don Flavio and Don Venancio, on theirs, four pack mules loaded with gear, five soldiers mounted on small mettlesome horses, and taking with them two extra mounts, unsaddled. One of the soldiers, Captain Fernandez, had been appointed in charge of the travelers, and it was he who would choose their resting places. He would select the camp for the night and appoint soldiers to keep guard over the night fire, and to cook simple food during the noon rest.

They started out with first light, before the rising sun could burn through their clothes. Nevertheless, the heat of the day descended on them swiftly, while they were still easing through the swampy lands of the coast toward where the Spaniards had traced a road and marked it with rocks they had limed, so as to make them shine white and indicate the way, for verdure grew so fast during the tropical rains that the trail might have been lost otherwise.

Captain Fernandez explained during their first rest stop that the Spaniards had simply followed the ancient trail used by the native Indians.

"The King, Moctezuma, in Mexico, had runners passing over this road in relays, bringing him fresh tropical fruits, and even fresh fish. The runners made short sprints, as fast as they could go, passing the freshly caught fish from hand to hand, and it is told that they often had the fish on Moctezuma's table by next day. Young boys were trained for this running from early childhood, and also they were given herbs, to strengthen them and increase all their capacities."

"Wonderful. Could we find and use some herbs like those? They would be a help to many people. Even to you, the soldiers of the King."

"The natives are secretive. It is not easy to convince them to share their treasures with us. Beginning with their gold. In spite of all our searching, we have never found the golden treasures of Moctezuma, and none of the natives will tell where it is, not even under torture."

"Oh, must they be tortured?" cried Guiomar.

Captain Fernandez looked at her in wonder.

"The King needs their gold," he explained curtly.

Fray Domingo took the trouble to address Guiomar and Judit when they made their first stop for the night. Captain Fernandez had chosen a flat and dry place, not far from running water, and there he made a circle of the tethered beasts with space for a good fire in the center. Here two of the soldiers set about boiling some water and cutting strips from a haunch of venison which they had brought with them. These they impaled on sharp sticks and roasted over the fire, the juice, as it fell on the coals, hissing and sending up a savory steam. Into the kettle of boiling water they stirred several tablets of a dark paste, which dissolved and colored the water a deep brown. This brew was served out in clay cups.

"You must sweeten it with a particle of this hard sugar," explained one of the soldiers, as he gave Guiomar her cup. "This is *chocolatl,* or bitter water, as the Aztecas call it. It is better with sugar, and milk, if you have it. We have none. But it is strengthening, and gives courage. Try it."

Guiomar tried it, and after a few tastes, found she liked the strange flavor.

"The men prefer wine, but we can't carry it on these journeys, and the *chocolatl* makes a good substitute," explained the soldier. "And it is easy to pack. One of these little tablets makes several cups of the brew."

"I will buy some for my father's household when I am in Mexico," planned Guiomar. "I expect to be his *ama de llaves.*"

Gonzalo had overheard her and he put in, "Ah, Guiomar, you won't have to work at all! Father has several slaves, and one is trained to the kitchen."

Guiomar paled and looked so distressed, that he continued hurriedly, "You will be in charge of them, of course, and no doubt you can teach them many new ways, to please our father."

Fray Domingo, who seemed always to be near, and listening, said severely, "I trust the slaves are being instructed in the True Faith."

"Oh, indeed they are. All have been baptized," said Gonzalo.

"They must be very carefully watched over and severely restrained from reverting to any pagan practices," went on the Dominican. "We . . . in the Holy Office . . . we are not permitted to subject the Indians to Inquisition. Therefore slaveowners must be very vigilant."

"The Inquisition . . ." murmured Guiomar. "Can it judge everybody else? Except the Indians?"

"Holy Office is determined to keep the True Faith pure and strong in this country, which is part of the realm of our Most Catholic Majesty," explained the friar. "Indians must be baptized and instructed. That is not my province. I must take care of adult Catholics, who may have lapsed into sin. Heresy is the worst sin, of course. But Holy Office is strict and severe with blasphemers (I hope the soldiers, who easily fall into this vice, are listening to me), with bigamists, and with immoral clergy.

"You see," intoned the friar, rocking himself back and forth from toes to heels, as if he were in the pulpit, preaching, and as if he had learned the words by heart, like Gospel, "being far away from Spain, some wicked men pretend that they were never married before, and take new wives, flouting the sacrament. They must be punished."

"And are the clergy, the ones who fall into sin, are they punished also?" asked Judit.

"Without mercy," pronounced the friar, with satisfaction. "Without mercy," he repeated.

Guiomar was silent, because his words chilled her. Mercy, she thought, is the sweetest of the Christian virtues. How can this friar be so rigid? But she held her tongue.

The two girls covered themselves in a blanket, and lay down together on a bed of boughs the soldiers had cut and prepared for them. Gonzalo and the men lay, wrapped in cloaks, their heads resting on the saddles from their mounts, with their feet to the fire. But all slept fitfully, the soldiers and experienced travelers like Gonzalo because the price of safety on the roads was being alert to danger and to any unusual sound, the girls because everything was new and strange, and they were unused to the discomforts of the road.

7.

The whole company was wakened an hour before dawn and given a cold breakfast, for, as Captain Fernandez explained, the soldiers would go ahead and hunt, bringing in some wild fowl, or perhaps even a deer, for the hot midday meal. Stiff and sore from the previous day's march and the unaccustomed ride on the donkeys, Guiomar and Judit made little conversation as they made ready for the journey. Under her breath, Guiomar prayed and offered her discomforts to the Crucified, while thinking aloud her gratitude for having come safely thus far. But Judit was dejected, and at intervals tears rose to her eyes and slipped down her cheeks.

Fray Domingo had passed a night of intense pain and misery, and despite all his best intentions to accept his suffering as a God-sent measure to help purify his soul, he decided that he ought to return to Veracruz (only one day's travel back along the road they had come on) and restore his health before undertaking the long journey to Mexico City. Besides, he thought, I should perhaps remain and investigate the passengers landing from the other ships, in case there are suspicious characters among them.

Being conscious of his *converso* origin (though he had successfully concealed this, so far, even from ecclesiastical authorities), he was fanatical in complying with all his religious duties, and he took his work as a spy for the Holy Office with the greatest devotion. For every secret or crypto-Jew he found and brought to trial, he felt safer himself, and he rejoiced in his heart that Holy Church was thus more nearly pure of any heretical taint.

Perhaps I can find that Dr. Morales, and be given some herbs to alleviate my illness, he thought. At least some ship's surgeon can bleed me. The fact was, he could not even walk, and had to be hoisted onto his mule.

"I will send one of my soldiers back with you, to protect you on the way," offered Captain Fernandez.

"No need," answered Fray Domingo, almost through clenched teeth, because of the ache in his limbs. "I will be safe. It is not so far, and I will put myself in God's hands."

Guiomar clucked as she saw him ride dejectedly back along the trail.

"He looks so sick," she murmured.

"Perhaps some pain will make him less cruel," commented Judit, coldly.

When the halt for a meal and rest was called, Gonzalo saw that the hunters had done well. Several fowls had been plucked and made ready, and water was boiling over the fire, into which they would be tossed and cooked.

"We dug up some of the roots the natives eat, as well," the captain told Gonzalo. "They are sweet, and very filling. We will dine well!"

As they all sat, at some distance from the fire because the day was hot and they had not yet risen above the tropical coastal plain, crashes and shouts were heard, and suddenly two mounted soldiers burst into the clearing where the little caravan had camped for their nooning.

Captain Fernandez rose and stood ready to question the men, who were wearing a uniform in red and black, not the King's colors.

They saluted and dismounted. Captain Fernandez offered food, which they accepted, but before they sat, they asked permission to join the company making its way toward Mexico.

"But we are proceeding slowly, on account of the ladies," explained Captain Fernandez. "You could make better time on your horses."

"But we are the front runners. Our company will be coming into sight in about an hour's time. We have prisoners for the Holy Office, who must be taken to Mexico for trial."

Gonzalo was silent, and the two other merchants in the party, who customarily kept quiet and attended only to their own beasts, made no comment.

It was Guiomar who broke into a cry of pity and distress when she saw the prisoners stumbling toward them some time later. They were chained together, four bearded men, whose clothes were in tatters, and through the rents of which she could see festering sores, on which flies clustered.

Two mounted soldiers, attired like the ones who had reached the caravan first, rode along beside them.

"Take them over there," ordered Captain Fernandez. He then gave the soldiers orders to dismount and rest their animals, and he saw that all, soldiers and prisoners, had bowls of broth and pieces of fowl to eat.

Guiomar put her hand on Gonzalo's arm. "Oh, brother," she began, "do you think you could get me permission to cure the hurts of those poor men? Look, they are almost fainting, and you can see that they are sick and in pain from their wounds."

Gonzalo would not look at her, for fear she would read the avid tenderness in his face, but he mumbled that he would speak to the captain.

Captain Fernandez thought the young woman might be planning to enter a religious order. Who but a nun would want to wash and lay healing leaves on those heretics?

"If you can heal them, it would be helpful," he said. "Otherwise, since they are prisoners of the Holy Office, we will be greatly delayed. It is obvious they cannot travel far in their present state."

So Guiomar washed the men's wounds, and their filthy faces, tried to comb out their matted beards and hair. Dr. Morales had taught her to use some leaves she found at hand, which absorbed the oozing pus and kept the flies away.

As she worked silently, not speaking to the men, Gonzalo went to the captain and guard of the prisoners.

"Where did you come from?" he asked. "Surely you have

come more than one day's journey, and Veracruz is but one day's march behind us."

"We come from Tampico," was the answer. The soldier dismounted, saluted, and offered his name.

"Captain Rivero, at your service."

"Gonzalo Montemayor. And our leader here is Captain Fernandez. But tell me, why have you come this way, to join us? It would seem to be out of your way."

Captain Rivero settled down, sitting back on bended knees, as horsemen do, to rest themselves.

"It's a long story. These"—he waved a disdainful glove at the silent, beaten prisoners—"are Lutherans, and pirates. English pirates. All the English are Lutherans." He spat in the dust to show his contempt.

"Tampico has been raided by the English pirates many times," went on Captain Rivero. "There is no real bay, but a broad entrance, by the river. Four times, pirates have put in, and sacked the town, taken on fresh water, and gone on out to sea again. But this time, we were ready. We had cannons ranged along the riverside, and we got them broadside. We sank the ship, we thought with all hands. At least, so we hoped. But about ten of the men who could swim got away, and were able to hide in the swamps. We were sent out after them, to hunt them down, and bring them to Mexico City to the Inquisition. It took us some time to find all ten. Two of them were dead already, from wounds, and one from snakebite. Others died on the march. We have only these four to take up to Mexico. If the señorita can keep them alive long enough to testify, we will be grateful."

Captain Rivero was young, but he already showed scars on his neck and on his brow that told of fights and violence. When he stripped to the waist to wash in the stream next morning, Gonzalo saw that his body bore further scars. The young man was proud of these, and told Gonzalo where and how he had acquired each one.

"But not from those Lutherans," he said. "By the time we found them they were half dead from the heat, and wounds, and they had been without water or food for days. They couldn't put up any resistance."

"What will happen to them?" asked Gonzalo.

"They will be tried. If they repent and accept the True Faith, they will be lashed and then sold as slaves, or sent to Spain, to prison. If they are recalcitrant and resistant, they will have to be made to do penitential duties," explained Captain Rivero. "And if they won't repent, but are defiant, they will be burned."

"Well, how can they explain themselves?" asked Gonzalo. "If they are English Lutherans, they cannot speak our language."

"Oh, there are very clever monks in the Holy Office," cried Captain Rivero. "Why, some even speak Arabic and Hebrew!"

Guiomar, washing and binding up with strips of cotton cloth the festering leg of one of the prisoners, saw him open his eyes suddenly, and they were blue as violets. She caught her breath.

"You are an angel," whispered the man, hoarsely. "I knew it when I first laid these fortunate eyes on you!" He spoke Spanish, with the accent of north Spain.

"In Seville, when I was boarding the boat," whispered Guiomar. "I remember you."

"God bless and keep you, kind angel," the man whispered again, and he turned to kiss the hand that was stroking an ointment onto his lacerated cheek.

"Do not speak. Try to rest," she whispered back.

Later, she questioned Gonzalo about the men, and he told her what Captain Rivero had related.

Guiomar did not confide in her brother; she worried about the fact of the young man's having been taken as a pirate—an English pirate—when she knew him to be a Spaniard. There was something wrong here. In the few short months since she had left the convent, candid and confident, she had learned to guard her thoughts that they might not show on her face, and to keep her own counsel.

8

Gonzalo suffered very much from a confusion of feelings, and longed for the journey to be over. Then he could put Guiomar into her father's arms, leave her there, and himself depart on his business trips, when he could forget her, and exorcize from his heart the intense attraction he had had for her from the first moment he saw her. Gonzalo had not received a strong education in any moral or ethical school; he had simply learned from his father, and had tried to imitate him, for Pedro Montemayor was a strong and kindly and successful man. Yet Gonzalo knew, deeply and instinctively, that the feeling he had for Guiomar was against the laws of men and the Church, that it was wrong, and he must never allow them to dominate his actions or his thoughts.

Realizing this, he never dreamed that behaving correctly would be so hard. But every day was a torment to him, especially as his sister was of an affectionate and demonstrative disposition, and liked to be near him, to serve him his meals, and to talk with him while she rode, or walked beside him.

In an attempt to spare himself, Gonzalo began to treat her coldly, which distressed her to such a degree that he saw that he could not keep up that pretense.

"But what have I done, brother, that you are angry with me?" she asked, again and again. "Tell me, so that I won't do it again! I want only to please you and be a good sister to you!"

Then Gonzalo hit upon the plan of paying attention to Judit, of seeking her company, to sit beside her when they stopped for meals, of walking with her when she was sent to gather firewood for the cooking, of riding near her. He saw then, with a wry kind of pleasure, that Guiomar accepted this as natural and right, and indeed, she seemed very happy to think that there might develop a real attachment between Gonzalo and Judit.

What Gonzalo did not see was that Judit had begun to blossom and expand, like a flower in the sun. Her cheeks showed a delicate pink, she took care to comb and tie back her hair with colored nets, and shyly, she began to seek him when, distracted, he had forgotten his plan. Her large dark eyes followed him constantly, and she was always smiling when he came near.

The company made way slowly, because of the weak, stumbling prisoners, but by the fourth day they had reached a high flat plain and a large settlement called Puebla de los Angeles. Captain Fernandez ordered a rest of several days, and made plans to turn the prisoners and their guards over to some other company. This was effected, as a new caravan was about to move north from the town, carrying two mortally sick officers by litter, and this company would of course proceed very slowly. Besides, they would go accompanied by more soldiers. Captain Fernandez had not ceased to worry that some one of the prisoners might be feigning and would try an escape. He had no doubt he could recapture the culprit should this happen, but he wanted no more delay than was absolutely necessary.

When Guiomar heard that the prisoners were to be transferred, she went to speak to the men, who had prospered under her care, and to give them portions of the ointments and packages of the leaves she had been using.

"You are better now; you can walk more easily," she said to them all. But she was looking at the man with the dark blue eyes.

They saw compassion on the face of the young woman, and despite the disarray the march had brought about in her clothes, the dirt and stains on her white covering garment, her beauty was arresting. Her clear golden skin, lit up by the large black eyes, seemed not to have coarsened or darkened. Her wide mouth was red and curved, and her teeth were flawless. A few long curling strands of her hair had escaped from the white hood, and shone in the sun.

The blue-eyed prisoner, and the one beside him, a dark man much older in years, spoke to her in hurried Spanish.

"We are innocent, Doña Guiomar. We are not Lutherans. We were captured from the sinking *True Cross*, by pirates, and enslaved. We can prove our innocence to the Holy Office." The other two prisoners, chained to them, did not understand.

"I will pray for your delivery and your safety," promised Guiomar.

"You are an angel! God bless you!" they cried, in unison.

"My angel," murmured Juan Palomar. Fermín García Mendoza echoed his words. "An angel. An angel."

9.

Captain Fernández delayed only two days in Puebla. This time he spent buying two new mules to serve as sumpter beasts, and a carefully planned body of supplies for the remainder of the march. The rains were beginning, drenching everything in the late afternoons, and he studied his routes again most carefully, from rough maps he had made on previous marches.

Guiomar, accompanied by a soldier, went to the native markets to look for the leaves, the grasses and seeds from which to make healing ointments and lotions, as Dr. Morales had taught her. To her astonishment and joy, she found him in the market himself, on the second day.

Running up to him she greeted him with affection.

He too seemed delighted to find her, and held her off for a moment to study her.

"You are well," he pronounced.

"We are all well. I have taken care, with the things you taught me, and I had to cure some prisoners who had been captured and were being taken to Mexico to be tried by the Holy Office," she confided. "They have gone on with another company now. Lutherans," she added, in answer to Dr. Morales's raised questioning eyebrow.

Dr. Morales asked about the prisoners at some length, and then about the other members of the company.

"And Fray Domingo?" he questioned.

"Oh, he left us, to return to Veracruz the very next day," Guiomar told him. "Didn't he find you? He intended to look for you in Veracruz. He was in great pain, from his legs."

"What a shame he did not find me," answered the doctor, "but I had left to take another path through the woods to Puebla, as I collect for my medicines on the way."

He said no more but after a few words with Captain Fernandez, he went away to fetch Gomo and his mules.

Gonzalo welcomed the learned doctor with pleasure, and reminded him of his promise to accompany him on a trading trip to the north, after a rest in Mexico City.

"I look forward to it," answered the doctor.

Guiomar, though she also was pleased to have the doctor's strong quiet presence near, wondered briefly why he had not joined them before when Fray Domingo had been with them. The friar's absence now seemed to imply that Dr. Morales had wished to avoid him. Perhaps he does not like people who work for the Holy Office, she thought. They make me uneasy, too. But the thought was fleeting, and she, with Gonzalo, listened carefully to all that Dr. Morales said, and was grateful to learn from him.

The whole company set out on the next day, before the dawn, and Dr. Morales was in the company. He rode beside Gonzalo, and Guiomar saw, with pleasure, that her brother drew closer to the learned doctor every day.

So they continued until they reached the village of Amecameca, where they were delayed for two days because of lameness of two of the mules. Dr. Morales knew ways to comfort and cure the animals, with poultices and drafts of a liquid he prepared, and he even had with him a strange sort of pipe, down which he poured the medicine, while Gonzalo held the struggling animal's jaws open. Captain Fernandez had the lame ones relieved of their burdens, and these were distributed among the other beasts. By then, the food supplies had dwindled, and there was less to pack.

By the time the company was but three days' march from Mexico City, the food had been consumed, so Captain Fernandez and two of his men went hunting. They came back to camp with a young deer, which they roasted, and all ate well that night. Their camp was pitched beneath pines for shelter, for they were in very high mountains by then, and it was extremely cold. Guiomar and Judit huddled together for comfort, and the men took turns keeping up the fires all night.

"I think I will never be warm again," moaned Judit.

"Where my father lives, it is not as high as we are now," Guiomar told her, for she had been consulting Gonzalo about the home to which she was going. His answers had been quick and clear, because he did not wish to stay near her, but Guiomar took no offense, believing that he was busy with many duties about the camp. She had gleaned the information that her father awaited them in a stone house with seven rooms, that he had four slaves, and that he carried on his leather-curing and sewing and cutting business in one of the patios.

Nevertheless, she was not prepared, when at last their company had reached the outskirts of the great city called Mexico by the Spaniards. The original Indian settlers had called it Tenochtitlán, a name hard to pronounce in Spanish mouths, and since the people who lived there belonged to a tribe called Mexicas, they renamed the city for them. Since taking the city over fifty years before, the Spaniards had built many solid square stone houses for themselves, some of them beautifully ornamented with carving, and they had set down cobblestones in the streets. Also, here and there was a small church, while masons were busily building a larger one, and hanging bells in the towers. As the company under Captain Fernandez entered the city, Guio-

mar saw that many of the streets were really waterways or canals, upon which many boats and canoes were passing.

Dr. Morales, walking near Guiomar's donkey, explained to her
that they had skirted the large lake of Texcoco, from which the
streams flowed, and had entered the city by land because of their
beasts.

"But I often ride the boats and cross the lake," he told her,
"especially when I am traveling unburdened."

Guoimar felt exhilarated, for the plain on which Mexico was
built was high and the breeze carried the fresh scent of water
from the canals. Passing near one of the waterways, they saw
boats piled high with flowers, giving off strong fragrance, and
then she saw, on the shore, a flower market, where every color
and kind of bloom was being sold.

Before they arrived at her father's house, though, they passed
through a section of the city which smelled rank and sinister, as
of burned flesh.

"Yes," explained Dr. Morales, "we are passing the *quemadero*,
where the heretics and witches are given to the flames."

Guiomar trembled.

"I cannot look," she whispered.

"Do not."

She dropped her eyes and folded a scarf around her face, and
did not unwind it until the clatter of the hooves of the horses
and pack animals ceased, and some of the beasts gave tired gusty
sighs.

"We are here," announced Gonzalo, helping Guiomar down
from her donkey. "We are home."

10.

Don Pedro Montemayor had not slept well in the last few nights,
because he had calculated that Gonzalo must soon arrive from

the coast with his sister. Inquiries in the city had yielded the information that the Fleet had arrived in Veracruz, and from the day and hour that he heard this, Don Pedro had been shaken by delight and by anxiety.

He had ordered his slaves to scour the house with lye and ashes, and to wash and air all the bedding. The female slaves consisted of three women, Tomasa, Leocadia, and Elena; he had baptized them Christians, and named them for the day on which he had acquired them. Tomasa was a woman in her fifties, taciturn, suspicious, and fat; she was the cook, and she had taught Don Pedro to eat many succulent and spicy dishes, which she had learned to make in her native village, before she had been captured and sold as a slave. Elena was a little girl of ten who helped her mother Leocadia. Don Pedro had bought them from a trader who told him that they had sold themselves voluntarily, because there was famine in their village. Both the child and her mother were thin, very dark, with bony noses and prominent lips, but with long shining black hair. The little girl resembled her mother and would look like her, but in her childhood, she was pretty, and she had endearing ways. Don Pedro was good to his slaves, saw that they went to mass, and did not demand too much work from them. But in preparation for Guiomar's arrival, he would not let anyone stop until the whole house smelled of sunshine and air.

He had laid in supplies of wheat flour and lard, haunches of bacon, and ham, and baskets of onions and the red fruit *tomate*, and the peppery chilies the Mexicans loved to use to season their food. In the large kitchen, Tomasa had been ready to prepare her most delectable dishes for many days, and she was growing angry and sullen at the delay.

Epifanio was the male slave, a man now in his twenties. Don Pedro had taught him the leather trade, and when Don Pedro was away, Epifanio was now capable of keeping the workshop active and producing.

When at last the great knocker on the wide front door sounded, and Don Pedro heard Gonzalo's shout, he and the slaves were immobilized for a moment before breaking into activity. Epifanio ran to throw wide the great door, or *zaguan*, and to guide the men with their beasts into the back patio. Tomasa blew on the charcoal under her cooking pots to redden the coals and start things boiling, and Leocadia and Elena stood ready to help the young lady into her room, where they had fresh towels ready, and a bed, invitingly turned down.

Don Pedro, walking stiffly because of the rheumatism which troubled him, embraced his son, and then eagerly looked beyond him, for his daughter.

Was it that slim dark girl, with the delicate oval face, and the black plaits of hair, so like his wife's? No! It was the tall girl with a tumbling mass of coppery curls that fell below her waist, who ran toward him with outstretched arms, a look of joy on her face.

Don Pedro, like Gonzalo before him, was unprepared for her beauty and for the strength and vitality that radiated from her.

"*Hijita*," he murmured, as he folded her in his arms, and he was thinking, *Dios mio*, what will I do with a goddess like this?

11.

In another part of Mexico City another reunion was taking place. This was more exuberant, for the two who met had been lovers for years, and made no secret of their relationship.

The woman was called Eulalia Monzón, but the whole neighborhood knew her as La Gorda. She was not fat, in truth, but only full-bosomed, ripe, and bouncy. While she was considered desirable by every male who met her or looked upon her—with her long curling black hair, sparkling eyes, red cheeks, and constant vivacious smile—they also feared her wrath, which was terrible, when she considered that she had been cheated, if only of a maravedi. She ran a boardinghouse for soldiers and as these were constantly returning from the wars against the Chichimecas, her business was lively, though it often included nursing as well. Her rooms were clean, and her meals were heavy and bountiful. She collected payment in advance. A careful administrator, she purchased everything needed in her house, worked her two slaves to the last ounce of their energy, and she was putting away several ducats a month, against her eventual return to Spain. She meant to marry her soldier then, and buy a *fonda* in Spain. This dream comforted her whenever she felt the weight of her thirty-five years, or lost a tooth. Usually she was cheerful, hardworking, and hopeful.

Gaspar de Oteiza, her protector, had been twice chastised and expelled from the army for stealing, as he could never restrain himself from laying hands on whatever was left about which he thought might turn out to be useful to himself. He was a stout, strong fellow of some twenty-eight years who had enlisted in Spain in order to avoid having to serve in the galleys, which would undoubtedly have been his fate had he been caught for stealing sheep and selling them. His new name, somewhat resounding, he had made up and assumed, and he was content to leave his real name, his family, and his past in Spain, forgotten.

Broad-shouldered, blond, and of a merry disposition, he never had any trouble finding friends, or partners in love. But La Gorda was possessive, and while he was in Mexico City, he took care not to make her jealous. He still carried a scar which had resulted from an attack by La Gorda, who had been chopping onions in a bowl, in her doorway, when he foolishly had dared to admire a serving girl, passing by in the street.

At about the time Guiomar had suddenly knelt and carried her father's hard, gnarled hand to her lips three streets away, Gaspar had arrived, somewhat furtively, for he had deserted. This never worried him overmuch, for there were not many soldiers willing to fight the Chichimecas, a crafty and cruel race of Indians, and he knew full well that when he wanted to join the ranks again the captain would accept him, though for discipline he would throw him into the *calabozo* for a day or two.

Gaspar, this time, had made his desertion worthwhile. It was not a simple case of haring after a pretty woman. This time he had stolen a load of hides from a traveler, leaving the victim unconscious in the road from the cudgeling Gaspar had given him. A load of hides was money, Gaspar had only to sell them, and he knew that La Gorda, with her keen commercial sense, would know where to go with them to get the best price.

After the first embraces and hearty kisses, and a few moments of tickling, and of disarranging La Gorda's blouse, Gaspar recounted his exploit.

"Where are they?" was her first question.

"Hidden."

"Far?"

"Not far. I could get them in an hour or two."

"Well, it would be better to bring them here after dark. So we have a few hours of daylight. Just time enough," she explained coquettishly, and led the way to her well-remembered bedroom.

Later, leaning back in his chair and patting his stomach, which was replete with three bowls of La Gorda's hare stew, he began to think about the stolen hides.

There were other lodgers at the table, and so he held his tongue, but before dark he strolled toward where he had hidden his booty under a big rock, north of the city, and on a road little traveled by any except Indian peddlers. And he was sure no one had seen him hide the bulky package.

He waited until the darkness had come down enough to blur images and deepen shadows, and then he quickly retrieved his stolen treasure. La Gorda waited for him, and whisked him in through her *zaguan* and into her bedroom, with no one the wiser.

She exclaimed over the hides, which had been delicately tanned, and were flexible and sweet-smelling, unlike the stiff odorous hides she had seen in the marketplace.

"I think they must be kidskin," she commented, fingering them. "For ladies' wear. And," she went on, "I think I know where we can sell them. Not you! I will sell them, and one at a time. I can say they have been left me, in lieu of payment, by one of my lodgers. Yes. There is a Spaniard who cuts and sews leather on Curtidores Street; I will try him tomorrow."

Gaspar was fond of La Gorda, but not entirely ready to give over his merchandise.

"I have to get back to the regiment in about four days, when they are sending out fresh troops against the Chichimecas," he mused, "and they need us old hands, who know the ways of the savages. I can't wait and sell my leather piece by piece."

La Gorda put her hands on her hips.

"You mean you think I will sell them, and keep back some of the money," she accused him.

He hotly denied this, but she insisted, and a blazing quarrel resulted, ending, as all their quarrels did, in blows, and then in tears and kisses and further lovemaking.

In bed later, exhausted but not convinced, Gaspar upbraided himself for having told her about the hides. He might have left them hidden a longer time. But no, they might have deteriorated. At last, unwillingly, he decided to accept her plan, but he made up his mind to follow at a distance, and find out the place where she intended to sell. He might even be able to overhear the bargaining, and thus know how to deal with any other windfalls that came his way.

In the morning, after feeding her lodgers (who were only three at the time, not counting Gaspar), La Gorda made ready to go to market. In the bottom of her basket, well covered with a fine cloth, she put the softest and tenderest of the hides. Gaspar saw her preparations, but he made no effort to follow her until she had bustled out, and could be seen leaping over the refuse in the street some distance away. La Gorda, unsuspecting, did not glimpse him among the crowds at the big *tianguis* (Indian market), where the Indians squatted with their mounds of vegetables and fruit. La Gorda took her time, choosing the firmest onions, the most shining and crisp peppers, the heaviest cabbages. With her basket well loaded, she hurried away in another direction, and Gaspar followed her, mixing into the crowds.

She stopped at a large square stone house and gave a mighty clang on the knocker, which was of brass, shaped like the head of a lion, with a circlet in its mouth.

And then something happened which was to change Gaspar's life. A young woman came to the door, young and tall, with uncovered shining hair, which fell to her narrow waist, in back. Her face was unlined, perfect, of a warm golden color, and her large eyes were black as velvet, under perfectly marked brows. She was wearing a dress of some blue stuff, and an apron. Gaspar breathed, "The Holy Virgin! She is exactly like the Holy Virgin, in the Church of the Annunciation, in my home village!"

Almost at once another young woman joined her, and they both looked at the hide La Gorda was showing them. But the new arrival was small and dark, like almost all the women of New Spain. Gaspar paid no attention to her. His head reeled with the beauty of the auburn-haired girl, and in some mysterious way she made him feel gross and dirty.

Marking the doorway well, he stumbled away and he mooned about all day, unable to eat.

La Gorda related her triumph.

"The leatherworking factory belongs to Don Pedro Montemayor, and his daughter has arrived to stay with him. She came with the Fleet. She was crazy for the leather, and he bought it for her. He will make her some dainty shoes, I presume. Though her foot, I noticed, is longer than mine!" La Gorda stuck out a short fat foot, and regarded it admiringly. "I got three ducats for your leather, my love!"

Gaspar held out his hand, and she put two ducats into it.

"One for me," she explained. "We are saving up for our inn in Spain, remember!"

"I remember," he answered dully.

That night, to La Gorda's annoyance, and his bewilderment, he could not make love.

He did not know what had happened to him.

12

The Grand Inquisitor, Don Pedro Moya y Contreras, was also the Archbishop of Mexico and Viceroy of New Spain. He had countless duties, and was obliged to make many ceremonious public appearances and to devise laws and regulations for the better governing of the colony, to think of and give impulse to new businesses (he had indeed imported large looms and started a useful commerce in woven woolens), and send troops wherever there were local disturbances. He had to write long reports to the Crown on almost every matter concerning the colonies, and the King was himself so methodical, careful, and detailed in his interests and instructions that the drafting of these reports took up a large part of his time.

The government of New Spain consisted of peak authorities (the King and his representative, that is, the Viceroy), with minor officials, in groups below these, always subject to the higher official and required to report regularly. The volume of correspondence from the Indies was enormous.

The army was under orders of generals and those below them in rank, but the Viceroy kept close contact with his generals, and could order and make countermands, at will (which of course had to be explained in detail, in a report to His Majesty). The civil law was well organized, and an army of clerks, scriveners, treasurers, judges, and lawyers was speedily growing in every city of any size in the New World. Above all these, and subject to the Viceroy (who was also Archbishop and Grand Inquisitor), were the clergy and the monastic orders which had come to teach, to build, to Christianize the natives, and to watch over the faith and morals of the colonists. Their task was an enormous undertaking, but the Church had accepted it with a will.

The Viceroy had, in fact, so many duties on so many levels that, like any good administrator, he named assistants to take over the active duties, for which of course, he himself was responsible to the Crown.

Most delicate and important of these, was the conducting of the Holy Office. Don Pedro could not possibly preside over the trials and Inquiries in person. He delegated a *fiscal*, or special prosecutor, to prepare the briefs and accusations, and named three Inquisitors from among the most trusted and vigilant members of the Dominican Order, to conduct the Inquisitions. The chief of those three was Francisco Aviles, who acted for him in perfect concordance with the Viceroy-Archbishop's beliefs and requirement. In fact, Fray Francisco was often sent to Spain, personally, with long reports on the work being done in New Spain.

The business of the Holy Office was conducted in a splendid building made of the red porous stone called *tezontli* used for the finest construction in the city. It was built around a central patio, for light and air, and the trial rooms, cells for persons being held while awaiting trial, archives, and copying rooms gave onto broad corridors with high balustrades. The building was decorated with sober Spanish elegance, but Fray Francisco permitted no luxuries within.

He had been away on a trip to Spain, and was awaited hourly, as it was known that he intended to return with the great spring Fleet, which had come into port at Veracruz. Fray Francisco was modest and quiet in the extreme, and was known to prefer traveling incognito. In this manner he avoided all unseemly honor and luxury, which he despised, for he had been educated in an order of the strictest discipline. At the same time, he could observe fellow travelers, ship's authorities, and others, who had no idea of his importance and power, while they acted and spoke naturally. He thus detected many a wretch in fearful blasphemies against Our Lord and Our Lady, and in other offenses. Fray Francisco in charge of the Inquisition offices for the Viceroy was particularly quick to perceive any ribald or licentious attitudes in the clergy, and when he did he was implacable. It was his deepest belief that Holy Church should be kept pure, stainless, perfect, and it followed that the clergy must also be devoted, chaste, and incorruptible. Whenever Fray Francisco found in judgment against a priest who had solicited women from the confessional, he did not hesitate to send him to the torture before shipping him back to Spain, to prison.

In the rooms of the Holy Office in Mexico City, there was an atmosphere of expectation not unmixed with fear, because Fray Francisco was expected at any moment. The stone floor had been swept, washed, and scoured, the chairs and tables had been rubbed with beeswax, and the heavy curtains across the barred windows had been taken down, shaken and brushed, mended, and rehung. Fray Francisco would tolerate no expenditures for comfort; there were no cushions on the chairs, and despite the bone-biting chill of the rainy afternoons, which were setting in with the summer, he would allow no charcoal fires, nor any sealed jugs of hot water clutched against bellies inside voluminous habits. One of the minor clerks, Fray Arnulfo, dared to harbor resentment about this. He was a copyist, and he could not write as perfectly, with the same pressure of quill against parchment, as he should, when his hands were stiffened by frostbite. And after all Fray Francisco had his cat, which sat in his lap, and kept his legs warm. Nobody else had ever been bold enough to bring his own cat with him. But of course, Fray Francisco lived in abject poverty in the small cell next door to his offices. His only concession to worldliness was the tiny square cut into the base of his wooden door, to allow his cat, Andúfar, to come and go. Fray Francisco frequently fasted, showing a white and haggard face to his clerks after three days of this self-punishment, but Andúfar was fat and sleek, never lacking his dish of meat in the morning, and his sup of milk at night.

Fray Arnulfo was painfully writing out a transcription of the anonymous denunciations that had come into the Holy Office in the absence of Fray Francisco. He was the first to hear the swift but quiet step of the Grand Inquisitor. Fray Francisco was dressed as a common sailor, in clothes that were dirty and tattered from months at sea. His hands had been roughened by the hard work, but his mind had been washed clean of all but prayer, by the winds and waters of the voyage. As he entered Andúfar rushed out to greet him, calling to him in loud meows. Fray Francisco picked up the big tiger cat, caressed him, and endured the whisker-rubbing and rough kissing of his pet. Then he gently put him down, and turned to the clerks. "Ave María Purísima," he said, smiling. "Thanks to God and Our Lady, I am safely home. I will go now and change into my habit."

Followed by his cat, he strode into his cell and shut the door. Emerging not long after, in his coarse black soutane, he engaged Fray Arnulfo.

"I shall dictate to you after I have gone through the records left me," he said.

Fray Arnulfo knew that this meant he would be busy for hours, as Fray Francisco had a prodigious memory, and he never forgot one name, or one offense against heaven. Fray Arnulfo enjoyed very much taking dictation from the Inquisitors, because he learned the names of all who were to be sought out and dragged before the Inquisition. Every person accused, or denounced, was investigated. And sometimes Fray Arnulfo could warn them. For a price.

<h2 style="text-align:center">13.</h2>

In the house of Don Pedro Montemayor, on Calle de los Curtidores, there was much obvious joy and festivity. Special meals were cooked to give pleasure to the Señorita Guiomar and the Joven Gonzalo, musicians were brought in from the street to offer impromptu concerts on their homemade instruments, and various old friends and cronies of Don Pedro were invited to meet his lovely daughter. These festivities occupied several weeks, actually well into the rainy season, and until the great feast day of Our Lady of Carmen.

As this was the favorite devotion of Don Pedro, the whole household attended mass on July 16, and spent the day in religious observances. Guiomar was touched and deeply reassured to learn that her father maintained a small chapel in his home, and kept a candle burning before an image of Our Lady of Carmen, day and night, and the altar was always decorated with flowers.

"And do you hear mass here, Father?" asked Guiomar, who at once took over the care of the small room, which was really no larger than a cell.

"No, though it was blessed, of course. It is my place for prayer," he told her. "I was once saved from certain death by my prayers to Our Lady of Carmen, and I thank her every day. And she brought you safely to me, over the waters. Though she denied me my wife, my beloved Leonor, perhaps because I had left her in Spain. I wanted her to come with me, but she was expecting you, and she would not. I wept for many days when I received the notice of her death. *Ay, hijita.* Did you visit her grave?"

Guiomar did not answer at once. She had feared this question, because she was not certain how she should reply. Her mother's fierce demand, on her deathbed, still worried and frightened her, although she had not promised to do what her mother asked.

"Let us sit quietly, in my bedroom, alone, Father, and I will tell you about it," she said at last. Don Pedro, limping because he suffered much pain in the rainy season, leaned on her arm, and they made their way across the court and into the large room that had been furnished with warm woolen rugs on the floor, and several good chairs, as well as with a wide bed and several leather-bound chests for Guiomar. She made her father sit in the chair that best suited him, and then threw a few cushions on the floor at his feet. Leaning her arms on his knees, she said, "Father, I was present when my mother died. I spoke with her."

"How could that be? She died when you were born! That is why you were given to the nuns, to rear!"

Don Pedro became very agitated, and his hands shook. Guiomar took his hands and kissed them, and held them to her neck.

"My mother was condemned to die, but she escaped. There was a false notice of her death. Many years later, she came to Seville and found me, and I saw her, when she was really dying, worn out from her troubles and fears."

"But how? Why?" Don Pedro was bewildered and upset. He half rose from the chair, but Guiomar pressed him back.

"Oh, Father, all the way here, on the sea all those many days, and all the way by land, I prayed and wondered whether I should tell you. But it seemed to me at last that I must let you know the whole truth. It is so painful, dear Father. Try to be brave, and listen!"

"You sound as if this is almost too much to be borne!"

"I hope it will not be, as now God has her, my mother, in His loving care, and surely He has forgiven her! For Jesus is all mercy and love, and teaches us forgiveness. How then can God not forgive?"

"Forgive? Forgive what—"

"My mother was a Judaizer. The Holy Office tried her and she was unrepentant, and they sentenced her. But with the help of other Jews, she was spirited away and hidden, and she lived all those years in another country. Only when she was dying did she return, to find me. And to give me a last message."

The old man sat silent, shaking, looking at her with anguished eyes.

"That message," went on Guiomar, in a voice thickening with held-back tears, "was that I must bring you and Gonzalo back to the old faith. She demanded that I persuade you to renounce Jesus Christ and Our Lady and return to the Jewish ways. She wanted me to swear."

"And . . . did you swear?" quavered Don Pedro.

"Father, I could not have sworn! Never! I love Our Lord and Our Lady. I could not have sworn! But I was saved from tormenting her; she died before my eyes, in my arms, before I could swear."

Don Pedro had covered his eyes with his gnarled, rough hand, and was silent for a long space.

"But I must tell you all. Mother and her friends—relatives, I think, Doña Carmen and Don Antonio—secretly kept the Jewish ways and pretended to be Christian, for safety. They thought I had sworn, and they brought a learned rabbi to the house, to teach me, so that I should know how I must instruct you, and how I must preside over your household, the traditions, the forbidden foods, the baths, everything. He was a gentle good man, and I listened and remembered, but in my heart I could never change. Father, I did not change!"

Don Pedro lowered his hand, and looked at his daughter's distressed face.

"Poor child," he murmured. "What a dreadful dilemma for you. But how did you come to be living with those people? Doña Carmen and Don Antonio. Was their name Mendoza?"

"Yes."

"Yes. Cousins of my wife. Second cousins."

"They took me from the convent by deceit, Father. Mother Superior was told that a bridegroom had been found for me, and a Dominican monk came to take me to the bridegroom's house." Guiomar shivered as she remembered following the monk through the streets of Seville, on a walk that she had thought would bring her to a wedding and a home and family life.

"But on the way, a cloak was thrown over me, and I was carried away to the house of the Mendozas. I think now," mused Guiomar, "that the monk was a secret Judaizer too, and part of the plot, and that the kidnapping was carried out in order to protect his position. The Inquisition is very jealous and severe in Seville."

"My poor child," groaned Don Pedro. "You must be careful and circumspect in everything, in case there may have been some suspicion, some shadow of doubt about you. The Holy Office here is jealous too. Ay!"

"About me?" murmured Guiomar. "But I am a True Christian." This fear had not entered her head, but now she felt a deep chill that seemed almost to stop her heart. She paled.

"Were there any religious on the ship, or on the journey here?" persisted her father. "Was there anyone who questioned you? Or seemed to be persistent in attentions?"

Guiomar could scarcely answer. "Yes, a monk. A Dominican. In Veracruz. And there was a doctor on the ship, a learned doctor—"

"The Holy Office has spies everywhere."

Guiomar took a deep breath.

"Do not torment yourself, Father. I am a Christian, and Our Lord and Our Blessed Lady will protect me."

"We will go to the little chapel and pray together. And say nothing to anyone, not to a single living soul, about what you have told me." They walked slowly to the chapel, where a candle burned, softly illuminating the dark, which had fallen with the sudden drumming rain.

"Except your brother, of course," said Don Pedro. "Gonzalo must be told. Gonzalo must know, and must be warned."

"I will tell him," promised Guiomar.

They prayed together for some time, and then Don Pedro had to be helped to his bed. He lay ill, without strength in his limbs, or the will to eat, for five days, and during this time Guiomar was never far from his side. She asked Judit to take over the supervision of the household so that she could nurse her father, and it was only after he had sighed and managed to take a little broth, and to walk a few steps in his room again, that she remembered her promise to tell Gonzalo.

He had been avoiding her as much as he could without drawing attention to himself, but one evening, after she had fed her father and seen him settled for sleep, she sought him out, and laid her hand on his arm.

"Gonzalo," she said. "Come with me to my room. We must talk. There are many things I must tell you."

Gonzalo went, unwilling, but willing, also. Trembling at his feelings, for he had had lustful dreams about her, he waited for her first words, hoping that she would not read his thoughts, of which he was bitterly ashamed and afraid.

"Gonzalo, my brother, our mother was a Judaizer," began Guiomar.

The young man started and stepped back. He had expected anything but such shocking news.

"Are you sure? How do you know?" he stuttered.

Guiomar told him everything, as she had told her father. "And Father knows," she concluded. "He warned me that I must be extremely circumspect in everything I say and everything I do, as the Holy Office may be searching for me."

"It may be suspicious of any of us. All of us," he said. "I knew," he told her, "that our family was *converso*. Our ancestors were Jews who went to Spain, oh, many generations ago, and decided to stay there to live. And they converted to the Christian faith. We can show *cartas de limpia* from as far back as our great-great-grandparents. Otherwise, Father could not have come out to New Spain. Jews are not permitted to emigrate here. But now . . ."

Guiomar clasped her hands together and tears gathered in her eyes.

"Ay, Gonzalo, I have brought a shadow with me, to hang over us all!"

"You could not help it," he said, in a low voice. "And how could you know that the Holy Office is so scrupulous about Judaizers here? I have been told that they think of nothing else but of rooting out heresies!"

"But nothing could happen. We are Christians," whispered Guiomar. "True Christians!"

"Ay, Guiomar, if they are suspicious of you and put you to the torture, you could say *anything!* The pain would speak, not you. They have horrid instruments, on which they stretch you, and they drip water into your mouth until you are choked, and they shame the women. They strip them to the waist, and . . . and gloat . . ."

He trembled, for he had envisioned her naked to the waist himself. Guiomar had instinctively crossed her arms over her bosom.

"You have filled me with fear, Gonzalo," she whispered. "I never felt like this before."

He drew a deep breath.

"As Father said, we must be everlastingly careful," he told her. "And do not say a word to anyone."

"Not even to Judit."

"Especially not to Judit! That name, Cerezo, is a Jewish name! The Holy Office probably has her on its lists already!"

"She is a Christian. I know. I was with her, close to her, on the whole voyage, and when her mother died. I know."

"Well, let us pray to God that no disguised spies have fixed their eyes on us. I am leaving on a trip to the north with Dr. Morales as soon as he is ready. Father is old and ill. You must be seen at mass daily, and also doing works of charity and kindness. As you would have been, in any case," he added at once, "for I know that you are good and true, sister. May God and His angels watch over you and protect you from harm!"

Guiomar jumped up and took him by the shoulders, and kissed him on the cheek. He trembled to feel her so close, her soft lips on his face, the perfume of her clothes and her person in his nostrils. He took himself away, brusquely.

Gonzalo had been struggling against the attraction he felt for Guiomar, a feeling he had never experienced for any other woman. Now, thinking about his mother, there began to seem to be a glimmer of something else, in the darkness of his mind, to take his thoughts away from his obsession with his sister. Around the misty image of his mother, he began to weave a mantle of mystical beauty, of heroism. A Judaizer, but a victim. His mother.

14.

Fray Domingo had endured the journey back to Veracruz only by the aid of constant prayer, and by liberal drafts of sacramental wine, which he had with him for the mass. The fumes of the wine helped, a little, to mitigate his suffering, but when he came into the city, after dark, he had to be helped down off his mount, and put at once to bed.

A doctor who had come in with one of the other ships (Dr. Morales was nowhere to be found) bled him, and though this was done at least every third day, he did not feel any better. Only weaker.

An Indian slave who knew something of curative herbs was found, and this quiet dark man, who spoke excellent Spanish, brewed teas, and made poultices for Fray Domingo's inflamed limbs. These at last began to afford him some relief. However, it was weeks before he could walk or ride, and he reflected that God wished him to carry out his duties here, in this place, until the rains were over.

A town was springing up, and more than one family had decided against settling on the cold high plain where Mexico was situated, but to remain close to the sea, where the ships came in, and where fish could be had for any meal. Trees in the forest round about gave abundant fruit, and there were deer and all manner of wildfowl. One need never starve. And business was active whenever a ship came in. It was a life very attractive to more and more of the Spanish colonists.

There were taverns, and brawls in the street, and more than once a day Fray Domingo heard blasphemies shouted by some roistering sailor, or a colonist. He carefully noted down names, dates, and the character of each offense. By the time he could plan on making the journey up to Mexico again, he would have a fat portfolio of cases that should be brought to the attention of the Holy Office.

Toward the middle of September, when the rains were beginning to slacken, Fray Domingo found a place with a number of soldiers who were going to travel from Veracruz to Puebla, and arriving in that city, he went at once to a house serving as a monastery for his brother Dominicans. He was very proud of his lists of offenders who should be investigated by the Holy Office, and made an occasion to show it to the Superior there. This man, a young and vigorous friar not long in the New World, read through the list, and did not at once burst into lavish praise, as Fray Domingo had hoped.

"Perhaps, Brother," he said to Fray Domingo, "this sort of work was all you had strength to do, for some months. But now that you are restored to health, do you not feel that we have more direct and important tasks to undertake for the glory of God? We must build schools, educate the Indians, preach the word of God to the godless. This list"—he tapped the parchment with a fastidious finger—"deals mostly with such things as a curse, or a person washing himself before meals—matters really of lesser importance in the eyes of heaven, don't you agree?"

Fray Domingo was hurt, and he remained silent, with hanging head.

"I only meant," went on the Superior, "that these things that you have concerned yourself with can be attended to *after* we have done all the other important works, built the schools, the churches, printed the books!"

"But what—but what about the ones possessed by demons?" persisted Fray Domingo after a moment. "Some of these creatures mouth the most frightful heresies."

The Superior was silent, in his turn.

"Since you feel this strongly, Brother, I am going to ask you to undertake a mission for me. There is a wretched woman near here who is possessed of a demon, and her brothers, who have her in their care, are distraught. They have no idea of how to relieve her, or to care for her, especially when she is in one of her fits. She is violent and screams in some strange language that nobody understands. Would you go to see this poor woman, and exorcise her?"

"Oh, gladly. It is true that the vanquishing and taming of demons is what interests me most in my religious work," agreed Fray Domingo. He happily wrote down instructions about where to journey to find the unfortunate woman. He was given a rough map, on a small piece of linen cloth, and a mule on which to ride, for the woman lived with her brothers on a ranch five leagues to the west of the city.

The trail, which Fray Domingo took early next morning, led away to several small Indian towns, where the people were engaged in weaving fine rugs and cloaks of wool, and farther along the way, Fray Domingo saw the flocks of black and brown sheep, from which the wool was sheared. It was a gracious countryside, watered by small crystalline streams and shaded by trees. As the trail rose higher, the trees became pines and other conifers and Fray Domingo drew in their sweet breath with enjoyment. He came at last to a wooden gate, marked (as he had been told, and clearly saw on his scrap of map) with a large *D*. Nervously making sure that there were no bulls in the fenced section, Fray Domingo guided his mule through the gate and down the path to a simple wooden house. He stopped, in front, and listened, but there was no sound, nothing but birdsong and the soft sighing of leaves in the breeze.

"Hola!" he called. "In the name of God the Father, who is here?"

He called several times, and at last saw that a man was coming in from the fields, followed by two large dogs. These began to bark and pirouette as soon as they saw the stranger, but they were ordered to heel by the man, in a rough voice, and both dropped down, belly to the ground, though they continued to look at Fray Domingo with fierce suspicion.

"Shall I dismount?" inquired Fray Domingo, really hesitating to do so, until reassured.

"Lobo and Leon, down. To your kennels!" shouted the man,

and the two dogs slunk away, looking back over their shoulders, to where a rough shelter of wood and thatch had been made for them.

"José Duarte," said the man, introducing himself, but not offering to help Fray Domingo down from his mule.

"I am Fray Domingo, and I have been sent here to exorcise a demon from a woman who is living here," he said then, sliding down off his mount.

José Duarte took the bridle of the animal and led it away, fastening the bridle to a small tree's branch.

"I will bring water for your beast, and a cover for him," said Duarte. "My brother will be in from the fields in a moment. We raise sheep and sell the wool, and then buy the woven garments, to sell in the cities. You will wish refreshment. I can only offer water and some boiled meat." He led the way into the house, which proved to be a simple one-room cabin, where the men slept, cooked, and ate.

"Please sit and rest. When my brother gets here, we will talk."

Meanwhile, the man José Duarte blew on some coals in the small stone fireplace, where a pot was hanging from a hook over the embers.

The other man came in, standing a few moments in the doorway, and making the room dark, as he was large enough to shut out almost all the light.

"Josué Duarte," he said, introducing himself as laconically as his brother had done.

Fray Domingo was happy to see that neither man went armed, not even with knives, for they were big, dark, bearded men, and he could draw no conclusions about their characters from their looks.

When the cauldron was bubbling, José portioned out meat and broth into three plain bowls, and then invited Fray Domingo to eat.

The friar blessed the food with prayer and made the Cross over it. Neither man crossed himself, but they seemed respectful enough. Perhaps they are simply uneducated, thought Fray Domingo.

"This must be difficult for you. Have neither of you married? There is no woman to help care for you and the sick woman?"

"We are alone."

"Let me see her." Fray Domingo's leg began aching again, due to the long ride. Because of his weight, his seat on the mule was far from comfortable, and he knew with certainty that he would pass a dreadful night of pain in this place.

"I will go to bring her," began one of the brothers reluctantly.

But Fray Domingo knew his duty. Despite his aching legs, he bustled up from his seat by the fire.

"We will go together," he said.

In silence the brothers led the way down the path, through the fields, which were heavy with grass and wild flowers, to where a few pines stood. There the men had built pens for their sheep, because the trees sheltered them from rain, and they went farther into the darkness of the forest. At last they stopped, and it was Josué who pointed. Fray Domingo looked. A deep pit had been dug, and the top of it partially covered over with laths and leafy boughs. Down in this pit, seated on the earth, her arms wrapped around an object which she cradled against her breast, was a young woman. She was very pale, with large dark eyes, and her long black hair, matted and caught in the rough wool of her garments, had not been combed or plaited. She looked up at the three men in silence, still protectively holding something against her heart, covered with a dirty woolen wrap.

"Sara," said José.

"Go away. I hate you. I shall die here," came the answer.

"You see," said José, helplessly. "She is unmanageable. Here we are, working, laboring, and she will not do anything to help us. She will not cook, or wash clothes, or weave, or sew. And she runs away. That is why we had to put her in the pit."

Fray Domingo saw that the unfortunate woman could not indeed escape from the pit; it was wide enough, and seemed not too damp, but it was deep. There was no way for her to scale the sides and gain her freedom.

"How did you put her down there?" asked the friar in sudden curiosity.

"We threw her in. We had to," answered Josué.

"So now we must exorcise her," pronounced Fray Domingo, "for I can plainly see that she is possessed."

"How do you do that?" began Josué, uneasily. "We only want her restored to sanity, so that she can help us, as she should. We only want her to be biddable and dutiful, as she ought to be."

"What is that which she hides and holds close under her shawl?" asked the friar.

José answered, "It is a doll she has made. She was married, but her husband was caught in theft and sent to prison, and she had a child. The child died, and that is when she began to behave so outrageously. She thinks this doll she cuddles is the child. And she keeps insisting on being loosened, to search for her husband, who died in prison years ago, of course."

"You must bring her up out of this pit for the ritual of exorcism," instructed Fray Domingo. "I cannot perform it from here, with her down there."

"If we bring her up, she will run away. And she is fleet."

Fray Domingo sent up a silent prayer for help but the answer, as always, was specific. Do your duty.

"Then you must arrange somehow to let me down to her. And to bring me up again, afterward," he added, hastily.

The brothers consulted, and at last one of them went back to the cabin, returning with a length of rope. Silently, he and his brother fashioned the rope into a sort of seat, with two loops for the arms.

"Can you manage in this?" asked Josué, anxiously. "It is the best we can do."

Fray Domingo tested the contraption, and decided that he must risk it. He had come to exorcise a demon, and somehow he must do it.

He told José to go back to his mule and bring what was in the saddlebag—his cross, his holy water, and his prayer book. When the brother returned, commending himself to Our Lady and St. Dominic, Fray Domingo put his arms through the loops and took his seat on the knotted rope. The two brothers carefully and slowly let him down into the pit.

The dampness and the odor of excrement was daunting, but duty must be done.

Not emerging from his ropes, Fray Domingo said, "Daughter, kneel. I have come to cleanse you."

The woman looked at him wildly, almost, he thought, with disbelief, and then she moved, and knelt. He could see that in spite of her rags and filth she was beautiful, or had been. She had strange eyes, one gray, and one brown.

"Give me that thing that you are sheltering under your shawl," he ordered.

Reluctantly and slowly, she unwrapped it. To Fray Domingo's consternation, he saw that it was a crude cross, two sticks bound together with cord.

"I kiss it and pray," the woman told him intensely, "and I ask Our Blessed Lord Jesus Christ to save me from those devils up there."

Fray Domingo was silent. His mind was racing. Had the brothers deceived him, or was the devil in this woman so astute, so bold, as to try to fight Holy Church with a cross? He did not know what to say.

"Save me. Help me, Father. Touch me with the holy water, I beg. I have endured and waited, and I know you have come to save me. Bless me, Father. Oh, bless me, and help me." And she began to recite her prayers, weeping, and lifting her clasped hands in supplication.

"But why have they done this to you?" he asked her, "if they are your kin, your blood brothers?"

"They are my step-brothers, and they are Judaizers," was the answer.

At this Fray Domingo felt a chill of horror. He was at the bottom of the pit with this woman, and up above were his enemies,

God's enemies. But he and the woman Sara had been speaking in
low tones, perhaps they had not heard. Trembling, he looked up,
and saw to his immense relief that the brothers were gone. But
also, he observed with horror that they had let the ropes slip
down into the pit. He was trapped. And, ears pricked and sensitive, he heard hoofbeats.

They have taken my mule, he thought. And we are here, in
this pit.

"Daughter," he said to her, "now we must pray indeed, you
and I, for they have abandoned us."

15.

Gonzalo had heard his sister's story with a strange sense of liber-
ation. He recognized this, but he could not explain it to himself.
And meanwhile, he could not overcome his feelings about Guiomar. He loved her, and he wanted her. Afraid of her and of himself, he spent all the time he could away from the house. When a
few days later, Dr. Morales appeared, with two loaded mules
and his slave Gomo, Gonzalo greeted him with joy. He would
join Dr. Morales on a trip away from Mexico, away from his ailing and sad father, away from Guiomar and away from little
Judit, whose big brown eyes followed him constantly, with avid
admiration and timid hope.

Guiomar welcomed the doctor warmly, and saw that the
kitchen slaves, who did not seem to mind their captivity and
who ate all day long, prepared tasty dishes for the evening meal,
which was taken just before dark.

The doctor was tanned and sinewy; he flexed his strong arms
with pleasure.

"Walking and living in the open strengthens me, and gets rid
of the softness and the puffy fluids that plague me on the long

voyage by sea," he said. "I feel myself again, able to run like a deer and leap over waterfalls!"

"Have you made a great collection of herbs and barks?" asked Guiomar.

"Indeed I have, and I will leave some with you. You can make a tea that will help your father very much," he answered.

Dr. Morales had noticed that Don Pedro walked with great difficulty, leaning on Guiomar, and that his hands were gnarled out of shape by his illness.

"The infusion that I will show Doña Guiomar how to make for you should be taken four times a day. It will startle your kidneys into function, so that they can begin to eliminate the poisons that have accumulated in your body."

"Where have you learned such things?" asked Don Pedro, wonderingly.

"About the plants? Oh, I have been coming to New Spain for many years, learning from the natives. They know much about body function, and about medicines. This little lady here"—he nodded toward Judit—"should take an infusion daily of a flower that the Mexicans use to stimulate the heart. They call it 'the little hand,' for it looks like a baby's hand, with curled fingers. The Mexicans say that this little hand will reach into your breast and squeeze your heart, and make it beat more strongly."

Judit had turned even paler at these words.

"Oh, don't be afraid," laughed the doctor. "It is only a tea, but if you take it regularly you will feel stronger, and you will breathe better." His bright large gray eyes had noticed that the young girl panted after even the simple exertion of bringing in chairs for the table.

"And do you have some herb for me too, Doctor?" asked Guiomar.

"None. You seem to be in perfect health! Something to thank God for. Now this young man, your brother. I find him too pale and nervous. But the journeying into the country with me will strengthen him, and I will cure him of all his troubles. Of *all* his troubles."

Gonzalo felt the doctor's eyes upon him, with that strange intent gaze, and his head swam. A little secret smile played about the doctor's mouth, but as he saw Gonzalo sway and seem about to faint, he lowered his eyes, and said briskly, "Young men often think they have troubles, when none are there."

"You seem young to me, Doctor," remarked Guiomar.

"Ah, but I am not. I am old. Old as time," laughed the doctor, and all laughed with him.

Don Pedro had secured a contract for leather vests for the soldiers barracked near the city of Zacatecas, which was rich in silver mines owned by the Crown of Spain. A tribe of fierce Indians who had never been subdued roamed about in the countryside nearby and sometimes made forays on the city itself. A constant flow of armed Spanish troops had to be sent to the area, and another constant flow of wounded moved back toward Mexico City for hospital care, though the one hospital founded by Cortés, the Conqueror, could not take care of all the men, and often those who were recovering were billeted in private homes.

Gonzalo loaded the leather vests on three mules, and packed a fourth with victuals for the journey. With Dr. Morales's two beasts, the cavalcade was made up of six animals, Gonzalo, and the doctor and his slave.

"But if you are going into this country, where the people are wild and hostile, will you be safe?" quavered Judit.

"We will be safe," answered Dr. Morales with quiet conviction. "I am friends with many of the Indians. We will not be harmed."

"When can I expect you back?" asked Guiomar.

"In three or four months. But do not count the days. We will just suddenly appear."

A strange tranquillity settled over the house when they had gone. Guiomar was at a loss to explain it. She had been ready to love her father and her brother with all her heart. Her father indeed accepted her care and her caresses; she was very demonstrative, feeling herself free to show her emotions in the safety and warmth of a home, after having been urged so long to control all her feelings in the convent, something she had never been able to do.

Gonzalo puzzled her, for she had often caught his eyes upon her with love shining in the dark depths, but when she approached him, he shied away and became cold to her.

Perhaps all men are this way, she thought to herself.

She had become familiar with the *tianguis* of the Indians, and had begun to learn a few of the words the natives used, and to cook and eat some of the strange vegetables and fruits they offered. Finding the kitchen slaves in tattered garments, Guiomar went to the textile market to buy cotton, and she and Judit cut and sewed new blouses, skirts, and aprons for them, before they began to make new shirts for her father and Gonzalo, and new clothes for themselves.

She went every day to mass, recited her prayers with love, and was happy and contented in her new life. With some effort, she wrote this out, made a fair copy, and arranged to send the letter to Spain, to Mother Superior of the convent where she had spent her childhood.

The only matter that troubled her happiness was the strange man who waited at the corner every day when she came by, and looked at her so avidly. Like the women of Seville, Guiomar wore a mantilla when she went out, and like them she often drew it across her face, leaving only her eyes free. When the strange man approached her with a large bouquet of flowers and attempted to speak to her, she drew back in momentary fear. He was, from the looks of him, a soldier.

He was a heavy man, with broad shoulders and thick arms. His face was young, above the blond beard, but there was a dark red scar on one of his cheeks, and Guiomar instinctively knew that there were scars on other parts of his body. A violent man.

As he came near, she shrank back, then murmured "Ave María Purísima" as a greeting, and hurried away.

She told her father about this man, at the evening meal, and he then sent Epifanio with her whenever she and Judit went out.

The life of the city fascinated the young women. They studied the silent Indians, in their white cotton garments, who came and went so silently. When they spoke, their voices were high and sweet, and their speech was full of musical cadences. The soldiers of the Crown, riding or walking stiffly on booted feet, were everywhere, in twos or sometimes in small groups, with a captain or leader. Sometimes they saw other soldiers, who wore red and black, instead of the King's colors. Everyone in the street shrank back, and let them past when they appeared, and Guiomar, by questioning another woman on the street, learned that these were soldiers of the Holy Office.

"Why are they here, on the street, like us?" asked Guiomar. "I thought they must stay to guard the prison."

"Oh, they are probably on their way to arrest some heretic, or a witch," she was told, and the other woman hastily crossed herself.

Guiomar, too, felt a chill of fear.

"And where is this Holy Office?" she questioned.

"There, near the church of the Dominicans. Down this street, and then to the left. It is not far from where they are building the cathedral."

The woman hurried away, her market basket over one arm covered with the end of her striped *reboso,* or scarf. Judit stepped closer to Guiomar.

"I can see that you want to go there," said Judit, "but oh, let's not! I'm afraid!"

"I only want to see . . ."

"Let's not!"

"We won't. Not today."

Guiomar herself could not tell why she wished to look upon the place. But she dismissed the thought. Judit was dear to her, and not to be frightened.

16

As Gaspar disappeared daily without having taken breakfast, and seemed uninterested even in the most delicious of the stews La Gorda contrived for her lodgers, she began to suspect that something serious was amiss.

At night, she begged him to undress completely, so that she could examine his wounds. All had healed, though the scars were dark and ugly.

"Is it these? Do they itch, or throb?" she asked.

He nodded his head dumbly.

"Does your stomach ache? Or your liver?"

Gaspar saw that he would have to think of something.

"My chest hurts," he said, laying one strong hand, tufted with short golden hairs, upon it.

"I will rub you with an ointment."

La Gorda rubbed happily, and bound Gaspar's chest with a linen cloth, but he did not improve in succeeding days.

Nor had his lovemaking improved at all. At night he lay inert and heavy beside her, unresponsive even to her most skilled caresses, and he often sighed. Once he even prayed aloud to the Virgin, and this she found most disquieting of all.

It was one of the lodgers, another soldier who had been sent back to Mexico to rest and recover from a dysentery, who told La Gorda what was the matter.

After Gaspar had left, in the morning, as he always did, "to take the sun," he said, this man laughed significantly.

"The poor benighted soul is in love," he commented.

This comment struck La Gorda like a bolt of lightning. It had never occurred to her, because she had felt so certain of her soldier. They had been so close, in boisterous lovemaking, in plans, in occasional evenings of near-drunkenness together. But now that she considered it, it seemed that all of Gaspar's symptoms were those of a man in the first throes of romantic love. She felt miserable for about an hour, and then she began to be angry. The more she thought things over, the more furious she became. After another chaste night, she decided to take steps.

Her first plan was to accuse him, and force him to tell where the woman lived who had stolen his heart. She therefore laid out wine, and a bottle of stronger ferment that she was able to buy, a drink the Mexicans made from the root of a plant, which was known as *tumba burros*, or "to knock down donkeys," and awaited the return of her erring sweetheart.

To her fury, he refused the drink, and informed her that he had reported to his superior officers, and was going out again, to the north, with a detachment of soldiers, to fight the Chichimecas. His crimes were all forgiven (as he knew they would be), because he was useful, a tough and trained soldier.

"When do you leave?"

"Tomorrow, at dawn."

La Gorda was dismayed and frightened.

"And I suppose you have a woman, there in the north!" she burst out. That must be what had been the matter with him; he was pining for some sweetheart he had met on the northern campaigns.

Gaspar saw the look on her face, and he knew what she was capable of. The instinct of self-preservation is strong in soldiers.

"Yes, I do. Forgive me!"

La Gorda emitted a strangled sob.

"And I, do I count for nothing?"

Gaspar put his arms around her.

"You are the one I come back to, isn't that so?"

"Will you come back this time?"

"Yes. I will only be away on campaign three months. I will come back," he promised.

He managed to please her that night, though he himself was unsatisfied, and sad. But instinct had told him to beware. If La Gorda ever suspected that it was the lovely lady of Curtidores

Street he dreamed of, she was capable of doing her some damage. This must be avoided at all costs.

When he left, before light the next day, he left La Gorda steaming about a rival in the north, but unsuspecting of any woman in the city. Gaspar thought that he had escaped just in time. He would have three months in which to figure out a plan. Bitterly he repented of ever having involved himself with La Gorda. He would think of a way to disentangle himself.

"Virgencita, show me!" he begged, and he began daily to say his prayers again, the ones he had learned in infancy. "Jesus, mighty Jesus, help me!"

17.

Gonzalo enjoyed walking beside his loaded mules. He was responsive to the delights of the countryside, the smell of fresh green grass springing up after the rain, the scent of wild flowers, the dappled shade of trees upon the sunlit road.

They were making their way north.

On the second day a detachment of Spanish soldiers of the Crown, marching swiftly, the officers mounted, passed them on the way.

Dr. Morales often stopped to examine a plant, or to take bark or leaves from a special tree. He talked entertainingly to Gonzalo, and taught him much of the lore of medicine.

"You are very wise," said Gonzalo, after a week in the learned doctor's company.

"I have learned wisdom," was the quiet answer, "and God has taught me to read faces, and to read hearts. You, I know, are deeply troubled. You love your sister, isn't that so?"

Gonzalo sat, pale, astonished, and a little frightened.

"Oh," added the doctor swiftly, "no one suspected, I am sure.

Not the young lady herself, who is so candid and open that she
would never think of anything hidden, in any case. It seemed to
me that you behaved with great skill, hiding your feelings from
everyone. From everyone but me."

Gonzalo was silent a long time. They had sat to eat their noon
meal beside a little brook that ran gurgling àmong stones and
ferns. Dr. Morales had provided his saddlebags with small cakes
made of corn and dark sugar. They kept well, and were very sus-
taining.

"What can I do, Doctor, except run away?"

"You can be cured," answered the doctor, softly.

Gomo had brought them water in small jars from the stream.
When they stopped to sleep at night, Dr. Morales cut the
round prickly leaves from the cacti that grew everywhere. He always wore a broad-bladed, short, very sharp knife at his waist,
and with this he stripped off the spines from the fleshy leaves,
and then he cut them into strips, and boiled them. They exuded
a milky, sticky liquid, which he drained away, and then he
cooked them in a pan with some dried peppers and dried fish,
making a very tasty supper. He set Gomo to cleaning further
cactus leaves of their thorns for the beasts who munched the tender juicy fodder with apparent enjoyment.

"Can I be cured? With some one of your magical herbs?"
asked Gonzalo with a gentle smile.

"Oh no. But there are ways. One nail drives out another, they
say. The little one, Judit, she has big eyes for you. And she is a
sweet child, tender and good, but with powers of character nobody has called forth, as yet."

"Indeed, you see beyond the flesh," commented Gonzalo.

"And there is another way, better still for a man of your sen-
sibilities. Religion."

"You mean, go as a friar?" The idea was not appealing to
Gonzalo. "That would be unpleasant for me. Oh, I am a
believer, yes. But I would find the obedience very chafing. I like
to go my own way, write my verses, think my own thoughts."

"I did not mean to go as a friar. Have you not wondered about the religion I practice?"

"No. I did not wonder. I have seen you praying."

"My religion is all-consuming. Demanding. Strong and firm."

"I wish I had such faith as you. I believe . . . but sometimes I have doubts. I mean, I wonder."

Dr. Morales studied Gonzalo for some minutes. Then he glanced up at the sun, which had passed the zenith.

"It is time to rise and continue our journey. You and I will talk again, thus. Man to man. Heart to heart."

The words comforted Gonzalo.

"I did not mean to go as a friar. Have you not wondered about the religion I practice?"

"No, I did not wonder. I have seen you praying."

"My religion is all-consuming. Demanding. Strong and firm."

"I wish I had such faith as you, I believe ... but sometimes I have doubts, I mean, I wonder."

Dr. Morales studied Gonzalo for some minutes. Then he glanced up at the sun, which had passed the zenith.

"It is time to rise and continue our journey. You and I will talk again, thus, Man to man. Heart to heart."

The words comforted Gonzalo.

BOOK THREE

Juan Palomar

1.

Juan, who had left the convent an innocent boy, optimistic and trusting, had become a man, and one who trusted no one. The terrible fight with the pirates, who had taken him prisoner and then beaten and enslaved him, making him work at the most dangerous tasks on their vessel, giving him little food and almost no sleep, had washed from his mind every gentle and poetic instinct.

He pretended that he did not understand English, and thus forced the pirates to order him about in Spanish. Their use of that language was so ludicrous that he got a few moments of bitter and contemptuous enjoyment from it, the only pleasure he experienced on that hellish voyage. Poor Roque had died on the third day, and had been simply tossed into the sea.

When their ship was fired on in Tampico Juan was overjoyed, and with his companion, Fermín García Mendoza, who had been taken prisoner with him at the same time, he spoke swiftly. They made plans to jump overboard and swim for shore at the first chance. That chance came sooner than they expected, for the vessel soon took water and began to tilt and sink. The pirates were distraught, and many of them jumped into the sea as well.

Juan was a good swimmer. He had learned in his youth, in the cold waters off his native Ireland, for the curraghs his people used could capsize in a storm, and Juan's father had all his men taught to keep afloat in the water and to swim. Fermín García Mendoza, who had been as taciturn as Juan, as heavily worked and as often beaten, was a poor swimmer, but he managed to flail about in the water and progress slowly.

"Let us swim out toward sea," cautioned Juan, "as the pirates are making for the nearest shore, and they will be captured and killed."

Fermín, silently striving, followed instructions. Juan stopped frequently to allow him to rest. They barely managed to get away from the tremendous tow and tug of the waves that pulled down the ship. All around them were floating wreckage and shouting, drowning men. Juan turned his eyes away from them, and devoted himself to making for the sea, and to trying to help his companion breast the heavy waves that rose and fell in the wake of the ship's foundering. From shore, they were still cannonading, and this roughened the waters further. Despairing screams of the dying and of wounded men sounded in Juan's ears, but he was not touched. He was bent on saving himself and, if he could, Fermín.

But Fermín could not keep up. Juan saw himself forced to seek land, though he tried to choose a place where he thought they might be able to hide. At last they made shore, where there was a wide white beach. Fermín staggered a little way up the sand, but he could not walk any farther. Exhausted he lay, letting the last of the waves from the bay curl around his inert body. Juan saw that he had been wounded and had lost blood, as well. He dragged his friend (for they had become close in adversity) up the beach, and into a clump of bushes, where there was a shifting thin shade. The day was very hot, and sand flies buzzed around the two men, who were salty from the sea, and sweating.

Fermín slept, making the snoring noise of a man at the end of his strength. Juan rested near him. Sounds of the battle still came to his ears, though now the shouting and the shots seemed far away. Juan knew that he must venture out, to look for water and food, and to ask for protection. He hoped it would be offered, as soon as he explained that they had been enslaved by the pirates.

He tried to rouse Fermín to tell him that he was going to seek help, but at last he decided that he must go, even though the exhausted man did not hear him.

Juan found that his legs were unsteady. The hard labor and poor food, the days at sea, and the exhausting swim had weakened him beyond what he had imagined might have happened. He had to stop often to rest but he kept on doggedly, until he came to the cottages at the outskirts of the town. There were no people in the narrow muddy streets; no doubt they had locked themselves in, fearing the pirates, who were accustomed to sack captive towns, house by house. After what seemed hours of walking, Juan came to the square, and he saw with relief that there was a building where soldiers paraded on sentry before it. He went up to them, and asked to be taken to the Commandante.

Juan was escorted by a soldier into the building and instantly thrown into the *calabozo*. Three pirates, two of them in poor condition, wounded and sick, were already there.

"Please," called Juan, "go to find my companion and bring him." He told them where Fermín was lying, and in about an hour's time Fermín, stumbling and dazed, was also brought in, and summarily thrust into the cell with the others.

Juan did what he could for the wounded men, and was pleased to be given water and bandages by the guard.

"I suppose we are all to be tried as pirates," Juan told Fermín.

The guard overheard him, and laughed in derision.

"You are to be marched to Mexico City and tried by the Inquisition!" he shouted. "For you are all hated heretics. Lutherans! And I hope the Holy Office will burn every one of you!"

At this, one of the pirates burst into noisy tears and began calling for his mother. The others tried to comfort him, but he sobbed and wailed all the night through. Fermín, who had begun to gather a little strength, since the prisoners were well fed and given all the water they wanted, explained to the terrified pirate that the Holy Office would be lenient if he repented and accepted the Catholic Faith.

"They want faithful Catholics," he explained, "and they will give you a teacher, to instruct you, if you ask, and if you seem sincere about accepting the Faith."

"How do you know all this?" asked one of the others, in suspicion.

"Because I knew someone who had been subjected to an Inquiry, a Jew, and he repented and took the Faith, and he was let off."

"Set free?"

"Not exactly. He had to wear the penitential garment for two years, and give money to the Church for candles. But otherwise, he was free. So you see . . ."

The men from the ship, with whom Juan and Fermín had been working for weary weeks, were simple fellows. Two of them began to take hope, and to ask many questions about the Faith. But one was stubborn.

"I will not repent! I am no Lutheran," he announced, firmly. "But I am no papist either and I will not worship the so-called Virgin Mother. A virgin mother . . . pah! Who ever heard of such a thing? We all know what takes place before there is ever any birth!" And he laughed derisively. Juan looked at him closely. Could he be the pirate captain? Juan thought he must be Captain Trout.

"You said you had never heard of such a thing," repeated Juan. "But then you deny that God is all-powerful? God made the rules of life; He can suspend them!"

"But why? Why such a ridiculous arrangement? That the woman should not even have pleasure to remember when the pains of birth take her?"

Fermín broke in. "I advise you, not to try to argue with the Inquisitors," he remarked dryly. "You will answer questions only. And receive instruction. There will be no arguments."

In the morning, after a terrible night of horrid dreams, Juan called out to his jailer, "When are we to be taken to Mexico?"

"As soon as they catch the others, who scrambled to shore and have hidden in the swamps. It won't be long," he added, with satisfaction. And indeed, that very afternoon, four haggard men, starving and with their clothes in tatters, were herded into

the building. There was no room for them in the *calabozo*, so
they were chained together, and held in a corner of the large
waiting room, guarded by soldiers with long swords, and with
the broad thick knives that they had found to be so useful in
their journeys through the forests. By the next morning, two had
died in the night. When they were unchained, and a detail of
soldiers was sent to bury the cadavers, Juan and Fermín and the
others were brought out and chained to the survivors. They were
then seven men. Before noon, in the worst heat of the day, the
march began.

The soldiers who were to guard the prisoners under Captain
Rivero on the way to Mexico City were mounted, and wore protection for their heads, having learned of the mortal effects of
too much sun. The prisoners, chained together, stumbled along
in the greatest misery.

When camp was struck for the night on a small dry hillock,
in the middle of a fetid swamp, the men were unchained so that
they could relieve themselves and also lie flat to sleep.

There was another reason for unchaining the men, which presently became obvious. Two of the Englishmen, finding themselves freed of bonds, stumbled away into the swamp, in a feeble
attempt to escape. The soldiers calmly took aim and shot them,
leaving the bodies where they lay.

Juan, who had spoken up several times, since he was fluent in
Spanish and could converse easily with the soldiers, asked, "Are
we to bury them, Captain?"

Captain Rivero answered easily. "No need. There are vultures
here who will take care of the dead for us. Look."

Already the sky was darkened with black wings, as large slow-
moving birds descended. Juan saw them, but he would look no
more, and he tried to stop his ears from the tearing sounds he
supposed he heard, as the great black birds settled on the bodies.
The vultures took their time, looking about, but rending and eating steadily. They were still busy with their feed when darkness
fell.

Captain Rivero's face, young and handsome, wore a look of

satisfaction. The fewer prisoners he had to shepherd all the way to Mexico, the easier was his task.

Assigning the other soldier to keep watch, he lay down near the fire which he had ordered built, not for warmth, for the evenings were almost as hot as the days, but to keep the flies and mosquitoes away. The prisoners lay face downward, attempting to keep their flesh away from the ravening insects.

On succeeding days, another of the pirates died, and Juan received a deep gash in one leg from a sharp-edged plant. The wound festered, and he began, reluctantly, to lose hope.

Juan prayed with all his might. But he was afraid that he might be in hell already. Could it be worse? Hell is a place where God cannot reach you, the old abbot had taught him. Surely this was hell, this swamp, this awful pilgrimage, chained and suffering.

Some days later, when they had reached easier ground, could breathe in the clean forest air, and somehow even managed to stumble forward with less pain, they joined the caravan of some merchants, for a few days.

A young woman, clothed in white against the ticks and flies, came, with sorrow and compassion, to wash the wounds of the men, and their filthy faces. She even tried to comb out their matted beards.

It was the girl he had seen ready to board ship south of Seville. It was that same beautiful lady. Juan's heart expanded in joy and his prayers to God were full of gratitude that night.

"You are an angel," he managed to whisper to her, and she had looked at him with tenderness, tears in her large dark eyes.

The vision of Guiomar was with him the rest of the way, helping him to endure.

They were taken to Puebla, and later, still chained, but equipped with cheap clothes to cover them, they continued their journey to Mexico. Captain Rivero was glad to have fewer prisoners to attend, but he did not bring in men unable to withstand the trials (and the tortures) of the Holy Office. Those who were left were well fed, washed, and covered. If they were to burn, they should be able to walk in the penitential procession, he had determined. Captain Rivero greatly enjoyed the processions and the burning. He felt strong and virtuous and proud of his True Faith, as he saw the heretics and traitors, for traitors they were, taken away to their deaths.

2.

Fray Domingo, at first terrified in the pit with the woman, overcame his fears, and turned to prayer.

He gave himself to this intensely, repeating with fervor all the prayers he knew, and then turning to supplication in his own words. As he became more and more emotional in his colloquy with God, the woman turned her strange eyes toward him and began to listen carefully. Suddenly she chimed in with him, adding her own pleas to his. In a moment when he stopped, with heaving breast, she continued in prayers he knew, though here and there she had forgotten a word, and then she hesitated, or put in some other word as a substitute.

"We are two Christian souls, Lord," cried Fray Domingo to the patch of heaven he could see from the hole they were in. "Make haste to save us!"

When he finished all the prayers he could think of, and had wearied, from sheer emotion of his own, he stopped. Tears were streaming down his cheeks.

The woman spoke to him, and though they had told Fray Domingo that she was mad, she seemed rational at the moment.

"I could not get out alone," she said, "but now we are two. The walls of this prison they dug for me are as high as I am, and once again my height. But if I stood on your shoulders, I might reach the top."

Fray Domingo looked at her and listened in surprise, and then he began to consider her words.

"We must try," he said then.

He was not a tall man, but he was broad, and though his life had not developed much physical strength in him, walking for many leagues over the byways of Spain had kept him from becoming as soft as some of his brothers who sat all day at their copying desks in the convent. Yet his legs were still inflamed and swollen from his illness on shipboard.

He bent down, and the woman, weakened though she was from months in the pit, was able to get to her feet. She struggled to mount his back and stand on his shoulders, as Fray Domingo crouched and tried to make it possible for her to climb up. But she was hampered by all the heavy skirts and the many woolen wraps she had twined around herself.

"You must take them off," he said.

"Ay, Your Honor!" the woman cried, and hid her eyes from him.

Fray Domingo asked heaven for help again.

"I am a religious," he said to her, "and I am chaste. God knows that I have been chaste all my life. I have struggled to this perfection, and I will not relinquish it for any woman whatsoever. I swear on the Cross that I will not think of you as a woman, without your clothes. But we must try to get out of here, or we will both die here, and then neither one of us is of any use to himself or to Holy Church!"

The woman listened. Then she silently began unwrapping herself from the woolen shawls, and unfastening her skirts. There were many, and they were thick with grime and redolent of the earth and of her long confinement. When she had dropped them she stood forth in a thin woolen shift and long woolen trousers, tied at the ankle. She unwound the strips of cloth that had bound her feet and served as protection in lieu of shoes. Then, breathing hard from the exertion, she managed to clamber up Fray Domingo's broad back, and set her feet on his shoulders. Bracing her hands against the sides of the pit, she righted herself, as he slowly and gingerly did the same. She gave a sharp cry of disappointment. She lacked about a foot of being able to reach the top. Fray Domingo slowly bent, and let her down again. They sat, desperate, unwilling to believe that their efforts would not get them out to freedom.

Suddenly Fray Domingo spoke. "We will dig up the earth here and build it up as high as we can manage, and then we will try once more."

She understood at once, and they began, with their hands, to rip at the floor of the pit and dig up the earth. The floor of the pit had been hard packed for months, but they persevered. It took them some time, but at last they had built up a mound that seemed higher even than they would need. This made their maneuver more difficult, as Fray Domingo had to stand upon this mound, while Sara scrambled up his back, and this time, being near the wall of the pit, he could not crouch. After several attempts, heavy breathing, and murmured prayers, they managed. The woman tremblingly stood erect upon Fray Domingo's shoulders, and she could almost reach the top. But not quite.

"We will make our mound higher."

Hours went by, in their toil and their attempts. They began to be irritable with each other, and feel almost hopeless. But she insisted that they try again.

"If you could give a little jump, and try to throw one leg up over the rim," he cried.

They tried again, almost exhausted, but she managed at last, and with a strangled cry of triumph she gained the top of the pit, got to her feet, and stood free. Immediately she disappeared. Darkness was falling fast, and Fray Domingo feared that he was abandoned again. He began to weep, snuffling and sobbing as he had not done since he was a child.

But then, after what seemed a very long time, he saw the woman's face at the top of the pit.

"Throw me the ropes now," she directed, "and I will try to pull you up."

"You are not strong enough," he cried.

"I am very strong, and besides, you will try, hanging on the rope, to climb up the wall, your feet upon it," she ordered.

They tried this, but Fray Domingo was too heavy for her.

"Wait," she directed calmly, "and don't cry anymore." She spoke as if to a child.

Then she set to her work, splicing the ropes, to lengthen them, until she was able to reach a sturdy tree, and loop and tie the ends firmly there.

As the moon began rising over the dark trees of the forest, Fray Domingo managed at last to get out, and to feel the good earth under his feet. He pulled Sara to her knees, and together they sent up a fervent prayer of thanksgiving.

"Now, we had better shelter in the house for the night, and then tomorrow at dawn we will take the road for Puebla," he said.

Since the woolen garments she had formerly wrapped herself in were at the bottom of the pit, Sara shivered until her teeth chattered. Silently she went about gathering up wood, until she had enough to make a fire. But there were no glowing coals among the ashes in the fireplace in the cottage. And Fray Domingo had no flint. Seeing his duty, he unwrapped the woolen outer panel of his habit and passed it to Sara, who wound it around herself, and so managed to warm herself. She settled herself into a corner of the cottage and fell almost at once into a deep sleep, partly from exhaustion and partly from relief and joy.

As dawn touched their eyelids, and they wakened, Fray Domingo said firmly, "We must thank God again for our safety, daughter, and say our prayers. And then you must tell me about yourself and how you came to be the prisoner of such wicked men."

"First let me fetch water," answered the woman, but respectfully. "We must drink something, and I will see if I can find something to eat."

She brought water from a stream, and they drank, and washed. "Ay, I will never get myself clean again," she mourned.

"But we must get away from this place. Who knows where my step-brothers have gone, or when they will come back?" She found remains of a barley loaf and they munched the dry hard bread. Then, as they began trudging toward the road, she began to tell her story.

"My name is Sara. I come of a Christian family, but my people had been Jews a few generations back. Our name was León. When my father died my mother was sought after by other men because she was beautiful, and she had wealth. My father had been a goldsmith, and he had trained many young men in the art of working gold and silver. She chose to marry a Portuguese named Duarte. Ay, and then our troubles began. Because this man, this Duarte, a widower with two sons, though he pretended to the Faith, was an ardent Judaizer, and he insisted that we, my mother and I, return to Judaism. His cruelties to my mother broke her spirit, and she gave in to him, or seemed to. But I ran away and married a young man, a Christian, from a New Christian family, who had worked in my father's *taller* [workroom]. His name is Fermín García Mendoza. He had loved me for years, he said, and I soon began to love him too, with all my heart. But my step-brothers, those bad men, accused him of theft, and got him sent to prison, and they made a captive of me. They kept me tied up, and all of them—my foster father and those two—they did all but kill me, to make me renounce my Faith. Yet they dared not denounce me, for the Inquisition would have taken them at once. Nor did they dare to put me out and pretend that I was dead, as the Jews do, for the same reason. But they feared me because I was defiant, in spite of their shouts and blows and insistence. When my foster father died, they thought they could manage me if they took me far away, but I was a continual trouble, and so they decided to come to the New World. The rest you know."

"Ave María Purísima," cried Fray Domingo. Sara thought his exclamation was in pious thanksgiving for her escape into his care. But it was also a heartfelt ejaculation of joy, because he had learned that the mysterious Mendoza, the person he had been told to watch and trace, was a True Christian. Fray Domingo, being a Mendoza by birth, was forever anxious about the beliefs of any other person of his name, as it was a name immediately connotating Judaism, in Christian ears, despite the fact that several of the family had reached high places in Court, and even in the Church.

Before they had been long on the road, Fray Domingo was able to hail other travelers, explain their plight, and acquire food. Munching as she trudged, Sara began making plans.

When at last they arrived in Puebla, Fray Domingo took Sara at once to the convent where Dominican nuns lived and taught.

He blessed her, as he left, commenting, "No doubt you wish to become a member of this holy sisterhood, and spend your life in good works, as an act of thanksgiving."

"No, Friar. I will do all the good works I can, and will thank God every day that I am free of those wicked men. But as soon as I am strong enough, I shall search for my husband. I feel certain that he is free and will try to find me, and he will come to the New World, looking for me."

3.

Gonzalo helped Dr. Morales with his collection of herbs, seeds, and bark and enjoyed learning of their medicinal uses. But also, whenever they came to a village, he was eager to sell his wares, and to search for skins and cured hides that he might purchase for his father's business. In the evenings, when he and Dr. Morales slept under the stars, or in some hut or cottage, he composed poems, most of them full of sadness and renunciation. Yet he seemed to enjoy finding the right words to express these feelings, and the best rhymes and rhythms for his poems.

Dr. Morales listened quietly, when Gonzalo read him these

verses, and made few comments. Yet one evening, when they huddled near a campfire (as it had grown cold on the plain, which they were crossing on their way toward Zacatecas), he said, "I believe you should try to take your mind away from these thoughts of love, which haunt you."

"I know I should. But I cannot."

"If you like, I can help you put them out of your mind."

"How?"

"Make yourself very receptive to me. And look deeply into my eyes. I have a powerful mind, and I will draw those unhappy thoughts out of your brain, and send them away on the wind. You will not think them again."

Gonzalo tried to do as he was instructed. Looking into Dr. Morales's large gray eyes, he seemed to lose himself, and after a little time, he no longer saw the shining whites of the eyes and the gray iris, but he saw deep, deep into the black pupils, into another world. Everything seemed to fall away and become mist. He sank into slumber, and when he awakened in the morning, he remembered nothing.

They came to a village the next day where Dr. Morales was known and had many friends. People ran out to greet him, with happy cries.

"Let us rest here with my friends for a few days," suggested Dr. Morales. Gonzalo was glad to agree.

The day was a Friday.

That evening Dr. Morales and Gonzalo went to the stream nearby to bathe, and to change their clothes. As they walked back to the village they saw that there were candles in the cottages, and the tables were spread with white cloths. Many delicious aromas from the kitchens greeted them, and Gonzalo was prepared to enjoy a rich feast.

"We fast tonight," explained Dr. Morales, gently. "Tomorrow at sundown, we will eat. It is the custom of these friends of mine." He looked deeply into Gonzalo's eyes, and the young man again felt the earth spinning away and leaving him. Nothing that happened subsequently seemed strange to him.

"Remember the Sabbath, to keep it holy," he had been taught. Thus these friends of his much-loved mentor the doctor kept the Sabbath. He joined in all the festivities with devotion.

"He is one of us," Dr. Morales explained quietly, to their host at the Saturday-evening feast.

4.

Don Pedro complained increasingly of the pains in his legs and back, and the day came, after a very heavy rain, when he could not leave his bed. Guiomar remembered what she had done to help Mother Superior, when the old nun had found it almost impossible to leave her pallet during the winter rains and cold, and she was able to comfort her father with hot packs of wet towels, and many hot drinks.

Talking with Judit at night after the evening meal, and after she had seen her father fall into a troubled sleep, Guiomar said, "Ay Judit, with my father so ill, and Gonzalo gone, who will rule this house? I think we must try to divide up our time and our efforts to keep this home in order and the business going. Can you think of some ways we might do it?"

"The business part must fall to you, Guiomar," answered Judit, "since it belongs to your family. I think you must go to the best worker, perhaps the oldest one, and learn what they do and how they do it. Learn about the hides and the leather, and the way they cut and fashion them. Then it would fall to me to learn how to manage the servants, and to oversee the kitchen and the cleaning and washing. And the buying of supplies, and the sewing."

"You are so sensible, Judit!" cried Guiomar. "Can you do all this?"

Judit turned a flushed and shy face to her friend.

"Ay Guiomar, can you not see why I want to learn to be a good housewife, a perfect *ama de casa?*"

Guiomar had noticed Judit's interest in Gonzalo.

"I know," she answered gently. "And if ever you and Gonzalo—"

"Stop! It might be bad luck to say our names together," whispered Judit.

"Then I will say only that I would love to have you for my true sister!" was Guiomar's answer.

The very next day, after Guiomar had taken her father his breakfast and made him comfortable, she and Judit began to undertake the preparation they knew they must undergo. With the oldest of the kitchen slaves, Tomasa, who was a glum and sullen woman but a good cook, and who knew all the Indian names for vegetables and fruits, and where to buy them, Judit studied the market and made the acquaintance of the best suppliers. Fruits, onions, potatoes, sweet potatoes, carrots, and large peppers were arranged in mounds of varying sizes. Housewives bought the mound; nothing was weighed.

The purchasing of meat was more complicated, for the slaughtered animals were hung up, and cuts of flesh or joints could be purchased, but only what was left on the carcass, until it was all sold. Only then would another slaughtered beast be brought out for sale.

Chickens, pigeons, and wildfowl of various kinds were sold, some of them live in cages. There were lizards, too, and certain snakes, but Guiomar and Judit avoided these with shudders of distaste and fear.

Judit, taking her work very seriously, then spent almost all of the rest of her morning in the kitchens, watching how the food was prepared. Tomasa was not pleased to have her in the kitchen, and spoke in an undertone, in her own language, to Leocadia, but Judit persevered. Only when Tomasa, in a rage, began breaking some of the clay pots she used, did Judit suddenly summon her own strength.

To Tomasa's surprise, for she had never been whipped in Don
Pedro's house, Judit came back from her room with a leather
whip.

"There will be respect in this house. Respect for me, and for
the dishes and the food in this house," she announced. And she
vigorously brought the whip down over Tomasa's shoulders. Tomasa, startled and scared, fell to her knees, and began to cry and
beg pardon. Moving on her knees, she made her way to Judit,
and took Judit's skirt in her hands, and pressed the cloth to her
forehead.

From that moment forward, Tomasa was dutiful and even
affectionate, and in her turn she watched over Leocadia and
Elena with sharp eyes and gave them buffets with the side of her
hand when they did not perform their duties to suit her.

Judit recounted this at night to Guiomar as they lay in bed.

"I wish we could get a black slave," she mused. "They are
wonderful cooks, and very strong and faithful. We had one in
Spain, but we had to sell her, to get the money for our trip here.
I wonder, Guiomar . . ."

"What?"

"I wonder if I really have relatives in Zacatecas. Do you think
someday I should look for them?"

"Someday. Do not think of it now. This is your home. And besides, I need you."

"I have no wish to leave," murmured Judit.

Guiomar, in the meantime, was learning the business of the
leather, how to be certain it was ready for cutting, which sections had to be reserved for "harness" or for protective cuirasses,
which left for the making of armbands, holsters for swords,
shoes. Much of Don Pedro's business consisted in providing for
the army. But he also had a thriving business in saddles,
harnesses, and all other leather gear for horses, for riders, and
for work animals. The Spaniards settling in the New World had
brought donkeys and oxen for heavy farm work, but there was a
steady demand for horses and all their accounterments, as well.

She was humble and diligent in her studies, and the workmen

respected her, both as lady of the house and, since Don Pedro continued ill, as employer. Epifanio helped and defended her.

One day there was a loud, peremptory banging of the knocker on the big *zaguan*. Judit went to open it, and was startled to see two soldiers of the Inquisition there.

"We have come to arrest Eladio Muñoz," was their taciturn greeting.

Judit flew to find Guiomar, who then came to the door. Eladio Muñoz was a skilled leatherworker, but a brawling, impetuous fellow. Guiomar meant to defend him if she could.

"Why, what has he done?" she asked.

"It is not our business to know what he is charged with," was the curt answer. "We have been sent to bring him in for questioning, and he must come."

"But why? He is working here; I need him."

"He must come with us," the soldiers answered.

"Who accused him?" she demanded.

"Señorita," began the spokesman, patiently, "we do not know. Nor of what crime. But when the Holy Office receives an accusation, we are sent to arrest the accused and produce him for questioning. Is that clear?"

"And he doesn't know who accused him, nor of what?" she echoed, unbelieving. "Why, that is"—the word "monstrous" was on the tip of her tongue, but she clamped her lips together. The Holy Office brooked no criticism, no contempt, no questioning, on the part of citizens. It did the inquiring; and when someone was brought in for questioning, he had to wait his turn in the prison of the Holy Office. The Inquisitional authorities indeed had only a few cells for their prisoners, although sometimes the accused were held for weeks or even months in cells called *secretos*. Guiomar had heard of this, had understood it from overhearing scraps of whispered conversation in the market, or among the workmen at her own workbenches in the patio.

"I will go to call him," she said only, bowing slightly.

Entering the patio, where the men were busy, she called, "Don Eladio! You must come. You are under arrest."

All the sounds of work stopped, and there was a heavy silence.

Eladio put down his tools, took up his woolen poncho, and followed her. Reaching the *zaguan,* the soldiers placed themselves on each side of Eladio. Without a word spoken, they started away down the street.

Guiomar went back to the patio, intending to tell the other workers what had happened. But her throat filled with sobs, and she could not speak. A fear beyond what might happen to Eladio had taken possession of her, as she remembered her mother, the sentence against her, and the piteous woman who had died in her arms.

One of the other workers, Remedios Torreblanca, rose and helped Guiomar to a seat.

"What, what could he have done?" she tremblingly asked. "He is not a Judaizer. Of this I am certain."

"Probably he got drunk and bawled out some blasphemies," said Remedios. "So do not grieve, Doña Guiomar. They will not burn him for that. They will make him do penance, but that is all."

"What kind of penance? Will he have to wear the sanbenito?"

Hung up near the main altar in the part of the cathedral where masses were sung, awaiting the termination of the building, Guiomar had seen the yellow and green tunics, with their tall peaked caps. These sanbenitos had to be worn by penitents who had been tried by the Inquisition, and given duties and penances instead of being turned over to the civil law for execution. Holy Church did not countenance the shedding of blood, and never passed sentence. On the other hand, the civil law was savage enough when a prisoner from the Inquisition had been judged intransigent, and so labeled. Then indeed the punishments were spectacular and ritualistic, it being thought that observing the torments of unrepentant sinners might draw potential heretics and blasphemers back into the Faith.

"Probably he will only have to give wax for candles, or silver for a chalice. If he is sensible, and shows himself humble and repentant."

"But . . . if he does not? If he is defiant?"

"It would go very hard with him."

"But would they torture him?"

"Not unless he is thought to be a heretic, Doña Guiomar. If they think that, they would put him to the torture, to find out the names of others, of coreligionists."

Guiomar began helplessly to weep.

"I know much about these arrests and the trials," continued Remedios, "because a cousin of mine was denounced as a Lutheran. They gave him a lawyer, and his advocate was able to prove that the denunciation came from a relative who owed him two hundred ducats. And the judges then set my cousin free, because they try to be fair. Only, because they cannot bear to make a mistake, and let some real heretic go, they made my cousin wear the sanbenito for a year, and walk in procession every Sunday."

"I will pray for Eladio," said Guiomar, and she rose and went to her room, where there was a large Crucifix on the wall. There she remained in prayer until dark. But her prayers were not all for Eladio. They were also for the soul of her mother, and for the health and peace of Madre Superiora, and for the safety of her brother and Dr. Morales on their journey. And for the poor prisoners she had tended, on their journey up from the coast.

5.

Every day Gonzalo was drawn deeper into the intimacy and devotions of Dr. Morales and his friends. He found them comforting and strengthening; they helped him to dominate his chaotic feeling about his sister, which had troubled him so much. He began to write many verses and parables, and these he read

aloud to the doctor, who often corrected him gently, but with
authority and taste.

They never stayed in *fondas* or inns anymore, but at the conclusion of their business. Gonzalo was occupied selling and buying, as he had been accustomed to do for many years, among the
native villages, where the people were avid for the oriental products brought into Mexico by the Manila galleons, and with
which Gonzalo went well supplied. Laws prohibited the Indians
from going unclothed, as some of them had preferred to do, and
they admired the brilliantly colored cottons from India and the
Philippines. They also, when they could, bought fans, buttons
made of pearl, and necklaces. Dr. Morales confined himself to
treating the sick in the towns, and to seeing and talking with
families he knew from previous visits.

It became clear to Gonzalo that Dr. Morales was, above all, a
teacher. In fact, the towns where they lingered for some days
were always eagerly awaiting him, and there were rooms set
aside for his talks and lectures. After a time, Gonzalo was invited
to these, which he found of absorbing interest.

Gonzalo loved study and cherished his books, but he could
not afford many, and the learned teachings of the doctor satisfied
his longing for them. Dr. Morales, in his talks, spoke often of the
Psalms; he told the history of the ancient peoples, and more and
more he began to criticize Christians, explaining how their
cruelties were against the laws of God. He lectured on Christian
hypocrisy, which seemed to him monstrous, and he spoke with
passion against the system of the *encomiendas,* which had been
devised and protected by the colonial government in New Spain.
The *encomiendas* permitted a Spaniard (not a Creole, for
Spaniards born in the New World had few rights in comparison
with Spanish-born immigrants) to own large tracts of land, and
the natives upon it. These people, sold with the land like cattle,
were forcibly baptized and then simply used as labor, and often
so cruelly that they died of exhaustion and melancholy while still
young.

Gonzalo pondered these thoughts and found that in his heart

he must agree with Dr. Morales. He began to take note of the groups of people who always gathered to listen to the teacher.

Whenever they reached a town of any size (and sometimes in small villages and on isolated ranches) these talks and prayers and the songs the teacher taught them (leading them with his strong vibrant bass voice) took place in a small inner room, painted white, and furnished with benches. Usually there were no windows in the room—at first, Gonzalo thought, for warmth, as the evenings were cold, the farther north they traveled. It began to become clear to him that the quiet inner rooms were basically for protection.

Always, on the Saturdays, or the Sabbaths, there were delicious feasts of special foods, which he enjoyed. The friends of Dr. Morales used a kind of bread made without leaven, flat and crisp, and wonderfully tasty. There were always stews of chicken, some green leafy vegetables, sometimes also sweet fruit wines. Generally he and the doctor (or teacher, as he now called him) were so busy with errands, prayers, and important calls that must be made upon the sick that they forgot to eat on these days, and the evening banquet, set upon a snowy cloth, and lighted by a strange and beautiful artifact which contained seven candles, was impressive and also beautiful, as well as a delight, for his having waited all day for food.

Gonzalo realized now, though as yet he had not openly acknowledged this to himself, that the teacher was a Jew. A rabbi, as some of the people called him. When he taught, he wore a fringed garment around his shoulders and a little cap. Such caps were always quietly passed out before the meal to the men of the family. Gonzalo took part in the feasts and attended the lectures, and learned the prayers and the songs. And yet some shyness, some curious reluctance, held him back from actually asking Dr. Morales why he was admitted to the inner rooms, why he was invited to the lectures and the feasts.

The learned rabbi's strange eyes, with their power to ease his mind and calm his tumultuous desires, could induce in him a state of calm and peace with a glance. It was no longer necessary to stop what he was doing, and ask the doctor for his help, in producing that euphoria. Gonzalo was grateful for it.

As for Judaism, it attracted him. The ancient poetry of the chants and prayers appealed deeply to him. The strength and power of the laws, the way in which they could enhance and give meaning to every act of the day—from washing and eating, to study and rest—attracted his consent. His own training in Christianity had been slight. A busy father had seen that he attended mass and kept the feasts; the rules of behavior he had passed on to his son had been personal, those of a good man. A man of honor. Don Pedro had not thought to color them with the Faith.

Gonzalo spoke of this with the rabbi.

"But the rules you learned, the wish to be a good upright man, this is the teaching of Jesus," pronounced Dr. Morales. "And Jesus was a Jew. And he said, 'I have come not to break the Law, but to fulfill it.'"

"Then you do believe in Jesus?" cried Gonzalo.

"As a great and good teacher, yes. Remember, he was called 'Rabbi.' But as the Son of God? No. I await the true Messiah. He has not yet come to save our people. For . . . look at us. Are we saved? Are we not in misery and pain and trouble, persecuted and ridiculed and spat upon? Tortured, and burned?"

His light eyes seemed to blaze with anger, and Gonzalo felt momentary fear of him.

Yet, thought Gonzalo, these people, these Jews, hidden and in danger, have accepted me, and they trust me. I could never betray them. Besides, my mother was a Judaizer. And I? I feel that I am closer to her now than to any other person.

On the road, as they sold their products, and Gonzalo bought hides and wool and woven woolen cloth from the people, and as the teacher-doctor continued to collect his seeds, barks, and leaves, they never spoke of their occasional stays among the friends the doctor called "my people."

It was in a village a few leagues south of Zacatecas, their final destination, that Gonzalo accepted that he had been taken com-

pletely into Jewish ways and that they deeply filled a hollow in
his heart.

They were met by friends playing upon stringed instruments
that they themselves had made—primitive harps, and guitars—
and all were singing. There were some fifteen persons, men,
women, and children. Clearly, this was to be a special festival.

Dr. Morales first went to bathe, and a large wooden tub of
water was brought for Gonzalo also. They washed, modestly,
with their backs to each other, and then both were given clean
white garments to wear. Their own were travel-stained and full
of sweat; a woman took them away to be washed.

After they were clean, Dr. Morales put on his ceremonial garment. With Gonzalo following quietly a few paces behind him,
they were shown to a clean large room where basins of water,
and clean white bandages were set out. A young woman, dark-
eyed and pale, but smiling with joy, sat holding a small infant on
her lap.

There were prayers and a curious ritual. The baby was
unwrapped, and proffered by the mother. A knife, glinting in the
light and very sharp, seemed to be blessed. It was passed to Dr.
Morales, the rabbi. The baby cried, with a surprised strangled
sound, and then steadily, as if in pain and rage. It was taken to a
corner and comforted and suckled by the mother, and immediately there was much rejoicing, dancing, and singing. A basin
with blood and bits of skin was taken away, where, Gonzalo
learned, it was to be buried in the earth, as all blood must be returned to earth, and covered over.

Gonzalo joined in the festivities, and enjoyed the feasting and
the drinking of wine afterward.

"Another Jew, to praise Jehovah, the one God." The father of
the infant went about to his friends, saying this and receiving
embraces and congratulations. Many were in tears.

"Another Jew to suffer in this world, and eat the bread of bit-
terness," said one, and immediately all the others were silent,
and wagged their heads, and many said, "True. True." Then, as
one man, all cried, "Hear, O Israel, the Lord thy God is One."

Gonzalo said no word, but he was deeply troubled, and confused. Much of what Dr. Morales, the rabbi, had taught him he had received as reasonable and sensible. He would eat no pork, for hogs fed on carrion and garbage; he would not mix milk and meat in the same meal, for that law protected the flocks, and permitted their increase. The ablutions before and after meals, and after any act which might contaminate the purity of his hands, he accepted wholeheartedly. The idea of God as One, and not God in Three Persons, he was able to accept at once, as the mystery of the Trinity had always seemed to him a strange and difficult conception. Why attempt to separate God into parts? God is One, agreed Gonzalo, with all his heart.

Later that night, when all had said good night and were ready to go to their beds, he asked the teacher, Dr. Morales, to walk with him in the moonlight a little way, and answer a few questions that perplexed him.

"Gladly," answered the rabbi, laying aside his ceremonial garments and making ready to stroll about the village. In the few houses, candles were doused, and there was a gentle silence everywhere, broken only by the sleepy murmurings of chickens roosting in trees, and by the occasional stamping of horses and donkeys in their compounds.

"I realize that you have been teaching me to accept your faith," said Gonzalo, "and I am greatly drawn to it. It seems to me austere, just, and reasonable. You do not accept Jesus as the Messiah, although He said He was. I have not thought too deeply about this. I suppose you do not accept His miracles."

The rabbi said quietly, in his deep voice, "I have been trying to help you, Gonzalo, as I go about celebrating the faith with my fellow Jews, and bringing back into Judaism the ones who have fallen away, or who have accepted Christianity because of fear and in order to take advantage of the fact that it is protected by the Crown and the army. I am also trying to return to the heart of Judaism men like you from *converso* families, whose hearts and minds are Jewish, but who have been inducted into a foreign faith by their forebears, in order to save them from suffering and persecution. From the beginning, I knew that you had courage, that persecution would not terrify you, not even the torments of the Inquisition, which keeps after us all like a great black cloud or hurricane, ready to lift us up into the whirlwind and dash us against the rocks below."

"Perhaps you think too well of me," murmured Gonzalo. "I have never been tried."

"If you become a Jew, with us, you will be tried," announced the rabbi.

A chill of fear made Gonzalo tremble.

"But the circumcision, what you did today to that infant, this is required?" he asked.

"Not really required of a convert, unless he asks for it," explained the rabbi. "The circumcision is an ancient sign, a covenant, which holds us all together, and makes us brothers in our faith. Did you feel that it was cruel?"

"The baby cried."

"In a tiny infant, the pain is momentary, and the healing is fast and without problems. Adults suffer, yes."

"It seems a . . . a savage kind of covenant."

"As I explained to you about many of our practices, there is reasonable and sensible hygiene beyond the ritual," began the rabbi. "The cleanliness of the member, the holy member of a man, from which life can spring, with God's help, is important in God's eyes. And this operation helps prevent lubricity and sexual itching, and therefore helps keep a man chaste, in his marriage, and before."

"It has this effect?"

"Assuredly."

Gonzalo pondered these words, and found comfort in them. And yet he could not bring himself to ask for the operation, which would keep him pure and prevent his overwhelming love for Guiomar from frightening her and shaming himself.

"I was sent to you," the rabbi announced to Gonzalo, when they were alone on the road again.

"Why, how could that be?"

"Your kinsmen, in Seville, are secret Jews. They begged me to protect and watch over Guiomar. She had been well taught and they trusted her to keep her promises, but they feared her convent upbringing. As do I. If I had more time to talk with her . . . but I can never stay in the city, in any city, very long. The Holy Office suspects me, and twice they almost captured me. If I manage to escape them this time, I will not again come to the New World."

"But," began Gonzalo unhappily, "how can we protect you, here? You seem to be so well known in these towns of the north."

"I have many disguises. Soon I will adopt one and keep to it until I can get to the coast. Meanwhile, Gonzalo, though I grieve for Guiomar and your father, I rejoice that you are one of us. As you are, now!"

"As I am," agreed Gonzalo, giving to the words his ardent heart's dedication.

Later, when they were traveling again, he asked the rabbi if there was anyone with whom he could continue his studies in Mexico.

"There is a teacher to whom I will recommend you in the city. He is thought to be a devoted Catholic; he attends mass every day, and belongs to many sodalities and walks in the processions. He has been able to deceive them—the Church authorities— because he is old and venerable in appearance. But he is a rabbi. He teaches secretly. You must continue with him."

"Then he is in danger, too?"

"Perhaps. But he is very clever, and nobody suspects him. We have many like him. The Church has no idea how many of us are here, working, teaching, sometimes even acting as priests!"

"Then their Holy Office can never really catch up, can it?"

Dr. Morales smiled.

"It tries. But it cannot. There is no better way to strengthen a people in their beliefs than to attack them and punish them. No better way."

6

Sara stayed with the nuns for three months, devoting herself to prayers of thanksgiving and to the luxury of keeping clean. She was given cloth by the nuns, which she cut and sewed to make herself garments, and they found wool for her to knit, to make herself a cloak.

Sara ate slowly and carefully, watching to make sure that she did not take more than her fair portion of what the nuns had for their table, but the food strengthened her swiftly and she began to feel healthy and agile, and ready for anything.

She did not deceive the Mother Superior, who had taken a fancy to her and wanted her to stay.

"I am married, Reverend Mother, and I must find my husband, who surely is searching for me."

"But, child, you have no idea where to look for him."

"My wicked step-brothers threw my husband into prison, but he was innocent and he would know how to defend himself, and to secure release, or escape. Then he would look for me. My step-brothers always took me with them on their journeys, and could not someone search for a party of three . . . of two gold-smiths, and a woman? Fermín will search for me."

Sara spoke calmly but with deep conviction.

"Then where will you begin?" asked Reverend Mother.

"Here. In New Spain. I will go first to Mexico City, where all travelers go, and I will search for a silversmith. Fermín will have to earn his bread, and that is his trade. See my bracelet? My husband made it! He works silver, as my step-brothers work gold. They are artists. But they left it and tried to farm, in order to keep me hidden and secure. They made sacrifices for me, I confess it, in order to try to make me renounce my Faith and become once more a Jewess. But Fermín and I love our Christian belief as my step-brothers love their Jewish religion."

"If they are so determined to bring you back to their ways, they will search for you, too."

"Yes, perhaps," Sara whispered. But then she drew herself up, and squared her shoulders.

"But I shall be on my guard," she said.

"You will need money. We cannot give you any."

"I can sing. I will sing in the streets."

"Oh, my dear child. That is dangerous. You will be assaulted. By soldiers, by drunken men."

"I can't do anything else. And maybe I could earn a few maravedis. There are always beggars, aren't there? And Christians must always give to them. I was taught this. I cannot sell my bracelet. I may trace him through it."

"But if you are young, and able, and beautiful . . . as you are . . . they will not like you to beg."

"Then I must disfigure myself."

"No. I forbid it."

But the Mother Superior could not detain Sara, and on the next day she set out, walking toward Mexico City. She kept her head tied in a cloth, and whenever she met strangers on the road, she dropped the cloth to hide most of her face. She could see through it, though mistily.

Standing on the road, with her eyes covered by the cloth, she began to sing, a very old sad song, and she held out her hand to the passersby. There were not many, but a company of soldiers came abreast of her, and one of them tossed her a coin. With this she trudged on, entering a village by nightfall. The coin bought her a bowl of beans and two corn tortillas, and a corner inside a hut where the native woman allowed her to sleep, warmed with a woolen spread that also covered her three-year-old boy.

In the morning Sara thanked her, accepted two more dry corn tortillas, and then continued on her way.

7.

La Gorda was awakened by a pounding on her *zaguan,* in a rhythm she knew. It was midnight. She hurried to pass back the heavy bar and open to Gaspar. He entered hurriedly, breathing in a hard, rasping way, and together they dropped the heavy bar back into place.

"What is the matter? What happened?" she whispered. She had never seen him in such agitation.

"Later. Get me something to eat. I am famished."

La Gorda quickly heated milk, beat two eggs into it, and broke him a thick chunk of bread. She had gone to the public ovens that morning with her loaves, and had fine fresh rounds of good bread.

She sat quietly waiting for him to finish eating and begin to recount to her his trouble.

"We had a discussion, the captain and I, and I raised my hand against him."

She knew something of military discipline.

"Did you strike him?" she asked, afraid of his answer.

"I killed him."

"*Dios Santo!* You must escape."

"Yes. Will you help me?"

"Of course."

"I thought . . . I will take ship for Peru. You can make fortunes in Peru, they say. I will have to go disguised. But how?"

La Gorda began to think furiously. Gaspar was fair, gray-eyed.

"Perhaps as a woman. That way, you could ride. I could get a horse for you, and you could join a cavalcade going to Acapulco."

"As a woman?" Gaspar's look was incredulous, and also full of distaste. "But I could not keep up such a disguise all the way to the coast. I would be discovered."

"I will think. You must not be found here, of course. This is the first place they would look for you."

"I know. I will leave at once. But where can I go?"

"Some charcoal burners are bringing me a load of charcoal tomorrow. You might go back with them . . . to the hills, where they have their ovens . . . Going out of the city, you could be as dirty, as black with their dust, as they!"

Still thinking and planning, she hustled him off to bed, and was not importunate with him, knowing him to be exhausted, though she longed for reassurance of her love, for his strong masculine caresses.

Gaspar slept deeply, and content.

He had lied. He had not had a quarrel with his captain, nor struck him. He had simply deserted, as he had before, as the soldiers constantly did, for a few days at a time. Their officers winked at it, because so few soldiers came out to the New World who were brave, trained, and clever. Mostly they were young fellows in search of adventure, or criminals in hiding, or old soldiers so ruined by the campaigns that they were almost useless.

Gaspar had spent the days away from Mexico City longing for the sight of the girl with whom he had fallen in love. Marching, camping, occasionally fighting, all he could think of was how he might see her again.

It had come to him like a revelation from above that he was single, and she was single. Why not openly court her, ask for her hand?

At this thought, a revolutionary one for him, as he had had lovers from the time he was sixteen, a sudden great horror of himself had overcome him. He spent sleepless nights repenting of his former life, and especially of La Gorda. Little by little, he worked out a plan. He would return, tell La Gorda that he had to escape, and he would go to Peru and make a fortune, and then he would come back and court the beautiful, the most beautiful, Guiomar.

There was danger, he knew. The worst danger was that she would be married to someone else before he could return. Deep in his inner being, he knew that he would be successful and rich. He was clever and ruthless, and he had never really tried before, but had been content to go soldiering and live from day to day. But now he had something to strive for.

Part of the plan had worked perfectly, even better than his original idea. La Gorda had accepted his story at once; he had been afraid, with her suspicious nature, she would see through it. Lying awake in the morning, before she stirred, he wondered how he might manage to speak to Don Pedro, Guiomar's father, before he started for the coast. Ships for Peru departed Acapulco every few months.

It turned out to be amazingly easy.

La Gorda rose, dressed quickly, and departed. She was arranging for the clothes of his disguise and perhaps some supplies. He thought of asking her for the money they had been saving, but he knew she would not give him all of it. If he said nothing and left it to her, she was likely to give him more than if he asked for it.

He got up quickly, dressed, and hurried out before any of the servants knew that he had been in the house. It was not far to Curtidores Street, and his breath grew shorter with each step he took that brought him nearer to where Guiomar lived. He was not sure just what he intended to do; he was not clean, nor dressed properly, and besides, at this early hour he could not hope to be admitted to speak to her father. But he might catch a glimpse of her.

There was no activity near the Montemayor house. All was quiet within. He did not even see workers arriving to begin their labors on the skins in the second patio. Puzzled, Gaspar hung about, walking up and down, for some time. At last one of the Indian servants emerged, and began hurrying along the street toward the *tianguis*, or great market, carrying her empty basket. Gaspar followed her, and stopped her.

"What has happened in the Montemayor house?" he asked her directly. "Is someone sick?"

Plague was never long absent from the city, and Gaspar's heart stood still with fear for an instant. It could not be that he had lost Guiomar before she even knew of his existence.

The Indian woman jerked away from him, but he caught her arm again in his strong grip.

"The patron . . . the patron is dying," she answered at last. "Everyone is praying. But the people have to eat, someone has to bring food."

Dying!

Gaspar gasped. If he could not ask for Guiomar's hand, he could not depart for Peru tranquil knowing that she would wait. It seemed he would have to beg leave to court her from her brother. That would be much worse, he realized, as brothers were often more jealous of their sisters than fathers could be, who were usually prejudiced in favor of early marriage for their daughters. And Gaspar had heard that young Montemayor was not a roisterer, or a drinker, or one who could be easily cozened. He was a serious youth, well behaved and dutiful.

Gaspar turned back toward La Gorda's house. But he was deep in thought, and worried, and wondering how to plan. He did not see that she had followed him and stood, suspicious and angry, watching him until he turned and strode away.

She pretended, when she saw him later, that all she could think of was to get him away safely to the coast. Gaspar had to allow her to shave him very close, and to dress him in many skirts and several loose blouses. That very night, powdering him heavily with soot from charcoal, and dirtying his face and hair with it until he was unrecognizable, she waited with him until the charcoal burner came by with his burros and his loads. The bargain had been struck: La Gorda paid the charcoal burner to take the bulky, dirty "woman" with him on his trip out of the city, and many leagues along the road to Acapulco. The charcoal burner was an Indian who knew little Spanish, only a few words, but he did know the value of the maravedis pressed into his filthy palm. With the charcoal burner was a boy, a mute, who helped guide the beasts, and in response to signs brought water and occasionally tethered the beasts for a rest on their journey. Gaspar left them, without thanks, when they reached Taxco.

Taxco lived from silver mines; houses were tumbled about on the hills, like a child's blocks tossed down helter-skelter. As Gaspar departed, the dirty charcoal burner gave a deep sigh of relief and directed himself toward a house he knew, on the outskirts of the town. As the *zaguan* swung open to receive him, he murmured "Shalom" and was greeted with the same word.

"Now I can wash. Thank God," sighed Dr. Morales.

The disguise of the charcoal burner was one he used most effectively, and most often.

8.

La Gorda had held her tongue with an immense effort of the will, and had contracted the first Indian she found in the market, with his sacks of charcoal. She had bundled Gaspar away with this taciturn native, and was able to go to bed tranquil, certain that Gaspar would soon be far away from whatever it was that drew him so often, and so mysteriously, toward Curtidores Street.

The Montemayor house seemed to be the one he watched, and there were two women there, besides the Indian slaves. La Gorda writhed with jealousy and longed to know which of the two was the one who had attracted Gaspar's roving gray eyes. It must be the small dark one, thought La Gorda. She seemed pale and uninteresting enough, reflected La Gorda, but men were strange; sometimes they fell in love even with crippled women, and that insipid, thin girl might be the one. She had lovely long black plaits, remembered La Gorda, who had seen her in the market, and noticed the braids. La Gorda's hair was thick and curly, and she was certain that long lank braids were unattractive. But then . . .

It couldn't possibly be the other one, she mused. The one with the horrible red hair that nobody could admire. Besides, that girl was big, tall, and wide in the shoulder. She seemed to have little curve to her hips or bosom. And big feet! La Gorda had noticed the feet. She was proud of her own small, almost square feet. Like many women of her class, La Gorda admired only her own type, and could find little to admire in women who were different from herself. Her ideal was of a short, full-bosomed woman, with thick curly hair and snapping dark eyes, a vivacious and bold glance. Like herself.

It seemed to her incredible that Gaspar should have fallen in love with either of those two—the little wraith, with the moon-pale face, or the tall one with the beet-red hair. But still, just to be sure . . .

She sat down, and with great pains and care she wrote out two denouncements. The two women who lived in the Montemayor house, in Curtidores Street, should be investigated by the Holy Office. One was a witch, and the other was (she stopped to consider how to spell the word she wanted) a Judaizer.

9.

Guiomar had not left her father's side since he had taken to his bed. It was evident that what he had thought was rheumatism was something much more severe. He was rapidly losing strength in his limbs, could no longer stand, and groaned continuously with the pain. He could not hold his mug to drink, or a dish from which to eat. Guiomar fed him tenderly, washed him carefully, a section of his pain-convulsed body at a time, as she had learned to do with suffering old nuns in the convent. Judit, from the kitchen, sent in delicate egg custards and nourishing drinks, some of them made with the bitter Mexican *chocolatl* that stained the milk dark brown and, sweetened with honey or dark sugar, gave a strange and delicious flavor. But Don Pedro was losing ground.

As his limbs became rigid and increasingly painful, he was almost paralyzed. His bodily functions, too, began to fail, and Guiomar was desperate for some medicinal herbs to afford him relief.

When she heard Gonzalo's voice in the hall, she flew out to him and threw herself into his arms.

"Our father, he is so ill," she sobbed. "I am doing what I can, but, brother, he is slipping away from me. Where is Dr. Morales? He might be able to help, to cure . . ."

Gonzalo had loosed her arms, and stood away from her, his heart beating fast.

"Dr. Morales has gone on south," he said. "But maybe I can find something to help. Dr. Morales taught me much of his lore. I will go to my father at once."

Gonzalo hurried into his father's bedroom and threw himself on his knees beside the bed. His father lay, wasted and weary, his face turned away from the light.

"Father, I am home. I am here," said Gonzalo.

Don Pedro slowly turned his head.

"I am dying," he whispered. "Get a priest."

Gonzalo went out at once, and hurried toward the cathedral, where, in one of the chapels, Guiomar heard daily mass. He found an old priest there, Father Anselmo, who tremblingly made ready the holy oils and bundled up his vestments. He was slow, and there was a delay in finding the acolyte to accompany him. When at last they were ready to proceed to Curtidores Street, at least an hour had gone by.

The worst had happened. Guiomar met them at the entrance to the house, weeping and wringing her hands. Judit, pale and frightened, stood by her side.

"Oh, Father," began Guiomar, falling to her knees and pressing the old priest's hand to her lips, "my father has died. Can you shrive him? His soul departed but moments ago."

"I can say prayers for the dead, *hija*. And if, in his soul, he repented at the last moment, and called on Our Lord, he will be saved."

Controlling herself, and clinging to the hands of Judit and Gonzalo, Guiomar heard the prayers on her knees. When the priest had gone, she sent her brother and Judit away.

"My poor father was so ill, so weak, that he lost all his powers," she explained. "I must wash him and make him ready for burial. Please send Tomasa to me, with cloths and basins of warm water and soap."

Murmuring her prayers, and asking God for strength, Guiomar uncovered the old man's body, which lay in a pool of his excrement, and quietly, with respect, she took away the soiled sheets and clothing, and washed and arranged the limbs, and gently closed the eyes. She laid coins on the eyelids, and bound up the chin in a silken cloth. She had been taught in the convent to do these last offices when they were necessary, and she did not shrink from any part of her duty.

When Don Pedro's body was ready and dressed in clean garments, she called Gonzalo to help her lift him onto the table in the hall, which she had covered with a black-velvet cloak of her own. She set blessed candles at his head and feet, and she prepared then to remain with the body throughout the night, praying for her father's soul. All the household was called to come and kneel and pray, at intervals, and so they passed the rest of the day and all the night until dawn of the next morning.

Gonzalo had gone to arrange for the burial, and shortly after first light the same old priest from the cathedral arrived, in black robes, to accompany the body, carried on the same table by the house slaves, to the cathedral, where the mass for the dead was to be sung.

Guiomar, fainting from her vigil and all her tears, was scarcely aware of the ritual. When it was over, she went back to their

house, with Judit and the female house slaves, to pray. It was not
the custom for women to accompany the dead to their burial.
This duty fell to Gonzalo, the leatherworkers, and the male slave
Epifanio.

It was late in the afternoon when Gonzalo returned, exhausted
and sad. Guiomar had ready a hot meal for him, knowing that he
would feel their father's death even more than she did, for he had
lived with him all the years of his childhood and youth.

"How kind you are, Guiomar," he murmured as he tried to sip
some of the hot broth. "Kind as you are beautiful." He said the
words sadly, and turned away from her.

She left him to his sorrow, and went to her own room, where
she knelt at her *reclinatorio*. There, still kneeling, she fell asleep
from weariness and tears. Judit helped her to bed.

10.

Captain Rivero arrived in Mexico City with but four of the captives from the pirate ship. One had broken away, but had been
recaptured. It was night, and they were sleeping on the cold
ground, in a forest. Juan and Fermín had tried to cover themselves with leaves, and had managed to warm themselves. The
captain had ordered a fire, and the glowing coals sent off a little
heat, although the prisoners were not allowed to lie too close to
it. "It will freeze tonight. This is the highest point of the trail.
Tomorrow we drop down into the valley of Mexico."

The next day, at first light, they were given bread and a tot of
wine to warm them. The captain's mount had been watered and
given corn. Captain Rivero forced the prisoners to follow at a jog
trot; he was anxious to finish his journey and deliver the heretics
to the guards of the prisons of the Inquisition. However, when
he reached the outskirts of the city he slowed down, and pro-

ceeded in a stately manner. He liked it to be known that he was a real defender of the Faith. His exhausted prisoners stumbled along behind, their chains clanking. It was an impressive sight, and slaves hurrying toward the market, ladies with covered faces returning from rosary, and bystanders, stood still to watch them go by.

To Juan's surprise the Inquisition was housed in a large imposing building. They entered a wide patio, which was sun-flooded after the brief rain that had fallen. Their cell (into which all four were pushed) was dry, and there were benches on which they could recline. Their chains were struck off, the door, of open ironwork, clanged behind them, and a soldier, in the uniform of the guards of the Inquisition, took a station before it.

Fermín and the two sailors who had survived their long and grueling journey lay down on the benches. Juan, giving thanks to God that the galling chains were gone, lay on the floor. Almost at once, all slept.

11.

At almost the same hour as Juan and the other prisoners, Fray Domingo had arrived in Mexico City, astride a mule loaned him by the brothers of his convent in Puebla.

He was very eager to present himself to the Grand Inquisitor, and to arrange to make himself useful. He had already taken some steps that he hoped would result in the capture of the two insane Judaizers who had lowered their Christian sister into the pit, and who had tried to kill him, Fray Domingo, as well. Clever spies and informers of Fray Domingo's own order, which had dedicated itself wholeheartedly to seeking out heretics, had been alerted to search for the men who called themselves Duarte. No doubt that was not their real name, nor was it likely they would be using it at the present time, either. Every departing galleon from Veracruz would be searched for them. Fray Domingo made checks against their names on his list. His list was growing; he hoped to capture enough of these hated traitors to the Crown and to Holy Church to justify a great auto-da-fé, an act of faith and discipline to purify the hearts of all Christians.

Fray Francisco received Fray Domingo courteously. Quietly he listened to what Fray Domingo had to say, and silently he examined Fray Domingo's list. Gently putting Andúfar on the floor, he ruffled through some documents on his desk, and then drew out a stiff long sheet of parchment, on which there was another list. He passed it, without comment, to Fray Domingo.

"Your Reverence, with such a list we should be able to hold an impressive auto-da-fé, with many penitents."

"These names are of persons who have been denounced, but not yet brought to trial."

"But an auto-da-fé—"

"Some of these persons may be innocent," murmured Fray Francisco. "All shall be heard. All shall be offered the opportunity to repent."

Fray Domingo felt an edge of reproof in the soft voice. He looked up suspiciously. Fray Francisco's dark eyes, in his pale thin face, gazed at Fray Domingo with an expression not easily identified.

"Further," went on Fray Francisco, "some of these suspected persons have not been apprehended."

"I could perhaps help in that task!" offered Fray Domingo, hurriedly.

"Thank you. But I will need you here. Fray Arnulfo has been doing much of the secretarial work. You will take his place, for I am sending him to Zacatecas, to the mines, to assist the treasurer there. I think perhaps he needs a rest. There have been some, let us say, curious delays, even errors, in his work."

Fray Arnulfo, who had been listening just outside the door, as he always did, felt a sudden chill. He had been found out! God knows what the treasurer at the mines would expect him to do.

Go down into the pits? For a moment, he thought of throwing himself on his knees to Fray Francisco. But the impulse passed swiftly. Fray Francisco was cold, he was utterly attached to the law, to his duties, and to his religion. He was exquisitely just but he was not merciful. Fray Arnulfo gave himself up to despair.

"I will appoint some assistants for you when the time comes to attempt to apprehend persons who have been denounced," Fray Francisco now told Fray Domingo. "In the meantime, there is a great deal of office work that must be done. I wish to prepare a list of all persons denounced, the result of their trials, the persons wearing the sanbenito, when their term of wearing the garment has been terminated, and many other important details which shall be a guide for the Inquisitors who come after me. In four months I am to return to Spain, and my place is to be taken by three new Inquisitors of your order, Fray Domingo. That is all."

Dismissed, Fray Domingo felt rebuffed. He had come with a full heart, bearing much information, ready to do his work with a will. Fray Francisco seemed not to accord him any prominence at all, nor any praise.

Bowing speechlessly, Fray Domingo left. The Inquisitor had not even asked where he was lodged. On the contrary, he had lifted his cat from the floor, and seemed to be thinking of something far away, as he scratched the purring animal behind the ears, and stroked it, nose tip to tail.

In fact, Fray Domingo meant to lodge with some members of his order, who had cells in a convent building they occupied behind the Church of Santo Domingo. Disconsolate, Fray Domingo turned his steps there; it was not far.

Fray Francisco, in the meanwhile, began looking over the notes he had made on data supplied by a soldier of the Crown who had come into the city with four Lutherans, the only survivors of the pirate ship that had been sent down in the waters off Tampico. Also, there was a trying note on several blasphemers, who must be frightened into the behavior of decent Christian gentlemen.

12

Gonzalo, in his sorrow at his father's death, and struggling against his unlawful passion, remembered the name of the person Dr. Morales had recommended to him.

"He lives as a devout Christian, and no one suspects him," Dr. Morales had told him. "But on certain days, he receives a few young men who wish to study, and leads them in chants and ritual, and instructs them, and they read the Torah."

He had told Gonzalo the address, which was a house near the famous Salto del Agua, where water from the great aqueduct was brought down into a basin, from which people could take water away in buckets for their use.

Gonzalo knew the way, crossing a canal and continuing along behind the enormous lands of the Franciscan convent. When he knocked at the modest *zaguan*, a woman in middle age opened to him. She was thin and pale, with silver strands in her dark hair, and she squinted against the light, as if her eyesight were failing.

It had been raining, and Gonzalo on his walk had seen many small puddles in the streets. Noting that they, which lay in dirt and filth, reflected in their shallow waters the purity of the blue sky and the perfection of the floating white clouds, he was moved to poetry, and he stood for a few moments after the door was opened, forgetful of why he had come.

Rousing himself, he said, "I am a friend of Dr. Morales, and he said that I might be welcome here."

The woman opened the door wider, as if to allow him to pass, but then she drew it half shut again, and stared at him curiously.

"What is your name?" she asked, abruptly.

"My name is Gonzalo Montemayor."

"You may come in."

Gonzalo entered, feeling somewhat reluctant. It was obvious that he was going to be subjected to some sort of scrutiny. He had hoped that he would simply be welcomed.

Just before opening another door from the corridor into which they had stepped, the woman turned to Gonzalo and said, "My name is Isabel. My father is José Acevedo. He receives visits for a short time only, as he is very old, and very delicate in health."

The truth of Isabel's description of her father was evident at once. The old man was sitting up in bed, wearing several shawls around his thin shoulders. Two young men were sitting on straight chairs at his bedside.

The old gentleman extended a thin shaking hand toward Gonzalo, but it was not to press his palm. It was to wave him to a seat in a third chair, which Isabel hastily drew up.

"Sit down there, where I can look at you, young man," he said in a surprisingly strong bass voice. "A friend of Dr. Morales, you say? Where is he now?"

"He is returning to Spain," answered Gonzalo.

The old man agreed, shaking his head.

"That is so, that is so," he echoed. He smiled suddenly, and Gonzalo saw that while the skull and features gave an impression of great age, the teeth were firm and young.

"I am often in bed, as I suffer from fevers," Señor Acevedo said. The other young men had said nothing. "Young friends come in to see me, and to read poetry and history to me," went on the old man. "Will you continue, Don Nemesio?" And Señor Acevedo settled back on his pillows and closed his eyes. The young man addressed as Don Nemesio began reading, in a singsong voice, from a small book which seemed to be a compendium of lives of the saints. After about a half hour of this reading, the old man in the bed waved his hand, turned away among his pillows, and seemed to sleep. The visitors quietly gathered up their books and wraps, and silently departed. Gonzalo went with them. Outside the door, in the street, they turned to say "Adios" and to press Gonzalo's hand.

"Come again. Soon," said one of them, in an intense voice.

It was the memory of the intensity in the young voice that drew Gonzalo back, day after day.

It was on his ninth visit that Señor Acevedo suddenly sat up in bed, drew a book out from under his pillow, and announced, "Now I will read to you from the book of wisdom. The Talmud." And, swaying and intoning the words rhythmically, he began to read.

Gonzalo stumbled home afire with dedication.

I am a Jew, he thought, exulting. I am a member of this sad and brilliant and persecuted and resilient race. I will be as brave, as stubborn, as discreet as they. And my God will help me to overcome all my weaknesses, and be strong.

Later, he began to notice Señor Acevedo's daughter Isabel. She was suspicious and dour, and it became apparent, as days went by, that she did not trust Gonzalo. This deeply worried him.

13.

It was a September day when Juan, Fermín, and the two sailors were led out of their cell into the sunlight. Chained once more, they walked slowly across the patio and along the short way to where they would be subjected to the questions of the Inquisitors.

Juan drew a deep breath of the winy air. It had rained the night before, and small patches of water on the ground shone blue as the sky above. Thick white clouds raced across the sky, and a light, swift breeze carried away the foul smells of their long hard journey and the days of confinement afterward.

The two sailors were solemn, but Juan felt a lifting of the heart. He was a good Catholic and he had no fears about making the judges realize that his plight was accidental.

From the sunlight, they passed into an arcade, and thence inside, along dark corridors. When they entered the Inquisition Room, Juan was startled and depressed to see that it was draped in black, and that behind a table covered with a black velvet cloth, the three judges sat, dressed in black garments and with black caps on their heads.

Captain Rivero was waiting, wearing his resplendent uniform of the King's army. He looked very proud of himself as he addressed the judges.

"Your Honors and Reverences, I have here four men from the captured pirate vessel which was sunk in the waters off Tampico. There were many others captured as well, but some died of wounds in Tampico, and others were unable to withstand the rigors of the journey. These men are Lutherans, deadly enemies of our King, His Majesty Philip II, and of Holy Mother Church. They know very little Spanish, and I am here to translate their words, whatever they may be."

It was Fray Francisco who spoke. He sat in the center, with Fray Artemio and Fray Anselmo, the other judges, one on each side.

"Let the men tell their names."

This was translated, and the two English sailors answered.

"Harry Cate."

"George Trout, captain of the *Mary Ann*." He spoke up stiffly and proudly.

"Fermín García Mendoza."

"My name is Juan Palomar, and I need no translator. I am an Irishman, and I studied in the seminary at Valladolid. I know Spanish. I am a True Catholic, and I was taken prisoner by this pirate captain and made to work on his ship, when they fired on and scuttled the galleon the *True Cross*."

Captain Rivero looked at him in consternation; Juan had carefully concealed from the pirates that he knew English, and when captured, he had never spoken so that the guards could hear him. Captain Trout looked at him with intense hatred.

Fray Francisco said, "Do you wish to continue speaking for yourself, or shall I appoint a lawyer for you?"

"I will speak for myself, Your Reverence."

Fray Francisco turned to Captain Rivero and ordered him to ask the other prisoners if they wished to have the help of a lawyer.

Weeping, and speaking through muffled sobs, Cate asked for a lawyer.

Captain Trout proudly refused one, but he demanded another translator. "That man, Rivero, is capable of turning my words into lies," he averred.

Fray Francisco listened without change of expression, as these words were translated literally by a gradually reddening Captain Rivero.

Fray Francisco quietly sent for one of his clerks, who came silently into the room. It was a young friar, in the Dominican habit, tonsured, meek, and obedient.

"Fray Basilio will serve as your translator," Captain Trout was told. Fray Francisco then began, in a quiet, careful voice, speaking slowly so that the translator might get all his meaning.

"You are here to reply to our Inquiries. These Inquiries are for the purpose of establishing the truth of your activities and of your beliefs, and to learn whether you are enemies of the One True Faith and of the Spanish Crown. You are urged to speak the truth, and to plead for mercy, and you are assured that this Court will be merciful, if you ask it in all humility. We will begin with the sailor Harry Cate. Are you a Christian?"

"Yes, Your Honor. Always have been."

"Were you a pirate, on the *Mary Ann*, of your own free will, or were you forced?"

"Forced by hunger, Your Honor. It was the sea or starve."

Fray Francisco was silent for a time, pondering. The other two judges sat with impassive faces. They knew their duties, but they were as yet inexperienced in the Inquisition Courts.

Fray Francisco, due to depart before long, would have liked very much to hold a great auto-da-fé before leaving—an impressive parade of penitents, in sanbenitos, the penitential garments, flagellating themselves as they walked and chanted their repentance, a solemn mass before the platform of the spectators and the burning of two or three of the defiant ones, to teach the public that God sees all and is a just judge.

But he feared that he would not be able to organize one in time. The law strictly required him to give sinners time and instruction; he was required to bring them back into Holy Church. It was evident, now, that this man, this pirate, was going to repent at once. Fray Francisco looked at him with a disillusioned eye.

"I only did as I was told, on board ship," blubbered Cate. "I had to eat, Your Honor. What else could I do? The captain is a cruel man, Your Honor, with a belaying pin and his cutlass."

"Do you know your prayers?"

"Somewhat. But I can learn, Your Honor. Only teach me."

"You shall be taught."

Fray Francisco made a small gesture with his head, and the guards took Cate, each holding one arm, and marched him back to prison, where he collapsed, weeping in his cell, and where he began praying aloud, with such words as he could dredge up from an imperfect memory. He was terrified.

Captain Trout stood with curling lip.

"As to what you are about to ask me, here is my answer," he said. "I am a free Englishman, and I do not believe with the Papists." He spat.

Silently, the three judges leaned their heads close together and consulted. One of the judges kept shaking his head, in disagreement. Trout stood, defiant, and spat again. At this the three judges seemed to agree. Fray Francisco signaled to two enormous men, with naked arms bulging, to take Trout away. He was led away into an inner room, from which, later, issued groans, and then screams of agony. The three judges then went into the inner room, and there was a murmur of voices. Then further screams. At last, the two who had taken Captain Trout away brought him back. But by then he was no longer defiant, nor did he spit. He was half dragged, seeming unable to move his legs, his head drooped, and he was deathly pale. From his slack mouth issued a dribble of saliva.

"Will you accept instruction?" asked Fray Francisco, waiting, not looking at Trout, while these words were translated.

Trout made no answer, but he lifted bloodshot eyes toward where the judges sat.

"Return him to his cell, after properly dressing his wounds," ordered Fray Francisco.

Turning to Juan, he said, "You are Juan Palomar. Repeat what you said previously, and slowly, so that the clerks may write it down."

Juan did so, striving to remember his exact words.

"And so you see, Your Reverence, that it is an accident that I was aboard the *Mary Ann*. I was taken prisoner, and so was my friend and companion, Fermín. We are True Catholics."

"Recite the Confiteor."

Juan crossed himself, and began the words. Also crossing himself, Fermín joined in.

Fray Francisco asked for several other prayers, and both men recited them faultlessly.

"What is your history?" asked one of the other judges, turning to Fermín.

"I am lately freed from a Portuguese prison, Your Honors, where I was thrown by my brothers-in-law, relentless Judaizers, who hate me because I married their sister. My wife is a Christian, like me. They stole her from me, and God knows where they have her now. I followed a clue that made me think they had come out to New Spain with her. But on the way, as my friend told you, our vessel was attacked and scuttled by the pirates. They kept me and Juan, as they said, to work until they could sell us as galley slaves. But when the *Mary Ann* was sent down, Juan and I managed to escape, because Juan can swim. I cannot, but he saved me. He kept me afloat."

He fell silent, and the three judges consulted quietly together. Then one of them spoke.

"Give us the names of these brothers. They shall be found and interrogated."

"The name they used in Portugal was Duarte. What names they would use here, I do not know. And I am searching for my wife, Your Honors. If they have her, I want her back!"

"If your story is true, you shall have justice," he was promised. They turned then, to Juan. "And you, Juan Palomar. You sound plausible, but there is no way in which we can prove your story unless by writing to Spain. Which we will do. The name of your convent, and of the abbot . . ."

There was a bustling from the shadows in the rear of the courtroom, and Fray Domingo came forward.

"I know this young man," he said, pointing to Juan. "His story is true. I can vouch for it. I gave him my place on the *True Cross,* and because I did, my life was saved, for the pirates would certainly have killed me. As for the other one"—he turned to look at Fermín—"I do not know him."

"But I can swear to him," put in Juan. "We were shipmates."

"However," went on Fray Domingo, "I have reason to believe that this man, Fermín García Mendoza, has told the truth." And he went on to relate the story of his capture by the Duarte brothers, his miseries in the pit, and his final escape.

The three judges again silently conferred.

"The men will be returned to a cell, but separate from Trout and Cate," ordered Fray Francisco. "Fray Domingo, please come with me, and recount what you have told us to the notary, who shall record it in his book. This matter will be given over to the civil arm of the government, so that they may capture and bring to justice these wicked men."

"And my wife . . . my wife?" cried Fermín. "Where is she?"

"Safe in the Dominican Convent in the City of the Angels," Fray Domingo told him. "Safe."

"Thank God. Thank God," cried Fermín, and he fell on his knees and crossed himself.

14.

Guiomar was still thin and exhausted from her long vigil by the bedside of her dying father, when there was a loud beating on the knocker of their *zaguan*. One of the Indian house slaves, Leocadia, went to open it, but as soon as she saw the soldiers of the Inquisition, she fled, moaning, toward the kitchen. Guiomar, supporting herself against the wall as she walked, wrapped in a black shawl, went to see what had caused the commotion.

"Doña Guiomar Montemayor and Doña Judit Cerezo are required to accompany us to the Courts of Inquiry of the Holy Office."

"Am . . . am I . . . are we accused of some work against Holy Church?" questioned Guiomar, unbelieving.

"You have been denounced, and must accompany me at once to give evidence."

"*Dios mio!*" Guiomar knew that she must not give way anymore to tears; she controlled herself fiercely, and managed to say, "Please wait here, while I call Doña Judit."

Judit broke into noisy lamentations, as Guiomor told her what they must do.

"No, no. Pray and trust in the mercy of God," cautioned Guiomar. "And let us take warm shawls, several each." She feared that they were to be imprisoned. Leaving instructions in the patio, where several men were working, and in the kitchens, where the slaves were hovering around Tomasa, she put Epifanio in charge of the house.

"And tell Don Gonzalo to come for us as soon as he arrives home," were her final words.

Then, drawing herself up so as to rise a half head taller than either of the soldiers, and taking Judit's weight against her shoulder, she proudly walked between the two black-clad soldiers.

As she had feared, they were taken first to the cells of the Inquisition and left there. Presently water and a piece of dark bread was brought to them.

"Eat it," commanded Guiomar, and she made Judit choke down every morsel of her share. Then she persuaded the shaking, weeping girl to lie down on the wooden bench in the place, and she herself lay on the floor, wrapped as warmly as she could manage. She tried with all her strength to imagine who might have denounced them, but all she could lay hold of was the thought that Tomasa might have denounced Judit, out of resentment. But Tomasa had nothing against Guiomar, who had cured her of a heavy congestion in the head with a tea made of Dr. Morales's herbs.

Dr. Morales? Impossible. But whom else did they know? There was no one.

Commending herself to God and His Blessed Mother, at last she slept.

In the morning, she made an attempt to smooth back and plait her hair, and, when the guards came to take them to the Inquisitional Court, she told Judit to hold her shawl over her head and halfway around her face, as she herself was doing.

Guiomar's prayers had strengthened her, and she walked into the dismal room and faced the three black-robed Inquisitors, almost with curiosity.

After they had told their names, Guiomar asked, "Why have we been brought here, Your Reverence?"

"I ask the questions, young woman," answered Fray Francisco testily, for he was tired, and Andúfar had not come home all night. Fray Francisco feared for his pet.

Besides, he was angry and irritated, because Fray Artemio had told indecent stories over their frugal evening meal, and had demanded extra wine. Fray Francisco was impervious to compassion in the carrying out of his duties, but he held close to the letter of the law, and as a religious, he was shocked by lechery. Whenever he heard a case of a clergyman soliciting women from the confessional, he ordered him flogged, and if he discovered a priest living in sin with a woman, he was capable of sending him to the rack.

He saw now, with a quiver of disgust, that Fray Artemio leaned forward and ordered, "Drop your shawls and uncover your faces."

The two young women obeyed, and Fray Francisco saw that they were well favored, and that one was beautiful. He was going to have a bad time with Fray Artemio. He greatly regretted that he had called him to sit in Inquiry with him; he might better have handled this case alone.

"One of you is a Judaizer," went on Fray Artemio. "Which one of you is it?"

Guiomar spoke.

"We are pious Christian women, Your Reverence, and this accusation against us in a calumny."

"That must be proved," put in Fray Francisco. "I will continue the questioning, Fray Artemio." The third judge, who was somewhat hard of hearing, cupped his hand around one ear and leaned forward.

"Let them repeat the Credo," he ordered.

Judit and Guiomar repeated the prayer faultlessly, and several other prayers, as requested, as well.

Fray Artemio said, "Perhaps we should apply sterner measures. These women are simply denying the accusation. It is incredible that they should have no idea who might have accused them. They are withholding information, perhaps the names of other Judaizers. Let them be stripped."

Two strong guards stepped forward and forcibly pulled down the blouses of Guiomar and Judit, exposing them to the waist. Judit cowered and tried to cover her breasts with her hands, but her hands were caught and held behind her back. Fray Artemio looked closely and with pleasure at Judit's small white pointed breasts and Guiomar's round breasts with the tilted pink nipples.

Guiomar stood straight and proud, and she spoke in a clear voice, directing herself to Fray Francisco.

"Is this the manner in which men of God treat Christian women? Shaming them before men? This seems to be the work of the devil, for how could it be the law of God?"

Fray Francisco was white with shame and anger; Fray Artemio red with lubricious enjoyment.

"The women will cover themselves," ordered Fray Francisco. "But, señorita," he added, turning back to Guiomar, who was buttoning her bodice, "you speak boldly and with authority. Have you been questioned before the Holy Office before?"

"I speak boldly to defend my honor," she answered, lifting her head. "My father is late in his grave, my brother is away on business, and who will defend me but my guardian angel and what he tells me I must do? I but obey what my angel whispers in my ear, in response to my prayer."

Fray Francisco rattled the paper of his notes.

"Your father was ill for a long time? What was his disease?"

"He had pains in his limbs, and eventually they would not bear him, and he lay at last unable to move, on his bed. And there he died."

"And when you prepared him for burial, what did you do?"

"I washed him, and straightened his limbs, and combed his hair, and put clean clothes on him. Then we laid him in his coffin. I kissed his forehead for farewell, put a rosary in his cold fingers, and so I let him go." Guiomar sobbed once, but controlled herself.

"Don't you realize that washing the body and dressing it for the grave in clean linen is a Jewish custom?"

"How can that be? In the convent, we never sent our dead nuns to the grave in the filth and sweat of their final agony," protested Guiomar. "I would not leave my poor father in his misery without washing him, alive or dead."

Fray Francisco murmured, "The young woman's answer is reasonable."

"You did not dose him with any nostrums?"

"I made him soups and broths, and the juice of pressed fruits, and a tea made from herbs, against the pain. You think I may have poisoned my father? But what for? He was good, and I loved him. And now I have no one to defend me. Why should I deprive myself of my only friend? Besides, it is a calumny that I ever Judaized—or that I am a witch. Somebody hates me, I don't know why."

Fray Artemio spoke.

"It may be," he said (for he was still smarting from the reproof Fray Francisco had dealt him), "it may be that someone hates you because you are beautiful, and a snare for the souls of men."

"I am only as God made me," replied Guiomar, "and I behave myself as I was taught by the good nuns of the Convent of Our Lady of Pardon, in Seville."

"Take a note," Fray Francisco ordered his clerk. "Write to the nuns of the Convent of Our Lady of Pardon for information about the señorita Guiomar Montemayor. But you"—he turned to Judit—"where were you reared?"

Haltingly, and in a timid voice, Judit recounted the short story of her youth. "We lived in Jaén, my mother, my father and I. My mother taught me and I made my first communion there, and we went daily to mass. When my father died, and his debts were paid, we had only a few ducats, enough for our journey to New Spain. We planned to search for my father's brother, who lives in Zacatecas. But my mother died on shipboard, and I came to live with Guiomar as her companion. I have not tried to find my uncle, for how could I go searching for him alone? I have been happy to remain with my kind friend, who is like a sister to me."

Fray Francisco again turned to his clerk.

"Write to the representative of the Holy Office in Jaén, and require information about . . . your father's name, señorita?"

"José de Jesús Cerezo."

"The name Cerezo has a Jewish sound," commented Fray Artemio.

"But José de Jesús does not," interposed Fray Francisco, who was disgusted with Fray Artemio, and was planning to have him watched. Such open lechery might be taking secret forms that could be used to eject him from the order.

Turning back to Judit and Guiomar, Fray Francisco said, "I hold in my hand these serious denunciations of you both. It will be months, perhaps a year, before I can gather any information about you from Spain. Therefore, in the meantime, I will sentence you to work as nurses, three mornings every week, in the Hospital de Jesús, caring for the sick and wounded of His Majesty Philip II's soldiers. You will report to"—he turned, and consulted his lists of father confessors—"you will report every Friday morning to Father Felipe, at the Church of Santo Domingo."

"I would be willing to confess the young women, and guide them, myself," put in Fray Artemio.

"They will report to, and confess to, Father Felipe," repeated Fray Francisco firmly.

I feel it my duty, he thought to himself, to apply for a change in plans, as someone with Holy Church at heart should be in authority over this questionable friar.

That very night he wrote to his Superior, and requested an extension of his duty in the New World.

15.

Gaspar disappeared in Taxco. That is, a buxom woman, careful of her appearance, and always modestly covered, and half veiled, disappeared. Not long after, a strong-armed young man applied for work in the silver mines, was accepted and given a cap, with a candle set in at the brow, his pick and shovel, and told his duties. It was very hard and dirty work, but Gaspar was strong and tireless, and he was studying all the possibilities afforded by the mine. He quickly learned that inspection of ore mined was made only at the usual exit, but that there were others, frequently left without guard, where he could escape with some stolen ore of high quality. The problem would be to find someone who would smelt it for him secretly. After he had begun some quiet investigation, he found a man who could be bribed to cooperate with him. Gaspar was diligent and careful, and he began to realize a steady and considerable profit. More, he reflected that a man who would compromise himself in this way, risking detection and disgrace, had probably done so in the past, and might even be on the suspect list of the police. So, carefully and quietly, Gaspar began studying his accomplice.

He was an old man, bearded, swarthy, and laconic. In the town, he was known only as a silversmith, and he regularly took a few crosses, chains, brooches, and bracelets to a little stall near the church, which was being built in the small square. Gaspar soon learned that he had few friends, and almost never went to the *fonda* nearby to drink or to eat the delicious roast pork, which was always available.

The man's name was Mendizabal, a good Spanish name of Arabic origin, and indeed the man's accent proclaimed him to be from southern Spain.

He never invited Gaspar to his house, and was often ill of a Friday, unable to work, or to eat. It came to Gaspar, like a sudden clap of thunder, that the man was a Jew. That would explain all his peculiarities, including even his assiduous molding and modeling of crosses, for it was well known that the secret Jews made great public pretenses of Christian piety. And Don Melchor Mendizabal took all his crosses to the priest to be blessed before he offered them for sale.

Gaspar was jubilant.

He saw his fortune growing, and he was safe! Safe! For he could always denounce Mendizabal.

16

Juan and Fermín were taken again to the Courts of the Holy
Office, and there heard sentence.

Fray Francisco ordered them to work three days a week, giving the money earned for candles for the altar at the cathedral;
the remaining four days of the week they were to act as orderlies
at the Hospital de Jesús, scrubbing the floors, carrying out the
slops, and otherwise obeying the doctors and clergy in charge.
And they were to report on the first Friday of every month to
Fray Domingo for instruction and confession.

"Your sentence is light," Fray Francisco told the two men,
"because I believe that you were, in fact, captured by this pirate, Trout, and that you are true sons of the Faith. But in case I
should have erred in my judgment, I impose this sentence, which
can do no more than improve your souls. At the end of one year,
you are to come before this Board of Inquiry once more, for a
further investigation of your beliefs and behavior."

Fray Domingo was waiting for the two men as they were set
free. He spoke kindly to Juan, and told the two that he had
found them work as masons, in the building and repairing of
walls and chapels for the Dominican Order, which was extend-
ing and conserving its large monastery and the other buildings
which belonged to the order. They would be paid twenty maravedis a day, and they were to oversee the work of the Indian masons also employed by the church, and keep their ears and eyes
open for any pagan practices among them, and report them to
Fray Domingo.

"For, you know, it is our custom to use broken stone idols and
the obscene gods of these people, in the foundations of our
building," explained Fray Domingo, "to impose the authority of

Christ Jesus upon them, and to make the natives see that their old gods are powerless. But sometimes they try to rescue their gods, or even to secrete them, whole and blessed by their incense and flowers, within the walls, to counteract the power of the Cross. You must be vigilant to watch for these things, and you are never to wait for first Friday, but come to me at once to report if you find any evidence of pagan activity. Is it understood?"

"It is understood. But, Father," continued Juan, "could you not give us some idea of where we might lodge and eat? We haven't any money at all, nor do we know the city."

"I will take you to the house of a good Christian woman who provides meals for little money, and you may sleep where you will be working for us. There will be places where you can shelter. Come with me now, so that I may get you started."

Juan and Fermín followed with high hearts.

In the meanwhile, Captain Trout stood before the Inquisitors to hear his sentence.

"You are to receive instruction in the True Faith from Fray Domingo, who will visit you in your cell every day at an hour to be arranged. It is devoutly to be hoped that you will repent and accept the Faith before you die."

"I am a Christian, but no Papist. I will not change," answered Trout. His usually stout figure had wasted to gauntness, but he stood very straight.

"You are to be given the opportunity to save your soul," went on Fray Francisco, "in which case you will be given a speedy death. Otherwise you will be given alive, to the flames. In any case, you are to be burned until nothing is left of you but ashes."

Trout heard his sentence without moving. Then he gathered spittle in his mouth, and expelled it toward the judges. The guards at once felled him from behind with a blow to the ear.

"Revive him," ordered Fray Francisco.

Water was brought and poured upon the prone man. He was

prodded to his feet. In silence, he was led from the courtroom and taken back to his cell.

Fray Francisco felt a gentle rubbing against his ankle, and then a soft sound, between a mew and purr. In pleasure, he lifted Andúfar to his knees, and stroked him. He felt something sticky by the cat's ear and, bending close, he saw that Andúfar had been injured.

"The Court will conduct no further Inquiries today," he announced, and rising, he carried Andúfar into his own small cell, where he cleaned and put medicine on the cat's wound, speaking softly and affectionately to the animal, which lay quiescent under his hand, even though the medicine stung.

17.

Gonzalo lived for his visits to the Acevedos. His avid mind, of a literary turn, and much given to poetic musing, found sustenance in the reading of the great Psalms and of much other material which Don José Acevedo declaimed, on some occasions. Sometimes, when there was a new visitor, the old man sent word that he felt very ill, and would keep to his bed.

Isabel, who had seemed to him to be middle aged and worn, on first appearance, began to change notably. Her hair, which had been gray, was now a raven black; she had dyed it with the juice from a cactus, which had been sold her for that purpose by an Indian woman in the market. Instead of her nondescript gray clothes, or rough homespun, now she often wore her dress of bottle-green velvet, with a ruffle of cream lace at the neck and wrists. Her large eyes, which Gonzalo saw were a light green, were often on him. Her looks were usually amorous, for she had fallen in love with him, but at the same time she feared him, because she did not fully trust him.

Gonzalo began uneasily to become aware of her intense interest in him. One evening, when he was the only visitor, he tried to entice her into conversation.

"You must be lonely for women friends," he commented. "Have you no sisters, or other relatives, to help you in the house?" He knew that the Acevedos lived very simply, without servants.

"My two sisters are married. One is living in Nuevo León, and the other in Zacatecas."

"Undoubtedly they are friends of Dr. Morales."

"Yes, we all are. And you, of course."

"He has opened the door for me to a new life, and given me hope. Studying the Jewish faith of my ancestors, and returning to their ways, I feel strength and virtue again. I was so miserable! And the Christian saints did not help me."

"Why, do you have some deep trouble? An illness?"

"Not an illness of the body."

"Of the soul, then?"

"Yes."

Isabel had turned an ugly dark red, but she persisted.

"An unhappy love?"

"Yes."

"She is married?"

Gonzalo looked up at her. The pale-green eyes were intense. An instinct to dissemble made him say, "Yes. Lost to me."

"Time will heal you," she suggested softly.

"Why have you not married, Doña Isabel?"

"I am needed to care for my father," she answered. "But when I marry, I must be very sure that my household will be pure, uncontaminated. And many men," she went on, angrily, "come here to the New World, and pretend that they are marriageable, and they look for wives and dowries. But at home, in Spain or Portugal, they already have wives, and families! It is iniquitous!"

"Indeed the Inquisition . . . the Holy Office . . . is terribly severe with them whenever it has a proven case."

Isabel now turned pale.

"What do you know of the Holy Office?" she asked, in a choked voice.

"Only that they are very vigilant, and they never give up," he answered, sadly. "I have seen an auto-da-fé. Have you?"

"No. God forbid," she whispered.

Don José Acevedo appeared, from his inner room, and said, "I think it wise that we be seen together in church. Could you meet me here tomorrow morning, and go with us to mass?"

"I will do it if you wish."

"We must. The spies of the Holy Office have made some inquiries about me. I have been made aware of them. I will not receive young people for visits or readings again for some time, and we must all be seen at mass. Those are my instructions," he added sternly.

"I will obey," murmured Gonzalo, taking his leave.

Walking home along the canal, he pondered his situation, and he recalled again the unholy scene of the auto-da-fé. He had been very young, in his teens, when the procession took place through the streets of the city, the heretics and blasphemers dressed in the high conical hats and painted tunics of the sanbenito, or penitential garment. There were four of the wretches, one of whom had been broken on the rack until he could no longer walk, and had to be taken to the place of execution on a mule. They carried candles and chanted prayers as they walked, and the guards occasionally flicked at their legs with whips.

The procession, observed, it seemed to Gonzalo, by all the city, wound its way to the square in front of the Church of San Juan. There a great platform had been built in two sections. The lower section was draped in black velvet, and there, in their black robes, sat three Inquisitors. Above them were seats for spectators, especially the notables of the city—the Viceroy and his family, his subordinates, and many of the heads of the important families, as well as the military, and minor clergy. Hundreds of spectators sat around under the trees of the shady Alameda, where Gonzalo himself stood, waiting, with terror and fascination, for the final rites of the ceremony.

An altar had been set up, topped by a crucifix, beneath the seats of the judges of the Holy Office, and black-robed celebrants moved about, chanting the sacred words, while the prisoners knelt. Three stakes were ready, and close by each one, chains to bind the men, and stacks of resinous wood that would catch fire at once.

Gonzalo could recall the hour of the mass, the growing excitement and fear of the entire crowd. He remembered hearing one of the prisoners plead for mercy, vowing to Jesus and Mary and all the saints, that he was a Christian, and would never again fail in his duties. Nevertheless, he was led away and bound to one of the stakes, after the last blessing of the mass.

Then Gonzalo had seen that one of the masked executioners whipped out a flexible wire, and from behind, passed it around the weeping man's throat, and strangled him. It was over in a moment, and the body slumped within its chains.

One of the four prisoners had not been chained to a stake; he stood apart. Gonzalo had asked about him, of one of the crowd nearby.

"Won't he be burned too?"

"He has been pardoned. They will flog him . . . fifty lashes . . . and he will be sent back to Spain, to prison. But watch! Now the torches are being set to the wood!"

Gonzalo could remember no more except a feeling of sickness, and a smell of burning flesh. His own horror had erased most of that final scene from his mind. Walking home, he made an effort to recall it, but he could not.

"It was too cruel to watch," he murmured under his breath. "In my new faith, we do not torment those who do not agree with us. I am strong in my new faith." And intensely, but silently, and with all his heart, he said, "Hear, O Israel, the Lord my God is One!"

Nevertheless, as he remembered the terrible fear and excite-

ment of that auto-da-fé, he trembled, and the thought intruded,
But am I really strong? He forced the thought away.

18.

On the road to Taxco, the charcoal burner had seemed to be on
his way south to the port of Acapulco, from whence the Manila
galleons set out across the Pacific for Spain's other lands in the
Orient. But he did not continue to the south. With his mute companion, still driving one burro, still powdered with the black
dust of the charcoal, they set out upon another trail, across the
mountains. They slept at night under the stars, wrapped in their
woolen sarapes, crowding close to the tired little beast's warm
flank; they ate simple barley bread and drank water, unless they
were invited to share some villager's boiled beans. Eventually
they came out upon the Puebla road, and then they hurried toward Veracruz. Dr. Morales was planning to return to Europe. In
order to do so, he had to change his disguise, and he had pondered, during the long walk across the mountains, just how he
might accomplish this, and also deceive the spies of the Inquisition, who were on the watch for him.

Making his way to the home of a trusted friend, who, though a
devout Jew, had protected himself and his family by taking Holy
Orders and acting as priest in a small parish in the city, Dr. Morales passed an evening of great spiritual delight. For behind
drawn curtains, and in perfect peace, he and his friend, Father
Pablo, washed themselves and ate, prayed and sang together.
Dr. Morales explained that he must walk most carefully for fear
of the Holy Office.

"But, my dear friend," answered Father Pablo, "they are afraid
of *you* now! They have almost caught you, so often, and always

you slip away! They think now that you are the Wandering Jew!"

"And so I am," agreed Dr. Morales, with a wry smile. "In case they are looking for me, as a man traveling with one black slave, I would like to ask you to keep Gomo for me for a few months. Can this be done without endangering you? He can make himself useful. And you know that he is mute."

"He must not stay with me. But I can place him in the home of a lady who needs household help. He need not be seen about on the streets. But you, how will you manage to take passage again?"

"As a Spanish gentleman, but blind. You will see, my friend, that with the eyes covered, one is not easily recognizable. I will use a black bandage."

"But something you can see through?"

"No. I shall indeed be blind, for a time. It is the only way in which I can be completely . . . authentic . . . shall we say? I have some drops, which will close my eyes temporarily. What I shall need is a white companion-nurse. Can you find such a one for me, who would like to cross the sea and visit Italy?"

Father Pablo sat, swaying back and forth. In his small quiet house, there was no one to see, to watch, or to listen.

"I will have to have a few days for this. But I believe I will be able to find someone."

Bathed at last, and in clean garments, Dr. Morales slept deeply that night.

My hour has not come, he thought gratefully, as he turned on his bed and slept again in the hour before dawn. The bells of Father Pablo's chapel were announcing the first mass.

Some ten days later a soberly dressed Spaniard, wearing a tall crowned black-velvet hat, with no plume, and a thick half cape, took passage on the galleon making the return voyage across the sea to Spain. He was accompanied by a pale young apothecary student who guided the elderly, failing Spaniard with great care, for he was blind.

19

Fainting along the road to Taxco, for she had not eaten for two days, a woman, in travel-stained and torn garments, staggered the last few leagues toward the white houses, with their red tiled roofs, which already showed against the green of the hills roundabout.

I will find some nuns here, she thought, and they will give me something to eat. But her strength failed her, and she fell to her knees on the stony road. There a miner found her, as he was returning home after his day's work, for his cottage was a little distance from the main town. He raised her and asked her her name. As he lifted her, he saw the finely wrought silver bracelet on her arm, with its fiery green stone. He thought, fleetingly, that she might easily sell it in Taxco, where the silversmiths would like to copy the design.

"My name is García Mendoza. Señora García Mendoza," she whispered. "I am looking for my husband."

"You are too weak to go on," he said.

The man was an Indian, coppery-skinned, with coarse stiff black hair, and a very scant beard.

"I am only hungry. I have not eaten."

Wordless, he opened his shoulder bag and took out a few tortillas that had been left over from his lunch. The woman took them eagerly, but not before she had thanked him, and blessed them, making the sign of the Cross over them.

"When you feel better, I will help you to find a place to stay," he said then.

"You are so kind. God bless you," she whispered. Then, after she had eaten, slowly, chewing each bite as if to extract the fullest savor from it, she said, "If there is a convent in the city, I could go there."

"I know where there are nuns. But wait here. My house is not far away. I will send my wife with a jar of something hot for you to drink." And he strode away swiftly before she could ask his name.

Sara's experiences on the road had taught her that there are many who are unexpectedly generous and compassionate, and many who are deceitful, cold, and evil. She sat to wait on a rock by the roadside, thinking that if the miner did not return within a half hour, he had not intended to, and she would struggle on into the town alone.

It was a lovely countryside and she had learned to take joy in the beauties her eyes revealed to her each day. She looked across a chasm, filled to the brim with ferns and climbing vines that broke into sky-blue flowers, to where the green wooded hills rose in endless lines as far as she could see. The town, white against the intense green, shone with brilliance in the last rays of the descending sun. Sara sat entranced, watching the shadows fall swiftly, and suddenly she was aware of a presence by her side. A woman stood beside her with a steaming clay jar of some drink that smelled of herbs and flowers. She offered it shyly, making friendly gestures, and Sara took it gratefully. She drank slowly, feeling a delicious warmth steal over her. When she had drained the jar, the woman handed her, again with gestures and looks, a package of fresh tortillas, still warm from her hands and from the pan on which they had been cooked. They were spread with a paste that tasted salty, but which seemed to Sara the most delicious food she had eaten in months. She said, "You are so kind and good. Tell me your name, so that I may bless you in my prayers, every day for the rest of my life."

The woman cast down her eyes and shook her head and Sara realized that she did not speak Spanish. However, she put out a small dark hand, and patted Sara softly on the shoulder. Then she pointed toward the town, and started forward on the road. Sara understood that she was to follow. Painfully she rose to her feet and took the first steps, gathering strength as she went. The

Indian woman, in her voluminous skirts, with her hair in two
tight braids, kept patting and encouraging her. The short walk
took some time, but as darkness and the chill of night fell
upon the two women, they arrived at a doorway, and the Indian
woman beat upon it with strong small fists. A little window at
the top, protected by an iron grill, opened, and a face seemed to
float in the aperture. Sara spoke.

"I am a poor Christian soul, needing shelter for the night,
and this kind woman has brought me here. Will you open to me,
in the name of Jesus?"

The door slowly swung open and Sara passed through. As she
turned to thank her guide, the woman had disappeared, melting
into the darkness.

"I come from the Dominican nuns in Puebla," Sara told the
dark-robed nun who had opened to her. "My name is Sara
García Mendoza, and I have been walking the roads of this
country searching for my husband."

The nun pressed a finger against her lips, but signaled for Sara
to follow.

She learned that this was an order of religious devoted to silent prayer for many hours in the day, but the Madre Superiora
spoke with her, and extracted from Sara the story of her long
wearisome search, and her sufferings on the road.

Sara remained there for several weeks, going out every day
to ask among the silversmiths who were working at benches in
the square, about her husband. For her keep, she worked for the
nuns, who supported themselves by doing the washing of the
many men who toiled in the mines.

Sara grew strong again, with regular food. As soon as she
could, sustained by hope and prayers, she made farewells, and
started out on the road to Mexico City.

20

Juan and Fermín worked at the construction, as Fray Domingo had ordered them to do, and listened to his teaching daily.

The walk to the Hospital de Jesús, where they were to work, was a pleasant one, along one of the main canals. Barges were coming into the city in the early morning, just after sunup, loaded with fresh vegetables, and with flowers. From both there wafted across the water a gentle fragrance. The rainy season had come to an end, and the days were bright with a thin golden sunlight. Nights had grown colder, and both Juan and Fermín had begged permission to use a few maravedis of their pay to buy woolen ponchos, and Fray Domingo had gone with them to the great *tianguis*, where they had bought them. As they walked silently beside Fray Domingo (both Juan and Fermín wore cloth shoes, with rope soles, bound on around their legs, with strips of woolen cloth), Juan began to sing a ballad he remembered.

"Hush, hush," cautioned Fray Domingo. "You are under sentence. Do not, I beg of you, make it appear that the punishment was not harsh enough! Can't you sing a religious song?"

"Oh yes, I will sing Amen!" And trilling and turning around the syllables, with flourishes and cadences that he made up, Juan walked along singing, almost happy. He was young, the morning was fair, and the idea of helping care for the wounded appealed to his tender heart.

Fermín trod by his side, serious and sad. He was planning to ask for permission to go and search for his wife, but he could not decide whether to ask boldly and no doubt be refused, or to wait and beg the favor, as a reward for good behavior. Or to run away. His mind played around the latter idea most frequently, as he realized how easy it would be to escape Fray Domingo, who had gained back his plumpness, and who breathed hard even now, as they leaped over the rough stones of a new building being constructed. Heaps of materials had been dumped in the streets. The three skirted puddles and even clusters of women seated before their wares spread to sell: clay pots, copper jars, mounds of wild plums, little heaps of medicinal herbs.

The Hospital de Jesús, built and founded by Cortés, was always busy because of the continuous fighting against the savage and desperate tribes of the north. The Crown had trouble keeping its soldiers, and desertions were heavy, because the tribes, among them the Chichimecas and the Yaquis, were terribly cruel to captives, and whenever an encounter seemed to be going against the Spanish arms, the soldiers were few indeed who stood and fought to the end. The wounded streamed into Mexico City steadily, and even as far away as half a league, one could hear the groans and cries of the men enduring amputations, or the swabbing and cleansing of festered wounds. The smell of sickness and corruption, too, came out to meet the three as they drew near to the entrance corridors.

A friar sat at a desk in the doorway, to ask their business, and write down their names. Fray Domingo bustled Juan and Fermín through these preliminaries, and turned them over to a thin, bony friar, who wore his sleeves turned up as far as his shoulders, and whose apron, arms, and hands were bloody.

As they passed the doorway of one enormous hall, where nuns were working over women on pallets on the floor, Fermín gave a strangled cry and broke away. He went hurriedly into the room and seized a slender dark-haired woman who was feeding broth to a sick patient. In his eagerness, he caused her to spill the broth, and she looked up at him with an angry cry. It was Judit, who, with Guiomar, was carrying out the duties imposed by the Holy Office.

"I beg pardon, I am so sorry . . . I thought, for a moment, that you were my wife, the wife I have lost," began Fermín. But a stern nun came toward him, and swung him around, and directed him to the door.

"Leave at once," she ordered. "You have no business in here."

Juan, who had witnessed this scene, stood transfixed, and had to be taken by the arm, and shaken, quite severely, by Fray Domingo. For he had seen Guiomar.

"My lady of the *Paloma del Mar*," he murmured. "Now God be thanked, for bringing me near her again, my lovely maiden, my apple-blossom lady, with the copper hair!"

As he was dragged down the corridor by Fray Domingo, who was much mortified by the behavior of his two charges, Guiomar looked up from a tray of bandages she was carrying and stared straight into Juan's blue eyes.

Juan did not see her again for several days, though he kept himself alert for every chance that might bring them momentarily face to face. But now Guiomar's face was again in all his dreams, and in all his thoughts.

21.

Fray Francisco had hoped that his letter asking to be allowed to remain at his post a year or two longer, might be acted upon favorably. His departure would leave Fray Artemio in charge of many Inquiries, under guidance of the Grand Inquisitor, and Fray Francisco had no confidence in him at all. In fact, he despised him for a lecherous and a bad priest, and he also feared that the power of the Holy Office, in hands such as Fray Artemio's, would result in misuse. Fray Francisco felt deeply that the Faith must be preserved in its purity and loyalty in the New World, and that all who underminded it with treachery, with heresy, or with witchcraft, should be made extreme examples of and severely punished. The New World was populated by indigenous peoples who should be brought into the Faith; New Spain must become a bulwark of Catholicism. Fray Francisco had scrupulously followed the law in regard to the Holy Office. The Indians were never to be brought before the Inquisition; all to be tried must be given every opportunity to defend their behavior, or, if they had erred, they must be urged back into proper devotion with instruction and with carefully chosen penalties. Naturally, if they were defiant and irreconcilable, they must be destroyed before they could do any more harm with their errors to other Christian souls. This Trout, for example. He must be sent to the stake. But the young woman Guiomar, who had spoken up so boldly (something Fray Francisco did not approve of), was undoubtedly the victim of some jealous woman who hated her for her beauty. The judges of the Holy Office must be firm, absolutely chaste, and honorable. Fray Artemio, he thought for the hundredth time, would bring the honor of the Inquisitional Court very low.

But Fray Francisco received no answer to his pleading for an extended stay. He was ordered back to Spain and he must go.

At least, he thought, when I am in Spain I will explain my reasons for distrusting Fray Artemio and I hope they will recall him. I will beg my superiors to take more care in selection of their judges.

Begging pardon of the saints for his lack of charity, he dismissed the matter from his mind, and began preparations for his journey. The first thing that had to be done was to design and have made a carrying box for Andúfar.

While Fray Francisco went out to find a carpenter who could build what he wanted, Fray Artemio began going over the cases pending in the Court. The list was long, beginning with all the accused who had been "reconciled," in the words of the Holy Office, and were receiving instructions from the priest to whom they were required to report weekly, and continuing with the tried and sentenced who were to be returned to prison in Spain. He noted that there was only one who might be burned, in an auto-da-fé. Fray Artemio was determined to organize a great auto-da-fé, and for this he needed more than one recalcitrant heretic.

He made careful comments, writing in his beautiful hand on fine sheets of vellum, and going through the lists name by name. The police and spies of the Holy Office were urged to redouble efforts in order to find, and bring in for Inquiry, any and all suspicious persons.

I might even, he mused, burn some of these heretics in effigy if they cannot be found. And dig up and burn the bodies of others, on whom proof was found too late, to punish them in life. In this way, I think I might prepare a great auto-da-fé by the spring.

Again he went over the lists, noting especially the women who had been accused. Calling in his clerk, he required that the women who had been denounced be visited again, in order to learn their ages.

"We must examine these first, of course," he explained virtuously, "because, being young, they have their lives to live, and must be made firm in the Faith before any more time goes by."

Yet, to his disappointment, the first woman to be brought for questioning was a dry, middle-aged creature, trembling with terror, her face all blotched and swollen with tears.

"Your name?" he asked, coldly.

"Isabel Acevedo."

"You are accused of being a Judaizer. What have you to say in answer to this?"

Isabel fainted.

"Revive her," ordered Fray Artemio.

Water was thrown on her, and sobbing and shivering, she began reciting prayers, in a loud, hysterical voice.

Fray Artemio listened for a while.

"Strip her," he ordered. Sometimes these old women were still appetizing, naked.

Isabel resisted frantically, struggling against the guards, who ripped her blouse down the front and pulled it about her hips. She stood trying to cover herself with her hands, weeping desperately.

She was nothing to look at. Her breasts were flaccid and with dark nipples and aureoles. Unpleasant.

"Are you a Judaizer?"

Often, in order to save themselves from further exposition to the eyes of men, these women would break down and confess at once. But Isabel shouted, "No! No! I swear by Jesus and Mary, by all the saints, by my immortal soul, that I am a True Christian!"

Fray Artemio considered. He had had experience with Judaizers in Spain, and he flattered himself that he could smell them, right through all their pious pretense.

"Let her go," he ordered, not looking up, as she hastily tried to cover herself and adjust her torn clothes. She was pushed toward the door, and looking about, in fear, she finally understood that she was free to go. Then she hurried out, stumbling in her haste, and she ran through the streets, crying. Deep instinct told her not to go straight home. Instead, she went into a church, flung herself on her knees, and remained, as in prayer, for a long time.

She was watched, and finally followed to her home, when she had at last decided that it might be safe to go. Fray Artemio had said, "Follow that woman and keep watch on her. I want to know the names of everyone who goes to her house, and every house she visits."

Fray Artemio reflected, comfortably, that he would catch many in his net through this Isabel Acevedo. The more desperate and vociferous they are, the more likely it is that they Judaize, he thought. Now that bold one who answered back, the beautiful one, I believe she is a Christian. He stopped going over his lists for a few moments, in order to give himself the pleasure of remembering her. Lovely, he thought. I wish . . . But no. Fray Francisco had ordered her to confess to Fray Felipe. Well, there would be other ways. Other occasions. He returned to his lists.

22

Guiomar worked among the wounded at the hospital with much skill, and even stayed longer than she was required to do. Judit was clumsy, and made ill by the sight of blood (a weakness Guiomar had overcome), and the nuns in charge sent her instead to help in the kitchen, and to wash dishes. As Guiomar bandaged, or helped hold heads while dressings were removed, or wounds swabbed with caustic, she often thought of the young man with the blue eyes, who had looked at her with such joyful recognition. She did not remember him.

If he is sent here to work also, he has been suspected, as I was, she thought. But I wonder what he might have done to arouse the ire of the Holy Office. He is not a Jew, certainly. Perhaps he is a Lutheran. She came to this thought reluctantly, for she had been taught that the Lutherans were the most heinous of traitors to Holy Church, and they constantly worked trying to destroy the Faith. They were even worse than the Judaizers, who, from all she had been able to learn, merely wanted to be let alone, and never tried to destroy anything.

She met him in the corridor one day as she was hurrying away with soaked and sodden bandages. He was on his knees, in a puddle of dirt and foam, washing the floor. He swept a wave of it away, so as not to soil her shoes as she passed. She remembered then that she had nursed him and cured him when they were on the road to Puebla. So! He was one of the pirates! An English pirate. A Lutheran! But he had whispered that he was innocent.

It seemed that the young man read her thought, for he said, aloud, "I am a devout Christian, lady. Trained in a seminary. I am Irish; we are strong Catholics!"

Guiomar listened, she smiled, but she made no answer. It was not seemly to be surprised in conversation with anyone but the doctors and the nuns.

And yet she began to look for him whenever she was on duty at the hospital. And soon she learned how to know where he might be, for he began singing, and she could hear the sweet, lilting voice. Sometimes he sang in Spanish, sometimes in Latin, and sometimes in a strange tongue she did not know.

As for Juan, he blessed the Holy Office for making it possible to see her, to mark where she stepped, to gather up into his memory visions of her bending over a sick soldier, washing filthy arms and hands, and drying sweaty brows, of Guiomar hurrying, with her swift graceful step through the corridors. He sang from a full heart, and his prayers at night, and during the day, were that the saints should somehow contrive that he might speak to her again, might be near her, for a little time.

Guiomar, too, began to think often of the young Irishman who had been captured by the pirates. She believed him when he averred that he had the True Faith. Because she was curious about him, she allowed herself to linger, when he passed, with baskets of filthy clothes, and dressings, which he had to wash in the patios.

Impulsively she asked, "May I know your name, young sir?"

"My name is Juan Palomar. That is, that is the way I turned my real name into Spanish. My baptismal name is Columb. I was given the name of an Irish saint. To serve you, my lady."

"My name is—"

"I know your lovely name, Doña Guiomar. I bless it every day, for your kindness, and your beauty."

She dropped her eyes then, ashamed of having been so bold and immodest, and hurried away. But Juan sang joyfully the long day, as he soaked the bloodied and filthy cloths and garments in water mixed with the ground root of a plant that gave off a hissing foam that lathered better than soap. The solution was hard on the hands; even Juan's hands, used to the sun and to rough work, felt the sting of the *amole*. But he felt little, because he was thinking of Guiomar, of the velvety darkness of her eyes, of the red full-lipped mouth, of the little dimple near her eye.

Guiomar, walking back home with Judit after their labors, longed to speak about Juan, but she decided to keep silent. It was difficult. Time and again, she caught herself about to make some confidence to her sister-friend, but she bit the words back. They were under surveillance, spies were everywhere, and many a wretch in prison had done nothing worse than speak carelessly, she knew. She had heard the workmen in her patio talking, and she had questioned Gonzalo.

I must not even stop to speak to him anymore, she resolved.

As for Gonzalo, he suffered keenly that Guiomar was under suspicion by the Inquisitors, for he did not for a moment believe that her labors in the hospital would exonerate her. On the contrary, he had heard rumors, at the Acevedo house, that the new Inquisitor was the worst Mexico had had. The others had been fanatical, but just, according to their laws and regulations. But this Fray Artemio was known to be as lecherous and tricky as he was cruel.

Isabel had told the scholars studying Hebrew with her father that Fray Artemio took the form of a black bat at night and flew about the city, making his way into the bedrooms of the young virgins and listening to every word men said to each other while drinking in the taverns. He played with his victims like a cat with a mouse, she told them. He let them think they were free, but he had them followed and spied upon incessantly. Her voice trembled and she rolled her eyes upward, as she said these things.

Don José, who preferred to teach while in bed, sat straighter against his cushions.

"He is evil, yes, but he does not become a bat," he admonished his daughter.

"But he does! And he follows me everywhere! I am tortured, for I see his eyes everywhere! And someone—one of your pupils perhaps?—" she cried, "betrayed me. Else why should they ever suspect me? I am daily at mass, and at evening service."

Don José said, "We are in danger, all of us. It would be better not to meet here anymore. But I will lend you my precious books for your private study. I have four. You must take turns. Arrange to meet in church; then one who has studied can pass on the book to another one. And now, leave us. One by one."

He turned to the wall, and would not say another word.

Isabel let them out quietly, first two, then later three, then one. They all thought that they were unseen, that they were taken for simple young men, out for a drink or a game, or a quarrel, in the night streets.

Isabel had told her father of her experience before the Inquisitors, but she had not said that she thought Gonzalo had betrayed her.

Gonzalo, though he felt himself deeply committed to his new faith, which was of course, the old faith, had hoped his dedication to the disciplines and austerities it required would exorcise his forbidden love. With devotion he recited his prayers mentally; on Fridays he fasted, usually by pretending to have business outside the city, so that no one would notice. Though pork was often served at home, he managed to avoid it.

Guiomar, since her father's death, had turned to him more and more completely, and with innocent love kissed him in greeting, and for farewell.

Gonzalo longed for Dr. Morales, who could guide him and steady him. In the meanwhile, he poured out his troubled heart in verses. These were usually philosophical in tone, as he tried to strengthen himself and remake his thoughts and sentiments around some figure other than his sister. But sometimes he wrote erotic love poems, unable to stop himself, though he never mentioned the name of his beloved.

Guiomar saw him writing, changing words, thinking, drawing consolation from the tasks he set himself. She never disturbed him, though she shyly asked if he would read his work to her. He refused, somewhat curtly. This gave her the sudden illumination that he was indeed writing love poems. She decided that, of course, the verses must be inspired by Judit.

Gonzalo felt that he could not leave the two girls alone in the house, after his father's death, before he had found and trained another guard besides Epifanio. He went to the slave markets whenever they occurred, but he had not yet found the strong, sensible sort of man he felt he could prepare to defend them in his absences.

Cut off from his evenings with the Acevedos, he sometimes visited a friend or two whom he had met in the old rabbi's house, but usually they seemed to meet by chance in the street. Sometimes, they met by appointment, usually inside a church.

The churches were multiplying all over the city, replacing the first quickly thrown up edifices. Now the cathedral was finished, and there were other splendid churches within easy walking distance in many sections of the city. For these meetings in a temple, where they would whisper together, the students of Rabbi Acevedo never chose churches near where they had formerly met, in his house. They never saw Isabel, who tried to go about her daily duties as if nothing had happened. But she was terrified, not only for herself but also for her old father, whom she idolized.

She thought about Gonzalo constantly, and wept often. She loved him, and she had nourished hopes that he might notice her, even ask to marry her. His pale oval face, his great dark eyes, his slimness and grace, obsessed her. At the same time, she constantly fought the fearful anxiety that he might have betrayed her. Her emotions undermined her health, and she fell ill of a strange fever, which sapped her strength and ate away the momentary bloom her love had bestowed.

Gonzalo feared the Inquisition, but his newfound faith demanded a fierce loyalty of him—loyalty, plus secrecy, skill at dissembling, and courage. All these things appealed to his fervent heart. He wanted to be worthy of the men who taught him and who risked torture and death to do so.

The thought came to him that he must be circumcised, so that he could bear in his flesh the sign of his faith, the mark that

united him to all who believed as he did. But for some time, this
thought was merely a passing fantasy.

Once, on a cold and wet evening, when he came home very
late to the house on Curtidores Street, Guiomar, who had been
worried, threw her arms around him, and begged him, tearfully,
not to worry her so again. His physical response to her round
warm arms, the loving expression on her face, frightened him. He
could not control himself. He decided then, that when Dr. Morales returned (as he had promised to do), he would ask him to
carry out the circumcision.

23.

Judit saw that Guiomar lingered in the corridor whenever she
had to pass through it, with dressings, or to perform some errand
for the surgeons. Often another worker in the hospital, now pro-
moted from washing floors to assisting the surgeons at their amputations because of his youthful strength, would contrive to
pass at the same time, and always he leaned his black head toward her, and whispered a few words. These always brought a
blush of deepest crimson to Guiomar's neck and cheeks.

If only Gonzalo would look at me like that, she thought, for
the hundredth time, as she saw Guiomar and Juan pass each
other once more.

Gonzalo had changed so much since the first days when she
had known him, on the road from Veracruz to Mexico City. He
had become deeper, more serious, and somehow more secretive.
She thought that this must be simply part of the masculine character. Having been brought up by a widow and carefully kept
away from contact with strange men by her vigilant mother, she
had known only Dr. Morales, Gonzalo, and Don Pedro Montemayor. Not one of those three had revealed to her, openly, the

essence of masculinity—Dr. Morales because he lived many lives within the disguises of others, Gonzalo because he was torn in emotional confusion by his forbidden love, and now by his forbidden religion, as well, and Don Pedro because he had been sick, able to think only of his infirmities.

Judit longed passionately to become a part of the life of another person, not in the role of sister to Guiomar, but as the wife or the love of a man, into whose strange fascinating world she would be taken integrally, to be part of him, of his body, and of the pattern of his existence. Gonzalo, whose sporadic attentions to her had seemed to promise that metamorphosis, was in her thoughts constantly. She listened for his footstep, and for his voice. She took tender pride in washing and starching his shirts, and mending the laces he wore at his cuffs. She knit hose for him, and put her dreams and hopes into every stitch, as she sat with Guiomar, talking about the workmen in the patio who were stitching and pressing designs into the leather, or about the cook and the kitchen slaves. Under all her daily life, with its ordinary tasks and duties, lay the fabric of her imagined conversations with Gonzalo, and, as time went by, her timid but ardently dreamed scenes of love.

24.

Guiomar began to think very often of the young Irishman. His open, declared devotion embarrassed her, because she had no experience of men, and felt sure she should not even listen. Yet, deep inside, she felt a little fountain of happiness, of joy in being admired and sought. She determined to consult Gonzalo about this, for Juan Palomar had begged her to agree that he might call on her when their sentences imposed by the Inquisition tribunal had been satisfied.

The fact that both of them had fallen into the bad graces of the Inquisition shadowed everything with a combination of resentment and fear. It might be wise, she knew, for she had a strong practical sense, to have nothing whatever to do with anyone who had been subjected to the Inquisition. And yet an instinct for justice worked to make her determined to live courageously, and not to allow anything or anyone to force her into behaving like a craven. November had passed, and the weather had turned cold, though the sun shone most of the day. It was a thin, fine sunlight, which did not warm the stones of the buildings, and in the shade one felt miserably stricken, especially if the wind was blowing. Nights were bitter, and people retired very early to their beds, to wrap themselves in sarapes and fur rugs, to keep out the chill.

In the house on Curtidores Street it was not long after sundown, one day in winter, and Guiomar had heated clay basins of water to hissing, and carried one into each bedroom, to try to heat the air while they changed from heavy day clothing into their night dress. Busy about her tasks, she did not hear the discreet knocking on their *zaguan*, but Gonzalo, who slept in a bedroom nearer the front entrance, did. He had retired, but he rose, taking his bed coverings with him, still wrapped about his body. At the door, he cried, "Ave María Purísima! Who is there?"

"Sin pecado concebida," came the answer, in the known and loved voice, and Gonzalo joyfully threw back the bars and opened to Dr. Morales. He slipped in quietly, followed by Gomo. They were wearing thin and dirty white cotton garments and huaraches on their cold bare feet.

"Come! You are frozen! Come into the kitchen!" cried Gonzalo. "Welcome! I am overcome with happiness to see you again!"

Dr. Morales laid an admonitory finger across his lips, and Gonzalo lowered his voice.

"Let me change, before the young ladies see me," he whispered. Gonzalo hastily led the two into his bedroom and shut the door. The basin of hot water had dispersed a little heat and steam, which was comforting for the doctor as he stripped and washed. In the pack which Gomo had been carrying on his back were warm woolen clothes, in the doctor's customary dark homespun. Gomo, too, took off the soiled cotton he was wearing, and put on plain dark clothes. The two men drew chairs close to the pot of hot water, and talked softly.

"I was desperate to hear from you," confided Gonzalo. "We have had so much trouble here. Guiomar and Judit were questioned by the Holy Office, and have been sentenced to labor in the hospital—"

"Why? Who accused them?"

"We don't know. Guiomar was accused of witchcraft and Judit of Judaizing. The accusation could not be proved, but the judge sent them to work at the Hospital de Jesús, anyhow. There was a farce of a judicial questioning . . ."

Dr. Morales wagged his head in confirmation of his distrust.

"They never set anyone free," he commented. "Never. Suspicion hangs over them forever. Now you will all be suspect. Everyone in this household."

"And all the Acevedos," went on Gonzalo. "They questioned Isabel, too, and stripped her—the monster strips every woman to the waist, to shame them, hoping to force confessions—but she was set free."

"Then God save us all. For if they set her free, they are having her watched, and we will all be caught in the net. We must leave at once, you and I. I knew I was needed; I thought I heard you calling me in my dreams. So I went only as far as Hispaniola, and then returned."

Gonzalo went to find Guiomar, and begging her to be brave, he made her sit and listen.

"We must leave at once, sister, and secretly, the doctor and I. Because, Guiomar, I have returned to the old faith. Dr. Morales is a rabbi, and I believe with him. I am a Jew."

Guiomar slipped to her knees, and joined her hands in an attitude of prayer. Tears streamed down her face. Shocked, at first she could not speak.

"No, my brother, no! You must not. You must hold firm to Jesus and the Church! I beg of you. Do not be misled, do not walk into this danger. Let the doctor go, if he must . . . Oh, stay and come back to mass with me. I beg of you!"

"No," was the calm answer. "I belong to my mother's faith and my mother's people. I will be faithful to her memory. I will be a good Jew."

"But the Inquisition! They meant to burn her! Oh no, Gonzalo. No, my brother . . ." And Guiomar could not hold back terrified sobs. She clung to his knees, and continued to implore, stammering in her distress, unable to contain her tears and her fear.

But he would not yield, and with terror she saw the determination in him.

"Then I will pray you back! I will pray every day and make sacrifices, and plead with the saints, and they will answer me, and they will save you!" she cried. "I will not rest until I have saved you!"

"No, sister. I only came to tell you that we must go. And why. I will take bread from the kitchen. You are to say only that I have gone to Veracruz to meet a ship and buy merchandise. Say that."

She threw her arms around him, to hold him close and kiss him goodbye. Gonzalo yielded, for one moment, to the joy of that sweet embrace. Then he loosed his sister's arms and slipped silently away.

Guiomar, in such distress that she could scarcely stand, feeling the world spin around her, made her way to the chapel and spent the night on her knees. The next day she would not eat, but was in church all the hours she did not have to work. At the hospital she went about her duties with glazed eyes, seeing no one. And again, she spent the night in intense prayer, falling asleep on her *reclinatorio* and awakening only to redouble her pleas to heaven and the saints.

Fainting and desperate, it seemed to her at last that she could take comfort.

Her mind and her body, rejecting the thought that Gonzalo had jeopardized his soul and had placed himself in awful danger, came to the belief that her prayers had been answered and that he was saved.

Then suddenly, she was able to eat and to resume her duties. But she said nothing to Judit, or to anyone about what had happened, nor of why she had been in such pain of spirit.

25.

Fermín and Juan had to report weekly to Fray Domingo, who counseled them, and made them recite the Confiteor and the Credo, and who dedicated himself wholeheartedly to the task of making sure that the two men would be loyal sons of the Church, upon their release.

Fermín had pondered for a week on how he might attempt to convince Fray Domingo to give him leave to go to Puebla to look for his wife. Wisely, he waited until Fray Domingo had heard their prayers and delivered his sermon, and had asked all the questions his conscience had dictated. Then he said, in a plaintive tone, "Father, I am so sad and desperate, some days, that I fear I may not survive."

"Why? How can this be?" inquired Fray Domingo, in great anxiety. He prepared his sermons with care, and devoted hours to the questioning and guiding of his wards. He longed to see them reinstated, in full devotion, to their Faith. He hoped to bask in the glory of having saved two Christian souls, for is it not written that he who saves another soul saves his own?

"I have no news of Sara, my wife, and you have told me that she suffered terribly under the domination of those monster step-brothers of hers. And that they put her into a well . . ."

"Yes, yes," answered Fray Domingo, with a shiver, as he re-

membered the awful time down in the pit, when he had despaired of getting out, and thought he must die there, like an
abandoned animal. "But," he said, "I told you that she was safe
now with the good nuns. As soon as your penitential work has
been completed, I will accompany you to Puebla, so that you
may identify her. However, my dear son, you should first find
some steady work, and have a home to which to take her. A delicate woman . . ."

Fermín interrupted impatiently. "Identify? You yourself said
she spoke of me, and that she has one gray eye and one brown!
How many beautiful women are there in the world, so marked
by God, different from any other? And my Sara is strong, she will
come with me wherever I go. Did you not say that she struggled
and worked with you until you could get out of the pit? Did you
not—"

"Yes, yes. All that is true. But you must think of other things.
When you reclaim your wife, you must form a home. There will
be little children, no doubt, and they have to be protected."

"Yes. But I must find her! I must see her! I must . . . I believe," pursued Fermín, insisting, "that Mother Catholic Church
would not approve keeping me from my lawful wife."

"But Mother Church has imposed your sentence. I am sorry,
my son. But how much time remains of your sentence? It will
soon be Christmas. Then there will remain seven months more.
Not so long, when you count it against a lifetime. I'll tell you
what I will do. I will go to the Inquisitor and plead for you and
ask that your sentence be shortened. This I promise!"

Juan had listened to this conversation in silence, but his heart
was full of hope for his comrade, and of envy, too. For Fermín
has married his love, thought Juan, even if now he is separated
from her. Whereas I . . .

He was determined to go to ask permission to court Guiomar,
but he was very conscious of his poverty and his lack of any
powerful patron to speak for him. And she, the lady Guiomar,
was daughter of a prosperous merchant, and sister of another.
Juan sighed.

That night, as he and Fermín lay shivering in their rugs in the lean-to near the church where they were working, Juan said, "You have only to be patient, my friend, and you will have your love in your arms again."

"You know nothing of love," answered Fermín, "if you think being patient is part of it. I have made up my mind to leave, to go to her."

"Oh no! You would be caught and sent back to the Inquisitor, and God knows what would happen then!" implored Juan. "Don't do it. Don't leave. It is better to conform, to placate the judges, to let them forget about you."

Fermín groaned and tossed.

"I know it. But Puebla isn't so far from the sea. We might be able to get to a ship . . . for Spain, or Peru, or Hispaniola . . . somewhere . . . before they caught up with us."

"And make your wife a fugitive too?"

He was answered only by another groan.

"Why not write to her?"

"I cannot write. I can make my name, and add and subtract, and read a little. But I cannot write. And maybe she cannot read. I don't know. Juan, I am thirty-four years old. I am old! And Sarita is not more than twenty. She was sixteen when we married. You know, as well as I, that most men die before fifty, and many in their forties. How much time does that leave me?"

"Still, if you are patient—"

"You say this because for you there is no alternative. The lady you long for is here, in Mexico, and you can see her, touch her hand as you pass by. I have watched you, and I have seen how you love her."

"I pray to her every night, as I pray to the angels and the Virgen María."

"She is beautiful."

"And she is good, and kind, and tender. I have watched her with the injured. And with the girl she has protected. I have listened to the gossip of the hospital, for any crumb of knowledge about her. The little dark one, Doña Judit, lost her mother on shipboard, and the lady Guiomar has been a loving sister to her ever since."

"And does the gossip mention any suitors?"

"Yes," admitted Juan. "They say a man high in the court of the Viceroy comes often just to look at Guiomar, and that as soon as her sentence and her mourning is over, he will ask for her."

"Mourning?"

"Yes. Didn't you notice that her clothes are all black? Against the dark color, her glorious hair and her clear skin are even more startling. And she has never had the pox. Not a scar. I had it. Look. Under my beard, and here on my forehead, you can see the marks. And on my shoulders. We all had it at the convent, and half died."

"I had it when I was a child. My mother told me. But I outgrew the pits."

And then they spoke, sleepily, of other things.

Juan was sad but not surprised when, a few mornings later, he woke to find himself alone. Fermín had gone, taking the road to Puebla.

26.

Tied in a thin cloth and bound against her body, covered by her voluminous clothes, Sara had money enough to buy bread and a drink of goat's milk, as she toiled along the mountain paths from Taxco until she came at last to the Acapulco highway, where the *diligencias* passed at intervals of several days. The walking was easier and once in a while she was offered a ride in some cart, or behind some gentleman who was traveling by horseback and wanted company. Sara never told her name nor where she was going but she always asked about towns where there were silver-smiths or metalworkers. To her dismay she learned that there were no more until she arrived in Mexico City, where there was

a whole street of *plateros,* or workers in silver. And her progress
was slow. By the time she reached a village where the workers
went out daily to tend the plantations of sugarcane, her money,
which she had saved so carefully, was almost gone, and she
knew that she must again seek work. There was no use asking
for employment in the miserable cottages where the peasants
lived; she was forced to take the long, tree-bordered road to the
stone palace where the rich *hacendados* lived who owned the
broad lands set out to the sugarcane.

The building was enormous, with towers on each side flanking
the broad expanse of stone. Along the flat roof were dozens of *al-
menas,* or battlements behind which defenders could shelter
while firing down at invaders. It was fortress, church, and habi-
tation for the *hacendado's* family. That it had been subjected to
attack was evident from the places on the façade where the thin
covering of clay or stucco had broken away, showing the rough
fieldstone of which the walls were constructed.

Sara hoped that there might be some work in the enormous es-
tablishment, but she knew she had to skirt the building and look
for some woman worker in the rear, where clusters of stone cottages and rooms and stables customarily could be found. As she
passed the side of the hacienda building, a pack of dogs came toward her, roaring defiance, though some of them wagged their
tails at the same time. This had happened to her before, so she
knew what to do. She stood perfectly still, and allowed the creatures to come to her, to sniff at her skirts and hands, and to decide that she meant no harm. She was frightened, because some
caporales, or hacienda managers, trained their dogs to fierceness,
and expected them to leap upon and tear unknown visitors. But
these animals evidently had been petted and cozened by someone, for even as they padded around her, looking at her with suspicious eyes and dropped ears, they continued a vague, propitia-
tory wagging.

A man dressed in the country clothes of the winter—tight
pants of woven striped wool, a dark woolen shirt and short
leather vest—appeared, and called to the dogs. When they had

left Sara and gone to mill around the man who called them, he approached her, and courteously asked what she wanted.

"Ave María," whispered Sara. "I am tired and hungry from the road, and I hope you may have some work that I could do for some food and a few centavos."

The man bowed his head, and murmured, "Purísima. But, señora, why are you on the roads? You do not seem to be an Indian. Have you met with some accident? Where are your people?"

"I have met with several accidents," answered Sara, "and I have been robbed. I go to seek my husband in Mexico City. But I am fainting, and my money is gone."

The man stared at her. The voluminous black skirts provided by the nuns in Puebla had been washed many times, and were dusty and faded, and around her black blouse she had wound a sarape in stripes of black and cream. Her long black hair lay in two thick plaits on her back. The wretched clothes could not hide her lissome strength of body, and her pale small face was lit by the strange eyes, large and expressive.

"This is the Hacienda de Nuestra Señora de la Purísima Concepción," he told her, "and we have no work here for strangers because the people who live on the hacienda lands do all the work. But you are welcome to our charity, for no strangers are ever turned away from here, without having eaten and rested."

"I am grateful," murmured Sara. "May I know your name?"

"Miguel Bonilla, to serve you. I am the *caporal* here."

"My name is Sara Duarte de García Mendoza," she answered.

"Welcome," he said again. "Follow me."

As he led Sara toward the rear patio where there was much activity—women washing, others preparing vegetables in enormous clay cooking pots held between their knees, men working at carpentry benches, and others at a forge—she felt drawn into a varied and active village life. Miguel Bonilla was thinking furiously that he would like to keep this lovely woman near, somehow. What could he devise that she might do?

"Come to the kitchens," he said, and he led her to where there was a group of three rooms, open at one side, with a row of tiled charcoal stoves set in a line, against the wall. A small Indian girl stood there, fanning the coals with a woven straw whisk.

At Bonilla's orders, the girl brought Sara a bowl of a stew made with meat and vegetables, and several tortillas. Bonilla brought a bench for her, and after making the sign of the Cross over the bowl and murmuring a prayer of thanks, Sara ate. The *caporal* seemed busy about giving orders in the stables and directing some work there, but he was conscious of her, saw her gratefully receive another helping of stew and eat slowly, savoring it, as a hungry person does, after the first hasty mouthfuls. As she finished, he appeared at her side and signed to her to follow him. He led her across the patio, scattering some chickens out of his way with his hat, and they skirted the rear buildings and outhouses. Sara saw that he was guiding her to the chapel, the doors of which stood open. Inside, there was an altar, on which candles burned, and a large crucifix hung above it. Four *reclinatorios*, upholstered in velvet, were evidently for the use of the patron; the workers no doubt stood, as there were no benches. Sara knelt and crossed herself, praying with fervor to be led to her love, her husband, to journey's end.

When she had finished her prayers and rose to her feet, Bonilla accompanied her outside.

"I have thought of something you might do. Are you a seamstress?"

"I can sew and embroider. But I have been doing very rough work. Look at my hands!" She held them out: the nails were broken and the fingers red and swollen, the skin chapped.

He smiled.

"A little oil or suet would fix your hands. If you care to stay a few days. I think we should have an embroidered altar cloth, and vestments for the priest to use, when he comes. Sometimes he brings only his holy oils."

"I can make such things for you. If you have the cloth and thread. And if I can soften my hands. Could I sleep where the women do?"

"Of course."

"And . . . while I will gladly do what I can to pay for my food, could you not spare me a little money, if my work is good? I shall need it to continue my journey."

"An embroidered vestment for the priest, and an altar cloth, would be worth much more than a few bowls of beans." He smiled again, and Sara dropped her eyelids. She saw something in his eyes that she had not seen before in all her journeying. Sara had walked with her face covered when she could but sometimes she had stood and sung for centavos, and men had approached her, and tried to ingratiate themselves. Indeed once, she had been overpowered and abused, but only once. Usually the travelers on the roads were as tired and hungry and hopeful of reaching food and a bed as she, and uninterested in dallying. But this man Bonilla looked at her with admiration and respect. I must not stay here long, she thought.

And yet she did. She made friends with the women servants, who told her the patron was severe but fair, and never stinted on their food. They ate meat every day except on the great fast days and during Lent, and the *caporal* was a good man, who never flogged the workers. There were other haciendas where life was a martyrdom, they told her, and some of the servants here at the Purísima had come to them, fleeing from other cane fields. The *patrona* was sickly, and they almost never saw her; only the house servants who waited on her told that she was gentle and uncomplaining, but that she could hardly walk, and lay most of every day on a couch, with her rosary in her hands.

Sara's hands softened, and she was able to pare her nails and even them around her fingertips. Linen cloth, silk, and velvet were brought to her, silk threads and silver and golden threads. Sara settled to her embroidery, sitting on a bench outside, in the shadow of the overhang from one of the balconies, so that her work was in good light, but not in the direct sunlight. Bonilla stopped by every evening, to see what she had done. So she remained at La Purísima through the Christmas celebrations, and through the New Year and through January.

27

Fermín had taken the Puebla highway, and he was not long in finding a place with a caravan on its way to Veracruz. Because of bandits, who so often lay in wait for travelers on that highway, almost any group of travelers was glad to add another man to its numbers. Fermín had no weapon, and was not given one, but numbers are impressive, and his duties were only to help with the horses, cut wood and bring water, help men harness, and grease the axles of the cart, whose wooden wheels screeched abominably by nightfall. He was strong and willing, and he had no trouble at all earning his keep as they progressed toward the coast. He became more and more nervous and excited, as the miles streamed out behind the caravan, until at last the mountains gave way to sunny plain, and Puebla of the Angels lay just ahead.

It was not difficult to find the convent of the Dominicans, and Fermín felt his heart almost ready to burst from his chest as he laid hold of the great knocker on the *zaguan,* and gave it three strong strokes. At last the small barred window within the heavy door opened, and a nun's face was framed within it.

"Hail Mary," she said. "What brings you here?"

"I am Fermín García Mendoza. Fray Domingo told me that my lady wife was lodged here with you good nuns. God bless you. I have come for her."

There was silence to answer him, and the small door of the peephole swung shut. Desperate, Fermín pounded again and again, with the knocker. At length, the small window opened once more, and another nun's face looked out at him with compassion.

"I am the Madre Superiora, my son. I regret to tell you that

Doña Sara left us more than three months ago. She insisted that she must go to seek you."

"But it can't be! She must be here! I have come for her!" he pleaded, unbelieving.

"As God listens to me, I am telling you the truth. I am very sorry, my son. God bless you." And the small window closed firmly.

Fermín knew that it would do no good to insist anymore. Overcome with disappointment, he sat down on the ground outside the convent door and wept.

"Which way could she have gone?" he mused at last, aloud. And he rose and knocked again, with all his might.

The small window opened.

"Which way did she go?" he asked quickly. "To the sea, or toward Mexico?"

The window closed. But this time Fermín waited, and in due course the Mother Superior's face again appeared.

"I cannot say for certain. But I believe she meant to go to Veracruz, to keep watch near the boats. How else? A lone woman on the roads . . . I begged her to stay, I assure you. But she was impatient. I am sorry."

Fermín could not make up his mind which way to go. At last he decided that Veracruz was nearer. He would go there first. And if he could not find her, then he must take the road for Mexico again, even though the Holy Office would be on the watch for him there.

It did not occur to him that Sara might try to find him in the towns where there were colonies of silversmiths, until he had reached Veracruz and spent many weary weeks helping load and unload the galleons that berthed there. When this thought suddenly crossed his mind, he set out for Taxco.

In the meantime, Sara had reached Mexico City at last, and had found asylum with the Dominican nuns there, who sheltered her for a time, and then recommended her to the household of a silk merchant, whose wife was delicate, and who longed for food cooked in the Spanish way. The merchant had despaired of teaching his Indian slaves to please his young wife, and Sara was employed to prepare for her delicate baked *flanes*, and *horchatas* made of ground almonds, and *alboronías*, cooked daintily without any chili. However, after a month of searching the silversmith shops and streets, and of going every morning at dawn to the main roads which departed for the coast, Sara left her employment, and took the road for Veracruz once more.

She did not really give up hope of finding Fermín, but the vision of their reunion faded gently into the mists which were growing thicker in her mind. She spoke little, only to ask her way or to beg a meal, or a place to lie down to sleep. Sometimes she sang on a street corner, and usually she could pick up a few coins that were thrown to her. She was not molested, for in time she was thought to be a madwoman, and the holy innocents are God's children, and should be fed and covered.

On the day she arrived in Puebla again, it was spring. And that day Fermín, in rags, with his feet bound in cloth, and sick with disappointment and rage, left Taxco, where he had been robbed of the earnings of the last month, and set out on the road back to Mexico.

Fray Domingo, during the months that Fermín was gone, had changed his mind many times. As an officer of the Inquisition, he was responsible for Fermín's soul, and no doubt he should have reported him at once, so that the police of the Holy Office would apprehend him. But Fray Domingo knew that Fermín was a distant relative (they were Mendozas) and he did not want their name to figure in the lists of heretics. Also, he truly wanted to save that unhappy soul, and so he had kept silent about the absence of his charge, waiting in daily hope for his return. However, as spring came in with its softer days, the time of Fermín's sentence to labor would soon be over, and Fray Domingo would be obliged to give an accounting of him.

Praying until his knees were sore and fasting until his usual plumpness had faded, he walked about, a small unhappy friar in folds of skin where fat had covered him pleasantly. He had made up his mind to give notice to the police at last, and was about to do so. Juan Palomar and he had spoken of Fermín many times, and Juan had promised on the Cross to advise Fray Domingo the moment he had any news of his absent comrade. On the very day that Fray Domingo meant to go to the Inquisition offices to denounce Fermín, Juan came to the Dominican convent to ask for the friar.

"He has come back," Juan said. "He is there, where I sleep, and he is very sick."

28.

Gaspar had stolen enough ore, and had accumulated enough smelted into silver, for a moderate fortune. His intelligence told him to take it and flee before he was found out, and he made careful plans. Wearing his silver bound against his body in a woven belt, he left one black moonless night. He had bought a mule, and stabled it outside the town, so it was not difficult to get away without anyone being aware of his departure until morning light. Even then, little thought was given to his disappearance. He had taken care to make few friends and to say little. In a farming village south of Taxco, he traded his mule and some silver for a horse, and so he made his way to the coast, to Acapulco, where all the galleons from the Orient came in with their cargoes of silks and spices, ivories and porcelain, fans and embroideries.

Gaspar learned that a smaller galleon, bound for Peru, was taking passengers and cargo. His silver found him a place at once, and he took his horse aboard, thinking, wisely, that the animal would be more than an asset in Peru, where there were no riding beasts save those brought in from Spain. And the horses brought from Spain were often so thin and ill from the long sea journey and the transfer to another ship that they were of little use; they often died en route, or shortly after landing. To this end, Gaspar tended his horse carefully every day, spoke to it and comforted it, saw that it had water and oats. Fortunately the voyage south was uneventful, and the horse, which he had named Buho (Owl) because of its light-colored eyes, did not suffer from the ship's motion.

Gaspar had made up his mind that he must return to Mexico with a fortune, but also with a new name and a new personality. He planned to cease forever being a soldier, and he intended to become a gentleman. A *caballero*. Now he had silver, and a horse. It was a beginning.

In Peru he called himself Diego de Castañeda. On the coast he took his time, informing himself of possibilities, and finally he decided to move toward the gold mines, and begin trading there. Accordingly, he invested his silver in necessary goods, bought a sumpter mule, and another riding horse, and set out for the east. As Diego, he hired a manservant, a taciturn, short, and bow-legged Indian of the region, and though Diego gave himself airs of aristocracy, he lived very simply, and saved with the single-minded tenacity that had characterized his peasant forebears. Whenever he had an excess of what he needed for the simplest food and shelter for himself, his man, Imo, and his animals, he bought gold.

It did not take him long to accumulate the fortune he wanted, and before many months had gone by, he was ready to return to Mexico, to present himself as a suitor for the lovely Guiomar.

And he thought, If she has already married, I will hire an assassin to kill him, the husband, and I will have her for myself. His plans were firm, and he undertook the return journey with a high heart.

29

Lying between sleep and waking, night after night, Guiomar decided that she must give some explanation to the household, of her brother's absence. And, she thought, I must devise some new way of earning money for our bread, because now we have no one who can sell the leatherwork: the saddles and bridles, and leather stirrups and the *gruperas*.

On the fifth day after Gonzalo and Dr. Morales had fled the house, Guiomar called Epifanio and Tomasa into the small office where she did her accounts.

"The patron, Don Gonzalo, has gone to Veracruz to open a business there," she said steadily, "and I am to carry on here. I need your help. Epifanio, you are to be in charge of the patio, where the working of the hides, and sewing and cutting is going on. We will clear out one of the dispensas, and use it as a storeroom, for we may not be able to sell our leatherwork, but we will save it until Don Gonzalo returns for it. In the meantime, I am going to start making sweets to sell, and Tomasa and Doña Judit will help me. Tomasa can take them to the market, and sell them for us there. You may go, Epifanio. Tomasa, stay. We must make lists of what I will need, and we must buy in quantity, to save money. I will need sugar, honey, nuts, and the shredded meat of that tropical fruit, the coconut. And you must buy some of the fragrant beans of the vanilla orchid . . . I will need them, too. And eggs. We must buy them at first, but I shall arrange a place in the rear patio and raise chickens myself."

Tomasa began giving advice with great enthusiasm, and later she set aside a special charcoal burner for the making of the sweets, and they cleared certain shelves in the larder for their supplies.

"I hope to make enough profit on my sweets, to buy the daily food," confided Guiomar. "For it may be a long time before Don Gonzalo can return for the leather goods."

And so they settled into a routine.

Guiomar began raising her chicks, which soon enough became pullets and layers. Early mornings, after she had heard mass (her face entirely covered with a black veil), she went to the hospital to do her work. In the afternoons, before darkness fell, she boiled her sweets and spread them on platters to dry. And every day Tomasa brought home a few more maravedis. They invented candy using the thick sweet root called *camote* and they cooked fruits in honey and syrup until they were crystalline. Little by little, the stall where Tomasa sat, her sweets spread out on a clean cloth and covered with a very fine transparent sheet of muslin, became known in the city, and the day came when the Viceroy himself sent an orderly to the stall to inquire the address of the house where the confections were made. Tomasa would not give it until she had asked permission of Guiomar. But Guiomar told her to treat the Viceroy's emissary with respect, and when he again appeared, a few days later, Tomasa gathered up her unsold confections, and led him to the house on Curtidores Street.

Guiomar met him and explained that she had learned to make the sweets in a convent in Spain; the nuns sold them, for their keep.

"Ours was a penitential order, and I was never allowed to taste the confections," she told him, "but I remember the recipes."

"The family of the Viceroy would like to arrange that you supply them daily with an assortment of your candies," she was told, and a price was quoted that would more than recompense her for the sales in the market. Besides, she would not have to deliver them; someone would be sent from the Viceregal Palace every day, to bring her ducats, and to carry away the sweets.

Thus Judit and Guiomar began to develop a profitable business, and they were no longer worried at not being able to send out a man to sell the leather goods to the army.

"When will Gonzalo return?" Judit asked constantly.

"I don't know," answered Guiomar. "But we must wait for him."

Their sentences at the hospital were almost finished, and both Guiomar and Judit had been good, humble pupils of the old priest to whom they had been sent for confession and instruction. A day came when they were told to report once more to the Inquisitorial judges.

Both young women were trembling and unsure, inside their thick dark garments, and wound in their black veils. Had some other unknown denounced them? Judit struggled to keep from sobbing aloud, but Guiomar looked about, in the black draped room of the Court, and was surprised to see that the young Irishman, too, had been called into the presence of the judges.

Fray Artemio was not present, but only two old priests of the Dominican order, one of whom seemed unable to read the documents in front of him. He held them up close to his eyes and moved the parchment from right to left. At last, in a trembling old voice, high as a woman's, he read out, "Guiomar Montemayor, Judit Cerezo. Are you present?"

"We are present," answered Guiomar.

"Juan Palomar, Fermín García Mendoza. Are you present?"

"I am present, I, Juan Palomar, Your Worship," came the Irishman's strong clear voice. "Fermín García Mendoza lies ill, unable to walk or to be present."

Fray Domingo, who had accompanied Juan, spoke. "Fermín García Mendoza is under my care, Your Reverence. He is gravely ill."

"Do you respond for him?"

"I do," answered Fray Domingo, firmly. He had prayed for guidance, and had seemed to hear a heavenly voice which told him that mercy and forgiveness were his duty, and that he must do what he could for this erring man, whose only fault was that he longed for his wife.

"You have completed your sentences. Letters have come from Spain, in the case of Guiomar Montemayor, and in the case of Juan Palomar, whose true name is Columb O'Carolan, convincing the honorable judges of this Court that they are True Catholics, not heretics, and not liars. There is as yet no report from Jaén on Judit Cerezo. She will continue to go to her confessor until further notice. The others are free, and may confess wherever they choose, but they are strongly recommended to continue to pray with and receive instructions from Father Felipe."

The old friar rose, trembling, from his seat, and leaning on the arm of the young clerks, he left the room.

Guiomar drew a deep breath. She was free! Judit sobbed aloud. They hurried from the courtroom, into the corridor, and along it, and out onto the sunlit street. Juan Palomar came close and said, "May I accompany you ladies to your home?"

"We are accustomed to walking by ourselves," replied Guiomar.

But Juan was not repulsed.

"Since I am now free, as you are, I was hoping that I might be able to serve you in some way, Doña Guiomar," he said. "I have learned that your brother is away on business. There must be things for which you need a man's strong arm!"

"I have slaves, thank you," replied Guiomar.

"But there may be something . . ." he persisted, and all his hope and longing was in his voice.

"What is your skill, your office?" she asked him, pausing, and reflecting that it was never wise to push away a helping hand.

"In the convent, I learned to write and to figure, and"—he paused—"and I am very good with animals. Horses especially. If you have no stableman . . ."

"Please accompany us," said Guiomar, after a moment, "and we will speak, in my home, of how you might help us."

The three walked in silence to the house on Curtidores Street.

Epifanio answered their knock and threw open the door of the *zaguan*. The unmistakable smell of leather came to Juan's nostrils.

"Your slaves, what work do they do with the hides, with the leather?" he asked.

Guiomar sank onto a wooden bench in the hall, and Judit sat down too, huddling close to her. Guiomar lowered the veil she wore in the street.

She searched Juan's face. To her, it seemed to reflect only his admiration for herself. But also, she thought, it is a candid face, open and honest, and, best of all, merry. How pleasant it would be to hear him singing about his work, in her house!

"We make saddles, bridles, all the equipment for horses. My brother sells to the King's army. They are always in need of these things. Oh, and we make leather jerkins too, and coats, for protection of the soldiers."

"Well, then I am your man, to help you!" cried Juan. "For I know horses and all the requirements of horses, mules, and asses. If you can tell me the names of the officers who purchase for the army, I can carry loads of your leatherwork, and sell it. I could help you thus until your brother returns from his business. Of course," he added swiftly, "I would at once place myself under his orders, when he arrives."

Guiomar said, "If I let you go away with a load of our product, you might never come back. I do not know you." Her words were severe, but her tone was not.

"Perhaps you should not trust him," put in Judit. "Mexico is full of schemers and adventurers."

Juan looked downcast. He had no answer.

"I have no one to speak for me," he said. "No one. Except Fray Domingo . . ."

Guiomar rose, and indicated that he might leave. As Juan turned to go, she said, "Ask Fray Domingo to come with you, to speak with me. I will listen to him."

She had behaved correctly, she knew, with prudence and caution. And yet her heart began to sing. She knew that he would become part of her household. She was sure he would be a help, and a support. She had not a moment's doubt. In her sudden complete confidence was the beginning of her love.

30

Gonzalo and Dr. Morales hid by day, and walked by night. Their way took them steadily many leagues to the north. They did not even talk very much, saving their breath for the journey, which was often arduous. When at last they came into the desert lands beyond Zacatecas, Dr. Morales allowed a rest of a few days in a village where there were people he knew, his people.

It was then that Gonzalo approached him, and said, "Rabbi, I want to be circumcised."

Dr. Morales was silent for a time, and then he asked, "Why?"

"I am one of you. I am a Jew."

Dr. Morales shook his head in negation.

"No," he said. "We still have far to travel, and if I circumcise you, you will be unable to walk for days. The operation is severe for an adult. And we must go east now, toward the sea, and then south once more, along the coast. It is jungle land, heavy with undergrowth and trees, and we must hack our way part of the time. I cannot risk delay."

"What is the plan, Rabbi? Are we to return to Spain?"

"On our way. The moment we land in Spain, we must look for passage to Italy."

"But—"

"I have hidden money, and jewels. I can pay your passage, Gonzalo."

"But they, the Holy Office, they will be searching for us."

"I will teach you how to disguise yourself, I will make you into a hunchback, and we will go as Indians. Spain welcomes the natives from this country; they are treated as one might cozen a pet bear."

"I had thought we might hide, for a time, until the situation was better, until we might be forgotten. I had no thought we were to abandon New Spain."

"The situation, with regard to us, will not change," replied Dr. Morales. "We will be sought as long as we live. We will not be forgotten. We are Jews, heretics they call us. And I am a teacher, a rabbi. They call me 'traitor.' If they catch me, I will be tortured."

Gonzalo had no reply. He went apart and sat down, and tried to put his chaotic thoughts in order. The thought of leaving Mexico, his home, perhaps forever, was terribly disturbing. He had never lived in Europe, and even his newfound loyalty to Judaism, he feared, would not be enough to sustain him through the loneliness of trying to make a new life far away. The thought came to him that, rather than endure a long-drawn-out exile, he would prefer hiding, somehow, in his own home. Guiomar, so tender and kind, would be there. But his presence in the house on Curtidores Street might compromise her with the Holy Office; he could not bear that. Yet . . . perhaps they could make a small hidden room for him, in the back patio, where he could live, hidden and quiet, reading his books, writing, praying. As he sat on, through the hours, he came back to this hope again and again.

The next day he said, "Rabbi, I must go back. I cannot go to Europe. I must stay here, in my own country."

Dr. Morales studied Gonzalo closely and saw again, so clearly, what he had noticed in the young man's face when first he had met him. He saw idealism, sensitivity, gentleness, intellect. But he did not see great strength.

He sighed. God is mysterious, he reflected, and marks out for each one the path he must take.

"Then, if you wish to return," he said, "I will help disguise you now, and teach you how to defend yourself."

There followed two days of painful instruction, and of even more painful disguise, for Gonzalo. His normally pale olive skin was stained reddish brown; his beard, never heavy, was plucked, so that only a spare mustache and a thin strip of beard were left.

His hair had grown long on the journey, but it was washed and heated with irons to make it perfectly straight. A slit was cut in his back, and a sponge inserted, that gave him, when it healed, a hunchbacked appearance. At last, in his dirty white cotton clothes, with sandals on his feet, Gonzalo indeed looked like the occasional tired Indians they had passed on the road.

He realized that his appearance was being changed, but he was unprepared for the change in the rabbi. When an old, stooped Indian with dark skin and black eyes came toward him, he could not believe it was Dr. Morales.

"But . . . even your eyes . . . your gray eyes, are dark!" exclaimed Gonzalo.

"Some drops I put into them. You look convincing, Gonzalo. You are to take a burro, loaded with some faggots, and if anyone stops to talk with you, do not look at them, mumble only 'Vuestra merced' or something, and do not talk. Many of the natives cannot—or, better, will not—speak Spanish, unless driven to it. If you do as I say, I believe you may be able to get back to your home safely. But then you will have to stay hidden for months. I pray that no one in your household will betray you."

The parting was very hard for Gonzalo, who had come to love the rabbi for his wisdom and his valor.

"I will be lost without you," he said.

"No, no, son. You have reserves of strength in yourself. You must find them. You do not need me anymore. Only remember . . . Be merciful, be just, be humble." He did not add aloud what he would pray for daily for his young friend and convert. "Be courageous, Gonzalo. Be strong. Hold to the truth with courage, with inflexible will." The rabbi knew that courage was the quality any true Jew had to have . . . he had to cling to it and augment it if his valor was small or flagging, had to hold and keep it with determination and prayer, if his courage was high. Jews, especially secret Jews, walked on a precipice every day, every hour.

Gonzalo turned backward toward Mexico, thinking longingly of Guiomar and of home. However, halfway along the road, realizing how complete and convincing his disguise had been, he began to worry about returning to Curtidores Street. In the evil event that he was betrayed, or if the Holy Office in any way came upon evidence of his hiding there, he would bring trouble and danger down upon his sister. He decided that for her safety he must never go near her again.

But then, where would he go? With whom could he find refuge for a few days until he could devise a way of making a living and hiding from the spies of the Inquisition? The Acevedos were his only hope. They at least were Jews, they knew his problem, his danger. And no doubt they knew possibilities.

Gonzalo did not want to do as they did, feigning great devotion to the Church in which they did not believe and which they had every reason to fear and distrust. He preferred actually to live out his life as an Indian. The Inquisition officers had been explicitly forbidden to molest the native Indians. The Pope had given instructions that the duty of Holy Church toward the pagans was to convert them, not to frighten or punish them. Gonzalo at last made up his mind to remain in his role of an Indian, living in cold and near starvation, humiliated and spat upon by the arrogant Spaniards, used as a beast of burden, or as a servant only. He could endure such a life; he had his secret book hidden inside his clothes. And he could write secretly.

Reflecting on these matters, he came at last to the conclusion that he could not approach the city of Mexico either. He therefore turned his steps toward Taxco and the hills. As he trudged, gathering firewood on the way and selling it for a few tortillas and a sup of vegetable stew or a drink of milk, sleeping in the open beside his little burro, he decided that when he had managed to win the confidence of the villagers, he could teach them Judaism, carrying on the work of his beloved rabbi, Dr. Morales. Thus comforted, he followed a trail into the hills, and after several days he came upon a village where there were at least a dozen huts, several kilns for making charcoal, and a spring, or "eye" of water, which gushed fresh cold water all day.

Knowing something of Indian customs, he did not ask for shel-

ter or for food, but sat beside his beast, where all could see him
and where all would pass by. On the second day, an Indian
woman silently brought a bowl of food and a few tortillas. As
silently he accepted, and though he was ravenously hungry, he
ate as the natives did, slowly and daintily, tearing off bits of the
tortilla and rolling morsels of food in them. On the third day, as
night was falling, the same woman came, and made him signs to
follow her. He had watered his small donkey, and taken it to
crop the rich grass that grew nearby on the hillsides, and now he
rose, and leading the little beast, he followed. The woman
quietly tethered his burro near one of hers, and gave it a few
corncobs to munch. She indicated that Gonzalo should enter her
hut, which he did. It was dark and smelled of the roughly cured
hides of sheep, which served as the woman's bed. Gonzalo saw
at once that she lived alone in the hut; there were no signs of
any man, or of any children. At once he knew that the woman
had chosen him to be her husband.

She brought him a clay bowl of hot food and tortillas, and he
ate. When full dark had fallen, she lay down on the sheepskins,
and he lay down with her. She took him into her warm arms,
and held him, and Gonzalo wept with gratitude. He was able to
make love to her, and she sighed happily before sleeping.

The woman's name was Sochil, she told him. She had a few
words of Spanish, and Gonzalo avidly learned the words of her
language. Sochil had been widowed before she had been able to
conceive, and this was considered bad luck in her village. No
other man would have her. She had a few sheep which her father had bought from Spaniards, and he had left them to her
when he died. She pastured them in the mountain meadows, and
sheared them and wove sarapes from the rich brown, black, and
cream wool. Once a year she went down to Taxco to sell them.
She told Gonzalo that he would be her man, and she would be
faithful to him. She asked his name, and he told her, Gonzalo,
but she could not pronounce it, and called him Shalo. Gonzalo,
when asked his name afterward, as the people of the village

came to know him and accept him, always gave his name as
Shalo.

Now Guiomar will think me dead, he thought. I shall be forgotten. This seems to be what God wants me to do—to live forgotten and humble and poor. But I have a mission. I must teach
these people to love God. I will teach them to be Jews.

31.

Guiomar had accepted Juan Palomar as her employee, and she
sent him out to sell the saddles, leather cuirasses, *gruperas*,
and other goods still being manufactured in her patio under the
trained and watchful eye of her slave Epifanio.

"I am trusting you," said Guiomar to Juan, simply.

He dropped to one knee, took her hand, and kissed it with
fervor.

"I am honored by your trust, dearest lady, and I will not fail
you," he said.

"Besides selling these goods, and taking orders for more," she
went on, "please, on your return journey, look about for good
hides, especially ones that have been softened and aired, so that
they do not smell, and buy them. Don Juan, I am conferring on
you the responsibilities of my brother, who has gone on a long
journey."

"I wish him speedy and safe return," said Juan, and he added,
boldly, "for there is something of great importance to me that I
wish to discuss with him."

And he looked up, his eyes telling Guiomar what lay behind
the words. That she knew and understood he saw, for the warm
color spread up from her neck and made her face and forehead
rosy.

Judit had stood near Guiomar, pressing close to her, for she felt some fear of the strange young man who had so quickly become a member of the household. When Guiomar went back to her room to rest, after making the confections for the day, Judit followed her and sat upon her bed.

"Oh, Guiomar, will Gonzalo be away so long, then? I thought he had gone only to start a business near the coast!"

"I have heard nothing from him for many months," answered Guiomar. "I do not know where he is. We are alone here, Judit, and we need someone to lean on. A man. My father is dead. Gonzalo is . . . somewhere. Dr. Morales comes no more to visit us. We are alone. I am afraid sometimes."

"You are never afraid," answered Judit, loyally. "But I am. I am not sure I feel that this young man, this Juan, should be in your confidence. Ay, Guiomar, he eats you with his eyes!"

"I think he is in love with me," said Guiomar. "And that is why I trust him. How could he harm us, if he feels affection?"

Guiomar thought often of Juan, and considered the love she saw in his eyes and in his attitudes, and in his wish to serve her. From her need of him, and her trust, love for him began to grow. In her loneliness, she nurtured it.

"I would rather Gonzalo were here," murmured Judit, disconsolately.

"I know," said Guiomar, "that it is Gonzalo you love."

"Have I been so bold as to show it? Has Gonzalo noticed? Oh, I am ashamed!"

"Perhaps he has noticed," mused Guiomar. "Perhaps that is why he has been away so much, and has seemed so thoughtful. No doubt he wants to accumulate a fortune before he asks for you!"

"Oh," cried Judit, "I don't want any fortune! I would be so happy to stay here with you, and with Gonzalo, in this house! We do not need more! I would be happy even in one room with Gonzalo!"

"I know that. But perhaps he does not. Young men, they used to tell me in the convent, want to lay treasures at the feet of their brides! They always told me to fear a young bridegroom, because they are adventurous and desperate. Take an old husband, the nuns said, who will be quiet and tranquil, and kind to you."

"But you—"

"I would have a young husband, adventurous and desperate," laughed Guiomar, "if I could! But who will come to sue for us? We shall die old maids, Judit!"

"Not you!" answered Judit. "Not you!"

And, despite her words to Judit, Guiomar knew that she need not die unmarried. The future began to beckon, to promise happiness.

BOOK FOUR

Guiomar

1.

Fray Artemio, who took care of the most important business of the Holy Office because Don Pedro Moya y Contreras was occupied extensively with the duties of his archbishopric, as well as with the pomp and activity that was his in his role as Viceroy, was plagued with a mountain of details. Don Pedro, who lived in the most extreme poverty, disliked the luxury of the Court, and was delighted when he was replaced by Don Alvaro Manrique de Zúñiga as Viceroy. Don Pedro remained as *visitador*, or inspector, of the works of the Holy Office, and as Archbishop of Mexico. To his work of religious organization, he gave wholehearted attention, and he was a hard taskmaster. He was often away, supervising the activities of even the humblest priest, for the flame of his faith was strong and pure. He loathed lechery and self-indulgence and heretics.

Fray Artemio was scolded for gluttony and required to put himself on short rations. His robes and belts grew loose, and his temper short.

Although the letters from Spain had forced him to free Guiomar and Juan, in *absolución del cargo* (free of all accusations), in accordance with the rules of procedure of the Inquisition which had been set down by Fray Torquemada in Spain, he did not cease to think about them, especially Guiomar. He had a long and tenacious memory, and he kept watch over the incoming mail whenever a galleon from Spain brought documents. He intended to call Guiomar before the Court again as soon as he had any word about the young woman Judit Cerezo.

However, chance gave Guiomar into his power before the awaited letter.

The old priest, Fray Felipe, to whom Guiomar had been sent to make confession, died. Fray Artemio immediately named himself in Fray Felipe's place.

Fray Artemio had no use for those *confesionarios* which screened the penitent from the priest; he preferred to look into the face of the kneeling sinner, and decide whether he told the truth or not.

"It is amazing," he told Don Pedro, "how often I can see through a lie, or an incomplete confession, by studying the face of the penitent, and thus I am able to spare Holy Church the impertinence of a false confession."

Don Pedro considered, and finally nodded his head in agreement. Possibly what Fray Artemio said had value. Possibly.

When Guiomar came into the chapel and knelt before him, Fray Artemio felt triumph. He was certain he could catch her in some sin that would merit a penance he might devise. For some obscure reason, which he did not acknowledge, he wished to hurt her in some way.

But she was humble and low-voiced, and careful, and he could not find any fault with her recitation of small sins of omission, of being late in writing to her beloved Mother Superior in Spain, of being sharp with the servant when she spilled the sugar, and so on and so on.

He gave the penance, and let her go.

Patience, he muttered to himself, patience.

2.

On shipboard, sailing up the coast from Lima, past Panama and the wild lands south of Mexico, Diego de Castañeda had made friends with Fray Feliciano, who was leaving Peru and returning to labor in New Spain. Fray Feliciano was a mystic, given to seizures when, he said, the saints appeared to him, and gave him celestial messages. He insisted on obeying these voices, and he had been told that he must go to New Spain, where he would find a blood descendant of Our Lady, a damsel who was sinless and pure, and who would give the world great prophecies of the Second Coming.

In appearance, Fray Feliciano was no different from thousands of young religious, who kept their vows of poverty and chastity and obedience to the letter. Of Spanish origin, he was short and slender, with a heavy beard, rosy cheeks, and bright brown eyes. He walked about on the heaving deck singing songs of praise for Our Lady, and saying his prayers aloud, peppered with many ecstatic short pious ejaculations.

Diego watched him carefully and thoughtfully. He was drawn to the friar because of the man's merry eyes, frequent laughter, and appearance of certainty. Fray Feliciano accepted everything —any food that was offered, any mishap on the decks, a fall, for instance, or an occasional blasphemy overheard—with a laugh and a blessing. He seemed absolutely certain of his life, of the world around him, of his future. For Diego, this was enviable; he himself spent so much of his time plotting out the days to come, the hours ahead. At first cautiously, and then with a rush of confidence, and even affection, he began to cultivate the happy little friar.

Diego, having been a soldier, living a rough life, was not immediately convinced of Fray Feliciano's spirituality. It even crossed his mind that the friar might be a holy innocent, a gentle madman. It was true that Fray Feliciano seemed to belong to no known order, and indeed, his simple rough habit looked homemade. He could have sewed it himself. And yet, there was such joy, such candor, in Fray Feliciano's ways and his words, that Diego was ashamed of his doubts. And little by little, he began to believe in the friar's obsession that in New Spain, in Mexico, he would find the sinless precursor of the new appearance of Our Lord.

They talked often at night, on deck, when the heaving sea and

the shining stars in the immense darkness of the sky gave pon-
derance to the friar's words.

"How will you look for her?" asked Diego.

"I will be guided," said Fray Feliciano, with confidence.

"But do you know what she will look like? How will you know
her?"

"Oh yes, I have seen her," proclaimed Fray Feliciano. "She
came to me in a vision."

"Was she . . . beautiful?"

"Lovely as an angel! She is tall, with a fair face, tender and
kind. Her beauty is that of the young Hebrew women of the
years of Our Lord. Her hair is a coppery cloud . . ."

"Stop!"

Diego shivered with shock and recognition. The friar was de-
scribing Guiomar! It must be she that he was seeking. But Diego
did not speak, did not rush to divulge what he knew of the
sinless, beautiful girl. Suspicious and secretive, he held his
tongue. Besides, in his lonely work in Peru, and his parsimonious
living there, he had been sustained by his obsessive dream to
win Guiomar. He could not give up the idea. If she were discovered by this friar, and told of her importance to the world, and
became known as a prophetess, he would lose her. He could not
bear the thought.

So he continually asked questions of Fray Feliciano.

"What will you do when you find this pure angel?"

"I will worship her," was the simple answer.

"But what of the prophecies you say she will make, about the
Second Coming?"

"I myself will go about in the world repeating what she tells
me. I will be her humble servant, her messenger," replied Fray
Feliciano.

"Perhaps," ventured Diego, "she may need protection. A bodyguard. There may be people who will talk against her. Prophets
are not always appreciated for their purity and worth."

"God will send a cloud of angels to hover over her and around her at all times, and protect her from evil," averred Fray Feliciano with certainty. "The saints have told me so."

"Where will you begin to search?" persisted Diego.

"In the city which they call Mexico now," was the immediate answer. "My saints have told me that she is there. I will find her."

Diego lapsed into silence and into unhappy premonitions. He decided that he must stay close to the little friar and somehow keep him away from Curtidores Street.

3.

When Fermín had recovered his strength, he applied to a silversmith on Plateros Street for work in his *taller* and was given a trial. Because of his skill and taste, he was quickly elevated to one of the best benches, and he began to turn out beautifully worked crosses, pectorals, collars, and bracelets. He still slept in the lean-to near the Dominican convent, though Juan had departed for the north with his burro loads of worked leather. Fermín saved every ducat he earned, setting aside only the most minute allotment for his food, and the one ducat he gave every month to the Santo Cristo in the cathedral, with his fervent prayers, that the Lord help him to find his lost Sara.

In the spring, he left his bench, and started out on the roads again, as before, searching, searching. He passed the Hacienda de la Purísima, on his way to Taxco. But Sara had left by then, and had made her way toward hot springs where, she was told, everyone came to bathe and regain his health after the rigors of winter. She was able to get work for a few maravedis and her food, washing the towels of the bathers, and she stayed there for several weeks, questioning every party of visitors from Mexico City. She showed her bracelet and asked about silversmiths, and begged to look at the silver ornaments worn by the ladies. This became troublesome, and one lady from the Court of the Viceroy complained about her. She was hustled away and not allowed to go near the baths again. She sat by the roadside for a while, wondering where to turn her steps, when a carriage, drawn by six horses, and apparently loaded with children, came down the road. From inside the carriage, Sara heard sounds of blows and then desperate screaming from a child. With a screech of wheels, and the horses snorting and tossing their heads, the carriage was brought to a stop, and a lady dressed in silks and velvets, with a plume on her hat, descended.

"You!" she shouted to Sara. "Come here a moment."

Sara rose and approached the lady, who was rolling her eyes and pressing her lips together, as if she were making a great effort to control herself. Sara was clean; she had washed her clothes and she had bathed. She looked decent and willing.

"Are you married?" the woman asked Sara.

"Yes, Your Mercy. But I am alone. My husband is living elsewhere."

"Then are you free to undertake some work? Are you employed somewhere?"

"I was employed as a washwoman, but I am not working now."

"Then come and work for me. I need someone desperately. You look to be a decent sort . . ."

"What kind of work?"

"Taking care of my children. God has seen fit to send me two sets of twins, for my sins. There are two boys, aged three, and two girls, aged ten months. I have come here, to the baths, to await my husband, and the Indian *nana* I had ran away. I am utterly spent. Can you manage children?"

"I could," said Sara. "For a little time, not too long."

"Anything, I must have some rest, or I will look like a witch when my husband arrives. I will pay you well. What is your name?"

"Sara de García Mendoza."

"Sara. I am the Condesa de Calatayud. The children are in the carriage. Come."

And so Sara remained at the baths, not far from Mexico City, for some weeks, living in pleasant rooms, and well fed. She found the children obstreperous, and she was not allowed to discipline them in any way, but she soon learned how to win them, with games, and songs and little treats, and with stories she invented, always leaving them at an exciting point in the narrative, so that they should be willing to go to bed next evening. She seldom left the rooms and the garden where she looked after the children, and she did not see Fermín, when he went past the baths, in the cavalcade, on the way to Veracruz.

4.

Fray Artemio had ordered that Isabel Acevedo be watched; his instinct for divining heresy had told him that the woman dissembled, and he did not believe her. Because old José Acevedo had dissolved his small group of students, and was seen daily at mass, there was no evil reported about him, and some months went by. The winter crept into the city, blowing icily under doorways and around windows, and the houses with their thick stone walls at last began to give off all the heat they had stored in the warm days of late September and October. In the patios, the leaves on the plants turned yellow and fell; only the glossy leaves of the small orange trees remained green.

Then the spy whose duty it was to watch the Acevedos came to Fray Artemio with the news that José Acevedo had died, and was to be buried that day.

"Attend the funeral, and learn what you can about what rites were followed in his household when he died. Make friends with a servant, with some relative. You know what you must do."

But the reports were of a deeply Christian and pious man. José Acevedo had been laid out in the robes of a lay Franciscan, with all the rites of the Catholic religion, and had been buried in blessed earth, *campo santo*. The daughter, Doña Isabel, was inconsolable, and spent all her time in church on her knees sobbing and praying.

Fray Artemio, hungry from his forced fasts, and angry because none of his suspicions could be proved, pondered the case at intervals. In the confessional, he questioned Guiomar about the Acevedos.

"I know no one of that name," was the gentle but firm answer.

The young woman, Judit Cerezo, insisted that she did not know the family either.

"But your brother, Gonzalo, does he know these people?" persisted Fray Artemio, to Guiomar.

"I do not know. My brother has been gone for many weeks, on a business trip to the coast. I have never heard him mention them."

But Fray Artemio had remembered a remark from his spy, that Don Gonzalo Montemayor had been seen leaving the Acevedo house months before. Fray Artemio worried this information, constantly, in his mind, and at last he decided to call Isabel Acevedo before the Court once more, to question her.

She was sent for.

She was wearing black, and was wound in a black woolen shawl that seemed not to bulk, but to emphasize her thinness. Very pale, she looked at the judges with terrified eyes.

The questioning, carried on by Fray Artemio, did not trip her; her answers were respectful and no amount of repetition evoked any suspicious answer. Reluctantly Fray Artemio let her go. As before, the spies sent to follow her reported that she had gone straight to church, and had remained there, on her knees, until dark.

"She is stubborn," Fray Artemio said to the other judges. "But she lies. I am certain of it."

5

Diego de Castañeda had sailed from Peru, for Acapulco, as a gentleman, with his horse Buho, another horse named Muñeca, and a good cargo mule known only as Mula. They all made the journey without mishap, but Diego began to brood very much about Fray Feliciano. All day long they heard his songs and prayers, and his expression of mystical joy made his face radiant at all times.

Also, to Diego's great interest, and fear, Fray Feliciano performed miracles. There were a number of these. Once he mysteriously caused the excessive salt in the soup to disappear and another time he cured a sick sailor by laying hands on him. But the most unusual miracle was the one he carried out on the madman who was being sent back to Spain. This unhappy creature, prancing, gesticulating, screaming, and frothing, was enclosed in a stout wooden cage with bars. As he was completely naked, the cage was lashed to the deck, so that it could be sluiced clean at intervals with sea water. The man had been an important officer of the Crown, and therefore was being returned to Spain; his wealthy family required it. He was bearded and long dark hair grew on his arms and legs as well.

Fray Feliciano went, on the very first evening, to wrap the cage about with covers from his own bed, to keep out the cold, and instead of laughing and pointing at the madman, he talked with him kindly, and prayed with him, though the afflicted man gave no response. However, little by little, he quieted whenever Fray Feliciano came near. Imo, too, Diego's slave, felt sorry for the madman, and often squatted near him, crooning some song in his own language. And this too, seemed to calm the caged creature.

But the miracle came shortly before landfall at Acapulco. Fray

Feliciano had remained with the madman all night, praying by his side, in a loud voice. Suddenly the man shook his head, looked about with wild eyes, and cried, "Why am I here? Where are my clothes? What has happened?"

"You have been sick," answered Fray Feliciano, "but now you are well. I will take you to my cabin, to dress and shave." Another miracle was the one in which Fray Feliciano touched the heavy lock on the cage, and it opened at once. He led the trembling man, who was trying, in shame, to hide his genitals with his hands, and in an hour's time they returned to the deck. With Fray Feliciano was a pale, quiet man, dressed in a suit of Diego's, too large for him, but adequate.

He bowed ceremoniously to the captain, and to Diego, and ate his meal with the others, showing delicate manners.

"I am forever grateful to you," he said to Fray Feliciano, "and I will pray for you every day of my life. You drove the demon out of me."

"Pray constantly, and the demon will never return," counseled Fray Feliciano. "My saints have told me so."

Diego's attitude toward the little friar became one of intense and fearful respect, although Fray Feliciano seemed not to feel that he had done anything spectacular.

Diego's worry now was La Gorda.

Would she remember him?

He considered taking a habit, such as Fray Feliciano's. But he rejected that scheme almost at once. He had labored and saved in order to launch himself as a gentleman. He possessed gold, a servant, and horses. After much pondering, he decided to wear an eye patch, and to dye his hair. This was easily achieved: Imo (who had learned rudimentary Spanish in his service) found out from Indians in the market what herbs to use, and he himself turned Diego's fast-graying blond hair into a black mop, and his trimmed mustache into a small neat black horseshoe, just below his nose. Diego decided to trust in this disguise, and indeed, within a few days he had begun to like himself in his new appearance and to discard the eye patch. Fray Feliciano seemed

not to have noticed any change. His joyous face beamed on
Diego as it always had, and he made no comment.

Fray Feliciano, who depended entirely on Diego for food and
protection, made no impatient comments on their delay. His
saints spoke to him and advised him to be patient, and he was.
When at last they set out, in the company of several clerics and a
half dozen merchants who had arrived laden with goods to sell
in the capital, he was pleased but he did not caper. And Diego
found, to his pleasure and comfort, that he himself was accepted
at once for what he said he was: a visitor, bound for Spain, returning from Peru, but eager to stay a few months in Mexico.

The madman, recovered, said that his name was Melchor Contreras, and that he was a native of Seville. He was a quiet, con-
siderate traveler. His plan was to report to the Viceroy in Mexico
City, and then take a place in a group making for Veracruz,
where he would take ship for Spain.

The cavalcade progressed safely into the uplands. The bandits
who lurked in the mountains having just attacked a large cavalcade and made away with horses, baggage, and quantities of
ducats, the travelers were not molested.

Diego felt his heart beat strongly in anticipation, when at last
they began the drop down from the mountains toward the valley
of Mexico, where the lake sparkled blue in the sunshine, and the
canals shone like satin ribands, binding the green meadows into
a design.

Carefully avoiding the parts of the city where La Gorda might
be, Diego found lodging for himself and Fray Feliciano near the
Salto del Agua. They gravely made farewells with Melchor Contreras, and Diego, like any schoolboy, became at once restlessly
eager to look for Guiomar, yet reluctant and afraid to find her.
For one whole day he sat inactive, worrying, wondering.

Then, as he prepared to set out to look for her, to approach
her door, Fray Feliciano detained him, his hand on Diego's arm.

"Not today," he said firmly.

Diego obeyed him.

6

Fray Artemio felt himself secure enough, after reading his spies' reports on Isabel Acevedo, to call her in for further questioning.

"This time she will break," he announced, "as she has lost her father, and is alone. He was buried, in a Franciscan habit, in the *campo santo*. But I am certain he was an active Judaizer."

Fray Artemio, since the departure of Fray Francisco, had completely cowed and dominated the other two Inquisitors who were his assistants.

When Isabel Acevedo appeared, trembling and white, before him, he felt a surge of power that always came to him just before questioning an obviously recalcitrant and lying suspect.

"You have appeared before us previously, Isabel Acevedo."

"Oh, don't make me show myself naked again," she babbled, "I beg of you. I am a True Christian woman . . . I have done nothing wrong."

"You are a Judaizer."

"No! No."

"Examine her," Fray Artemio ordered the physician, who stood by in his black velvet clothes, with his case of knives and bandages, sutures and salves.

"Why? Why should he examine me?" screamed Isabel.

"The *fiscal* has decided to put you to the torture, to find out the truth," answered Fray Artemio sternly. "For you consistently lie. The physician will establish whether you can resist the torture."

Weeping and praying, Isabel was pushed toward the small room beside the courtroom, and there subjected to a cursory examination, consisting mostly of listening to her heart, looking at her eyes below the eyelids, and peering into her ears. Isabel fainted. She was quickly revived with a tumbler of water, and dragged inside to the *potro*, the preferred instrument of torture for women. This was a framework of wood, with places to which arms and legs were tied, and then subject to screws, which tightened, inflicting intense pain. The *potro*, or rack, could break bones if utilized to its fullest. Fainting and weeping, Isabel was tied into position by two black-masked, black-robed men, and the screws were attached. Fray Artemio stood by, expectant.

At the first turn, Isabel screamed and fainted. She was quickly revived.

"Confess," urged Fray Artemio.

Screaming, Isabel declared herself to be a Christian, and implored the saints to come to her aid.

But at the second turn she begged for mercy.

"I will confess, I will confess," she babbled. She was not untied, nor allowed to rise from the rack, but Fray Artemio continued questioning her. It took the threat of another turn of the screw to bring her to complete submission. Sobbing and hiccupping, she recounted her training in the Law of Moses by her father, who had since gone to his rest.

"But I will change, I will repent, and become a good Christian," she wept. "Only let me go. Only let me go."

"Now," said Fray Artemio, motioning to his scribe, "you must tell the names of the other Judaizers who came to study the Law of Moses with your father."

"No, no. You would torture them. Besides, they are all gone away. I don't know where they are! O God, help me!"

"The names," insisted Fray Artemio. "We can find them. The names."

"No," cried Isabel. The torturers received a nod from Fray Artemio and again the excruciating pain was delivered to Isabel's arms and legs.

"I will tell you! I will tell you! Only stop, stop. And let me go. Ay . . ."

Her screams rang into the courtroom, through the half-open door.

Isabel, sobbing, limping, with lacerated arms, was led into the courtroom to testify. She gave the names of all the young men who had frequented her father, among them that of Gonzalo Montemayor. She also named Dr. Morales.

"We know of him," she was told. "We have sought him. But how does he escape? Does he have magical powers? Does he call on the devil?"

"Yes, yes," muttered Isabel. "He is a devil. Oh, let me go!"

7.

Sara had some difficulty persuading the Condesa de Calatayud to pay her; she was constantly told to await the Conde, who was momentarily expected. But the weeks went by, and Sara saw that the Condesa received visits from other gentlemen, obviously not her husband. She began to despair. When the sixth week had crawled by, and Sara was desperate to leave, she again asked the Condesa for her payment. The Condesa made a brave show of calculating what it must be, at a real a month, less half that for her board and room, less a few maravedis for a broken comb (which had been broken before Sara used it on the children, but she was so eager to be paid and be gone that she did not contest the point). At last the Condesa agreed that she owed two reales. However, she did not produce them, but again insisted that Sara must await the arrival of the Conde.

That night Sara took one of the Condesa's silver hairpins and departed, leaving the children quietly sleeping and well covered in their little beds. To avoid capture, she took the road to Mexico again, where she was sure she could hide for a time before deciding in which direction to go, to continue her search for

Fermín. A friendly muleteer, who was driving his beasts to market in Mexico, allowed her to mount one of them and ride with them. To protect his animals, he did not take the road used by the *diligencias,* but a trail over the mountains, which dated from pre-Conquest days, and Sara was glad of the chance this gave her to get away. She frugally shared the muleteer's wine, bread, and sausage, and when they reached the first of the canals she dismounted, thanked him, and went to beg a ride on one of the vegetable barges, which were on their way to the market.

Having left the Condesa, Sara again fell into her dreamlike attitude, singing to herself and noticing little of anything around her. This was the only way in which she could endure her anxiety and impatience, and gradually nature helped her by blacking all thoughts from her mind except a joyful anticipation of her meeting with her husband, at last. She began to be sure, each day, that the next day would bring him into view, and her songs became more joyous, her looks more strange. The Mexicans, who respected mad people, or "innocents," as they were called, gave her food and helped her. Her hair grew long and matted; she ceased to care for her appearance, and her skin, normally fair, was tanned and thickened by the weather. Her clothes were tattered and dirty from her journeyings, and sometimes she had sandals on her feet and sometimes not. Her feet grew calloused and were protected by a thick layer of grime.

She became known on the roads as "La Loca," the madwoman. This troubled her not at all, and as she walked, or rode a mule, or sat for a little time in a cart or a canoe, she sang.

Fermín heard of La Loca, but it did not enter his head that the madwoman might be Sara. He continued to seek the lovely bride of his memory . . . slim and fair, the perfect oval of her lovely face lit by the strange eyes.

8

Fray Artemio had little trouble apprehending the men Isabel had named. They were easily caught, put to the torture, and further names wrung from them. Weeping and praying, they sat, some of them badly broken, in the *secretos*, or holding cells, of the Inquisition prison. As Holy Church wished to save all erring souls, they were visited daily by priests, whose duty it was to exhort them to repent and return to the True Faith.

Fray Domingo was one of the Dominican priests on whom fell the duty of teaching and guiding those who had fallen into the grievous error of heresy, and he worked with all his soul and all his might to draw these lost sheep back into the fold.

To his deep satisfaction, he was able to save the six men who sat in the *secretos*. They wept and repented, and were willing to accept instruction. After Fray Domingo was convinced of their conversion, they were sentenced to wear the sanbenito, to walk in procession dressed in the penitential garment on Sundays and feast days, and to give three hundred wax candles to the church.

With trembling hands the young men dressed in the shaming red-and-yellow garment and affixed the peaked hat, with its design of flames, on their heads. As sentence was read out to them, they learned that they must wear this garment for a full year, and that when returned to civil life, they must never expect to hold any office, or to dress in velvet or silk, or to wear any jewelry whatsoever. These terms were to keep fresh in their minds the possibility that they might once again slip into error. Should that happen (God save us all!) they would burn as recalcitrant and unredeemable heretics.

Isabel, wearing the sanbenito, heard with horror the sentence passed upon her dead father. His bones were to be disinterred, and shamed, and thrown into the pit for common criminals.

However, none of the best police of the Inquisition could locate or even find any reliable news of Dr. Morales, or of Gonzalo Montemayor. Of Dr. Morales, it was agreed that he had a pact with the devil, and probably was the Wandering Jew. The police soon tired of trying to catch a phantom. But they continued doggedly to search for Gonzalo.

9.

Diego studied Fray Feliciano with avid care, for the little friar had been certain he would find his Holy Woman, his saint, in Mexico City. Yet he seemed unwilling to look for her. Instead he spent most of his time in the churches, praying and singing, entering a state of ecstasy which frightened and awed Diego. One day he dared to ask Fray Feliciano about his search for the beautiful virgin who would give the world prophecies, to save it from destruction.

Fray Feliciano thought for some time before answering.

"I must wait," he said at last. "I will be given a sign. But she is here, my Holy Maiden. She is here!"

Diego himself went, as often as he dared (for La Gorda lived in the *barrio*, or neighborhood), to wait for Guiomar to show herself at her door. But now she seldom left her house. She was busy making the confections that gave them their livelihood, their daily food. Any money from sales of the leather, when at last Juan returned, would be set aside for savings, and used to buy new material. Leocadia and Tomasa were in charge of the little *puesto*, or booth, where the sweets were sold, and Epifanio accompanied them back from the market, in the afternoons, when they brought home the money from their sales.

Diego waited many days before he saw Guiomar, and then it

was only a glimpse, as she opened the great *zaguan* to admit
Leocadia, Tomasa, and Epifanio.

He had longed for a sight of her. Her image, beautiful as
the Madonna of his native village in Spain, had been with him
all the days of his labor and exile in Peru. When she stood for a
few moments in the doorway, furred with gold from the setting
sun, he dropped to his knees. Passersby might think he had
stumbled, or that he was looking for a dropped coin. But he had
knelt in adoration; his own idealistic love, plus Fray Feliciano's
obsession, had caused him to see around Guiomar a heavenly
light, and a halo. He struggled to his feet and went away to his
home like a drunken man, weaving and falling in the street,
gasping for breath. Unnoticing, he passed La Gorda, who looked
at him with interest, as she did any personable man, but she did
not recognize him, and he did not even see her.

When he found Fray Feliciano that evening, he said, "I have
found her. Our saint."

"I know," answered the friar. "But we must not approach her
yet. We must wait, and pray."

It came to Diego like a revelation that the riches he had slaved
to accumulate should not be used for the purchase of a fine
house and slaves, and for a wedding. Like Fray Feliciano, he
had been touched with a divine hand, and in a moment he decided to change his life. He moved to simpler quarters, and sold
his horses. He freed Imo, although the Peruvian paid no attention to this and refused to leave him, staying on to cook, care for
his clothes, and sweep out the simple lodging where Diego and
Fray Feliciano slept. The two spent many hours in prayer, and remembering the miracle of the madman on shipboard, Diego decided that he must build a hospital for the men stricken insane,
and pray with them. Fray Feliciano, he was sure, could save
them all. This decision came to him like a thunderclap, and like
any saint he acted upon it at once, believing it to be a direct
command from God.

The first thing to do, he knew, was to find a place . . . a house,

or a building. If these were not to be found, he must buy a piece
of land, and there erect his hospital himself. He already knew
what he would call it: the Hospital of Our Sweet Lady of
Heaven.

When he found an inn that was falling to pieces, having been
hastily built of the adobe bricks the people made from clay and
straw, he bought it, and with his own hands, and with Imo's help,
he began to reconstruct it.

"In the Hospital of Our Sweet Lady of Heaven," he told Imo,
"we will not chain the madmen, nor beat them with whips to
drive out the devil. We will keep them clean, wash them every
day, and caress them, and kneel with them to pray, and Fray
Feliciano will cure them."

Imo understood little of all this, but he was devoted to Diego,
and between them, they restored crumbling walls, repaired holes
in the roof, and laid heavy stone tiles for the floors.

"We will have shutters on the windows to keep out the cold,
but no bars," decided Diego, "and we will have a great *zaguan*,
but it will be closed and barred only at night. All day it shall be
open for the madmen to come in, or to leave, if they wish, but
when they see how we will love them and care for them, they
will not leave. The ones who are cured will stay and work with
us, and we will all sing, every day, the Divine Praises." He began
to sing as he worked, and Imo soon learned the words and the
tunes. When it became known what Diego was doing, and why,
the people began to call him El Santo Loco, or the Mad Saint.
He did not mind, and indeed, in the months of intense prayer
and hard work to which he dedicated himself, he began to forget
all the names he had called himself in his life, and in true humility, guided by Fray Feliciano, he began to refer to himself as El
Tonto de Dios, God's Fool.

He had never been happier in his life.

10

Juan Palomar had never traveled the road to the north, nor sold leather goods or any other thing, but he was young and hopeful, and he had a goodly share of native shrewdness from his own racial inheritance. He sang wherever he went, and his clear bright voice and the tunes he sang drew people to him, buyers or no. He did well, and he prudently bought whenever he could, so as not to be known as carrying money. What ducats he did earn in the sales, he bound into the woven "snake" he wore around his waist like all muleteers, and some extras he sewed into the lining of his breeches, which tied around his legs just below the knee.

"Faith, they may take my hat or my cloak, or even my *vibora* [snake]," he said, "but few now would take a man's breeches off him!"

Juan had visited many towns along the way, and had been asked frequently about Gonzalo Montemayor, and sometimes about Dr. Morales. But he could answer truly that he did not know where they were.

He pondered these requests, and the people who made them, and a small doubt began to stir in his mind. However, he put it aside, because most of the time he thought of his love, of Guiomar, and as he walked he searched about for fine land, with pasturage.

"If I could find a place to bring her as my bride," he planned aloud, as he walked, "I would raise horses. It is something I know well, and I could become a supplier of the troops."

He even took time to wander north of Zacatecas, into dangerous Chichimeca territory, looking for the kind of country he would need.

"And we could carry on our leather-making industry on a

ranch, as well," he mused, "and we could live peacefully and happily and raise fine sons and fair daughters and make good Christians of them."

There was lovely rolling land, well watered and with some trees, to the north, and Juan stayed there, and slept there, under the trees, dreaming that it was his already.

Well laden with new skins, and with ample ducats in his *vibora* and sewn into his breeches, he turned at last, and began the long journey south.

11.

"Bring Guiomar Montemayor before the Court for questioning," ordered Fray Artemio.

One of the assistants, who had a clerkly mind, protested. "She was given absolution of the charge," he pointed out.

"I shall question her about her brother, Gonzalo Montemayor, who has been denounced as a Judaizer, another matter entirely," pointed out Fray Artemio coldly. "Send for her."

Guiomar, surprised at her work over the cauldrons of boiling sugar, was taken before the Inquisition Court in her black mourning clothes, still wearing her apron of rough cotton cloth, and with no covering over her disordered curling hair that stood out around her face like a halo, and fell down her back in a river of bright metallic color.

"You are known to this Court," intoned Fray Artemio, "and you are exhorted to tell the whole truth, on your oath before heaven."

Guiomar had prayed deeply and constantly for strength when this moment came, as she had known it would come, ever since Gonzalo's confession to her. She had implored God to guide her, and she had come to the decision, unshakable, that she would stand firm. At all cost she must protect her brother.

She recited her oath in a quiet voice.

"Where is your brother, Gonzalo Montemayor?"

"My lord, I do not know."

"Of course you know!"

"I do not know. He went away to the east, but I have had no word or news of him for many months. Not one word since he departed."

From this she could not be shaken, though Fray Artemio worded his questions with sly skill. At last he lost patience, and barked, "Gonzalo Montemayor is a Judaizer."

"That cannot be true," answered Guiomar, firmly.

"He has been accused by Isabel Acevedo, under the torture, when even the devil speaks Truth."

"I do not know Isabel Acevedo. But she is wrong. Gonzalo is not a Judaizer, but a True Christian."

Guiomar had said countless rosaries to Our Lady, pleading that she turn Gonzalo back to the Church, and she had come to believe, with all her heart, that her prayers had been answered. Her faith gave fervor to her replies. As she could not be shaken, the assistant Inquisitors became restless, and Fray Artemio felt their unspoken annoyance. He lost his head entirely.

"Call the *fiscal*," he shouted, "and the doctor!"

After a few moments' confusion, they were found.

"This woman must be put to the torture, to force her to speak Truth," shouted Fray Artemio, who longed, somehow, to bring this beautiful girl to her knees. He desired to see her weeping, pleading, desperate. Deep inside he had coveted her from the first moment, and deep inside, unacknowledged, as his lust was unacknowledged, he knew that she scorned him, as a woman scorns a man toward whom she feels repugnance.

Guiomar was silent. Erect, with head high, she walked before the doctor into the examining room; she endured the prodding and thumping. They stretched her on the rack and bound her arms and her legs.

All her convent training had been against what she had determined to do, if she must. She had made up her mind, a stubborn and resistant mind despite the long-past efforts of the good nuns, to defy everyone, but not to send anyone she loved to the torture, not anyone. Especially not her own blood brother. On her knees, trembling, and with gritted teeth in her intensity, she had prayed that he return to the Faith, and she had asked the Virgin and the Angels to stand over her and guard her lips, should she be put to the torture. She knew they would defend her.

She was ready.

At Fray Artemio's orders to the masked torturers, they gave the screws a turn, and the flesh of Guiomar's arms and legs was pinched and wrenched. Her lips were clamped together and she made not a sound.

"Forgive me," murmured one of the torturers, when the signal was given for a second turn.

But Guiomar had sent her spirit into a far place, and even after four turns, when they had broken her arms, she did not cry out. The doctor ordered the torture to be stopped. Wild with frustration, Fray Artemio was about to resist, when the other two Inquisitors detained him.

"It is evident," said one, coldly, to the red-faced and trembling Fray Artemio, "that this maiden has been misjudged, and that she is innocent. It is clear that she knows nothing of the whereabouts of her brother. Set her free."

Guiomar had lost consciousness and was near death, the doctor pronounced, after listening for her heart. It fluttered feebly inside the cage of her body.

"She must be nursed here, because she cannot be allowed to try to walk now," said the doctor. He had been trained in Spain by others who had studied under the Arabs, and he was learned in treating wounds, as well as in estimating the strength or weakness of the heart, the kidneys, and the liver.

Guiomar's legs were torn, bleeding, and bruised, but the bones of her legs had withstood the rack; her arms had not. She had kept absolute silence during the torture but when the doctor

pulled her arms, to free the broken bones and allow them to settle together correctly, her screams rang out, and she returned
from wherever her spirit had been cowering. After the screams
she wept, and her wrenching sobs sounded all through the night.
The doctor had insisted that she could not be moved and that
some woman from her household be sent for, to attend her. Judit
came, and she sat by Guiomar, rubbing on the ointments the
doctor provided, bathing her forehead, crooning to her with love
and trying to silence the sobs. By morning Guiomar seemed to
slip into an uneasy sleep, and she slept until darkness fell. She
would not eat, but drank a little broth. It was not until the
fourth day that she was allowed to sit up, and on the sixth day,
tottering and scarcely able to set one foot before the other, leaning on Judit and on Epifanio, she made her way slowly through
the rooms of the Court (which had held no hearings since the
one that had ended in her torture). Two of the clerks who were
busy working there looked up, full of curiosity. Few indeed were
the persons who resisted torture.

No woman ever had.

They saw a gaunt woman, with dark eyes set back into hol-
lows and surrounded by purple discoloration, as if she had been
bruised; there was a wide silver streak in the dark coppery hair.
She could scarcely walk. She moved, and she looked, like an old
woman who has gone through a deathly illness.

Outside the door of the Courts of the Inquisition, where at last
Guiomar felt the sunlight again, two men were waiting. One was
a monk and the other a workman, for though the clothes he wore
were those of a gentleman, they were worn and torn, and his
thick arms and calloused hands betrayed his manual labor.

As soon as he set eyes on Guiomar's face, which she had lifted
to the sun, eyes closed, a faint smile hovering on her lips, the
monk fell on his knees, and he took the hem of her garment,
stained and filthy though it was, to press to his lips.

"Blessed lady," he murmured.

Diego was too shocked to move. Was this travesty the lovely
girl of his dreams? What had they done to her? A fierce rage

began to rise from his very bowels to his brain, and he actually saw red.

Guiomar was made aware of the two men.

In a whisper, she said, "Kind gentlemen, leave us. Go away. Let me go home."

As they walked, slowly and painfully along, it was Judit who wailed and keened.

"Be quiet," whispered Guiomar, but the two men heard her. "Be quiet and say nothing. All this . . . is . . . as if it had never been . . . It is to be forgotten. And I am to be forgotten, now, thank God and all the Angels. Forgotten . . . I only want to be home . . . to rest in my own bed . . ."

Fray Feliciano remained on his knees, and when they were at last out of sight, around the corner, he kissed the earth where Guiomar had walked. He rose to his feet, his face glowing with love.

"Was this . . . your Holy Maiden?" croaked Diego. "This poor broken . . ."

"Oh yes," answered Fray Feliciano. "But she said she is to be forgotten. I obey. Let us go now, Brother Diego, for there is still an hour or two of light, and we can accomplish some work . . ."

They strode off toward where Diego was getting his hospital ready for occupancy. Already two cells were in use, and Fray Feliciano bustled toward them at once, singing a joyful song as he went.

12.

As the months went by, the feelings of peace and tranquillity that had possessed Gonzalo in his life as a simple Indian peasant began to give way to vague doubts and disquietude. There was no one to whom to read his poems, or his ecstatic essays about the faith of his ancestors. He had taught the village people to wash before meals, to pray, to chant some of the Psalms, but he suspected that they enjoyed these things as they did any ritual, as much as they enjoyed their native dances and the rhythms of their great drums that they made from tree trunks, and covered with hide. Their language, as he learned it, was poetic, but limited. Naturally enough, it had developed to make possible communication about crops, about food, work, birth, and death. But though rich in delicate metaphors about nature, it offered little expression for philosophic comments and subtleties.

And, fearfully but strongly, Gonzalo began to long once more for the sight and sound of Guiomar. How was she managing, alone, with no man of the family to help her? Had his own defection, his position as a Judaizer sought by the Holy Office, brought any danger to her? At the thought he trembled with obsessive fear for her. He would not, for any price save that of his faith, bring any trouble upon that beloved person, who still haunted his dreams.

Not normally observant, because his mind was always concerned with thoughts and ideas about abstract matters, it was some time before he realized that Sochil was pregnant. At first the shock of this discovery was acutely unpleasant. Then he began to find in it the excuse for leaving, and he realized, with a start, that the plan to leave, to return to the capital, had been taking shape in his mind with insistent recurrence. Sochil would have no trouble finding another husband now that it was obvious that she was fertile, a complete woman. The possibility of her bearing a son disturbed Gonzalo, for any child of his loins must be brought up as a Jew, and properly instructed. But, he began to tell himself, he could come back and attend to this duty after the child was born. But now . . . he must go to Mexico City, he must learn what had happened to Guiomar in his absence. To the living, a duty; to the unborn, this duty was not yet imperative.

Unable to bear waiting any longer, he left one morning before dawn, taking nothing with him except a few tortillas tied around his waist with a woven belt. He trudged the road north, in his white cotton clothes, wearing sandals with a high binding around the ankle, and a woven poncho over his shoulders, to shield him from the rain, and to keep him warm at night. His skin had long since burned and tanned to an Indian brown, his lank black hair and sparse mustache were those of any native. When he passed others on the roads, or came abreast of a horseman, or a cart, he snatched off his straw hat, but made no conversation. Nobody paid any attention to a lone Indian going somewhere about his mysterious business.

On the roads, Gonzalo walked as he had always done, with long strides. But nearing towns, or when groups of people passed him, he eased into the little dog trot the Indians all used on their foot journeys. At a market in a town near Mexico City, he bought a woven sling that was held firm across the brow by a broad band of cotton, and filled the sling with *camotes*, or sweet roots. He could sell these or pretend to, if asked about his business.

Once he neared the city of his youth, his breath grew short and his heart beat strongly in his breast. So near to all he had loved, he hurried, almost forgetting the disguise he had worn, had grown into, for so many months. But caution rose into his mind, and he took a roundabout way. He passed a place where several men were working with bricks and mortar, repairing a wall. There seemed to be considerable work to be done. Gonzalo knelt to slip the heavy band off his forehead, and felt a kind hand bracing him, and helping him to rise.

A small shabby monk smiled at him, and asked, "How do you sell your *camotes, hijo?*"

Gonzalo did not speak, but held up one hand, as the Indians do, showing three fingers.

"Ah. Three for two bits [of a real]?"

Gonzalo shook his head.

"Ah. Three maravedis for one?"

Gonzalo signed assent.

"I will buy them all," said Fray Feliciano, "because they are good and nourishing and because you are tired from carrying them this long way. You have come far."

The money was counted out. Fray Feliciano was lacking several maravedis.

Gonzalo motioned to the work being done by Diego and a helper.

"You wish to work, to help us?" inquired Fray Feliciano.

"Sí, señor. Your Worship," mumbled Gonzalo.

"Come then and help. But first sit a little while and drink a cup of water."

That evening, after working all the afternoon, Gonzalo was given a sweet potato that had been baked in the ashes, and a clay mug full of unsweetened chocolate. (Fray Feliciano had no money for sugar.) And he was shown a place under one of the walls, in a room not yet finished, where he could sleep.

Gonzalo lay down gratefully. But before he drifted off to sleep, the thought crossed his mind that Fray Feliciano saw through his disguise. His eyes seemed to see through to the truth. However, he had said nothing, and Gonzalo believed that he would not betray him. He moved about, adjusting the straw on which he lay his tired body, and he knew nothing more until the sun rose next morning.

13.

Juan hurried along Curtidores Street with his laden donkeys, and his eyes found the well-known *zaguan,* with joy and anticipation. Guiomar! He would see her again, hear her step, listen to her voice.

But, when the wide door swung open, and Epifanio conducted his beasts through to the back patio, where he would stable them, Juan was conscious only of silence at first, instead of the busy sounds of activity he had expected. And then, occasionally through the heavy silence rang a scream, followed by muffled sobs. He stood still, chilled with apprehension.

Epifanio answered Juan's unspoken question.

"It is the señorita, *pobrecita!* The Inquisition came and got her and they put her to the torment because she could not tell where her brother Gonzalo had gone! She did not know, and she withstood the torture and did not cry out, until they had to make the torturers stop, for fear she would die. She kept silent through it all, but now that she is home, and safe from them, she cries all the time. *Pobrecita!*"

Juan could not answer anything in his distress. He rubbed down and watered and fed his beasts, and saw that they were comfortable. He unloaded and laid out the skins he had bought, and he would have liked to go at once to Guiomar to report and to hand her the money he had made on his sales. But those muffled sounds of weeping paralyzed him, and drained his will and his natural optimism. He went at last and lingered in the corridor near Guiomar's room, waiting for someone to come out. When Judit emerged, carrying a tray on which were a few cups and broken pieces of bread, he stopped her. But she quickly put a finger to her lips and signed to him to follow her. When they were in the kitchen she left the tray and went out into the sunlit back patio.

"My poor lady," began Juan. "What happened to her?" His eyes filled with tears, and Judit laid a kind small hand on his arm, in compassion.

"The wicked judge of the Holy Office made them torture her," she whispered. "She was so brave! She never gave in, but here, at home, she has been out of her mind with worry and fear. And with the pain, as her wounds are healing. Now she wants to go to search for Don Gonzalo, she says to warn him, and to take him money so that he can escape to another country."

"Does she know where he is?"

"No! That is the frightening part. But she insists she must go. She says she will go north, as that is where he started with Dr.

Morales many months ago. She will try to trace him. But ay, Don
Juan! The Inquisition has spies everywhere! They would soon
follow her!"

"What can we do, Doña Judit? What can we do? I would give
anything to spare her this suffering!"

The moaning from Guiomar's room had ceased, and Judit
whispered, "Perhaps she will sleep a little now. And I must
hurry to make the confections, so that we can have something to
sell tomorrow. We have been poor these last days, Don Juan. So
little money."

"But I bring much money back with me! I will give it to her
as soon as she can see me!"

"I will let you know when she seems stronger. Meanwhile you
must hide the money. Come, I will show you."

Hurrying, and watching to see that nobody followed, Judit let
him into the room where Don Pedro had died. With Juan's help,
she moved the heavy bed, and then they pried up one of the
flags in the floor. There was a small dry space underneath, and
into this Juan poured the ducats and reales he had worn around
his waist for so many days.

"Should you not take some money, for the household?" he
asked. And after thought, Judit did take a few coins.

"But now that you are here, you can help me, and I will have
time to cook the sweets, and we will send Tomasa and Leocadia
to sell them again. And now," she added, "you must be very
weary and longing for a bath and clean clothes. I will have
water heated for you, and I will send Epifanio with clothes for
you. Some that Don Pedro wore should suit you, for he was a big
man and tall, like you."

"They would be fine clothes," murmured Juan, "and I am not
worthy to wear them."

"Indeed you are," contradicted Judit, "for it is obvious that
you are a gentleman. And Gonzalo," she said, "is too short and
slim to wear them, if he ever comes home. How I have prayed
that he would come back to us!"

The next day Guiomar sent for Juan. She had risen and

dressed, in her customary black. Her pale face, with the purplish bruises beneath her eyes, her gaunt cheeks, her bound arms (so that the broken bones might knit), her thinness and trembling, but most of all, the droop to her wide generous mouth which she tried to control by clamping her lips together, all struck him with intense pain and sympathy.

"Juan, thank you. You have done so well, you have come at the right time, to console us and help us."

Juan dropped to his knees and pressed her hand to his lips.

"My lovely lady," he murmured brokenly. "My brave lady."

"Not beautiful. And not brave. Frightened and weak."

"Beautiful. And beloved!" cried Juan.

Guiomar stared at him in disbelief.

"No," she said gently. "No, Juan."

"Yes! Loved and adored! For years, and for always!"

Tears welled into Guiomar's eyes.

"Let us speak of what we must do. Let us not give in to thoughts that have no purpose now. You know everything about this house, and all our troubles. I must get strong, ready to travel. I must somehow find my brother and persuade him to escape. You must help me."

"But . . . perhaps he has already left these lands!"

"He has not. I know it in my heart. He would have sent me word. He would not have gone without sending some word."

"Well," said Juan, striving to make his words sound natural, "we must make careful plans. And first you must regain your health and the use of your arms. And the household should be set into motion again, the sweets made and taken to market, the skins I brought cut and sewn—everything made customary and busy as before."

"Juan, good friend," said Guiomar, "I will make you my majordomo now, the manager here. My father is gone, and my brother is alone and in danger, God knows where. You must be the strong man of this household."

"Count on me," answered Juan.

Guiomar sat on her bed and gave herself up to thoughts about

Juan. It would be so easy, she mused, to fall into his arms, take advantage of his love. And I feel such affection for him, such a need for him. Is this love? But I have nothing for him now. I am tired and sad and ugly. I only want to know that Gonzalo is safe, and then I can rest.

After Juan had left Guiomar, to arrange for the work in the patio, he cleared his throat and began a song. He thought, It is too sad here and there should be some joyful music, to lift our hearts. After the first notes, his voice rose strong and true, and he remembered an old ballad of his own country. The singing made him feel confident, and he went to find Epifanio and to discuss finding the workmen again, and setting in motion the long-delayed work on the leather. Then he strode into the kitchen, where he lifted the lids on the pots bubbling on the braziers, and laughed.

"Make something tasty, Tomasa," he cried, "for we must all eat well this day! And there must be noise and music in this sad house! Let us cheer the lady Guiomar and warm her heart!"

14.

Fray Artemio did not know what was the matter. His forced fasts had made all food, any food, taste wonderful before. But now every mouthful was as if he chewed grass. He was restless, and the hearings of the Holy Office bored him. It was not until a letter from Spain arrived, reporting that the family of Judit Cerezo was staunchly Catholic for as many as six generations back, that he began to find a way to calm his thoughts. He would go to the Montemayor house with this news; it was good news, for them, but his appearance there might frighten them, and they might let slip some word, some indication, or betray some attitude, which would justify his taking Guiomar, that strong, rebellious, and hated (he thought) girl into his power once more. He believed that his obsession was hatred; he ached with a longing to overpower and destroy her. Unlettered in sentiment, he did not realize that this feeling for her was as close as he would ever come to realizing that bond of unity with another being which is love.

It was a bitter day of driving rain and cold wind when he beat with his cane on the *zaguan* of the house in Curtidores Street. Epifanio opened the door, and then stood speechless, not allowing Fray Artemio to pass. The friar lifted his cane and dealt the Indian a sharp blow across the shoulders.

"I am from the Holy Office," he announced, "and I must question the two women who live here. Judit Cerezo and Guiomar Montemayor. Announce me at once. I am Fray Artemio, Inquisitor."

His voice was loud and harsh, and he was heard in the inner rooms. Judit came out at once, pale and obviously unnerved.

"I have information from Spain, which I shall read to you," pronounced Fray Artemio. "Where is Guiomar Montemayor?"

"She is weak and ill, she is resting—"

"Where is her bedroom? She has not come for confession and no doubt she has much on her conscience."

Striding forward, he threw open a door, and then another. At the second, he came upon Guiomar. She was half reclining against cushions on her bed, fully dressed and wound in a dark shawl. Her hair, which had not been braided as yet, lay across her shoulders and fell down below her waist. Standing near her was Juan Palomar.

At the sight of the Inquisitor, Guiomar struggled to a sitting position. With a respectful hand under one bound arm, Juan assisted her to her feet. She stood steadily staring at Fray Artemio, but she did not utter a word.

"I will have a chair," ordered Fray Artemio.

Judit hurried to bring one. The friar sat, arranging his long black robes around him. The tableau he had surprised had given him an inspiration.

"Who is this man?" he thundered. "Is this a house of ill fame, that young women consort in their bedrooms with admirers? There is no authority here as chaperone, I know, for Don Pedro Montemayor is dead, and the whereabouts of Gonzalo Montemayor is unknown, according to the sworn testimony of Guiomar Montemayor under the torture!"

Guiomar spoke.

"As I swore, and I maintain, I do not know where Gonzalo is living, nor have I heard any word from him for more than a year. And this man"—she turned to Juan—"is Juan Palomar, my majordomo, and my affianced husband. We are to be married as soon as the banns can be called. We are going to find Fray Domingo to ask him to call them, and to marry us, as soon as possible. We were about to leave when you called. And what is the reason for your visit, Your Mercy?"

Fray Artemio had first paled and then slowly turned a dark mottled red. He rose from his chair.

"My business is with Judit Cerezo," he said.

"I am here," quavered Judit.

"Information from Spain clears you of any taint of Judaism in your family."

Fray Artemio fumbled for his cane, took it, and leaning heavily upon it he went out, down the corridor and toward the door. Gesturing toward it with his cane, he waited. Epifanio opened the zaguan, and the friar passed through. He heard the bars being slammed into place after his departure.

That night he wrote to the head of his order in Spain, asking to be recalled. But it would be months before he would have a reply, and even then he might be ordered to stay. He sat at his desk, in his cell, for many hours, in a state of great unease. He could not even calm his thoughts enough to pray.

15

Fray Domingo had been present when Isabel Acevedo confessed, after the torture, and he had felt strongly that it was a
good thing that pain could be applied to release truth from unwilling lips. But when Guiomar withstood extreme torture, and
made no sound, and then, tottering on torn legs and cradling her
broken arms against her breast, had been exonerated of any
fault, his feelings took a sharp turnabout. Was it really God's will
to inflict such suffering upon people who swore that they were
innocent? Well, but Isabel Acevedo had lied and the torture
showed her perfidy to all the world. Yet the torture was far
worse for Guiomar, and she had not wavered. His head whirled.
Logically, then, the torture was a correct procedure. And yet, as
used against the innocent . . .

Fray Domingo was bedeviled with other doubts. But, bewildered and frightened, he pushed them to one side of his mind,
and concentrated on catching the faithful out in their many
small sins. Brawlers on the street shouted God's name in vain,
and drunken soldiers blasphemed. Fray Domingo, accompanied
by soldiers of the Holy Office, had them in cells, waiting for a
hearing, in swift retribution. He heard of, and tracked down and
found, a bigamist, and though he was usually correct in his procedures (for he respected rules and regulations), he allowed the
soldiers of the Inquisition to bully and push and mistreat the
man who had dared to try to cheat God, dared to use one of the
holy sacraments—marriage—fraudulently.

On a day in late summer he set out to investigate a rumor he
had heard that was disturbing. Two men, one of them wearing
the robe of some order, had been collecting madmen and women
off the streets, and incarcerating them in an edifice they had partially restored and constructed.

But why? And why had not this work of charity, if indeed that is what it was, been blessed by Holy Church and dedicated? And to what order did these men belong, that the Archbishop had never received them, or given them permission for their activities? There was something decidedly amiss, and Fray Domingo, to keep himself from worrying about theological uncertainties, intended to get to the bottom of the whole affair. As he walked across a wide square paved with stone and open to the sky, the dark clouds which had been hovering over the city burst with a sound like a million trumpets, a streak of lavender lightning cut across the livid sky, and a drenching rain fell. There was no time for Fray Domingo to escape. He was soaked, cloak, robe, undergarments, shoes, and tonsured head. The soldiers of the Holy Office, two of them, also thoroughly wet, walked stolidly behind him. Fray Domingo was near his quarry, the building where the two monks (if they were monks at all) carried on their strange business.

Pretending to a hardihood he did not feel, Fray Domingo strode forward until he came to the door of the building, where a sign, lettered on a plank and set over the door, proclaimed, "This house is dedicated to Our Sweet Lady of Heaven."

He went in, for the *zaguan* was open. At once a small dark man in a shabby robe came forward to him, with outstretched hands, and a smile of radiant welcome on his face.

"Come in, my son," cried Fray Feliciano.

"I am Fray Domingo, from the Holy Office. I have come to question you."

Still smiling, but making no answer, Fray Feliciano clasped his hands together and cast his eyes down.

"I say, I wish to question you."

"I will answer."

"Who are you?"

"A child of God."

"Your name?"

"They call me Fray Feliciano. But," said the little friar, "I am

not sure that is my name. Nor do I know to which order I belong. I forgot all those things long ago. I remember only what I
can do, and so I do it, for the glory of God."

"But what do you do?"

"We take care of the innocents," was the quiet answer. "We
feed them and wash them, and love them. And so God often
reaches down to touch them, and make them well."

Fray Domingo's robes were steaming. He shook his sodden
sleeves, unhappily.

"Come," said Fray Feliciano, and with authority he led Fray
Domingo into one of the small rooms. "Undress," he ordered. "I
will bring hot water, to warm you, and something in which to
wrap you, and a hot drink, and when your robes are dry, you
can put them on again." He left. Not long after, he reap-
peared, with some lengths of cotton and wool, worn but well
washed and dry, and he wrapped Fray Domingo, cowering in
his small-clothes, into them. An Indian boy of about fifteen followed with a bowl of hot liquid, which Fray Domingo drank
gratefully.

"The soldiers?" he asked, suddenly remembering them.

"They are being comforted in the kitchen. The rain is still
heavy and you cannot go out in it yet. So, sit still, and pray. Or
sing, if you like!"

"I never sing," mumbled Fray Domingo, realizing that he had
been taken charge of, while he had intended to take charge himself.

"Well, I do," cried Fray Feliciano, and he broke into a happy
song and even danced about. Fray Domingo saw that Fray Feliciano had no sandals, and no hose. Perhaps, thought Fray Domingo, in horror, he hasn't a thing on under that robe! And the
thought came, But he must be so cold, and uncomfortable.

"No," said Fray Feliciano. "I am not uncomfortable. I am always in good health, thanks to God!"

"It is strange, you seem to answer my thoughts," said Fray
Domingo. Might this be witchcraft? he wondered silently.

"No. I am not a witch," answered Fray Feliciano, matter-of-factly. "I am just a creature of God, and He has given me graces, so that I may serve Him better. You wondered about my clothes. Well, I have none. The robe covers me. If I could, I would go about the world naked, just as God made me, and once I did, when I lived in a forest. All God's dear creatures were my friends, and none of us had clothes. But here, God has called me to work in the city, and I must not give scandal. Now finish your broth, and then I will tell you answers to all these questions you are thinking." He took the emptied bowl and bustled away, humming softly.

He is an innocent himself, thought Fray Domingo, feeling the urgency of his mission fading.

"And how do you support this . . . this hospital?" he asked when Fray Feliciano returned.

"Diego gave me money, at first. But now it is gone, and so we beg. He is out on the streets now, asking for help. He will come in soon, and you will know him. He was a soldier, but now he is one of God's men."

"Is that the name of your order . . . God's Men?"

"No. We have no order. We have no Superior . . . only God, who tells us what to do. Would you like to visit some of our sick ones?"

"When I am dressed again."

"They would not know if you are dressed or not. They are out of their minds, from sorrow or love or misery or because they have done something wrong. But we pray with them and love them, and many return to their senses."

"It is not the usual way of treating the insane."

"I know. I was chained once to a wall, and beaten with whips to drive the devil out of me. But that did not help. Once we were to be moved, and so they unchained us, and that was when I ran away. That was long ago," he said, "and it was in a far country. Here, we do not chain anybody."

"But if they become violent, and try to kill you?"

"Not one has. But if that should happen, I would submit because it would be God's will. I trust that will not happen; it would be a heavy cross, a terrible cross, for the murderer."

"Fray Feliciano, you are a good man."

"I am God's man. Now. What else do you want to know? The soldiers of the Inquisition, what do they want with me?"

"Nothing, Fray Feliciano. They came with me, as sometimes I must take a heretic back to the Courts."

"Heretics," murmured Fray Feliciano. "Poor souls."

At that moment Diego returned, shaking rain and wet from his shabby clothes. Fray Feliciano made the sign of the Cross over him and then embraced him fondly.

"No money," reported Diego. "The rain kept people away. I'll go out again later. But a kind baker gave me all these loaves from yesterday's baking. We can feed all our *enfermos* tonight, and all will sleep well, with a full belly."

"How many are here with you?" inquired Fray Domingo.

"Seven," answered Diego, after bowing to the Dominican. "And we have several helpers too, who come in from time to time. All will eat tonight."

Fray Domingo took a plunge. He heard himself asking about what troubled him. "Then you, Fray Feliciano, do not believe in the torture? As used by the Inquisition? Even to find out the Truth?"

"No," was the gentle answer. "I believe only in prayer. You are thinking, I know, of the lady they tortured until the doctors made them stop, for fear of her death. You are thinking of the lady Guiomar, are you not?"

Fray Domingo was again astounded at the way in which his unvoiced thoughts were heard and answered by this shabby strange friar, God's man. An Indian, who was passing by with a mop, evidently bent on sopping up the rainwater that had dashed into the corridor, had stopped at Fray Feliciano's words, and stood as if frozen. The two friars paid no attention to him.

"Yes, the lady Guiomar. They broke her arms, and her legs were torn. But I think now she is recovering."

"Poor soul."

The Indian moved on and began his work. Yet he was not out of earshot.

"She was innocent," mused Fray Domingo aloud. "This is what has worried me so much. Never before has an innocent person withstood so much torture."

"And even the innocent may tell lies, so as to gain surcease from the pain," said Fray Feliciano. "I know, for I was tortured once. See?" He raised the loose sleeve of his habit, and showed livid scars. "It was in Peru. But I got away. I am safe here. For you will not ask me anything about myself, nor tell the Holy Office about me. I know that you will not."

Fray Domingo answered, "No, Fray Feliciano. I will not." His clothes, dried by the braziers in the kitchen, were brought him, and he dressed in silence.

At the door, before departing, he gave his blessing and made the sign of the Cross.

16.

After Fray Artemio had left the house on Curtidores Street, Juan turned to Guiomar, hastening to tell her that he knew she had said they would marry only to escape further difficulties with the Holy Office.

"They are terribly severe with anything immoral," he said, "and you saved the situation with such cleverness! But I am not deceived, my lady. I know that you do not wish to marry me. Or anybody else!"

Guiomar looked at him deeply. His words were open and he meant them, but also, she knew, he hoped.

"Don Juan, I am alone, and in trouble, and I need a protector," she began. "And whom can I trust? No one. Except, perhaps, you. Can I trust you?"

"Completely, my lady."

Guiomar's face had changed subtly during her torment, and in the days afterward. It was thin, showing the line of her cheekbones. Dark violet circles under her eyes made them seem even larger. The warm golden color of her cheeks was gone, and she was very pale. Her mouth seemed much too wide, and the corners drooped. Even her rich mane of coppery hair seemed to have lost sheen, save where a white streak showed above the temples.

"I would never take, or insist upon, a husband's rights, until you gave them," persisted Juan. "But I would be honored to protect you, to look after you and all your affairs, to serve you. But I would also pray, my lady, that someday you might turn to me. For I have loved you from the first moment I saw you."

"I know," answered Guiomar, simply. "But I am not fit for anyone's love now."

"You are sad and ill and frightened. But you will recover. You are not alone anymore. God will strengthen you."

Judit came close to Guiomar and put her arms around her protectively.

"With a husband here to defend us, we can wait for Gonzalo," she said. "Someday he will come. He has not forgotten us."

"May God hear you and listen," murmured Guiomar.

The banns were called, in due course, and on a Monday morning, Guiomar and Juan were married by Fray Domingo in the cathedral. Guiomar was still in mourning, but Judit persuaded her to wear a white lace mantilla over her hair. The morning was fair, the streets washed clean after a heavy rain, and many thick white clouds ran before a light wind, in the shining blue sky. Judit was Guiomar's attendant. One of the younger priests of the Dominican order attended the bridegroom, who had no friend to ask besides Epifanio, and he could not serve, being a slave.

The service was simple and quiet, before one of the side altars. Only a few persons had come to mass so early in the morning (it was just six), and they were mainly servants from houses nearby, and a few natives in their Indian dress. One, who sat at the back, keeping his head low, seemingly very devout about his prayers, was not noticed by anyone, though he was behaving in a manner seldom seen among the Indians, who were a stoical race. This man, in tattered and dirty white clothes, his black hair hanging long and lank over his shoulders, was weeping bitterly during the mass. Just before the elevation, he rose and hurried away into the street, and was lost in the early crowds on their way to market.

17.

Isabel Acevedo was not comforted when she heard that Fray Artemio was being recalled to Spain. She had been forced to put on the shameful sanbenito, that garment which told everyone that she had relapsed and was being instructed. She hated the dress, the greenish-yellow background, with the painted flames rising from the hem to the breast, and the horrid peaked hat. Obliged to wear it in the street, and having been ordered never again to wear silk or velvet, or any jewel, she always tore off the hated sanbenito the moment she closed the door of her house, and immediately put on an old dress of brown cotton, with coarse white lace at the neck. The dress was not becoming to her sallow skin, any more than the sanbenito, but it was old and had been used in happy days when she was mistress of her house, the adored and trusted daughter of Don José.

Isabel was receiving instruction, as required, for she was classified as one who could be saved and brought back into the bosom of the Church, as a *reconciliada,* or one reconciled. Her experience in the torture chambers was unforgettable in its horror, and she pretended, with all her might, that she was repentant and wished to be a dutiful Christian. Yet at night, alone in bed, she wept and stormed, and begged pardon of her father and of faithful Jews. Often she made up her mind to go and defy the priests and announce her Judaism, but she was never able to bring herself to the point of doing so.

Few of her father's pupils ever dared go near her, but once in a while a secret Jew would sidle close to her, at mass, or hurrying through the street, and whisper some word of news, or of encouragement. Usually she made no answer, and only hurried away, or pretended to be so deep in prayer that she did not hear.

"Our spies tell us that Fray Artemio is returning to Spain," one whispered. "Maybe things will be easier! The next one may not be so harsh! We might even meet and read our holy books again."

"Careful," she whispered back, terrified. "And stay away from me. Fray Artemio might prepare a great auto-da-fé before he leaves! God save us!"

The fear of an auto-da-fé had broken into her defenses. Not only would she be displayed in her shame and treachery to her true faith, but she would have to watch the final agonies of men and women stronger than herself, strong enough to risk everything, and endure frightful pain, for the glory of Jehovah and for His martyrs.

She was torn with remorse and weak in her terror.

18.

Fray Domingo had a small office in the Church of Santo Domingo, where he kept his ciborium, humeral veil, cope for bad weather, his breviary, and a few personal objects, such as his quill pen and a few leaves of thin parchment, on which, in very small letters, he wrote out his daily examination of conscience. He also noted down what progress he had made in drawing back heretics to the Faith, and his lists of suspected persons who might, by un-Christian acts or beliefs, attack or undermine the teaching of the Holy Catholic Church.

In recent weeks, he had noted, sorrowfully, that he had wavered in his devotion to honored practices of the Church, as he had begun to worry about the tortures used to cleanse the souls of heretics, or make them confess. Fray Domingo now harbored the sudden, terrifying thought that the Lord Jesus might not have approved of this practice. The idea was so revolutionary that he dared not confess it; instead he reexamined it every day, turning it about as one might a piece of colored glass in the sun. But he could not bring himself to square the idea of torment with Christian mercy. And yet, he himself had been a zealous pursuer of heretics, and a devoted worker to try to reconcile them and save their souls. For was it not said that if you saved one soul during your lifetime, you would save your own?

In this small office, surrounded by his books (which were few but important and inordinately cherished), he gave instruction to the heretics, blasphemers, and sinful priests who were turned over to him by the Holy Office.

Awaiting the visit of Fray Arnulfo, who had been excused from wearing the sanbenito but ordered to receive instruction for a year before he could be absolutely pardoned, Fray Domingo was aware of intense distaste. Fray Arnulfo had trafficked with the business of the Holy Office. He had delayed capture of known heretics and had received gold for withholding information about suspects. Such a capitulation from the requirements of the Church in its efforts to save souls, for the mere acquisition of gold, seemed to Fray Domingo heinous. Worse, the friar was a Dominican.

When Fray Arnulfo appeared and stood humbly in the doorway, Fray Domingo could not resist making him wait, immobile, for some time. At last he turned to him, and gave greeting.

"What are your thoughts today, Fray Arnulfo?"

"I have been wondering if I am to be ejected from the order."

"I have had no such notice. In any case, ejection would not affect your sentence. Please recite for me the Confiteor."

Fray Domingo carried out his duties carefully and completely, and then prepared himself with deep, intense prayer to receive the penitent Isabel Acevedo. He hoped to bring this soul into the safe and comforting arms of the Church.

She appeared on time, as she always did, wearing the sanbenito. As always, Fray Domingo was pleased by her piety and her humility, though disturbed and sometimes worried by her sudden attacks of hysterical sobbing. He set these down, and he was right, as remorse, but the remorse was for her treachery to her father and his disciples.

After she was gone, he sighed and prepared to make notes on his parchment. But another penitent had arrived.

Fray Domingo automatically murmured "Ave María" and was answered correctly, at once.

The man who entered the office was an Indian, seemingly young, and a laborer, for his clothes were dusty and worn, his hands thick with calluses, and his straw hat tattered.

"My son, what is your trouble?" asked Fray Domingo, for the Holy Office did not pursue the native peoples, but only sought to instruct them.

The man looked up and Fray Domingo felt a shock of recognition.

"I am Gonzalo Montemayor," said the man. "I have come to give myself up."

Fray Domingo could not even make answer for a few moments. His thoughts whirled in his head. At last he said, "My son, you have done well. I must turn you over to the soldiers, who will imprison you, but I promise to hear your confession and to instruct you and bring you back into the bosom of the Faith. All is not lost. You did well to come to me."

"May I ask you a question?"

"Anything."

"Why was my sister put to the torture?"

Fray Domingo took his time. He sensed the tension in Gon-

zalo's voice. It would not do to antagonize him, now that he had
come to surrender, to ask for pardon.

"I considered it too severe. She was questioned about your
whereabouts, but she insisted that she did not know. The Chief
Inquisitor did not believe her. But she endured the torture without a sound, and she was completely exonerated."

Fray Domingo observed that Gonzalo was making an effort to
control his tears.

"Has she—she has recovered?"

"Her arms were broken, and her legs injured, but the doctors
reset her arms and dressed her wounds. Physically, she is getting
well. My worry is—for I have just confessed her and married her
to Juan Palomar, a good Christian—my worry is that she has not
forgiven the judge nor the torturers. She resists talking about
this, and I suspect that she harbors deep resentment in her
heart."

Gonzalo made no answer. He seemed unable to speak. Fray
Domingo waited.

"She has more courage than I," murmured Gonzalo, finally.

"Also," continued Fray Domingo gently, "I believe that she is
extremely anxious to know about you. She does not say so, but it
would be natural."

"I have come to give myself up, so that she need never be
bothered anymore about me. Or taken prisoner. Or tortured," he
ended, in a whisper.

"Your sentence will be heavy," Fray Domingo told him, "but I
rejoice that you will be saved! Thank God!"

"But I shall not change," said Gonzalo firmly. "I am a Jew,
and I will not give up my religion. I expect to be burned. I am
ready."

"Oh no! Oh no!" cried Fray Domingo, in great distress. "You
must repent!"

"Hear, O Israel," chanted Gonzalo. "The Lord my God is
One!"

"No, no! Stop. Be quiet!"

Fray Domingo fell to his knees and began fervent prayer.

Gonzalo could have escaped, but he made no move. He waited patiently for Fray Domingo to finish and to struggle to his feet again.

"Repent, I beg of you! Say the Confiteor!"

"I do not repent."

"You oblige me to call the soldiers and turn you over to them at once. This would have to be done in any case. But I will come with you and I will strive with you, and I will not give up! I must return you to the True Faith."

Gonzalo made no answer, but he smiled compassionately at Fray Domingo. In his heart he was comparing this stout, babbling friar with the strong, dignified, and powerful figure of his friend and rabbi, Dr. Morales, and Fray Domingo's undistinguished pale face with the handsome, intelligent, and manly visage of the doctor.

Fray Domingo prayed once more, and exhorted Gonzalo with all his heart, but Gonzalo was silent, simply shaking his head in denial at every request. At last Fray Domingo went out into the street near the church and called in a pair of soldiers of the Inquisition in their black garb. He conducted them back to his study. There they formed a small procession, Gonzalo walking between the two soldiers, Fray Domingo following, carrying his pectoral cross high, and reciting prayers in a loud voice. He followed Gonzalo into a cell, and remained there with him, praying and begging him to accept instruction, until it was dark.

At last Fray Domingo stumbled away, hungry and worn out. He knew that he must inform the Holy Office and he must also let Guiomar know that her brother had returned, unrepentant. He felt unable to do either errand that night, and instead went to his pallet.

He knew that he was facing weeks and months of intense work and prayer. But he was too exhausted to do more than cross himself before he slept.

19

Juan took over all the important decisions of the household in Curtidores Street. He had never had to assume authority before, but it was in his character to wish to do so, and he made an ally of Epifanio at once. Carefully studying the production of the worked leather, he decided to confine the activities of the workmen strictly to accouterments for horses. Also he considered purchasing two more male slaves, and teaching them the trade. He had in mind a long-term plan: to move Guiomar and her household with him, far to the north, and to support them all by his trading with the army in horses and in leather.

He saw, with delight, that Guiomar leaned upon him more and more each day and was content to go to mass, recite her prayers, and watch over the small business of the confections. In his manner toward her Juan was always courteous, and deferential; he never stepped over the bounds he had firmly set for himself. And he saw, with inward hope, that Guiomar often stopped and studied him thoughtfully, as if making up her mind about him.

As master of the household, Juan could break into song when he wished, and he did so, sending out trills and long lines of melody, gladdening the solemn corridors of the house. He remembered many an old song of his boyhood, and sang them in Gaelic; he recalled the melodies of the chants from his seminary years and he fashioned the long phrases in Latin with great joy and care. His singing brought a new atmosphere into the house, which had been so sad and quiet. Now there was laughter in the patio where the men worked, and Judit and Guiomar and the serving maids went about their tasks busily and often smiling, instead of, as formerly, with drooping mouths and slow steps.

The rains had stopped. The first brisk days of autumn had come, and there was a winy taste in the air, and a brightness that seemed to fall from the swift silver clouds racing across the deep blue of the sky.

On such an afternoon, holding his black cloak close over his chest, for he had caught a cold, Fray Domingo took the knocker of the *zaguan* of the house on Curtidores Street, and gave three peremptory strokes. Epifanio opened and stood, for a moment, frightened, before he observed that the friar was not accompanied by any soldiers.

"I have come to speak with Doña Guiomar and her husband," explained Fray Domingo, and was admitted. He stepped into the corridor, where he heard the busy hum of work in the patio, and the joyful singing of Juan, as he helped cut the leather.

Guiomar, still wearing black for her father, but less wan than before, hurriedly came to greet him.

"Ave María Purísima," murmured Fray Domingo, and Guiomar murmured the response at once, going down on one knee and bringing the friar's hand to her lips.

"Come, Father, into the *sala,* and make yourself comfortable." She led him to the large carved armchair her father had used and which had become the accustomed evening seat of Juan Palomar.

"I will send for refreshment."

Fray Domingo was quiet as he savored the delicate cake perfumed with the vanilla orchid, and the foaming cup of chocolate. Judit brought him a bowl of warm water and a napkin for his fingers.

"Stay, daughter. And call your husband, please," said Fray Domingo to Guiomar. "I have news that all of you must hear."

When they had gathered around, he cleared his throat unhappily. He did not relish his errand.

"Your brother Gonzalo Montemayor is in the city. He came to me . . ."

"Oh, God be praised," cried Guiomar. "Where is he? When may I see him? Will he not come here, to his home?"

"He is in the prison of the Holy Office," stated Fray Domingo bluntly.

"Ay!" Guiomar and Judit both cried out at once.

"He is a confessed Judaizer. But wait, wait! I myself will undertake to instruct him and to convince him and to bring him back to the True Faith!"

But Guiomar could not restrain sobs of fear.

"Will they torture him?" she whispered.

"Not if he confesses everything willingly and fully."

"They will want to know where Dr. Morales can be found," cried Guiomar, in a broken voice.

"As to that, I know the answer," said Fray Domingo, "so they will not torture him to make him tell. Dr. Morales has escaped to Europe. It is no longer in the hands of our Holy Office to apprehend him."

Guiomar stood up.

"I must go to my brother! I must see him!"

Juan took her gently but firmly by the shoulders.

"No, *mi amor*. You will not go. I, your husband, forbid it."

Guiomar looked about wildly, but she did not twist out of Juan's hands.

"You have been questioned by the Holy Office and tortured. You will not do anything, or see anyone, who might again involve you with the august judges."

His voice was firm, and Fray Domingo saw that Guiomar was trying to be calm, and would obey.

"If there is anything we can do for my brother-in-law, Fray Domingo will surely tell us so that we may help him."

Fray Domingo rose. The pain in his chest seemed very sharp, and he coughed, a dry, painful cough that shook him.

"There is nothing to be done except pray for his soul, which I will try, with all my might, to save for Jesus and Mary."

As he departed, Fray Domingo heard a woman sobbing heartbrokenly. But it was not Guiomar. It was the young woman Judit Cerezo.

Poor child, thought the friar. She loves him.

He himself had never experienced love for any human being save his mother, for he had gone as a small boy to the seminary, and he was chaste. But he had seen what love could do, the misery it could cause.

He sighed. He felt very ill; there were stabbing pains in his chest. He hurried, to get out of the wind.

20.

Fray Artemio had received orders from the Superior of his order to return to Spain by the first available ship for questioning. He pondered the letter, and was puzzled and then worried, for the letter surely had been written and sent before his own request for recall. The two letters must have passed each other in mid-ocean. Realizing this, he spent several hours in meditation, and finally came to the conclusion that enemies had carried wicked tales about him. It was true, he had erred; he had solicited women, and he had visited women whose favors could be bought. He was a lusty man, and much tormented by desires of the flesh. But otherwise (though maybe he had been guilty of the sin of gluttony), he felt that he had been a good priest, vigilant for the Faith, and stern in his ecclesiastical duties.

It had come to him that he could rectify his position by organizing and carrying out a spectacular auto-da-fé, before making the return journey. Studying his cases, he saw that he had enough culprits to form a handsome penitential parade, and there were even two heretics who could be sent to the stake. This Lutheran Captain Trout had been held in prison for months, awaiting execution, and there was Isabel Acevedo. He was certain that she was a dissembler, a liar, a hypocrite. She complied with all the requirements set by the Inquisitorial Court, and pretended great piety, but he was certain that she would break under torture again, and if she was indeed Judaizing once more, or even sympathetic to Jewish practices, she could be sentenced as relapsed, and then burned. They made two. He needed another sinner for the stake; it was unthinkable to go to the expense of a great auto-da-fé without at least three to be immolated.

He wrote out an order to detain Isabel Acevedo once more, and gave it to his soldiers. That matter could be taken care of swiftly enough, he was certain.

Before a half hour had passed, he was able to add a third name to his list. Gonzalo Montemayor. And the man was like all of those Jews, stiff-necked, proud, and scornful. Fray Artemio would waste little time trying to reconcile him.

Happily and busily he began to make the plans for the auto-da-fé calculating the *varas* of black velvet that would be needed to cover the Viceroy's platform, the lumber, and the workmen required to construct the platform, in two tiers . . . one, smaller and nearer the place of execution for the Viceroy and his ladies, one larger, with at least fifty seats, for dignitaries of the Church and government. The stakes must be found and set up, together with the proper wood for burning, and the chains, to hold the prisoners fast. There must be refreshments for the Viceroy and his guests, and waiters to serve them. Perhaps a canopy against the sun? It might not be needed. Fray Artemio made himself a note to go and investigate the square in front of the Alameda. It was the usual scene of an auto-da-fé, and the small patio between the Church of La Santa Veracruz, and the Chapel of Los Desamparados (the Forsaken) was the perfect location for the platforms.

Fray Artemio bustled out of his office. He wished to choose the route for the penitential parade. It was a short distance from the prison of the Holy Office to the Alameda, but he believed it would be salutary for the populace if the parade passed through a good number of streets before arriving at its destination. The sight of the penitents in their sanbenitos, flagellating themselves as they walked, would inspire onlookers to spit at them and throw filth on them. These activities always gave the spectacle more meaning.

Later, after having decided on the streets through which the parade should wind, he realized that he must visit the Viceroy and secure his approval for everything. For after all the Viceroy was the Chief High Inquisitor. Fray Artemio thought that this would not present any difficulty, especially as he could lay before the Viceroy the plans all made, every expense calculated.

How fortunate that the winds had ceased. The weather would be perfect.

21.

Fray Domingo spent every available moment with Gonzalo in *los secretos*, or the secret prison cells of the Inquisition. Usually prisoners were kept incommunicado, and alone in a cell, but there were few cells in total, and another man was brought into Gonzalo's cell. He was small and dark, a simple artisan, but when they were alone at night, they spoke together in whispers, and Gonzalo rejoiced to learn that his cellmate was a fellow Jew. "I am called Mario, but my real name is Moses," he told Gonzalo.

"I shall abjure, and confess, and go through all their mummery," he told Gonzalo, "for it is meaningless to me. In that way, I will be given an easier sentence . . . maybe only giving candles to the Church."

"But—"

"I am a good Jew, but I can continue to be one, secretly. There are hundreds of us! Why should we not play their game, but keep our faith strong in our hearts? If all Jews gave up and were willing to die, our faith would die! No, Jehovah surely does not want that to happen, or why has He spoken to us, and given us our laws?"

"You are right," agreed Gonzalo.

But, he thought, my plan is to free Guiomar of any trouble and pain, and the best way is to die, to disappear.

He was much troubled in his mind, however, about how to die. It might bring too much shame on Guiomar if he was burned as a Judaizer; it might even bring down danger upon her again. That he could not bear.

If he did as Mario planned to do, however, the Inquisition would continue to watch him and to spy and probably they would set up vigilance over Guiomar and their home once more.

Sometimes he remembered his life as an Indian with longing and sadness. Sochil might bear a son. If so, the child would be instructed, as he had taught the people, but who would circumcise the babe, and give him the sacred symbol of his unity with all Jews?

"How did the Holy Office happen to suspect you?" he asked Mario. "What did you do, to arouse their suspicion? Or were you betrayed?"

"It was my own carelessness," he answered. "I went to bathe in the stream not far from my house, and some Christian saw me. Saw the sign in my flesh. I insisted my circumcision was a scar from a childhood injury, but they did not believe me, and then they began to question and to take evidence, and they became certain. So I cannot defend myself as a Christian. I will have to abjure, and wear their hateful garment, and mouth their vows and their prayers." He spat.

When Fray Domingo arrived to teach and to pray with them, Gonzalo marveled at the duplicity with which Mario could feign piety and penitence. Fray Domingo was completely convinced of the man's sincerity. It was this, the friar's acceptance of the acted role, that strengthened Gonzalo in his own stubborn decision. He would not give in. He would not be a party to this degrading kind of theater. He never made any answer to Fray Domingo's questions and hopeful assumptions; he merely smiled and waited.

One day Fray Domingo hurried in and reported that there was to be a great auto-da-fé, and that they, Mario and Gonzalo, would walk in it as penitents. They would wear the sanbenito, and carry green crosses, symbols of hope in salvation. Fray Domingo had labored to make sure that their sentences would be reasonably mild.

"Though," he confessed unhappily, "you will be given thirty lashes each, and required to make presents of silver chalices to the Church."

After he had departed, Mario laughed in derision.

"What did I tell you?" he said to Gonzalo. "If you give in to their requests, they think they have convinced you, and who is to say what a man thinks in his head? We will hear their solemn sentence, be told we may never be lawyers or notaries or wear velvet or fine jewels. What do I care? I never use those luxurious things anyway, and I am a stonemason. I wouldn't be anything else. And they will prohibit me from riding a horse. Who wants to take care of a horse anyway, great snorting animal, eating its head off in the stable, using up your savings?"

"But," remarked Gonzalo slowly, "my silence only convinced Fray Domingo that I will abjure. And I will not."

That night, as he lay sleepless on the vermin-infested straw, it came to him how he might convince Fray Domingo, and also strengthen his own will and courage.

22.

On Curtidores Street, Juan's singing and the feeling of happy business about the house had given way to a heavy worried silence. Guiomar strove to keep herself steady, not to give in to the seizures she felt of hysterical fear when she wanted to howl. When they came, she gritted her teeth and hung on to furniture until she could control herself. She realized that this effort to be strong was necessary; the household pivoted around her, and in the days when she had been helpless with fear and pain, everything had gone to pieces . . . no sweets were made, the house was not kept clean, the servants did little work. She knew, too, that she owed Juan some measure of help, as he tried to take over the duties of manager, and head of the home.

Juan was a comfort to her, and a source of valor. He seemed to know when she was about to fail, to give up and to cry, and he was then at her elbow, with a word of common sense about something they must do, an affectionate comment on something done.

Judit made Guiomar's struggle difficult. She had become useless; she wept and moaned, and could not sleep, nor eat.

"I love him," she had shrieked at Guiomar. "He is your brother, and you love him too, and fear for him. But I adore him! I have from the first moment. He is the only man for me. I want him for my husband! But now . . ."

And she would dissolve in tears again. Even household tasks did not help; Judit had lost strength in her hands and in her knees. She dropped things, she stumbled, she fell, and she wept incessantly.

At last Guiomar went to Tomasa in the kitchens and asked her if there were not some herb the Indians knew that would help calm Judit.

Tomasa nodded an affirmation.

"Then please go and get some in the market, or wherever you can buy it, and teach me how to use it. I need it for her, Tomasa, and God knows I need some myself, too. We are very sad and frightened here."

The Indian woman nodded again, and held out her small dark hand for coins. Guiomar hastened away to get them, and saw

Tomasa leave. She came back with a small package of leaves tied into a bundle and wrapped in a piece of cotton.

"I make the tea," she said. "Strong, for Señorita Judit."

Guiomar took a cup of the liquid to Judit, and insisted that she drink it. She was obeyed, though Judit made a wry face and choked, as she swallowed. But within half an hour she was drowsy, and Guiomar led her unresisting to her room, undressed her, and put her to bed. Deep shuddering breaths and strangled sobs still sounded for a little time, even in sleep, and then Judit drifted away into unconsciousness. Guiomar sighed with relief.

Juan, who had watched Guiomar's efforts with Judit, asked about the herb.

"Something Tomasa brought me."

"It must be powerful."

"Perhaps it is dangerous," worried Guiomar.

"Maybe. In large doses. But the native people know so much about these things, more than we do. And you, my lady. Do you wish to take some tea also, and rest awhile?"

"I will wait until it is dark," answered Guiomar. "I have still much to do. And I must pray."

"We will pray together."

On her knees in the small chapel in the house, Guiomar felt the familiar peace and hope come with the first words of her devotions. Juan, beside her, gave his whole heart to the Latin words, and he too, felt his faith well up into hope and comfort as the ancient phrases came to his lips.

23.

Fray Domingo lay ill on his cot in his monastery for some days, with the dreaded illness of the chest that clogs the breathing passages and makes the lungs labor painfully. His brother Dominicans nursed him as best they could, but even in the delirium of his fever he voiced anxiety for his charges in the secret cells of the Inquisition.

"Who will instruct them? Who will save their souls?" he continually asked.

"The Holy Office will send another priest to instruct the heretics and persuade them to abjure," he was told. But his worries delayed his recovery. When the fever had broken at last, and he lay cool and limp and tired, the Superior came with news that broke his heart.

"Brother Domingo, one of the prisoners you were instructing is dying, they say, of bleeding that cannot be stanched."

"Bleeding? How? Was there a fight?"

"No. But somehow, he managed to get hold of a razor; perhaps they let him have one to shave. And he has circumcised himself."

Fray Domingo left his cot and threw himself on his knees before his Crucifix. With streaming tears, he began to pray.

24.

The day of the auto-da-fé dawned cold but clear. In the Alameda, three stakes were ready, with the chains, and heaps of well-dried faggots placed at the foot of each one.

Workmen were finishing tacking the black velvet onto the great platform that had been constructed, in two tiers, the lower table and chairs for the Inquisitors and the Viceroy, the upper for distinguished guests, and their ladies. Down to one side, a temporary kitchen had been installed, with pots ready to be set boiling over the charcoal, heating delicious dishes for the spectators.

A large space was cleared for the penitents, who would stand while their sentences were read aloud. To one side was the stake to which those to be lashed were to be bound.

Over in the square before the Church of Santo Domingo, in front of the prison of the Holy Office, Fray Artemio was busy organizing the procession. All the penitents who had been receiving instruction had been ordered to appear before eight o'clock in the morning, and those who were late were sent for by soldiers of the Inquisition and escorted, with kicks and insults, to the square.

There were thirty-three penitents, wearing their smocks of green, painted with flames and devils, or with the extended red cross. These were persons who had blasphemed, or were bigamists. All the bigamists were Spanish soldiers of the Crown, who had come to New Spain for adventure, and to earn a few maravedis, but planning on remaining when their tour of duty was done, to farm or engage in commerce. And it had seemed easier to marry again than to go to all the expense of bringing a wife from Spain.

And there were persons who had been suspected of Judaizing, by having been surprised spurning a dish cooked with pork, or abstaining from work on a Friday, or washing their dead and binding them in clean linen. Most of these had repented at once, and had received instruction, and had been sentenced only to contributing a certain number of hours to labor on a church being built, or to buying wax for candles, or to a stiff fine. They fleshed out the procession, and made a good showing.

Among them was one penitent who wept and moaned incessantly; he was a priest who had been denounced for soliciting women from the confessional, and who had confessed. He was to be given thirty lashes. Not obliged to wear the sanbenito, he wore his own soutane, now filthy from many days in the cells.

Two strong young Spaniards, who had relapsed badly not once but twice, in blasphemy and taking the Lord's name in vain, had been sentenced to the galleys. They were not to be lashed, as the pain and wounds might impair their usefulness at the oars. They wore only chest covering, marked with the cross,

over their ordinary padded cotton doublets and long woolen
hose. The two walked despondently, for it was known that the
life of a galley slave was seldom more than five years once they
had been chained to the oars, and there were also the dangers of
shipwreck, pirates, thirst, and other terrors.

Fray Domingo, burning with fever but eager to do his part
and longing to induce the condemned to repent and take the
Cross before dying, hovered among the men and women in the
procession. Hoarse from the inflammation in his chest, he exhorted, prayed, threatened, and begged. He gave out small rods,
with leather thongs at the end, so that penitents could flagellate
themselves, as they walked, proving their sincerity.

When all the penitents save the three who were to be burned
had been assembled, Fray Artemio lectured them on their behavior in the procession. All were given green candles, to hold
aloft as they walked, and they were to follow his lead in loudly
chanting their prayers.

When all was ready, the acolyte with his tall processional
cross at the head of the group was followed by Fray Artemio,
who then ordered the prisoners from the cells to be brought out.

Fray Artemio was much annoyed to find that two of the heretics could not walk, but had to be dragged, supported by two
men, one on each side. They would have to be mounted on asses,
and someone would have to go to procure the animals. This took
time, and the sun had begun to rise higher into the sky. The
Viceroy and the guests would be waiting.

At last two sleepy little donkeys had been found and brought.
The beasts must be draped in green cloths painted with the
flames and devils, and it took time to find the proper coverings.
Fray Artemio was dancing with impatience when at last Gonzalo, pale and fainting, and Captain Trout, who seemed to be a
skeleton, with long lank beard and matted hair, were set upon
their mounts, and the procession could begin. Soldiers were dep-
utized to hold Gonzalo and Trout upon their donkeys, as they
had no strength, and would have fallen. Isabel Acevedo, the
third of the heretics to be burned, was dragged, screaming and

sobbing, and made to take her place in the procession. She began crying out that she had repented, that she would accept the Cross, that they must not burn her. No one paid any attention to her, but Fray Artemio was forced to take note, for if she persisted and accepted the Cross she would have to be garroted while bound to the stake. It was an act of mercy that the Church had ordered, so that the repentant heretic might not suffer the pains of the fire. It was devoutly to be hoped that the repentance was genuine, but of course, it was not always possible to know, time being short.

The procession began its slow parade through the city. The penitents were urged to shout aloud the nature of their transgression, and to follow this with the Confiteor and the Credo. Shouting and crying, they obeyed. Only Isabel Acevedo kept demanding that she be set free, that she had become a True Christian, that they must not burn her. Her voice became hoarse with her screaming, and before the procession had come into view of the Alameda, her crying seemed that of a wild beast.

The penitents, who to accord satisfaction for spectators had been lashed along the way by Inquisition soldiers, were spat upon, stoned and muddied from filth flung by hearty Christians.

It was almost the hour of noon when the penitents were at last lined up before the august judges of the Inquisition and of the civil court.

25.

All Christians in the city were obliged to attend the auto-da-fé, for the edification of their spirits and the strengthening of their devotion. All must see that Holy Church was vigilant in protecting the Faith from contamination and gnawing from within, from traitors, heretics, and bad priests. All must see and applaud the severity of the Church against each and every enemy of the Holy Catholic Faith, which had been given by God for the salvation of mankind through His only begotten Son, and for which countless martyrs had gladly given their lives.

No one must sympathize with the wicked men and women, recalcitrant and demon-infested as they were. No one must weep or grieve at watching the sentences carried out, for such demonstrations of sympathy for the convicted would be looked upon as highly suspicious, and worth searching Inquiry.

Therefore, Juan ordered all the household to attend the auto-da-fé. Guiomar and Judit, pale and trembling, made ready to obey. But Juan went to Guiomar and, taking her hand, said, "We will go very late, so as to find a place only at the farthest edges of the crowd. And here, drink this, my love. It will dull your senses, and help you to live through this ordeal."

He gave a cup of the soporific drink to Judit, too, but her nervousness, bordering on hysteria, was so severe that the draft seemed to have little effect. He took a few swallows of the drink himself, to help him through the awful hours to come. He grieved wholeheartedly for Guiomar, but he was afraid, too, as the Inquisition seldom relaxed its vigilance of any members of the family of a heretic. But Juan had made careful plans, and he hoped to be able to carry them out, as soon as the auto-da-fé was finished.

As they opened their *zaguan* and stepped out into Curtidores Street, followed by all the household, they heard, far off, the shouts and screams of the crowd, as the holy procession went by. Juan held them all back until the noise had died away almost to silence. Then, pacing slowly, he led Guiomar and Judit, Epifanio, Tomasa and Leocadia, and the other household slaves toward the Quemadero, or Square for the Burning.

The crowd was enormous, milling about with excitement. There had not been a real auto-da-fé for many years and the populace was keyed up and ready to enjoy every thrilling moment. Juan saw with relief that they could melt into the fringes of the crowd (which was close packed, struggling to get nearer to the platform where the judges sat, already very warm in their heavy black velvet robes and caps). It was better to be inside the crowd, close pressed against each other, though not too close to the stakes for burning. The spies of the Holy Office prowled around the edges of the multitude, looking with sharp eyes for anyone who seemed to feel sorry for the culprits about to be punished.

Juan saw a place near a tree with a wide trunk, and he pushed and shouldered until he came to it; it would do to shield Guiomar's eyes from the drama unfolding down before the platform.

By noon it was warm in the direct sunshine. Many of the ladies on the platform of the distinguished guests had their slaves hold protective shade over their heads; sometimes these were made of feathers, sometimes of cloth stretched upon a frame. Waiters were already passing to and fro among the rows of seats on the high platform, with drinks that had been kept in clay pots, where constant evaporation through the porous material made the contents pleasantly cool.

The procession came into view and was greeted with shouts, imprecations, and hisses. The penitents, most of them exhausted from days and even months in the cells of the Inquisition, or from terror of what awaited them, stumbled. Many fell and were hoisted to their feet again. A silence fell as the Civil Prosecutor stood and was about to read aloud the descriptions of the crimes of the prisoners, with their sentences, a silence broken only by the now harsh, almost inhuman noises issuing from the throat of Isabel Acevedo, who had not ceased to cry out.

The list was long, and before the Prosecutor had reached the more serious offenses, already delicious smells were being wafted across the park from the cooking pots on one side of the platforms. Lunch was being prepared.

The Prosecutor came to the matter of Padre Felipe Pardina Prunedo, who had confessed to the soliciting of women, for his pleasure, from the confessional. The sentence was read: "And upon the bare back of the said miscreant Padre Pardina Prunedo, the Court orders thirty-five lashes. Once lashed he is to be defrocked and required to beg for his sustenance for one year, after which time he may come before the Court to plead for reinstatement as a civil person, with the right to earn his living at physical labor."

Padre Pardina could not walk; he was sunk utterly in shame and fear, and the crowd laughed and jeered as they observed that he had lost control of his kidneys and bowels, while the soldiers of the Holy Office hauled him toward the whipping post. His robe was torn and pulled down to bare his back, and he was then tied with his arms around the post. When this had been done, the two soldiers who were to administer the lashing took their positions, one to each side, and they began methodically, one after the other, to lash the priest's naked back with their heavy, three-thonged whips. Great red welts stood out at once, and Padre Pardina howled like a dog, lapsing into a kind of grunt and scream, as the whipping went on. But at the nineteenth lash, he slumped, apparently in a faint, and the soldiers turned to the judges for instructions.

"Continue," ordered the Viceroy.

They continued, until they had delivered the thirty-five lashes. Then they cut down Padre Pardina. A half bucket of water was tossed over him to revive him, so that he might walk away. But he lay motionless at the foot of the whipping post. One of the soldiers knelt on one knee to examine him, and then stood up, hastily.

"Your Honors, the man is dead."

This annoyed Fray Artemio; he had made no provision for anything of the kind; the auto-da-fé was to culminate in the deaths of the heretics at the stake. He consulted hastily with the Viceroy, who waved a hand toward the patch of lawn in front of the stakes, with their high-piled faggots. Padre Pardina was dragged there; his torn robe was pulled up to cover his dead face.

The two young men who were to be sent to the galleys listened to their sentences impassively. They learned that they were to be taken as prisoners to Spain, by the next galleon departing from Veracruz, and there turned over to the King's navy, for service in the galleys. In the heart of one of them there blossomed a tiny hope; it was a long way to Veracruz, and then across the sea . . . a man might somehow contrive to escape.

The sentences had taken up much time, and the sun was high. Waiters were handing about plates of a savory stew of wild turkey in dark spices. The three judges also accepted plates and ate their luncheon; the prisoners, in the meantime, stood waiting in the sun, guarded by the watchful soldiers. The Viceroy gave the order to a small band of musicians to play while they ate, and the music almost covered the unnerving sounds of Isabel's sobbing.

After they had finished their meal, and rinsed their fingers in the bowls of perfumed water handed about, the judges returned to the business at hand. All the other sentences had been announced. Now the punishment to be meted out to the heretics was heard.

Captain Trout was first condemned because of his stubborn Lutheranism, and he was sentenced to be burned at the stake until his body had been consumed and fell to ashes, so that no breath of contamination from the rebellious demons of heresy should remain, and so that he should be an example to any others who supposed that they could thus flout the vigilance of Holy Church. As the sentence was read, Trout, who had been supported by two soldiers, suddenly cried in a loud voice, "I repent! I accept the Cross!"

Fray Domingo hurried toward him, and held the cross to his lips. The judges consulted among themselves, and then ordered that Trout be garroted as soon as he was tied to the stake. Sobbing with relief, Trout went willingly to the stake, and was bound, his arms behind his back. A masked and black-robed executioner stepped swiftly behind the stake, whipped out a flexible woven cord of thick firm leather, and pulled it taut. There was a moment's struggle, and then the body of Captain Trout fell limply into his chains.

Isabel was next. Weeping and stumbling, she was led to the stake and there fastened firmly with chains. Her crying stopped abruptly as the executioner garroted her.

Gonzalo, the third heretic, was bitterly accused by the judges, as Isabel had been, for being a relapsed heretic who had stubbornly returned to Hebraic practices, despite having been thoroughly tutored in the ritual of the Church. His death was to strike terror into the hearts of all Judaizers and cause them to examine their consciences and repent.

Gonzalo heard the sentence impassively. Fray Domingo, in tears, hovered near him, holding out the cross, begging him to kiss it, to accept, to escape the torture of the flames. Gonzalo had to be helped to the stake, where he was chained; he made no sound, and paid no attention to Fray Domingo's entreaties.

The signal was given for the torches to be put to the stacked wood at the base of each stake. As the first flames shot upward, Gonzalo lifted his head and shouted, "Hear, O Israel! The Lord our God is One!"

A shock of fear seemed to rivet the spectators, but afterward, there were shouts of rage and hatred and a buzz of excitement, a low growl of delighted vengeance. At this moment a young woman burst from the crowd, screaming, "Gonzalo! Gonzalo!" and she threw herself into the flames which were consuming him.

Two soldiers ran to drag her back, but her clothes had caught fire, and her hair was streaming upward in flame. She died shortly after they had quenched the flames in her clothing, and laid her on the grass.

26.

Juan had been shielding Guiomar from the pressing crowd, and keeping her close to the thick-trunked tree, which screened the place of execution from her eyes. He had not noticed when Judit had left them and begun to worm her way toward where the heretics were tied. When he heard her despairing cries, and then saw what had happened, he feared for Guiomar, but she stood silent, wide-eyed. Under his protective arm, he felt her tremble and then become rigid.

"Stay, *mi amor*. Be quiet. You can do nothing. It will soon be over." And a few moments later, as the stench of burning flesh reached them, he whispered, "There was much smoke. He suffocated quickly I think. Do not look. Do not think . . ."

Guiomar remained motionless; her staring eyes seemed not to see. She was like a sleepwalker. And like a sleepwalker he led her home, when at last the crowd began thinning out, and spectators, excited and with whetted appetites, began to straggle toward home and dinner. There would be much drunkenness that night.

With sure instinct, Juan led Guiomar straight to the chapel and *reclinatorio* in their house, as the *zaguan* slammed behind them, and as Epifanio shot the great bars across from within.

Juan knelt beside his wife, and there they stayed, deep in prayer, for an hour or more. Then Juan rose, and went to give orders for the household. He did not know what to do about Judit, and at last thought to send Epifanio to the Alameda, to find out. Indians were protected by the Holy Office. He could pretend to be merely curious. But when Epifanio returned, the slave said that he had not found Judit's body. No doubt it had been carried away, and would be thrown into the *fosa comun* (the common pit) if unclaimed.

"Shall we go to claim it, patron?" asked Epifanio.

"No," answered Juan. "We will pray for her soul, but we will not do anything more. Nothing to arouse the interest of the Inquisition in us. It would be dangerous. You must keep silent, and if anyone stops to question you, pretend not to understand."

During the night, while Guiomar remained in prayer, he went to accompany her at intervals, and he added the name of Judit to his pleas for mercy. Toward morning, Guiomar fell to the floor, fainting, and he carried her to her bed and tenderly covered her. While she slept, he began methodically setting about the tasks he had set himself. The finished leatherwork was sorted, bundled, and packed. He made lists of the most indispensable of household goods. He sent Leocadia to buy white cotton cloth, many *varas*, and bring it home, and he consulted with Tomasa about the cutting and sewing. Simple garments such as those the Indians of the countryside wear were to be made for everyone in the household.

Guiomar slept until the late afternoon.

Obediently, she sipped broth and ate bread that was brought her. That night, she did not go to her chapel, but she walked all night in the corridor, up and down, up and down, until she was unable to take another step. While it was still full dark, hours before dawn, she went back to her chapel and sank into prayer once more.

Juan was near her at all times, accompanying her often, a silent loving presence. He said nothing, but joined her in her prayers. On the morning of the second day, she rose from her knees, looked about, as if seeing where she was for the first time, and called out, "Juan? Juan?"

"I am here."

Mutely, she held out her arms to him, and he came at once, and lifted her and gathered her close. That night he slept with her, in her bed, not kissing or caressing her, but only holding her comfortingly, her head on his shoulder.

She had come to him, and he was content. It would take many months to heal her wounds of the spirit, and it would take all his care and energy and planning to remove her from where danger would always threaten her. But he was young and determined, and he knew that with God's help, he could do it. And someday she would be wholly his, he was certain.

27.

Fermín waited for a ship in Veracruz. He had searched diligently for his lost love, but suddenly he had become convinced that she was not in Mexico. He bought passage on a vessel making for Hispaniola. She might be there. She might have despaired, and have decided to return to Spain; he would continue his search there. It might take years. He was poor, but he was a gifted artisan, and he could always work silver and save his money, before going on to the next port.

When they set sail for Hispaniola, there was still hope in his heart.

28.

Fray Artemio could not delay, having carried out the splendid auto-da-fé, which would go down in history as one of the most spectacular and satisfying. He found a place with a caravan being formed of four well-to-do merchants who were bound for Veracruz to meet the Spanish galleon and receive the goods they had ordered. They traveled well protected, with six soldiers and two good cooks, who provided well-spiced meals when they stopped to rest or to sleep. Fray Artemio had been loaned a riding mule, and though he disliked the animal and resented the jolting and the uncomfortable position, he knew it was quite the best he could ask for.

He tried not to think of what awaited him in Spain. Even if the Superior had had news of his splendid auto-da-fé, something must have happened, some calumny must have been whispered in his ear, to cause this summary order to return. Perhaps he was to be sent as a missionary. This thought troubled him; he would plead ill health, if they meant to send him to some distant and dangerous place. He knew that his gifts were administrative and organizational.

The rigors of the mountains passed, the caravan came within a day's march of the City of the Angels, where they would rest, and bathe, and gather strength for the remainder of the journey. Stopping at a small village, the merchants found a room where they could all share a bed, and Fray Artemio lay down at once with a deep sigh, for he was very weary.

He was roused from a deep sleep by one of the soldiers, who had dared to come into his room, and shake his shoulder to awaken him.

"Father, come. Come at once. There is a poor woman dying in the street. You must come and shrive her."

The soldier was young, not more than sixteen. His beard was still soft and new, and his service in New Spain had not been long; he was still devoted to the rites of his Faith, still in awe of God's priests.

Fray Artemio labored to his feet. He had not undressed, in his haste to lie down, but he had to untie the straps around his bundle of possessions, in order to find the ciborium and his holy oils. Putting on his stole, he followed the young man out into the street. It was still dark, and he saw several curious people standing near what seemed to be a sort of roadside shelter.

"She is in there," said one, pointing, as Fray Artemio came near. He stepped inside, and instantly was aware of the fetid odor of the pox. He was terrified, for he had never caught it. The bundle of dark clothes on the floor stirred and he saw what had been a human face, now a swollen shapeless mass of putrefaction.

Quickly unstopping his vial of holy oil, he was about to shake a drop upon the woman when he became aware of the soldier and several others watching him closely. He would have to touch the woman. He would have to.

Moistening his finger in the oil he touched the woman's face on her closed eyelids, the ears, not easily found between the locks of dark dank hair, where the nose might be in the shapeless mass, the mouth. Then he must anoint the hands and the feet. As he moved the woman—surely she was now dead?—to free her hands, he saw the glint of silver, and of a stone, in a bracelet on the suppurating arm. No one would steal it, he thought, not even the gravedigger; it was imbedded in the rotting flesh. He quickly anointed the feet, thick with grime and calloused from trudging the roads.

Murmuring prayers, he left.

"She should be buried at once," he ordered, "and deep. She is dead of the smallpox."

Fray Artemio did not sleep that night, out of fear, and he prayed diligently.

But the days went by, and he remained in good health, eager for his food, a good sleeper. He began to be sure that God had spared him.

It was not until he was on shipboard that he experienced a sudden shaking chill, then a rising fever, and a backache that gave him no peace. It was the beginning.

He never reached Spain.

29.

The caravan leaving the house on Curtidores Street was a strange one. They set out in the blackest hours before dawn, and the mules and horses had hooves wrapped in rags; they made no noise as they went along the streets, and no lights sprang up in windows of houses as they went by.

Juan Palomar, the patron, sat a fine stallion, which had cost most of his money. But he had bought a brood mare, too, and Guiomar, dressed in the white cotton skirts and blouse of a country woman, her hair covered and tied back in a white cotton snood, rode the mare. Juan's plan was to raise horses, for which he needed the animals. But the stallion was most important; he could find other mares wherever there were Spanish soldiers, but to breed horses for the army, he had to have a fine stallion, and he was proud of this splendid three-year-old *alazan,* or dark chestnut animal. It was mettlesome, too, and intelligent, and Juan knew it would be affectionate. He had named his stallion Principio, meaning Beginning. Principio should mark the beginning of a new life for them all. Epifanio, the two women slaves, Leocadia and Tomasa, and two teenage Indian boys he had bought to be taught the leatherworking skills, came on foot, all dressed in white, all looking exactly like the slaves of a household. They walked beside the mules on which Juan had loaded the household necessities, food for the journey, and oats for the animals.

In case anyone should have noted their departure, he took the road south, but, after several leagues, and before they had passed two villages, he turned northward again. He was taking all his household and the wife whom he loved to the wild lands in the north, where the savage Chichimecas roamed. There he could trade, he thought, and the soldiers of Spain would be purchasers for his saddles and his horses, and they could all stay far away from the Inquisition.

He knew where he intended to settle. There was fine grazing there, and stands of trees for firewood and shelter. He had learned how to make bricks, working for Fray Domingo, and he would have Epifanio's help. They would build a house, with thick strong walls, warm in winter and cool in summer, and easy to defend.

They camped along the way, and ate sparingly. Guiomar

spoke little, but she seemed stronger in the sunlight of their journeying, and she turned her eyes to the north, with Juan.

He calculated that they would reach the valley he had chosen
for their home within a month's time. When they were far from
any village or town, he sang, all the songs he knew.

AUTHOR'S NOTE

Kind readers sometimes write asking me how much of my novel is "true." I attempt to be correct in background material, through careful study. And often I find, in the pages of history, characters and events that become essential parts of the narrative. This was the case with *Among the Innocent*.

I found my Guiomar in a tiny shop on the Ponte Vecchio in Florence. I never forgot her beauty.

But Dr. Morales was a person who lived in the late sixteenth century. He was indeed a learned rabbi, who went about in the New World, posing as a doctor, but striving to bring back to Judaism the members of his race who had slipped away. The Inquisition finally thought of him as the Wandering Jew, for they never caught him.

Gonzalo is based, lightly, on the character of Luis Carbajal, *Hijo*, whose sad story has been written up completely in Mexican archives. Gaspar is very like Bernardino Alvarez, a Spanish soldier, rough and savage, who made a fortune in Peru, and later, through sudden complete Faith, became a devoted Catholic and founded a hospital for the insane. (The largest mental hospital in Mexico today is named for him.)

Isabel and José Acevedo were based on persons who lived in Mexico City, as crypto-Jews, or secret Judaizers, and it is true that the body of the old rabbi was disinterred, and his bones were dishonored, after his death, by the vigilant Inquisition.

Other characters in the story were put together, in bits and pieces, from what I learned, in my studies, and from my imagination.

There was indeed a pirate ship that attacked Tampico and was sunk; its surviving sailors marched to Mexico to stand trial as "Lutherans."

What became clear in studies of the period was that all the people who lived in that time were fanatical and superstitious, in one way or another, and amazingly brave and resilient, and beset by the same longings, desperate hopes, and troubles that afflict countless people today.

Elizabeth Borton de Treviño